Hopelessly addicted to  **Kristine Lynn** pens hi[gh-stakes romance in] the wee morning hours [before teaching] at an Oregon college. Luckily, the stakes there aren't as dire. When she's not grading, writing, or searching for the perfect vanilla latte, she can be found on the hiking trails behind her home with her daughter and puppy. She'd love to connect on X, Facebook, or Instagram.

Kate MacGuire has loved writing since for ever, which led her to a career in journalism and public relations. Her short fiction won the Swarthout Award and placed third in the 2020 Women's National Book Association writing contest. Medical romance has always been her guilty pleasure, so she is thrilled to be writing novels for Mills & Boon's Medical Romance line. When she's not pounding away on the keyboard Kate co-runs Camp Runamuk with her husband, keeping its two unruly campers in line in the beautiful woodlands of North Carolina. Visit katemacguire.com for updates and stories.

Also by Kristine Lynn

Brought Together by His Baby
Accidentally Dating His Boss
Their Six-Month Marriage Ruse
A Kiss with the Irish Surgeon

Also by Kate MacGuire

Resisting the Off-Limits Paediatrician

Discover more at millsandboon.co.uk.

NINE MONTHS TO MARRY THE PRINCESS

KRISTINE LYNN

CITY DOC FOR THE SINGLE MUM

KATE MacGUIRE

MILLS & BOON

All rights reserved including the right of reproduction in whole or in part in any form. This edition is published by arrangement with Harlequin Enterprises ULC.

This is a work of fiction. Names, characters, places, locations and incidents are purely fictional and bear no relationship to any real life individuals, living or dead, or to any actual places, business establishments, locations, events or incidents. Any resemblance is entirely coincidental.

This book is sold subject to the condition that it shall not, by way of trade or otherwise, be lent, resold, hired out or otherwise circulated without the prior consent of the publisher in any form of binding or cover other than that in which it is published and without a similar condition including this condition being imposed on the subsequent purchaser.

® and TM are trademarks owned and used by the trademark owner and/or its licensee. Trademarks marked with ® are registered with the United Kingdom Patent Office and/or the Office for Harmonisation in the Internal Market and in other countries.

First published in Great Britain 2025
by Mills & Boon, an imprint of HarperCollins*Publishers* Ltd,
1 London Bridge Street, London, SE1 9GF

www.harpercollins.co.uk

HarperCollins*Publishers* Macken House, 39/40 Mayor Street Upper, Dublin 1, D01 C9W8, Ireland

Nine Months to Marry the Princess © 2025 Kristine Lynn

City Doc for the Single Mum © 2025 Kate MacGuire

ISBN: 978-0-263-32504-1

04/25

This book contains FSC™ certified paper
and other controlled sources to ensure responsible forest management.

For more information visit www.harpercollins.co.uk/green.

Printed and Bound in the UK using 100% Renewable Electricity
at CPI Group (UK) Ltd, Croydon, CR0 4YY

NINE MONTHS TO MARRY THE PRINCESS

KRISTINE LYNN

MILLS & BOON

To Cindy.

Thank you for helping make my writing fairy tale come true!

You're the best agent a gal could ask for.

PROLOGUE

EMILIA DE REYES stared down the long wooden bar. Each seat was occupied, the screams of laughter deafening, the rock and roll competing for space in each patron's eardrums. She took a deep breath and squeezed between two towering, bulky humans, trying to find enough real estate to flag the bartender down.

Neither gave Emilia a glance. She smiled.

This is amazing. I'm actually invisible.

A bartender materialized.

"Whadaya having?"

She glanced above him at the menu outlined in chalk—*chalk! How truly American!*—and thought of her "list."

"How about the Big Sam and an old-fashioned?"

The man nodded and disappeared. He was fully what she expected to find in a hipster bar like the one she'd chosen, with a loose bun piled atop his head and what might pass as a beard smattering his chin.

This whole scene—from the noise to the scent of something fried and delicious to the people casually dressed in off-brand clothing—was exactly what she'd hoped for when she'd chosen Minneapolis, Minnesota, for her obstetrics residency in the United States. When she'd dared to hope, that was.

When her stepmother had stopped seeking fertilization treatments after too many failed pregnancies, Emilia had worried that her let's-turn-the-princess-into-a-well-rounded-queen-to-the-people trip was *off the table*, to use an American turn of phrase. In a moment, she'd gone from hopeful that her life could be *guided* by royal protocol, rather than dictated by it, to *resigned*.

Her father and stepmother would never have a child of their own. Which meant...

Emilia was the sole heir to the Zephyranthes throne. And her dreams of picking a so-called passion project to follow for two years, as all Zephyranthian nobility did, was likely off the table. Emilia's health and safety could no longer be risked.

A patron at the bar whooped when some athlete competing in an American football match crossed over a line on a field. Emilia smiled, feigning interest in the television above her. At least one good thing had come from Luis's betrayal and her biggest mistake being plastered across the front pages of every European newspaper: he'd given her an out.

All that negative media coverage and her sudden disappearance from the limelight would have made it seem as if she were running away. Instead, her situation was rebranded as the start of her "queen in training" preparation.

It'd worked, too. Especially when the media got wind of what she'd chosen as her passion project. She'd be working toward a medical specialty in obstetrics in America, helping women like the late queen, who'd died in childbirth. She felt moderately guilty for capitalizing on her mother's death two decades earlier, but Emilia was also healing from a fresh betrayal there as well. There was so much her mother hadn't told her... So much she'd been blind to since she'd only been seven when her mother passed away. Now, thanks to Luis, all her past was on a world stage for everyone to read about in the scandal pages.

And Luis himself? Well, he was part memory, part heartache, and full regret at this point. He was banished from Zephyranthes, at least.

Her engagement to Luis might've left her with a decent heartbreak, but it gave her a chance to pursue more than just a passion project. Much more.

She *loved* medicine, and in that brief moment after her father had remarried and started trying to have more children, Emilia had allowed herself to imagine what life as a royal physician might have been like. But now she was back to her role as Heir Apparent, Queen-in-Waiting.

At least she had an American hamburger with *bacon*, not to mention a whiskey drink on the way. *Check and check.* Two things crossed off her list before she'd even finished unpacking.

This was a good idea, coming here.

The shout from the crowd was louder than the rock music; someone must have done something outrageously stupid or heroic on the TV. Her smile grew.

Emilia's stay would be short-lived, a mere two years, but she didn't mind. She loved her country, found honor in her duty, and would appreciate going back to meet the needs of the people counting on her.

But anonymity was a welcome respite. Well, sort of.

She stole glances toward the door. There, leaning against a post, was Chance, her father's answer to keeping her safe while allowing her to complete her OB residency in America. Without a drink of his own, and in all black, he looked more bar bouncer than patron.

Likely, he thought this assignment beneath him. Still, he could loosen up and try to enjoy being outside the gated walls of the castle. Wasn't he happy to be out from the stifling duties of her father's chief adviser?

When a large, male form almost brushed against her at the bar, her smile turned to shock at a stranger being this close to *her*. With Chance mere feet away. Out of the corner of her eye, she noticed Chance close the distance, but she shook her head. She was okay. No, she was better than okay.

I'm not in the castle anymore, am I?

Emilia tried to take in the man who'd somehow made the seas part for him, but he was too close and too tall—well over two meters. The gray sweater he wore swept across her skin, tickling it. It was soft, *expensive*. His broad chest and strong arms pressed against the fabric but didn't strain it. The sweater had been tailored for him—she'd recognize that kind of craftsmanship anywhere.

How interesting to find it in middle America at a local bar.

The muscles in the man's torso extended to his neck, his jaw, his cheeks.

But that's all she could see.

What she *felt* was another story altogether. She'd never been this close to a *man*—other than Luis, who hardly earned the right to be called as much. Luis had been attractive in the basic sense of the word, but masculine? Nothing like the man beside her.

She inhaled deeply, the scent of spicy soap overwhelming her senses. Romance had never been, nor wouldn't ever be, an option, if for no other reason than the crown didn't allow it. Not in the conventional sense.

Her royal obligations included a marriage of convenience that would benefit her country, which was sort of romantic if she thought about the centuries of tradition that supported the ceremony she'd partake in when she returned to Zephyranthes.

Then again, her father and stepmother hadn't expressly told her she couldn't pursue a *fling*.

In that case, a man as intoxicating as this one might make the top five list of things to do in America. Modern decrees had relinquished outdated policies about a princess's virtue, which Emilia hadn't taken advantage of. Yet.

As the velvety voice of the man next to her ordered his drink—something with *sour* at the end of it—a pooling of heat sank past her abdomen and into the place she longed to be touched.

Apparently, the things she'd learn on this trip wouldn't all be within the hospital walls.

No sooner was she handed a glass of amber liquid did the

hulk of a man back into her, spilling at least a third of it. And he didn't even bother to turn around.

Desire turned to ice, heavy and cold in her stomach. She tapped his shoulder. "Excuse me." He dipped his gaze at her angry words. "You spilled my drink."

She raised her chin and was met by a piercing gaze the same slate gray color as his sweater. The full force of his power and nonchalance was something she was all too familiar with in the world she'd left behind.

"I apologize. I didn't realize. Can I replace it?" he asked.

"No, thank you. This will be plenty, I'm sure. But you could be more careful. Someone might've been hurt."

"Were you? Hurt?" He handed her a napkin but didn't turn away.

"No." Her pulse beat loud in her ears. "Not this time."

"Good."

Emilia held his gaze. When his brows lifted in appreciation, she swallowed, her throat dry. All moisture in her body had fled south, it seemed.

"You're beautiful," he said.

"I know," she replied, crossing her arms over her chest. It wasn't as if she was unaware of her physicality. She was raised to consider its importance above almost everything else in her life. Yet, to see its effect without thought or care for what being caught gazing at a *princess* might do to his reputation—his *life*—was a heady thing indeed.

She also knew she'd chosen wisely when it came to the slinky jade green shirt with thin straps exposing her toned shoulders and her slim-cut black jeans. The former highlighted the jeweled green slivers in her eyes, the latter her figure.

He laughed, then, his stoic demeanor gone. "Where are you from?"

"Why do you assume I'm not from here?"

"The accent, for one."

She shrugged, conceding to that observation. She'd worked

hard to learn American English, but every now and then, even she heard the stray *theta* from her native Zephyr—similar to Spanish—that slipped through into speech.

"That's fair. And the rest?"

His eyes sparkled with recognition, and awareness prickled her skin.

"You don't fit in here," he said with a finality that left no room for an opposing opinion. A stab of something familiar and unwanted pulsed in her chest.

"Neither do you," she shot back.

She'd tried for *confident* and come up short. That was the problem, wasn't it? She didn't belong anywhere. Too wild for her royal existence, too proper for much else. If it weren't for years of training, the worry she couldn't be the princess Zephyranthes needed would have devoured her a long time ago.

He laughed again. "Trust me, it's a compliment. But yeah, this place isn't my normal scene. I'm supposed to be meeting a friend in a bit."

"A friend?" Why did a thread of jealousy tug at her heart? This man—this handsome stranger—didn't owe her anything.

"My buddy, Brian." Unexpected relief cut the thread. "But you still didn't answer my question. Where're you from?"

"Europe." She kept her answer simple, alluding to the story she, her parents, and Chance had worked out. It was tenuous, but at least they could count on Luis's silence from wherever he'd slunk off to. They'd paid handsomely for it.

"Spain?" he asked.

She shrugged, allowing the common misconception. Their language and culture were similar enough, buying her even more anonymity.

"*Encantado*," he said, dipping his chin. "*Me llamo* Aiodhán."

The accent and greeting weren't as fluid as Zephyr, but she didn't fault him for that. Hearing something close to her native tongue from his lips was thrilling. Whiskey did the job the desire started, and she had the sudden urge to give into the heat building at her core.

When she got bumped from behind this time, she careered into the wall of muscle in front of her. The arms that held her up were strong, warm, and wholly tempting. Kind of like the rest of the man.

Not yet, and not him. Besides the obvious—he was the first American she'd spoken to—she couldn't escape the feeling wafting off the handsome stranger. Aiodhán was trouble, and until she was sure if it was the good kind or not, she'd best keep her distance.

"Emily?" the bartender asked, breaking the spell she'd fallen under while under Aiodhán's gaze. She nodded. The nickname was one more buffer between her and her royal reality. Once someone associated her with the...*family obligations* she had back home, she would no longer be Emilia, woman and physician. Just *Princess* Emilia.

The bartender held out a brown bag. Perfect timing. Flirting with the stranger next to her had diverted her attention from the pangs of hunger she felt, but barely.

"Emily, huh?"

She straightened her shoulders, tossed her hair back.

"Yes. Well, nice to meet you, Aiodhán." She held out her hand to bid him good-night, but he ignored it. Fine. She turned to leave despite his breach of etiquette.

"You been here long?" She stopped short. What would five more minutes of chatter cost her?

"I haven't. This is my first day here, actually."

"Welcome to Minneapolis," Aiodhán said. "What brought you here?"

"Work. I start a new job Monday." The less he knew, the better. Only the CEO of the hospital system she was completing her residency at was aware of her real name, her credentials. And it would remain that way for the next twenty-four months.

His eyes narrowed. "Have you ever been to Minneapolis before?"

She shook her head. "It's a beautiful city, though." Nothing like the centuries-old spires in the center of Cyana, but modern, fresh, *new*.

"I like it. And I'm thinking you need a tour guide."

"Is that right?" The food bag hung at her side, all but forgotten under the intense gaze of this stranger.

"It is. How about after you dive into that burger we get you acclimated? As a resident downtown expert, I'm your guy."

"How are you such an expert?" she teased. It felt good. Freeing.

"I'm doing a project downtown with a new building, so I had to do market research. All boring stuff, but it did give me one gem." The look he sent her was primal, filled with adventure. Her skin prickled with awareness. "It's a fun place with some great music if you'd like to join me."

"What about your friend?"

He shrugged. "He'll live without me for a night."

"Well, I don't know you," she said, worrying aloud.

His smile didn't waver.

"That's why people go on dates, generally. To get to know each other."

A thrill whispered through her. *Dating.* What a wholly American—and ordinary—thing to do. It'd never actually occurred to her.

Didn't I choose to pursue my residency in the United States so I could learn about other cultures that might impact the way I lead one day?

Not exactly. However, she *was* there to heal from heartache and take on a passion project. Maybe there was another way to look at those edicts.

"Okay," she said, a smile working its way across her face. "I'm interested. But only after I've devoured this burger. I'm absolutely starving."

Aiodhán's laugh was throaty and thick.

"I'd never dream of keeping a woman from a meal." He swallowed the contents of his drink then placed the empty glass on the bar. The gleam in his eye was positively wicked, with a hint of feral desire she recognized from the men who'd coveted her on their supervised courting outings, men like Luis. Only this man wasn't aware of the fortune or title she carried like invisible, gilded baggage on her shoulders. He whipped out a credit card and waved at the bartender. "I'll take all this, too."

"You don't have to—"

"Consider it a welcome drink and dinner. Just sit back and enjoy."

Well, this is a pleasant surprise. For obvious reasons, she was usually left fronting the cost of all dinners out.

Another pleasant surprise? Aiodhán cleared the way for her to dive into her food, which she did with reckless abandon. Not one worry about dabbing her lips with a cloth napkin or if she looked silly crossed her mind. Aiodhán wiped a smudge of ketchup from the corner of her mouth, but otherwise let her eat in peace.

"Ready to go, Emily from Europe?" He leaned in close enough that the spice from his soap tickled her nose. She inhaled deeply, wanting to remember this scent—the scent of her first American date. Her first *real* date.

Excitement rolled through her chest, even as she allowed Aiodhán to believe she was someone other than who the world knew her as. She stole a glance at Chance. The plan forming in her mind was almost unfair to the stoic, frowning grump of a man, but that didn't deter her from putting it into action. After all, hadn't she slipped his watch countless times in Cyana as a child? She'd learned a few tricks since then.

"I'm ready, Aiodhán from Minnesota," Emilia said. "Let's go."

Her heart beat wildly as reality hit her. Yes, she'd been placed back at the top of the line of succession. But she was also free for *two whole years*. Sudden desperation for adventure beat in her chest. A date with an attractive man she'd met at a local bar seemed just the trick. The rest—her dream of working with new moms and women who needed her help to have the families they craved—was on the horizon. And the sun would rise on it tomorrow.

Right now, she was focused on the man taking her hand in his leading her out of the bar and into the magic of the unknown.

CHAPTER ONE

Emilia applied a thin layer of gloss on her lips before appraising her look in the mirror. It reminded her of the last time she'd applied makeup—the night she'd slept with the hot American she met in the bar two weeks prior. She shuddered but smiled, memories of the most delicious night of her life still tingling her lips, no matter how much gloss was painted on.

No time for that now. Even if she couldn't forget the spectacular way he'd wielded her body like a surgical instrument of pleasure, those memories stood in the way of what mattered. Namely getting ready for her first day of work, acclimating to this new life, and healing while she had the space to do so.

Oh, and finding a decent place to put on her makeup.

She'd moved into her apartment a week ago and still couldn't figure out the dimmer switch in the bathroom. Had she overdone the blush on her cheeks? Like many aspects of her move so far, she was both frustrated by small details and overjoyed at the freedom they represented. Sure, it would have been nice to have her consorts and lady's maid to assist her in getting ready, and ooh, she missed her Scandinavian LED makeup mirror.

But then again, wasn't it delicious to stay up all evening reading a *romance* novel instead of a foreign policy text by a stuffed-shirt scholar? She'd deal with poorly lit rooms for that unique pleasure.

This apartment *was* a cut above decent, considering they'd only decided Minneapolis was an option for her residency two days before she flew out. The hospital had accommodated her, no questions asked. But housing…? That had been a different story altogether.

Emilia giggled, recalling the king's beet-red cheeks as he was given the runaround by an apartment manager for luxury apartments near the hospital.

"I don't care if you're King George. I don't have anything for ya."

"King George has been dead for three-quarters of a century," he'd huffed. Emilia had wondered whether her father was more upset about the lack of options afforded a man of his position or that he was compared to a deceased ruler of a different country. "Do you have anyone more qualified than you to assist me?" he'd asked.

God love her father, but he wasn't immune to the blinders his power put on him. It was part of why this whole trip was so important to Emilia. She didn't want to get to the throne only to discover she didn't know her place or her heart's values. How could she be expected to lead without perspective and context for the rest of the world's issues?

"I hope this is worth it, Emilia. I don't want to see you hurt again," the king had said once a suitable apartment had been secured.

"It will be," she'd assured him. And so far, that was true, if only because it separated her from her mother's story, while giving her time to grieve. Not just the lie she'd been fed by everyone, including her father, but the life she'd had stripped away when her lineage had become more important.

Emilia's stepmother and the king had nurtured her dreams to practice medicine, but it always came secondary to trying for another heir. Emilia understood. A baby had been *their* dream, just as hers was making sure women had the kind of care denied her birth mother, despite being pregnant with the future prince. Her death had rocked Emilia's childhood.

It had also left a chasm of grief in her father's chest, in the country's memory, but both had been replaced. Her father's grief turned to love—deep love—with a woman in a graduate program at a Zephyr university he met at a summit. The country liked the new queen but kept Emilia's mother in its heart. That is, until Luis had somehow unearthed the unthinkable.

The baby her mother carried hadn't been the king's.

If Emilia had learned that as an innocent seven-year-old, she might've taken the news differently. But mere months ago? When she'd looked up to her mother her whole life, even altering her career choice to honor her mother's sacrifice?

The country's shock was nothing to Emilia's. Nor was their grief. Emilia was still reeling. She'd always assumed her parents had been happy. What else didn't she know?

Here, four thousand miles from her sandy shores, she could pick through these thoughts without the scrutiny of an entire country.

Emilia sighed, slipping on her tennis shoes. The one thing finding out about her mother hadn't shifted was Emilia's love of medicine. Learning bathed her grief in the salve of knowledge, tucked it away between the covers of science texts, in the conversations with her professors at the Royal Zephyranthes Conservatorium Medical School.

"It's finally here," she whispered to herself. Tucking an errant strand of hair behind her ear, she grabbed her phone and headed for the door. "Don't mess this up."

In the elevator on the way down from the penthouse suite, she checked her messages.

One from her stepmother, wishing her luck, and…that was it.

What exactly am I looking for?

Regret opened wide in her throat. She hadn't given Aiodhán her phone number, and why should she have? They'd shared a passionate night and nothing more.

In her world, marriage, romance, and love were mutually exclusive, but the latter two? They just weren't in her cards if nothing could come of it. Hope had buoyed her on more than one occasion, but hoping to find what her father and stepmother had was too much to put on the universe. She was lucky to be here, to study medicine, and that was enough.

Still, she hadn't counted on the after-effects of sleeping with Aiodhán. Her skin tingled with memory where he'd caressed it, her hands itched to move across the continents of flesh he'd laid open for her. Her body craved his, plain and simple.

And, like all tragedies, she didn't even have a last name to cyberstalk the man, or at least put Chance to the task of tracking him down.

Thank goodness, too. The elevator doors opened to her future—the lobby of the hospital. Who had time for a love affair when *life* was hers for the taking? And with a very definite timeline?

A smile bloomed on her face as the cool Minneapolis wind whipped her ponytail into a dance. She was going to learn and practice obstetrics in the United States. And under a pilot program called the Gold Fleece Foundation that had begun in LA for women who couldn't afford good care, no less.

Finally. Her future felt like *hers* for the first time. She tried not to think about it being the last, as well.

Inside the foyer she'd just entered, the only word Emilia could come up with was *vivo*. This place was *alive*.

The stories-high pale green walls surrounded a miniature city that pulsed with energy. People in different-colored scrubs—maybe delineating their departments within the hospital?—rushed across the sepulchral space as if their worlds lay on the other side of whatever doors they passed through. People like *her*, there to learn to save lives, or already well on their way to doing just that. It was loud, chaotic, but with a measure of reason and pacing that Emilia recognized. Everyone and everything had a place and a role. Stepping into her own would be adding another cog to the wheels that made this place run. Emilia gazed in wonder, a sense of something calm settling over her, despite the frenetic energy whizzing around her.

Home. She was home.

No sooner did that realization wash over her than a tap on her shoulder roused her from Minneapolis General's bustle.

It was followed by a bright voice with an accent different than the one she'd heard around the city. Those were all long *O*s, a lilt at the end of each sentence, turning them into questions. This was thick and sweet, a cup of sugary tea.

"Y'all new here, too?"

Emilia whirled around, a smile on her face. The *too* warmed her. So did the spritely blonde greeting her with wide blue eyes. There were a few other folks who looked like they were waiting for orientation as well, but they were all on their phones, serious expressions pinned to their faces.

"It's my first day. Are you part of the residency program as well?"

"Sure am. Straight from Georgia. I'm Bridget. Hoping to work in peds." *Georgia*. That explained it. After reruns of *The Golden Girls* as a motherless teen with too much time on her hands, Emilia recognized the southern accent.

"Emilia. Obstetrics. Nice to meet you."

"Same. Obstetrics, huh? No joke messing around with two lives at a time. I like it."

"Thanks. The Gold Fleece program is one of the best, so I'm feeling terribly lucky."

"I've heard the same. Say, where's that fancy accent from?" Bridget asked her.

"Um... Spain," she said, sticking to her lie by omission from the other night. "I've only been here two weeks."

"Wow. And you didn't want to stay there with all the Mediterranean men? I've been here since last Thursday doing my onboarding paperwork, and aside from the head of general surgery, it's like the Sahara desert—dry of anything resembling life."

Emilia laughed. "Trust me, the men over there aren't as interesting as you'd think."

An image of Luis's cold sneer flashed in her vision. Her only consolation from being duped by such a weasel was knowing he'd been vetted by the crown as well and, until proven otherwise, had passed inspection. At least he'd sold their secrets to the press before she'd actually walked down the aisle.

She shivered. It would be hard to trust the next man her father chose for her, but she knew he'd be a thousand percent more cautious. Neither her nor her country could survive another betrayal.

Too bad the only man she had trusted and felt safe with was the one she'd shared her bed with two weeks ago.

Aiodhán. A shiver ran up her spine as she recalled his hands sliding over her skin, his tongue tracing her anatomy, the way he thrust into her… She might not have had any *physical* experience with men before Aiodhán, but she couldn't imagine it got better than the night—and very early morning—she'd spent with him.

She shook the heat of the memory away.

"Anyway, I'm not here to date."

"So what *are* you here for?"

Emilia smiled, her focus on a woman with a gash over her left eye being led away by a young man in blue scrubs. She thought she'd figured out the color coding in the past few minutes of watching medical staff move in and out of the lobby, where they were told the residency coordinator would meet them. Pink was maternity, black for surgery, blue for the ER, and yellow for pediatrics.

"I want to work while I still can, travel if there's any time, and," she said, "have as much fun as possible. Dating would only get in the way of that."

Bridget eyed her through thick, fake lashes.

"Good," she finally said. "I need a wingwoman and if you're staying off the market, there's more hope for regular-looking people without Mediterranean accents."

"I'm happy to help," Emilia said, tossing Bridget a sly wink.

"Maybe we can start at this local bar. I met an absolutely beautiful man there the other night."

"We're gonna be fast friends," Bridget said, laughing and throwing an arm around Emilia's shoulders.

Emilia warmed at the idea of a friend. She'd never had anyone she trusted enough to let down her guard with.

"I'm glad you're enjoying yourselves, but I'd like to get started if that's okay with you?"

Emilia whipped around. The voice washed over her with eerie recognition.

Sure enough, the face staring back at her was as familiar as it was unnerving. Largely because she couldn't reconcile the strong shoulders, broad chest, and tree-trunk thighs draped in pale blue scrubs that brought out hints of robin's-egg blue in his eyes she'd missed the other night under poor bar lighting. The man standing before her was all rough edges and steely gaze, where he'd been soft and inviting mere days before.

"Aiodhán?" she whispered.

"*Emily*, is it?" His pupils dilated, but his lips remained pressed tight. The night they'd shared may not have meant enough to warrant a reaction from him, but heat singed her skin.

She shook her head. "Um, Emilia, actually."

"Hmmm." He looked away, but the heat from his stare still burned where it had caught her in the small, but meaningful, lie.

Emily was the name she'd picked for when she met people outside the hospital, but of course, everyone here would be aware of her name, if not her title. But other than the withering stare, he didn't comment.

That didn't change the way he stood over her. In her space. Taking up all the oxygen in the room.

"Like I was saying," Aiodhán continued, ignoring her, "I'm Dr. Adler, the chief of general surgery. I'll be running the clinical rotations, which means I'll get to know all of you in time, but right now, I'd like us to get started. Follow me."

Dr. Adler. Chief of Surgery. All things she should have

known about the man before sleeping with him. If only they'd spent more time talking and less time tearing each other's clothes off.

Emilia shivered.

"You know this guy?" Bridget hissed under her breath. "He's the general surgery doc I was telling you about. The only one hot enough to imagine breaking the rules for in this place."

"What rules?" Anxiety crept over Emilia's skin.

"You know, the *don't sleep with the boss* rules in every place of employment. Especially an ER where we'll spend sixteen hours a day together." Bridget laughed, but not one thing about this situation was humorous. How could Emilia have known he was her *boss*? Or the rules of employment when she hadn't been allowed to have a job until now? "Can you imagine if you slept with him and then had to see him at work every day? Awkward..." Bridget sang the last word.

Oh, God. That's exactly what Emilia had done, and *awkward* didn't begin to cover it.

Aiodhán—Dr. Adler—led them through the lobby to a room with metal lockers and restrooms.

"This is your break room and where you'll store your personal belongings during your shift. Take the next five minutes and change into the scrubs we've laid out for you, and then we'll continue our tour."

He left the locker room, and a collective sigh of relief escaped all of the residents' lungs. With the exception of Emilia's, that is. Pressure built up in her chest, making it ache.

"That guy's intense," one resident said. Others echoed similar sentiments.

"I thought he was hot. And you know him?" Bridget asked.

Emilia shook her head, willing her skin not to flash red with her newest lie. Oh, she knew the guy. *Intimately.*

"He looked like someone I knew, but he couldn't be that man—he was sweet and kind, and Dr. Adler doesn't seem like those adjectives describe him."

A small truth hidden in the bed of lies.

"Too bad—I kinda wish you could make a personal introduction. Adler is *fine*."

Emilia finished getting ready before the others but didn't dare step out into the hallway alone. Not when *he* was out there.

When Bridget was dressed, Emilia followed her out. She glanced up and caught Aiodhán staring at her for the briefest of seconds before his gaze shifted to the others. That small blip of recognition was all she saw reflected in his eyes before casual nonchalance took over. Anger, she could have understood—she'd lied to him, after all. But he was acting as if he barely recalled meeting her.

Her own anger surfaced.

Hadn't he lied to her, as well? He'd said he was working on a building downtown. *Ha!* This only barely qualified.

Please let this be some sort of cosmic joke. That she'd never set foot in that bar two weeks ago.

Except it had happened. All of it. Aiodhán Adler was her boss, and she had to spend the next two years with the man while he pretended he didn't recognize her.

She'd hoped for anonymity, but was she really that forgettable?

A flood broke through the dam holding Emilia's emotions back. Heat pressed against the back of her eyes, and her chest pulsed with regret. She'd slept with her boss and all but ruined any chance of being known for her medical aptitude. That, and she didn't have a single person she could ask for advice.

No, this was her mess, and she was responsible for cleaning it up.

Sadness washed over her, replacing the adventurous thrill from earlier.

Oh, my goodness. What have I done this time?

CHAPTER TWO

Aiodhán Adler stormed down the hallway. His steps were heavy, but not as weighty as the pressure building in his limbs, his chest, his head. Shaking his head at the charge nurse who seemed bent on getting his attention, he bypassed the beeps and trills of the nurses' station.

"I'll be back in a sec."

He just...he needed a *moment* to catch his breath, to think through how to handle this...*situation*. When he rounded the corner and found the first on-call room unoccupied, he breathed out a heavy sigh.

Emily. In *this* hospital. In *his* program.

Emily isn't even her name.

Fine. Whatever. Emilia-freaking-de-Reyes. He might have to call her something different, but the effect on his breathing, his memory, his heart was the same.

He snatched a pillow off the on-call bed and groaned into it. He'd let a moment of weakness and that damned accent snake under his defenses and ruin a two-year streak of saying no to his basest desires.

And, hell, was he paying for it now.

He inhaled deeply, letting the cool air in the quiet room calm his racing pulse. After the urge to run for the Canadian border passed, he placed the pillow back on the bed, straightening the sheets while he was at it.

Aiodhán fished out his phone and dialed.

"You know that woman I told you about?" he asked when his best friend answered.

"Hello to you, too," Brian said, laughing. In the background, Aiodhán heard another laugh he recognized.

"Tell Mallory *hi*."

"Ad says *hi*," Brian said. "She says *hi* back. And that she forgives you for skipping out on half our reception."

"I made it the whole way through the ceremony." He might not understand the desire to date, fall in love, and then commit to someone who could wreck your world if they left—by choice or chance. But Brian and Mal were his best friends.

"Anyway, what's up? You called about some woman?"

When Mallory snorted with laughter in the background, he grimaced.

"Can you take me off Speaker?"

"Sure thing." Aiodhán heard the door close on Brian's end. "Dang, man. This must be serious if you're calling me on my honeymoon and don't want Mal to hear."

"It's serious, but not like you think. Remember the woman I met at the bar that night?"

"When you blew off my bachelor party? Yeah, I recall."

"I didn't blow it off. I was there."

"For two minutes at the beginning to tell me you were leaving, and without the cigars you promised."

"Again, I'm sorry, but—"

"It couldn't be helped," Brian said, echoing the words from Aiodhán's text, sent from the elevator of his apartment when he'd kissed Emilia. But Aiodhán could hear the smile in his voice.

"No. It couldn't." Even now, he could feel the pull she'd had on him that night. It was magnetic and untamed: dragging himself away would have been like shoving a dead vehicle across the banks of Lake Superior. And worse? He *still* felt it.

He shook his head, willing it to dissipate. He was a brilliant surgeon at one of the nation's top hospitals. Why couldn't he work through his feelings for a woman he'd just met?

"So...you like her?"

"I did. I mean, I do." He exhaled a hiss of breath. "But we agreed it was only a one-night thing. She wanted to concentrate on her new job, and well, you know me."

"You want to concentrate on your job. Period."

"Yeah. Exactly." Brian and Mallory knew him best and loved him regardless of his work ethic, which others had dubbed *obsessive*. Aiodhán chose to think about it like a scientist: if a series of experiments all warranted the same negative results, the responsible thing would be to choose another course of action.

Life kept taking people he loved, so the answer was easy. Scientific. Clinical.

He simply didn't let anyone close to his heart.

"Bud, you're worrying me. Mind getting to the point so I know you're okay?"

"She's *here*." Aiodhán could feel her, even though half an ER separated them. She'd gotten too close that night. Her gaze had seemed to push through his walls. Worse still, he'd gotten the sense that, if he'd spent more time with her, she'd find the keys to the chains holding the walls up.

"Like, as in the hospital?"

"Yeah."

"Is she a patient?"

"Nope."

"A family member to someone you worked on?"

"Uh-uh."

There was a beat of silence on the other end.

"So she's...?"

"Yep."

"Damn."

Aiodhán nodded, even though his friend couldn't see him.

"That's an HR nightmare, isn't it?"

Aiodhán glanced at the pillow he'd taken his frustrations

out on. He wanted to either kick it, scream into it, or lie down on it and restart the day—back to a time before knowing the woman he'd had trouble getting off his mind was one of his new interns.

"I hadn't thought about that."

"Well, I'd suggest you start. If I were you—and brother, let me tell you how glad I am that I'm not—I would swing by human resources and file a We Didn't Know We Worked Together form."

"They have those?" How often did this sort of thing happen?

"No, they don't have them, Ad. My God." Brian laughed, and Aiodhán's frown deepened. This wasn't funny. This was his career on the line. "Just go to HR and tell 'em what happened. You didn't know who she was, it won't happen again, blah, blah. And let me get back to my honeymoon, please. I've got a gorgeous blonde waiting on me with a mai tai, and neither are getting any happier that I'm out here with you."

"Sorry to bug you. Thanks for the advice, though."

"My pleasure. You've given me things to talk about between meals and bed."

"Please leave me out of your pillow talk. I've got enough problems. Anyway, see you when you're back. We'll go out for drinks, my treat."

"You bet."

Brian hung up, and Aiodhán inhaled, letting the cool air filter through his lungs, waking him up.

Time to get to work. Relationships he couldn't do, but run a new intern program? Yeah, he was built for that.

Ripping open the door to the hospital's locker room, he called inside. "Let's go. Time's up."

"Most of us are here, Dr. Adler," a confident, *accented* voice said from behind him.

He wheeled around and froze. Emilia had been stunningly beautiful the night he'd met her, in a deep green tank top that showed off her toned shoulders and breasts he'd enjoyed the rest of the night.

That was nothing compared to how she'd knocked him on his ass just now. *Again.* Her wild crimson curls were pulled back, accentuating the flawless, smooth curve of her neck, but one errant curl framed her forehead. He clenched his fists until he felt the flesh of his palms sting. Touching her, even to tuck the hair back, was forbidden on so many levels.

Of course Emilia would make the pale blue scrubs and lab coat she wore look like something off the catwalk. They managed to accentuate curves he hadn't forgotten in the past two weeks. Curves that kept him up at night, dreaming of how he might trace them with the tips of his fingers once more.

But she was his intern, his physician-in-training, his employee. So that couldn't happen. Not if he wanted to keep his job as chief of general surgery or practice medicine anywhere ever again.

Even if she wasn't any of those things, I can't have her. I can't have anyone.

Why did it feel as if he'd have to remind himself of that more than once over the next month?

He needed to talk to her, acknowledge what had happened and see where she was at with it. Maybe then, he could work in peace.

"Emilia, can I see you over here?" He gestured to an open space near the nurses' station where they wouldn't be overheard, but where he could protect both of their reputations by not hiding behind closed doors.

However, even in view of everyone, he could feel the way his body reacted to Emilia, to her soft, sweet scent and confident demeanor.

"Dr. Adler," she said.

"I wanted to apologize for not telling you fully who I was the other night. I've gotten a lot of interest from women who like me for my position here, and I liked talking to you anonymously."

Her gaze narrowed. "I understand that," she said. When she didn't elaborate, he continued.

"I understand if you can't work under me or need to report this to HR, but I assure you I'll remain professional from this moment forward."

Even if I feel like I'm being eviscerated every time I imagine your lips on mine.

"I'm fine. Thank you for your concern, but I can be professional, too."

She was fine, wasn't she? In fact, she didn't seem concerned in the slightest.

A twinge of something—frustration, maybe—tickled his skin. He didn't want her hurt, or pining after him, but a little bit of acknowledgment would have been nice. He rejoined the herd of interns, confusion sitting at the edge of his thoughts.

"All right. Well, let's start the tour, then. Take notes because I'm not going over this material again."

Aiodhán strode off, the interns filing in behind him like ducklings. At the nurses' station, Emilia was the only one who pulled out a pad of paper and pen, ready to note down what he taught. She was the only one taking him seriously.

He thought back to the bar. She'd been jostled by him but kept her chin and chest raised. And in his bedroom that night…

She'd been serious then, too, but in the goddamn best of ways. He shook his head, disrupting the image of her on top of him.

The intercom shot to life.

"Code Blue. Team needed in the ER."

"I meant what I said. Take notes," he said to the rest of them, already taking off down the hallway. "Looks like we're learning on the go today. Follow me." They fumbled, while Emilia strode beside him, her shoulders thrown back in the same way as they'd been at the bar. No hurt in her eyes.

Good. Maybe there was hope they could work together, then?

The ER was pandemonium. At least three gurneys were rolled in by EMTs, and more sirens whined in the distance.

"Give it to me," he said to the charge nurse, Mary. "What do we got?"

An EMT cut in. "Six-car collision on the I-35. One car almost went over. Three dead on scene, ten inbound in bad shape. These three are the worst."

Aiodhán whistled as he washed his hands in the scrub sink. "That damned bridge is cursed. Where do you need me? I'll have an audience, but put me to work."

"Why?" Emilia asked.

"Because you're here to learn," he shot back. This wasn't the time to challenge him. Confidence was fine, but he needed their respect as a teacher, too. Couldn't she see they were in the thick of it?

"Why is the bridge cursed?" she asked, donning a surgical gown and gloves as Mary handed them out. The rest of the residents looked perplexed, for which he couldn't say he blamed them. This was a helluva way to start their time at Minnie Gen.

But not Emilia. She looked ready to go. Was there any place she didn't seem in control?

"It collapsed almost twenty years ago. Thirteen fatalities and a hundred and forty-five casualties. Every bed in every hospital was full. C'mon."

"That's horrible," she whispered. It had been. Even now, he could still smell the burnt steel, hear the screams of the victims. It'd been...awful.

For him, especially. That was the day he'd become an orphan. It was also his first month of residency.

Both his parents were gone, both in accidents, but a decade apart. Neither had seen what he'd accomplished in his own residency. Heat built behind his eyes.

"We don't have time to worry about that. Let's get to work.

De Reyes, you're with me. Everyone else, join us when you decide to get dressed."

He was too sharp, too short, but there wasn't room for his emotions or theirs. Only saving the patients mattered. Each life he saved added one to the scales against a universe that seemed hell-bent on taking from him for its own scale.

Emilia lifted the patients' eyelids and pulled out a penlight. "Unresponsive. No pupil dilation. Should I call for a CT?"

"Okay. Order it. And de Reyes?" he said as she headed for the nurses' station. She nodded that he should continue. "Get those other residents in here, stat."

Dammit. Forget overexaggerating his feelings. This was gonna be impossible, wasn't it?

He needed to figure out how to work with a woman who had such a visceral effect on him. And who understood medicine on a cellular level. The only other Minnie Gen resident who'd ever been as unfazed in the ER in the midst of a crisis was himself.

Three hours later the team was exhausted. Only one resident had thrown up when they'd had to crack a chest cavity in the ER while they waited for a surgical room to open up. Three others had blanched but held it together. Maybe they wouldn't be the worst group he'd had.

Especially Emilia. She'd performed CPR for twenty minutes on one of the crash victims and hadn't missed a beat until they'd had to call TOD from brain death. She only nodded, called it, and walked out to change her gloves before moving to another room.

She was efficient as hell. And would make a damned good doctor, especially under Mal's tutelage. He struggled to find fault with her, and he needed something—anything—to get her off his mind.

He sent them all to the skills lab and made his way back to the nurses' station.

Aiodhán rethought Emilia's performance today. It meant the possibility of her earning chief resident if she kept it up.

Working even closer with her was out of the question. He was already too distracted by the doctor.

But he'd never keep her from it, either. Which meant he needed to find some other way to distance himself from the woman.

A plan formed in his head, but it only covered the next twenty-four hours. Finish his shift, go for a long run along the river, then have enough whiskey to pretend the day hadn't happened. That Emilia de Reyes hadn't happened. It would work—hell, he'd done something similar when he'd realized he was alone in the world.

But it wouldn't last long, not with his liver intact.

And it had to. Not just for the next month, but for after that when his building—a world-class surgery and recovery center for victims of violence—was finished and he could start building a team to run it with him. It was all he'd wanted since he was eleven years old, and he'd be damned if anything pulled his focus. Even—*especially*—Emilia de Reyes.

But just saying it to himself didn't make it true.

Dammit. How the hell was he supposed to get through the next *two years* with this woman under his watch?

CHAPTER THREE

THE PERSISTENT BUZZING of her cell phone against her stomach made her cringe. She'd tucked it away in her lab coat pocket, silenced in anticipation of the work day ahead of her, but that didn't stop the outside world from encroaching on her.

"If you ignore them, Emilia, they'll only find other ways of reaching out. Ways you may not appreciate, *verdad*?"

"*Entiendo*. I understand." As crazy as Chance drove her with his helicoptering over her health and work, it was nice to hear snippets of her native tongue from time to time. "But they're going to have to wait. I have a busy day, and what they're calling about won't be fixed in the hundred meters to the front doors."

She stepped out of the car, waving him off. He got out anyway but stayed close to the driver's side.

"Don't you think they deserve to hear your progress?"

The thing was, she wanted to hear the only two voices who'd brought her any calm in the forest fire that had become her life. But what could she say?

I'm a disaster. I slept with my boss, I've barely eaten or slept since, and I'm thinking this was a mistake.

She couldn't let them down, not after her fiancé had thrown all their lives into a cyclone of grief and betrayal. The country was still reeling. *Emilia* was still reeling.

And she was *exhausted*. So much for healing and making this trip a restorative one.

"What progress? I'm two months into a two-year residency.

I've got a long way to go, and they'll have to get used to not hearing from me every day. I barely have enough time to manage two meals a day."

"And if they ring me? What shall I say to them? Aside from the fact that their daughter is skipping meals."

Emilia rolled her eyes and pointed a finger at her guard.

"You won't mention my meals, thank you very much. Just tell them I'm fine, but busy, and that I'll call them over video chat on my next day off."

"And when might that be, Princess? Next year?"

"Shh…" Emilia glanced over her shoulder. Only the head of the hospital knew who she was and had assured her that her title would be kept quiet, as it had no bearing on her status at the hospital. Emilia was one of the first to arrive most days, something she was grateful for today, as the employee parking lot was empty. "You can't go shouting that word, Chance. But no, I'll be off shift this Monday. I'll call then."

"Sorry, Your Highness," he replied, dipping his chin. She shot him a scowl, but it didn't do much to deflect the smile on his lips. A jet-black SUV drove into the lot, and Emilia stood straighter.

"I've got to go, but please convince my folks I'm doing well."

"As you wish," Chance said, dipping into a low bow just as the familiar SUV parked three rows ahead of her. She rushed to catch up to it, hoping to deflect from Chance, who was still midbow.

"You are *such* an arse," she whispered under her breath at the man.

"Excuse me?" Aiodhán asked, materializing before her.

She gaped up at him, wishing for all the world she didn't have the palest, most translucent skin in the Mediterranean. Right now, she wagered her cheeks were a deep crimson.

"Sorry, I wasn't talking about you."

Aiodhán nodded, locking his G-Class with a click of a button. Emilia tried not to stare, but the way his Henley collar stood around a neck she'd kissed and his form-fitting jeans hugged thighs that had wrapped around her waist made it nearly impossible.

She'd really slept with her boss, hadn't she? Two and a half months wasn't even close to enough time to forget the evening with Aiodhán, nor was she sure she wanted to. But it would be nice if it didn't consume her every thought whilst she worked alongside the man.

He glanced over toward the edge of the parking lot where her gaze had traveled from.

"Who is that guy?" Aiodhán asked. "And why's he always hanging around till you get off?"

Emilia hadn't thought anyone noticed. Chance was entirely chosen for his ability to fold into his surroundings.

"He's my roommate," she responded, her gaze locking with Aiodhán's. It was the party line she'd been told to spout if anyone asked, but it sounded trite. Who would believe a roommate would wait all day in the hospital parking lot so he'd be available when Emilia's shift was over? Not even a beau would be that dedicated. "He's using the hospital Wi-Fi to look for jobs in the parking lot. Says it's less expensive than finding a coffee shop."

"A roommate, huh? I guess that's better than the alternative."

The alternative? What might that be—a suitor? Aiodhán, who'd all but ignored her existence at the hospital except to bark orders at her, couldn't care about her dating life, could he?

Not that she had a dating life. Even if it *were* something she wanted, when would she find the time? No, she'd been married to her title and crown at home, and to the hospital here. It was fine. Real marriage would come all too soon. She somehow, even through her bone-weariness, thought she'd prefer this to sleeping beside someone other than Aiodhán. He'd set the bar rather high, hadn't he?

She would never show her distaste for whomever her parents

chose, though. It was her duty, and she was proud to do what she was able for her country, for her family.

But, oh, would she carry her memories with her! Even small ones, like catching Aiodhán glancing at her when he thought she wasn't looking. And the small touches, their hands grazing each other when she passed him a scalpel, the way he'd accidentally brush by her in the hall, their shoulders touching.

Was she imagining their effects?

When Aiodhán strode over to the Lincoln Town Car, a stone of dread—always at the ready at the base of her throat since she'd left home—fell to her stomach.

"What are you doing?" she said, hurrying after him. She'd only been at Minneapolis General for eight weeks. Getting found out now would be terribly inconvenient.

But he ignored her. Of course.

When he got to the car, he rapped on the driver's window. Emilia shook her head behind him as Chance rolled down his window.

"May I help you, sir?" Chance asked, his accent thicker than hers. Would Aiodhán draw the obvious conclusion or make up one of his own? Which would be worse?

"I'm Aiodhán Adler, a surgeon here."

"A pleasure. My name is Chance. And how may I be of assistance to you?"

Aiodhán chuckled, shaking his head. "Um, I just wanted to invite you to use the Wi-Fi in the lobby. It's only gonna get colder out here the closer we get to the holidays. Plus, I don't want someone to call the cops on you for squatting in the parking lot."

"Pardon me? Squatting? The Wi-Fi?"

Aiodhán glanced back at Emilia, a question in his gaze, and she jumped in.

"Chance, what *my boss* is saying is that you're welcome to come sit in the lobby to use the internet for your job search."

Chance's eyebrows reached comic heights, and the corner

of his lips twitched up into what she'd assume was a grin if Chance ever deigned to smile. Emilia held her breath.

"I see. Well, isn't that a kind offer? Though, I did think you told me not to come near the hospital entrance, Your—"

"Well, that was before Dr. Adler's kind offer, which I do *insist* you take."

Chance smirked. "Of course. I'll be in momentarily. I only need to finish this important call. About a *job* I was given to do."

Emilia's skin heated with a blend of frustration mixed with fear. Her lips clamped tight.

"Oh, you already found something?" Aiodhán asked. "Good for you. Well, nice to meet you, Chance. See you around. De Reyes, we should probably get inside."

"Of course." Emilia followed Aiodhán, awaiting his questions with bated breath.

"He's an interesting guy" was all that came.

Emilia breathed out a sigh of relief. "You have no idea."

"How'd you meet him?"

She decided on a version of the truth. "He worked for my father, and I needed a roommate to be able to come to Minnesota for the program."

She felt Aiodhán's gaze on her, but she kept her eyes locked on the entrance to the ER. She couldn't get there fast enough.

"Why'd you pick Minnesota General? Your skills are already honed. You could have had your pick of programs."

Was that a compliment from her stoic, terse boss? "Thank you. But I needed someplace…quieter. I'm only here to learn what I don't know yet and be the best physician I can be."

Aiodhán stopped walking and gazed down at her. His eyes flashed with intensity, and his brows were pulled together in seriousness.

"What drives you, Emilia?"

She froze, her cells locking up one by one under his scrutiny and such an intimate question. And he'd used her first name.

"My mother." The rest of the words choked Emilia, thickening in her throat. Those two words had shifted meaning in the past few months, but the answer was the same.

"She's a doc as well?"

Emilia shook her head.

"She died when I was seven." She stood taller, pulled her shoulders back. There was no reason it should still hurt, not when it had been two decades. But there was a raw wound over an old scar now. Damn Luis for finding and pulling the thread that had led him to her mother's hospital records. Because the queen had been at the university downtown when her bleeding started, she'd been admitted there first. While she and Emilia's brother had died at home later, the evidence was there—the father on record was a member of the guard. The King's Guard.

When Aiodhán's hand rested on her shoulder, warmth flooded down from the spot he touched, radiating across her torso. Though it did nothing to tamper the hurt living wild in her chest, it awakened other parts of her that had been asleep her whole life, save the one night she'd spent with the doctor. "I'm sorry to hear that. Loss is a helluva powerful motivator. But—"

"Adler. Get in here. Got a trauma and no surgeon," a man called out from the entrance, interrupting Aiodhán. What was the *but* he'd referred to?

His hand lingered for a brief moment longer before his eyes hardened into the stone jewels they usually were.

"Let's go, de Reyes." He took off toward the entrance, and she followed at a run. "Dress out and meet me in Trauma One in two minutes."

As she donned her scrubs and coat alongside the night shift interns, she ran through the words he'd been prevented from saying. Had he gone through similar loss? Sometimes, when they worked a trauma as a team, he got this faraway look in his eyes. She imagined he was seeing something she couldn't, something from his past.

Not that he'd share anything personal with her. No, he was too professional. Surgically efficient.

When the beeping from Trauma One grew loud enough to hear from the hallway, she put aside any thoughts of Aiodhán and his odd behavior.

It was time to do what she came there to do, and under no circumstances was a man going to stand in her way.

CHAPTER FOUR

AIODHÁN TIGHTENED THE tie around his neck and gave himself a once-over in the mirror of the on-call bathroom. He looked professional. Competent. In charge.

Giving his watch a glance, he bit the corner of his lip. For the next few minutes anyway. Why was it every time he was in the orbit of Emilia de Reyes, all that went out the damned window?

He'd never once suffered a crisis of confidence at work—until the redheaded temptress entered his life. Now he second-guessed every last thing he'd been taught, said, even wore.

"Get a grip," he told his reflection. "You're the goddamn chief of general surgery. You can handle this." If the last eight weeks were any indication, however, that wasn't entirely true.

Emilia had been *brilliant* in the ER the morning before. Quick reflexes, she'd anticipated his requests, and her calm had been contagious. He'd worked through the GSW with an energy and serenity he'd never felt in the ER. She was the best intern to walk through the doors of Minny Gen. Himself included. He'd picked it up—the rhythm, the work ethic—after a few months, but Emilia came with it bred into her. Nothing seemed to faze her.

And he'd tested that theory.

Eight weeks of routine scut work, never-ending rounds that residents had to make, even the toughest patients with horrible attitudes... Other interns were burnt out, and she smiled through it. Hell, she even got some of the hard cases smiling, too.

"Three things, Adler," Mallory had told him when he agreed to take over the residency program. "Passion, responsibility, and professionalism. You find a resident with all three at the end of their first year, don't let them go."

"I'm not an idiot, Mal." Of course he'd hang on to the good ones.

"That may be true, but you are—how should I put this?—grumpy enough to put Scrooge on the Nice List."

He'd balked at the accusation, but now he wondered. Was he pushing and testing Emilia, or driving her away? He hoped not. Wasn't he always saying that the job mattered more than anything else? And she was good for the hospital.

It wouldn't be the worst thing if she found another program.

Yeah, it would, his head argued against the criticism of his heart. *She deserves to be here*, the balancing scales in his heart argued. She helped him save lives, which was his only goal.

She also made him forget all about that goal one evening when they'd been locked in the skills lab together during a tornado warning. She'd bet him she could assess and analyze more correct case studies and he'd shaken her hand, taking that bet with the overconfidence earned by his years on the job. That'd been his downfall. Her scent had overwhelmed him, and to compensate, he'd gotten overconfident and misdiagnosed three patients.

Fake patients, but still. De Reyes was killing him. No, his reaction to her was killing him. None of this was her fault, something that bugged him more than anything: she was doing just what he'd promised he would and kept things professional since day one.

He'd truly believed he could do the same thing. That he couldn't had to imply some sort of weakness he'd not addressed in himself yet.

The speaker overhead blared. "Dr. Adler to the nurses' station."

He needed to forget Emilia and focus on the trauma building across the street and start the interview process for docs to join him there. Thank God the residents moved to rotations next month.

"Dr. Adler to the nurses' station." The page sounded again and he jogged over.

"What do you have for me, Kathy?" he asked, grateful for work to distract him from thinking of Emilia. Again.

Always.

He swallowed that and concentrated on Kathy's rundown.

"Female patient, twenty-three years old, trouble breathing. Your intern is already in with her, taking vitals."

"Isn't that your job?"

Kathy just shrugged. "Wasn't my idea. She was halfway through when I got here. Doing a good job, so I figured I'd let her finish."

"She?"

"That new doc from Europe."

Damn.

"Okay," he said. "Thanks."

He grabbed a tablet and headed to the room Kathy indicated. The interns weren't even supposed to be on shift till now, and it looked like she'd been here at least half an hour.

But sure enough, before he even walked through the clear, glass doors to the patient's room, Emilia's laughter rang out.

The laugh was so incongruous with the space, it rubbed him the wrong way. No, that wasn't wholly the truth. If he were being honest with himself, he was frustrated because everyone else seemed to get this side of Emilia—the fun-loving, effervescent one. Everyone but him.

"What do you see, Dr. de Reyes?" he asked, pulling up the patient's chart.

The woman was young—too young for the indicated hypertension.

Emilia's smile fell. What was it about him that forced her to hide that beautiful smile of hers?

Maybe it's a good thing. It's distracting.
And it wasn't his job to make Emilia happy…
But you wouldn't mind it, his heart argued.
Maybe not. But making her happy would lead to caring about her, and caring led to—well, it led to all kinds of places Aiodhán avoided.

"I've made the notes in her chart, but it looks like hypertension and some resulting complications," she said. When the patient's brows pulled with concern, Emilia added, "Ms. Delaney and I were just discussing the new dating show while I changed her bedpan and took her vitals. You're looking good right now, Ms. Delaney."

The patient calmed, as did her rapid heart rate.

"If only my husband agreed. He said these gowns make patients look like Monty Python characters."

The two women laughed. Her laugh might be yet one more thing about her that distracted him, but Aiodhán certainly didn't mind the way Emilia's skin flushed when she smiled, like her whole body wanted in on the pleasure. That is, when it didn't remind him of the way her skin had flushed under his touch the night they'd met.

Had that really been two and a half months ago? Why could he still recall each cell on her cheeks as they changed color for him?

He shook the images from his mind. He needed to keep this professional. In this case, he couldn't find fault in her job, either: she'd done good work.

Go a little easier on her. If this were anyone else, you'd be kinder, more patient.

When she got out a saline bag, however, he stopped her.

"You need to wait for the other interns. And this is a nurse's job. You're a physician." He argued with himself that was a fact, something he'd tell any of the interns.

Emilia's brows furrowed, and she hung the bag without attaching the IV.

"But if I can do it, and I'm available, doesn't it make sense for me to help out?"

"It's a precedent we don't want to set. There's a reason we don't cross-train here."

Emilia opened her mouth as if she meant to shoot back a retort but shut it again, shaking her head.

"I feel nauseous again, Emilia," Ms. Delaney said. Her color had indeed changed to a pale gray. Emilia had a bedpan under her in seconds, just as the other interns finally rolled in. Aiodhán checked his watch. Ten minutes late. Emilia was the only intern pulling her weight, and then some.

The patient vomited into the bedpan as Emilia placed the IV for fluids without asking for permission. Emilia breathed through her mouth, her own skin dappled with moisture and nearing the color of her patient's. Aiodhán didn't miss the way a wave of nausea rolled through her.

"Are you okay?" Bridget asked her.

"Yes, thank you."

Aiodhán moved beside her. "If you can't handle bodily fluids, de Reyes—"

"I'm fine." Her skin paled even more than the translucent cream it usually was, but she kept going until the line was placed.

Aiodhán inspected her work, then shook his head.

"It's not right. Try it again."

"Would you care to explain how? It's placed precisely where you indicated it should be."

Aiodhán took a moment to compose his response. She was right, on one hand. It wasn't that the line wasn't placed correctly, but it wasn't the way he'd have done it. And that's what mattered—consistency. Still, he had to admit she had an inherent skill the other interns were slow to come to. They were learning where she seemed to just…know.

"You've taped it incorrectly. On top of the arm allows for easier access to the port."

Warning prickled his skin when she scowled.

"This gives her more range of motion."

As if to prove her point, the patient vomited again, and the line didn't tangle or pull.

Thankfully, she didn't gloat about her win. Instead, she rubbed the patient's back, talking softly to her.

Hmmm. Good bedside manner, flexibility in patient care, top-notch skills... Mallory would be pleased. Why wasn't he?

Because you're afraid if she's too good, she'll get snapped up by another hospital after her residency. A more prestigious program.

That hadn't occurred to him until now. The only thing worse than having to work with Emilia for two years, all the while craving her in every sense of the word, would be to see someone else claim her.

He continued, his skin prickled with goose bumps. "Based on the medical history this patient shared, what's the next step in diagnostic reasoning?" he asked the room. The three other interns who'd arrived dove into the notebooks they'd taken to carrying with them since the first day, as if they might find the answer there.

Emilia's hand was the only one that rose confidently.

"Of course she knows," one of the interns mumbled under their breath. Another snickered.

"You two are jackasses," Bridget mumbled. Aiodhán bit back a smile. She was right on that count.

"If one of you has the answer, you're welcome to share it," Aiodhán told them. He might be frustrated by Emilia's natural proclivity for giving right answer after right answer if only because it meant he had to focus his attention on her, something he fought the urge to do day after day anyway. But for a lower-performing student to disparage her for it? Not on his watch. "Well, come on. Do you have anything?"

"I don't, Dr. Adler," the first said. When he trained his gaze on the man who'd laughed, the intern shook his head as well.

"Very well. What do you think, de Reyes?"

"Run an echo and electrocardiogram and have a full blood panel drawn."

"Looking for what, specifically?"

"Heart disease and a blockage that might explain the shortness of breath with the patient. Specific worry about a prestroke clot should also be watched over the next twenty-four hours."

He'd bet by the open mouths on the other interns' faces, their eyes wide with surprise, they were thinking of something lung-related. They'd have been wrong.

"Why is that?" he asked.

"The patient was on estrogen birth control until this month when she tried to conceive. In addition to trouble breathing, she presented with a family history of clots and a mother who suffered a fatal stroke at around the patient's age."

Aiodhán nodded. Most others would have missed the history of clots and birth control. Especially their first two months on the job.

"Good work." Giving her praise was awkward: he felt as if the whole room could see through to his feelings for the resident. But they needed to see what competence looked like. That was the job. "So, what are you waiting for? Order the tests, and check in on the labs. Report back on the results as they come in. You've earned it."

Emilia nodded and spun on her heels, and like everything she did, there was an air of confidence in her step, in the way her shoulders remained tall and proud even under his scrutiny. She was thinner than when she'd arrived, likely the demanding schedule. Her skin was pale, too. She'd adjust, but his heart tugged. He'd been working her too hard.

He sent the interns on rounds, then ran to catch up with her. "Emilia, wait."

She turned to face him. "Yes, Dr. Adler?"

What did he want from her? Nothing he could ask for, nothing he should pursue for so many reasons.

Walk away. And he almost did. Until his eyes caught the door to an on-call room. Her eyes flashed with something he recognized from their night together. Desire.

Before he could talk himself out of whatever it was he was doing, he pulled her in and shut the door. Emilia's back was to the wall and her eyes were round as she gazed up at him. Her chest rose and fell with each breath she took through parted lips. He knew the curves of her breasts by heart, even after only one night of giving them all the pleasure he knew how to give. But they appeared fuller, heavier. Maybe that was just his imagination that knew no bounds when it came to Emilia de Reyes.

Goddamn, she was stunning. His hand reached up of its own volition and wrapped around the base of her ponytail before his brain could redirect him to less dangerous ground. His thumb traced her pronounced cheekbone. She inhaled a small gasp, and color spread to her cheeks. But she didn't move out of his grasp or try to move away from him. In fact, she leaned into his palm, closing her eyes as a soft smile played at the corner of her lips.

That—the smile he'd missed on her lips for so many weeks now—undid him.

"I'm just Aiodhán," he whispered. "Not your boss or even someone you work with. Just the man you met at the bar that night."

"You...you can't be that. Not anymore."

A whisper tickled the back of his mind.

She's right. What are you doing?

What he'd wanted to do for weeks now but couldn't. Touch her, which he did, trailing his thumb along her full, pink bottom lip.

"Please," he whispered. She nodded. He dipped his chin and claimed her mouth, used his tongue to open her mouth so he could explore her.

She deepened the kiss by pulling him closer, and with her chest pressed against his, he didn't have any doubt—her breasts were swollen and fuller than they'd been. Goddamn. The desire ripped through him fast and hot until a Code Blue alarm sounded outside the door.

She shot back against the on-call bed, leaving him struggling to catch his breath.

Emilia's eyes grew even wider if it was possible, and her fingers traced her lips where his had just been.

"We can't do this. I—I'm not available, Aiodhán."

"You're with someone?"

She shook her head. "No. Not exactly. But I can't be with you. It wouldn't be fair." Those last four words came out as a whisper.

"I'm sorry," he got out through a ragged breath. "I don't know what came over me." He was her boss. Of course this wasn't fair to her. Jesus. What had he done?

If pretending he didn't want her was hard before, it was impossible with her taste on his lips. But he had to.

"I've got to get back." She opened the door just enough that the harsh fluorescent lights poured in through the crack, reminding him of what lay beyond the on-call room. Namely an unjust world where the one thing he thought he wanted most he couldn't have without risking everything he needed.

He left the small room, and the events of the past few minutes caught up to him.

What the actual hell did I do? Had he really just followed an intern on orders he'd given her, only to pull her into a room and kiss her within an inch of his life? Heat spread from his lips to his chest, then pooled low in his stomach. Yeah, that's exactly what he'd done.

Aiodhán shifted on his feet, tempted to follow her again to apologize, but how could he trust that's what he'd actually do when his real desire was evidenced in his lips that tingled with want, in his erection that wouldn't abate?

Getting a grip on both issues, he turned the opposite way

that Emilia had gone and strode back to where the other interns were finishing up.

Damn if pulling away from that kiss was the hardest thing he'd ever done, after burying his parents. What had come over him? It wasn't that he didn't want her, but that had to come second to letting her grow as a surgeon or physician. Which led to another problem. If she was incredible at what she did, and as passionate about it as he was? Well, he'd have a hard time talking himself out of wanting her the way he did each time she smiled with those full lips of hers while she worked, each time her independence and confidence won over a patient or resident, each time she corrected a misdiagnosis. He already lost control, and they'd only been working together for a matter of months.

"Thanks for making sure they stayed on task, Bridget," he told Emilia's friend, gathering the crew to finish the rounds. "As for the rest of you, it's time to learn what scut work is. You can go ahead and put those notepads away. You won't be needing them the rest of the shift."

When they all grumbled, doing what he asked at a glacial pace, he sent a glance to where Emilia had just turned the corner. An ache that only partially had to do with being surrounded by her lesser motivated, poorer substitutes filled his chest. He missed her, dammit. Her lips, her hands, her sharp wit. But mostly how she made him feel when she was around. And that wasn't going to work.

Not for so many reasons, least of which was her enigmatic pull on his heart. His new job, in addition to running the residency program and finishing up across the street, was finding reasons for distancing himself from Emilia.

More than just his career and dream project were on the line if he didn't. His heart was at risk, and he swore he'd never wager that again on a relationship. Not even for a woman as captivating as Emilia de Reyes.

CHAPTER FIVE

"CAN I GET you anything, Princess?" Chance called out from the next room.

Emilia shook her head, but that wouldn't suffice, would it? Not when he couldn't see her. But she didn't have the energy for much else.

"I'm okay, Chance. Thanks."

She sank into the couch at her new apartment, letting the soft leather act as a balm for all that ailed her. Her toes curled against the sharp pain emanating from the arches of both feet. Her back cracked in two places, providing little relief to the pressure built around her spine. And why—*why*—did she have to pee again?

Honestly, it was as if every organ and muscle in her body joined in mutiny against her singular dream to practice the kind of medicine that would have saved her mother. Not that she blamed her body for putting up a fight. Even her heart was weary, not entirely sure *this*—the sixteen-hour days, the painstaking work of putting into practice all she'd learned in medical school, the loss of patients she'd grown to care for—was worth it.

She'd thought she was made of tougher stuff than simply princess material. But maybe she'd been wrong.

Then there was the persistent *thump-thump* of her heart every time she had to interact with Aiodhán. From time to time she'd catch him staring at her, as if trying to figure her out.

It had only grown worse after their kiss. She put a finger to her lips and swore they still bore the heat that had passed between her and Aiodhán in that on-call room, even though it had been a month and he'd barely looked at her since.

She didn't blame him. She'd made it seem as if it would be unfair to her if they pursued a relationship. Even a physical one. But it'd been a lie, one meant to protect her cover. The truth was, she wanted him so desperately, she dreamed of his lips, his hands, his tongue…

But it would be so dreadfully unfair to him to let him in when the truth was she couldn't date, couldn't fall in love, couldn't have anything resembling a romance outside of her impending royal union.

That didn't stop the part of her that flushed with desire when she watched him work, when a hint of a smile graced his lips when he talked to a patient, or as he strode down the corridors of Minnie Gen. She still wanted him, whether or not she should.

And make no mistake, she *shouldn't*. In the past month since the kiss, she'd made sure to focus on work and work only. But in doing so, she'd become undernourished and overworked, with no time for the self-care needed to get back to full strength. Emilia picked up a pale green throw pillow that reminded her of the color of the Mediterranean Sea outside her family home and screamed into it.

It wasn't bad, but it wasn't *her*. She was a doctor.

A chime alerted her to the private elevator making its way to her penthouse.

Chance peered out from the kitchen, an apron tied around his waist.

"That's quite a look for you, Chance," Emilia said. A giggle escaped, earning her a frown from the uberserious adviser.

"Are you expecting company?" he asked, ignoring her quip about his attire.

"Relax. It's just a woman from my program. We're going to study and work on sutures together this evening."

"Do you think it wise to invite people here? Others knowing where you live puts you at risk, Princess."

"Well, luckily, that's what I have you for." Chance's scowl deepened if that was possible. "Please don't call me Princess while she's here, okay? It's just Emilia. Who cares where I live? If people find out who I am, *that's* when I'll be in trouble."

Chance didn't respond but went to the elevator doors that were opening on Bridget, typing something frantically on her phone.

"Okay, please explain why I needed a code to get in here—" She cut herself off as her gaze lifted. Her mouth dropped in surprise, and her long whistle echoed off the vaulted ceiling. "Holy crap. You live *here*? Why the hell are you an intern if you can afford to live like this?"

"May I take your coat?" Chance asked.

Bridget hugged her red pea coat close to her chest.

"Who is this?" she asked Emilia, jabbing a thumb in the direction of a wounded-looking Chance. Emilia sent the man a stare that hopefully expressed he was on thin ice. A roll of his eyes and quick turn on his heels and he was back in the kitchen.

"Never mind him. He's my roommate and comes from money."

It was a weak alibi, but when Chance reappeared with crudités on a tray, Bridget didn't question it.

"Oh, my *gawd*. We're never meeting at the library again. You've been holding out on me," she said, stuffing a salmon pâté cracker in her mouth. Emilia stifled a laugh. If life were any different, she'd love to take Bridget to see her home country. This penthouse was nice, but it paled in comparison to her coastal home in the south, or the castle in Cyana. Bridget would love it.

A small yearning to see it for herself nudged at Emilia's heart. She missed Zephyranthes, but this trip was important. She'd be back soon enough.

"I'm okay with that. Any luck on the moonlighting position?" she asked, grabbing a snack for herself. She had to give the guy credit: for all Chance's grumblings, he was a fabulous cook.

"Nothing yet. Aiodhán doesn't think I'm ready for the extra shifts here, so I started putting out feelers at hospitals outside the city."

Emilia bristled at the mention of Aiodhán. He took up so much space in her thoughts and life, but having his name spoken here filled the spacious room with an oppressively thick air.

"Yikes. Do you really need the extra work? I mean, we're barely off enough to sleep and get a meal on the run as it is."

Bridget shrugged. "I wish I could, but this city is expensive, and residency doesn't pay enough to cover rent."

Emilia curled up on the couch, her legs tucked beneath her. Other residents had expressed similar sentiments. This life—when one didn't come from her resources or wealth—wasn't for the weak of heart.

Was there something she could do to help, or would that come off as patronizing?

"I'm sorry," she said, but it sounded weak, especially since they were surrounded by Zephyr art and decor that cost enough she could have housed the whole residency for cheaper.

"It's fine. Not all of us are as lucky as you, finding your way into this life. You're like Minneapolis royalty up here."

A slow burn traced Emilia's skin, painting it red with embarrassment. She'd grown up around privilege and pomp and ceremony. Was she missing out by not adapting fully to life here? The truth was, she didn't know if she'd make it in the grueling residency program without Chance cooking for her and these comforts to come home to. As it was, she was barely able to stand.

"Well, my place is your place. You're welcome here anytime."

Two hours, three different appetizers, and one delicious chocolate mousse pie later, the women put aside their oranges and thread so Emilia could say good-night to Bridget. The poor fruit looked like something out of a horror film, with crude sutures stitched across their skins. But there was noticeable improvement.

A wave of pride washed over her own skin. Who cared what Aiodhán thought? She was good at this and, more importantly, she was willing to work and learn how to be better.

She stood up, prepared to head to her bedroom for the five hours of sleep she'd get if she fell asleep immediately but was rocked by a crippling wave of nausea.

Desperation to make it to the sink warred with her body's inability to move without a new crest of dizziness crashing against her. Immobilized, she vomited into the bowl still half full of gourmet popcorn.

"Chance?" she whispered. Somehow, the man heard her and was by her side in less than a breath's time. "I'm not well."

"No, you're not. You're pale, *Princesa*." He swept her up and before she could process what was happening, she was being tucked into her four-poster bed. She nestled between the down comforter and the pillowtop mattress, sleep claiming her as a final thought floated to her consciousness.

It's probably something you ate. You'll be fine in the morning.

With that, she fell into the deepest sleep since her arrival in America.

The next morning, feeling weak, Emilia sought out Bridget in the staff locker room.

"Are you feeling okay?" she asked her friend.

Bridget shot her a surprised look from under furrowed brows while she donned her lab coat labeling her a resident of Minneapolis General.

"Um, yeah. Why? Should I not be?"

Emilia shook her head, but the headache that had plagued her all night still pulsed behind her eyes.

"Of course not. I just felt...*off* last night and wanted to make sure it wasn't the salmon."

"Don't you dare blame that dish your roommate made. That was the best meal I've had in years." Emilia laughed, relieved. Her friend was okay. But if it wasn't the fish, what made her so ill so suddenly? "You're probably just exhausted."

"Yeah, you're probably right."

Bridget set down her stethoscope and appraised her closely. "You feel okay now? Because I'll vouch for you with Aiodhán if you need to take off today."

Emilia's stomach flipped.

"No, no. I'll be okay. I just want to get the day over with. Then I'm going home and going straight to bed."

The door to the locker room slammed open, crashing into the wall behind it.

"Let's go. You two are holding up the group."

Aiodhán. He hadn't heard anything they'd discussed, had he? If he had, especially after the week she'd had under his watchful eye in the OR, she'd never recover her reputation with him.

Why do I care so much what this man thinks?

Emilia's stomach flipped. Was it another side effect of whatever had upset her rhythm the night before? Perhaps she had a stomach bug that was a result of more than just dehydration and malnutrition. She tended to sick people all day, after all.

It didn't matter either way. She needed to get to work before Aiodhán found another excuse to be peeved with her.

As she stepped out into the light—far brighter than normal, wasn't it?—she swallowed back the pervasive nausea. Nothing was getting in the way of her dream that was so close she could touch it. Not even a little bout of stomach issues that would surely resolve in a matter of days.

CHAPTER SIX

Two weeks later, Aiodhán was actually worried. Emilia hadn't missed a shift or even been late once. But she wasn't herself either.

Outside the OR that morning, he'd been telling the intern class about fistulas and how to repair them, and her eyes had glazed over; she focused on the wall behind him and not the medical advice he was sharing. At one point, she sighed heavily and struggled to keep her eyes open.

Definitely not typical Emilia.

Then he'd offered the chance to scrub in to the first intern who could correctly name the four types of fistulas that might occur. The three residents all shot an expectant look at Emilia, as did he. After all, she was always the first to answer—correctly, too—when he posed a question to the cohort.

But nothing. Just another sigh capped with a yawn.

Definitely not typical Emilia.

"May I speak with you in the hall, de Reyes?"

She seemed to snap out of the stupor she was in and nodded.

"What's going on?" Aiodhán asked when they were alone.

"What do you mean?" The genuine look of surprise in her twisted brows and pursed lips didn't sit well with him. If anything, the woman was painfully self-aware. "Am I in trouble?"

"No." He shook his head, regret pulsing in his chest. He'd pushed her too far, and she blamed herself. "I'm sorry if I made you think you were."

"Then, I'm confused. Why are you pulling me aside? Did I miss a report?"

"No, nothing like that. You just seem…off. I asked about the four types of fistulas, and you didn't even glance over."

She frowned. "Anorectal, anovaginal, colorectal, and colocutaneous."

"Right." Of course she knew; he expected no less from her. *She'd be perfect for the trauma center. I want to take a resident or two, so why not her?*

"So," he continued, "as you know I'll be moving my practice across the street."

"To the Minneapolis General Trauma Facility?"

"Yep. I was wondering if you'd be willing to do an extended rotation there. I need a good resident, and you're the best."

Emilia's lips parted like she might answer when a Code Blue alarm went off. Aiodhán's gaze shot to Kathy at the nurses' station.

"Trauma Three," she shouted over the din and chaos of the ER.

He nodded and glanced down at Emilia. "Join me?"

Her forehead raised in question. Aiodhán had never asked her for anything before today, had he? Just demanded. Well, that would change. It had to if he didn't want to lose Emilia. As a doctor, of course. He didn't have any personal feelings toward the woman.

Liar, his libido chimed in. *You'd take her back to an on-call room in a second if you thought you wouldn't lose credibility or your job.*

Damn. That was true, but inconsequential. She'd shut him down, and thank goodness. If he still wanted her, it was his problem—not hers.

"Um…sure. For this case. May I take some time to consider the other offer? My heart is set on obstetrics as a specialty, but I'd like to weigh my options."

"Of course. You should know we'll have an OB wing there

for trauma cases involving pregnant women. But take all the time you need to consider the offer," he said. Aiodhán lingered a fraction of a second, only then noticing her red-rimmed eyes. "You sure you're okay to do this?" he asked.

"I am."

He saw what it cost her to throw her shoulders back and lift her chin. *That* was typical Emilia. She'd be fine with some rest and time off. He'd make sure she got both next week. No matter how he acted in person, whatever front he put on for show, he cared about Emilia. Seeing her like this was like a mirror to all his mistakes being held up in front of him.

He gestured toward Trauma Three and jogged over, Emilia close on his heels.

"What's the story?" he asked Rana, the nurse on call. She was up on the bed performing CPR, but the steady beep rang in the background, indicating no sinus rhythm.

"GSW to the right flank, no exit wound. Waiting on a surgery room to open up. Coded thirty seconds ago. No pulse."

"Another one," Emilia whispered, shuddering. She wasn't wrong. There'd been an increase in gunshot wounds the past week. He could triage those cases easier than he could the car-wreck victims, though. The latter came too close to home for him.

"Come on down and push two of epi."

Emilia was already charging the paddles to two hundred, anticipating his ask.

"Okay, we only get one shot at this. I want to get him back, then open him up."

"Here?" Rana asked.

"Do we have another option?"

She shook her head, putting the meds in the IV. "Not for at least an hour."

"This guy doesn't have that long."

"I'll call and get the team here, along with a portable surgery tray," Emilia said. Before he could comment on the sterile field he'd need to make, she added, "But I'll have them wait behind the glass divider so you can keep a sterile field."

"Go for it, but hurry back. I need you to assist." It was the closest he could get to what he wanted to say. *Thanks for anticipating what I'll need and being a helluva partner in the OR.*

Within ten seconds, the other interns flooded the room on the back side of the divider so they could observe but stay out of the way, and Emilia rolled in a tray. The patient had sinus rhythm back, so if he was going to do this—open up a patient in the middle of the ER—he needed to do it now.

"Iodine," he said as he grabbed the scalpel he needed, but Emilia already had it in hand and was dousing the patient's abdomen. "Thank you. I want a portable ultrasound brought up and a recovery room booked."

"It's already on its way," Emilia said. "And the room is reserved. It was the last one available, and I didn't want us to lose it."

Damn it. She really was magnificent. In so many ways...

"Okay, then. Let's do this."

Emilia adjusted the light, and Aiodhán stilled before he cut. Her skin was pale and dappled with sweat.

"You sure you're up for this? You can observe if you'd like."

"No," she said, swallowing hard. "I'm okay. How can you use me?"

"Suction, and watch the ultrasound for shards of metal or the bullet. Best case we find it intact, but I'm not betting the farm."

"The farm?"

He chuckled, as did Rana. Using the scalpel, he sliced a ten-inch opening for them. "It's an American English expression meaning I don't think we will. Do you have an idiom like that in Spain?"

"I'm from Zephyranthes, actually."

"Oh." She hadn't so much lied to him as allowed him to make assumptions. But why not share where she was from in the first place? It didn't make a difference to him. "So, any Zephyr idioms?"

Emilia's smile brightened the room more than the overhead surgical light. She suctioned, her eyes on the wound, and her hands moved fluidly like she'd been doing this for years, not months. "The closest I can think of is an old one. *El tapete le acabó con cuanto poseía.* It means *The man lost his fortune at the gambling table.*"

"I like it. It's a helluva lot classier than ours. Suction."

Emilia moved the suction to the bleed Aiodhán found. She breathed through her mouth, slow and deliberate.

"Zephyr idioms always seemed more like life lessons when I was growing up. Do this and lose your and your family's good name. Say that and drown in sorrow for eternity."

"Damn. Well, with one of the few countries left with royalty running the show, that checks out."

"What do you mean?" she asked. A hint of color flushed her cheeks, but he couldn't focus on that now. Nor what it did to the fluttering in his stomach.

"Nothing, really. Just seems like all those staunch royals make things more serious than they have to be. I saw the king on the news the other day, and he had way too many medals on his chest for a guy signing in a new law. Suction, please." She moved the hose to where Aiodhán worked. "Thanks."

"Maybe we should stick to talking about medicine and not something we know so little about," she said.

He moved the lower intestinal tract out of the way and still... nothing. Was Emilia really passionate about all that pomp and circumstance? "Found it." Relief washed over him. His patient was deteriorating fast. All he could hope for now was a clean bullet and no internal bleeding. Emilia handed him a set of curved hemostat forceps without taking her gaze off him. He retrieved the bullet in one piece, no signs of fragmentation present. "Looks whole."

"I guess you didn't lose your fortune," Rana said, an overly wide smile on her face. The nurse was only trying to lighten the mood, but as Emilia sutured the patient up, her scowl didn't budge.

What the hell had he said?

After closing, Emilia cut the thread and put the scissors down on the tray. "If you don't need me for anything else." She moved in the direction of the door.

"Emilia," Aiodhán said. He kept his voice level, even though an undercurrent of so many emotions ran below it. "Can we talk?"

She shook her head, her back to him so he didn't see her face as her shoulders slumped. What happened next was both in slow motion and at the same time too fast for Aiodhán to react. Emilia's legs gave out, and she bent over her stomach before crumpling to the ground. Though his arms were outstretched, desperation driving him toward her, he was too late.

Emilia's body bounced off the gurney, and her head hit the tile floor with a sickening thwack that reverberated in Aiodhán's chest.

As time sped forward again, he sprinted to her side, only one thought on his mind.

Oh, God. Please let her be okay.

"Everyone out. I need a gurney *now*," Aiodhán said. Emilia was unconscious but breathing. He'd done a quick workup, and there didn't appear to be any damage to her neck and spine. But her pulse was thready, and she looked like hell.

He cupped her head, keeping it stable in case he'd missed something, and despite the optics of the situation he stroked the hair off her damp forehead with the pads of his thumbs. He shivered, a dark memory of holding his father's head in his lap playing at the edge of his consciousness. He couldn't help then, but he'd be damned if he let Emilia suffer the same fate as his old man.

"Why isn't anyone moving? Get her help *right goddamn now*!"

So much was at stake, and they were deer in the headlights.

"I'll grab the gurney," Bridget said.

"Wait. Do you know her roommate?"

"The rich Zephyr guy with the fancy apartment? Yeah, why?"

Aiodhán frowned. That was a lot of information he hadn't been aware of.

Not the time.

"Sure. Yeah. He's in the lobby. Sprint down and grab him in case he knows how to contact her family."

"You got it, boss." Bridget sped off down the hall, and the rest of the room cleared out, the steady beep of the gunshot patient's heart rate monitor peppering the silence until he was moved to his recovery room.

"I've never met anyone like you, Emilia. You make me—hell, you make all of us—so much better."

The admission surprised him. It was all true, but he'd always been able to shove aside his feelings, his memories—anything that might get in the way of his job. Until Emilia. She blurred lines he'd thought were etched in steel.

The door hissed open, and a nurse rolled a gurney through.

"Do you want me to help you get her up?"

"No," he said, shaking his head, his gaze still pinned on Emilia's unconscious form. A proprietary sense of ownership washed over him. He couldn't relinquish her care to anyone else. "I've got it, thanks."

He tucked an arm under her legs and stood, cradling her neck. She was light but limp in his arms, and seeing her without her signature strength and sass bit the back of his throat, making it hard to swallow. She didn't stir as he set her down on the gurney.

"Make a room available in the west wing," he told the nurse. "I'll take her up myself. But let her roommate and Bridget know where we're sending her."

She tapped a few things on her tablet and left.

"I've got you, Emilia. I won't let anything happen to you."

He made a mental list on the elevator to the west wing of what he'd need to take care of Emilia. Basic labs to see how malnourished she was, an IV of fluids, a CT to check her head for a concussion.

And what she needed? A few days off and for him to finally let her hold on him go. Maybe if their shared night of passion wasn't so prevalent in his thoughts, he'd have recognized she was sick.

He'd be better. For her, because she deserved a teacher who could live up to the same level of professionalism she showed up with every day.

If she makes it, his brain chose that moment to chime in.
She will. She has to. She's just a little overworked, right?

But small memories perked up in the back of his head. Her puking a few weeks earlier after a patient was sick. Overhearing her tell Bridget she was sick before that. This had been going on for a while, but he'd been too stubborn, too hurt by her dismissal of him, too rigid in his attempts to keep her at arm's length that he'd failed to act on what he'd seen.

The doors to the elevator opened, and Chance was standing there, a grim look on his formerly stoic face.

"Where, may I ask, are you taking Emilia? And what happened to her?"

"She passed out in the ER. I'm taking her to a room so I can get a workup done. She hit her head pretty hard, so there are some tests I have to run."

"I'd like to see all the results."

Aiodhán maneuvered around Chance, realizing for the first time the girth of the man. With his arms crossed over his chest, he looked strong—strong enough to feel like he could demand the impossible.

"I'm afraid I can't do that. Family only. I appreciate your concern for Emilia's health, but—"

Chance slapped a folded sheet of paper against Aiodhán's chest as he walked by.

Okay, so the man didn't just *look* strong. Aiodhán coughed some air back in his lungs.

"This is her medical power of attorney, granting me access to her care, the decisions that need to be made on her behalf, and full rights to information until such time as her parents can be dispatched."

Until such time as *what*? Any other time, this guy's attitude and odd speech patterns would rub Aiodhán the wrong way, but right now? With Emilia's health on the line? It straight pissed him off.

"We're wasting time. Get out of my way before I call security."

Chance smiled in a way that sent a chill through Aiodhán's veins. It was less a grin and more a sneer.

"Do you think they'd like to learn you slept with Emilia the night you took her home to your apartment?"

Aiodhán stopped pushing the gurney and felt his jaw drop as his limbs froze.

"She told you?"

Chance shook his head. "She didn't need to. I make it a point to know everything Emilia is up to."

Aiodhán's finger was up in Chance's face before he could stop himself. The woman at the heart of the rage that boiled in his chest was lying unconscious beneath the men arguing over her care. Not okay. Not one bit.

"Now, listen here, you creep. If you don't move out of my way, I'll have you arrested for obstruction of care. Either way, I'm deciding whether to turn you in as a stalker. Call her parents, and stay the hell away."

His grip on the gurney tightened until his joints ached and his breath came in short bursts. That guy was a piece of work.

The room was set up already, Bridget hanging the last of the IV bags.

"Thanks," he told her. "I appreciate you working ahead of me. Can you order a set of bloodwork and labs? And schedule a CT. I want these yesterday, Bridget, with the results for my eyes only, okay?"

"Of course. I understand." Bridget's brows were marked with concern. "But, um, I thought you should know she threw up this morning and last night and wasn't feeling well."

A flash of anger singed Aiodhán's skin. Not at Emilia, for coming to work under the weather, but at himself for making her feel she had no other choice.

"I appreciate you letting me know. I'll swab her for the flu and run a couple other tests."

At the door, Bridget stopped and turned around. "She's gonna be okay, right? She's the only person willing to talk to me here and who studies with me after our shift. Emilia is my best friend and the best of all of us."

Aiodhán couldn't agree more with the latter. If only he'd let down his guard with her and appreciated more of what she gave to the hospital, to her fellow interns who were studying and thriving so they might have a chance at keeping up with her, to *him*.

"I'm not sure what's going on, but I can promise I'll take good care of her."

Bridget smiled and left, but the door didn't close. Aiodhán looked up and frowned.

"I told you, man, get out of here now or I'll—"

Chance held up a badge, stopping Aiodhán in his tracks for the third time in as many minutes.

"I'll be staying, thank you," Chance said. Where the man had been humorously unsure of himself in the lobby, since he'd come up to the west wing, he exuded a presence that sent a chill across Aiodhán's skin. "I need to handle the secrecy of this until Emilia's parents arrive. It's imperative we contact them in a way that doesn't alert the wrong people to her…condition."

"And who would those people be?"

"Sir, I trust you're good at your job, am I correct?"

"Yeah. You could say that."

Chance dipped his head, as if in agreement. It was his first deference to Aiodhán's status.

"And I'm *superb* at mine, which is why I was chosen to travel with Ms. de Reyes. Please lock down any access to these quarters until I've given the green light. If you check with your CMO, you'll see she is already aware of the protocols."

Aiodhán's brows were arched, his curiosity piqued, but Chance didn't leave room for misinterpreting his commands. Aiodhán might have been in charge of his hospital, but Chance was in command of this situation: that much was clear now.

"Okay. I'll check back in once I've alerted the nursing staff and Bridget not to say anything."

"That won't be sufficient. I'll have NDAs distributed immediately. I need a list of names of people who are aware of Ms. de Reyes's stay here."

"Sure. Yeah. I can do that." *Why?* he wondered but wouldn't ask. He wasn't clear about *how* exactly, but this was bigger than him.

Aiodhán's arms fell to his sides, a feeling of inadequacy plaguing him for the first time since he'd first declared he'd wanted to be a doctor at the age of eleven. He'd stood there in nothing but plain white underwear, a stethoscope around his neck like his dad had worn.

"I'm gonna save people like Dad," he'd told his mom.

She'd been so supportive of that dream, even as a grieving wife who'd lost her husband to a car crash, doctors unable to save him. When his mother passed away in the horrific I-35 crash, leaving Aiodhán an orphan, it had solidified two things: he'd be the surgeon he wished he'd been to help save his parents, and he'd never let anyone else into his heart, which was a recipe for heartbreak.

And yet… Here he was, this woman very much infecting his heart. To what degree he'd parse through later, when she was okay. But damn if she'd somehow snuck past each of his carefully constructed defenses.

"May I ask you a question?" Aiodhán said to Chance, who nodded. "Why'd you need to travel with her? Why couldn't she do this alone?"

Thick, heavy silence filled the room with an edge of foreboding as Chance folded his arms across his chest again and nodded at Emilia on the bed.

"Because she's the crown princess of Zephyranthes, and my only job as royal adviser is to keep her safe."

CHAPTER SEVEN

"THE CROWN PRINCESS OF ZEPHYRANTHES? Like...a *real* Mediterranean princess?" Aiodhán asked. The room took on an eerie glow along the edges of his vision, and damn if pulling a breath was like sucking through a straw. His intern was a goddamned *royal*?

And part of the royal family he'd just unintentionally insulted while they operated a mere hour ago? No wonder she looked at him like he was the plague just before she... He shook his head, begging the image of her slumping to the ground, lifeless and pale, to dissipate. He doubted it ever would, though.

"Your knowledge of geography does your country justice," Chance retorted. The quirk of his lips said otherwise.

"And there are a lot of them? Royals? You know, like, for show? Dukes and princesses and whatever?" Why couldn't he recall what the news story had said? He was a bumbling idiot, trying to keep his head above water.

Chance's smile turned to one of pity.

"No, sir. Just the one. And her parents. The king and queen of Zephyranthes."

Aiodhán's thin field of vision contracted even further as heavier truths settled on his chest. First, there were actually *royals* out there, walking among the mere mortals instead of just on television. Hell, not even Minnesota was immune. But even bigger? Emilia, the incredible woman who'd infected his brain with thoughts of ridiculous, career-ending things like lust and passion, was one of them. And he'd hooked up with her in a night he wasn't likely to forget.

Oh, damn... His brain stalled as it struggled to process the reality of that simple discovery and exactly with it meant.

I slept with the princess of Zephyranthes. And then kissed her, breaking every international-relations rule that existed.

But wait... He wouldn't have kissed her if he'd known who she was. Indignation rolled through him, hot and fierce.

"She's a princess, and no one thought to tell me?"

"Was there a reason she should have disclosed that?" Chance asked. "Would you have treated her any different?"

"I mean, *yeah*."

Chance's smile grew thin. "Do you think, perhaps, that the choices you made would have been questionable whether or not Emilia was of royal lineage?"

Aiodhán sighed and put his head in his hands. "Damn. I'm sorry." He'd messed up, not just with the princess but the woman behind the crown. She deserved better no matter what title she bore.

"You might save that apology for the princess when she wakes up. And her parents might deserve an explanation as well."

"Yeah. Of course." Nerves fluttered in Aiodhán's chest. "And they're..."

"On their way here, yes. I'm sure they'll be delighted to meet Emilia's..." Chance paused, giving Aiodhán a head-to-toe assessment. *One-night stand,* Aiodhán filled in for him. "Boss," Chance ended with, mercifully.

Aiodhán paced the cold white-tiled floor while his brain raced with myriad thoughts about this new information.

Emilia was the princess of Zephyranthes.

Like a crown-wearing, title-bearing *royal*. He laughed.

"Is something funny?" Chance asked.

Aiodhán shook his head. "Tragic, actually. I mean, if I had been paying attention, I probably could have figured it out. Her confidence, the way she can talk to anyone and make them feel like they're the most important person in the room. All of it."

"The princess is regal, through and through."

And Aiodhán had done his damnedest to work that exceptionality out of her. And all because he couldn't get the captivating woman out of his head—or other parts of his anatomy. Looking too close at how she was struggling meant looking too close, period.

He was a royal, too. A royal *ass*.

Well, she's definitely unattainable now.

Another laugh escaped his chest. To anyone but Chance, he probably looked like he was losing it, and to a degree he was. Everything as he knew it was…different now. Who she was—a princess, yes, but also a fantastic doctor—was lined with a thousand red flags telling him to back off.

But damn if not one of those flags took the edge off the pulsing desire the woman brought out in him. Not even her lifeless form tucked beneath wires and hospital blankets did that; all it did was add a layer of protectiveness to the wanting.

Too bad both were misplaced. She had Chance for the latter, and protocols against dating a commoner—an American commoner—no doubt.

"Why couldn't I know?" he asked. "I mean, I wasn't just her boss."

"Precisely. We couldn't take the risk. There was a man who took advantage of her—of the entire family, actually—so anyone outside the upper echelon of administration knowing was too great a risk. Especially someone as…involved with the princess as you were."

"I'd never hurt her."

"I don't believe you would, not intentionally."

The idea of Emilia with another man was hard enough to imagine—but one who'd take advantage of her kindness, her intelligence for his own gain? Good thing there was an ocean between them. Still, it begged a particular question.

"Is she..." Aiodhán asked, peeking out of the curtains to make sure there weren't any lurking interns outside the door, eavesdropping. "Is she supposed to be with someone back home?"

Chance regarded him from under bushy brows.

"You care about her?" he asked Aiodhán.

Though the answer came to him immediately, he let it sit for a moment so he could choose his words wisely.

"I do. I know I'm not supposed to, especially with this new information, but..."

"She's special."

"She *is*. In so many ways." The way she understood what he needed—what their patients needed—without nudging, the way she anticipated questions and answered them in advance. But mostly the way she smiled no matter how tired she was. All the medical stuff could be trained into someone bright enough to pick it up. Yet her bedside manner? That couldn't be taught, and it was more than special: it was rare and beautiful. "But she'll have to marry someone back home, right?"

Chance's subtle nod might as well have been a hurricane-force wind the way it bowled Aiodhán over.

"It's part of her duty to her country, to make a union that will strengthen international ties. Her parents will make sure it's a proper match. Especially after the last attempt failed so grievously."

"The hell?" Aiodhán asked. His pulse was tachycardic, and his fervent pacing along the edge of her bed matched the speed of his racing heart. A primal scream welled up in his throat, suffocating him, but he didn't dare let it out.

"Where your geography does you proud, your lexicon falls short, Dr. Adler."

Aiodhán glared at Chance and jabbed a finger at the hospital bed.

"You're telling me this brilliant woman, the top of her class at one of the best teaching hospitals in the country, with passion that actually matches her skill...you're telling me she's betrothed to a guy she's never met? And after being screwed over by the last guy? Did I miss the train taking us back to the Dark Ages?"

"While I don't expect you to understand royal protocols—"

"Oh, don't give me that, Chance. You know as good as I do that the woman lying in that bed is way more than a crown or somebody's arm candy. She's a damn fine doctor, and she'll be squandered if she goes back there."

A flash of something resembling understanding passed over Chance's stoic features but passed as quickly.

"Emilia is aware of her obligations and takes them seriously. And she was always going to leave at the end of her residency. A two-year passion project is all our nobility are afforded, I'm afraid. Though her health might predicate her early exit from the program."

All this time, he'd made choices about her related to *his* needs and responses to the night they'd shared. He'd worried Emilia would stay and be a constant source of temptation for *him* or leave for another hospital and leave *him* wanting. The third option hadn't occurred to him. She wasn't even going to stay in this country because the woman owed *him* nothing. She'd shared a night of passion with him he'd never forget, but they'd never once talked about more.

He was losing her, no matter what. Which meant the hospital was, too. Faced with that possibility, he knew what was best for everyone. She needed to stay, to pursue medicine as long as she was able, and he needed to get the hell out of her way.

Aiodhán couldn't find his breath. His vision narrowed. Was this what a panic attack felt like?

"If she's okay, if she heals quickly, will they let her stay?"

For the first time since he'd met the man, Chance's smirk dissolved.

"I cannot answer that, Dr. Adler. But I encourage you to consider her role if they let her stay. Because one is adept at something does not mean they should be run ragged completing that task."

A deep unease slammed against Aiodhán's chest, settling there. Chance wasn't saying anything Aiodhán hadn't dragged himself over the coals thinking about the past couple hours.

It didn't matter how he made it right. Whatever she needed, he'd give her, even if it slowly killed him in the process.

Space from him.

Turning down the trauma center job.

"I know. I'll fix it. Whatever it takes, as long as she can stay. I... I asked her to help me run the trauma center across the street."

"Even though she came here to study women's health?"

"She can do that there, too. It's a trauma center with a wing dedicated to women who need access to care but no means."

"That sounds like a cause our princess would champion. But the choice is not only hers to make."

Chance gave his curt, telltale nod, and both men focused on the woman lying on the bed. None of it mattered if the princess—Emilia—wasn't well enough to continue following her dream to be a doctor. If her parents dragged her back to sell her like chattel to the wealthiest suitor.

His pager went off, breaking his spiraling thoughts.

"Her results are in."

"Go," Chance said. "I'll keep watch over her."

Aiodhán nodded and took off at a sprint to the lab. Somehow, whatever pull he'd felt toward Emilia before had doubled since she collapsed. She might have an entire country—hell, an army—to go to war for her, but damn if he didn't want to be counted among those.

What's that supposed to mean? You can't be with her.

No, he couldn't. And he shouldn't even care about her, because...because he could *lose* her. That was all he needed to distance himself.

The lab tech handed over a sealed manila envelope and Aiodhán closed his eyes. His hands shook as he tore open the envelope. He read the results and then read them again. Then a third time.

No. This can't be...

His stomach dropped to his feet, and his jaw clenched with worry. His teeth clattered even though the lab was warm.

"Has this been verified?" he asked the tech.

"We ran it through three times." The tech shrugged as if the results weren't life-changing. Damning.

Aiodhán did some quick calculations and shook his head. It'd been almost *four months* since he'd met Emilia at the bar. Sixteen weeks if the tally he kept in his head was right, not counting the passionate kiss they'd shared a month ago. If those results were accurate...

"Run them again. I'll wait."

"It could take up to fifteen minutes for the results."

"I'll wait," Aiodhán said again.

He paced the hall, growing more and more agitated. When the lab tech signaled him over, he snatched the paper from him. It was confirmed. *Oh, God.* He tucked the paper in his back pocket and strode back to her room.

Emilia was...

Which meant *he* was...

He was going to be a *dad*. He knew it was his, in the same way he'd sort of always known Emilia was special, different. Maybe he hadn't guessed she was a princess, but he'd known something. And he knew this.

Oh, *God*.

Forget the distance—he was all-in now, whether he wanted to be or not.

A barrage of questions hit him like punches from a prizefighter. Had she had medical care since she arrived? Would she be able to keep it? Would her husband back in Zephyranthes raise Aiodhán's kid? Would Aiodhán be expected to participate? Did he *want* to?

He didn't know. It was…it was everything he'd avoided his entire life. But on the other hand, it wasn't just a woman who'd snuck past his defenses. It was a *kid*. *His* kid. *Their* kid.

It wasn't about Aiodhán anymore.

Worry pressed against his chest, but he pushed it down where he could ignore it. One final question landed, a sucker punch as he reached Emilia's door.

Had she known about the pregnancy? Scientifically, it seemed impossible to not know about this for sixteen whole weeks. But if she *had* known…

No. She wouldn't have. That wasn't like her. But how much did he really know about the woman who'd captured his attention?

Very little, it seemed.

He might not have any of those answers, but one came to him with startling clarity.

Emilia needed to stay because if she went home to Zephyranthes, that was most likely the end of everything she cared about.

And quite possibly the same for him.

CHAPTER EIGHT

EMILIA'S EYES FLUTTERED OPEN. The view in front of her was immediately recognizable. The vantage point was not. She gazed up at the bright white lights she'd worked under for months now, the machines beeping and purring at her side like a familiar voice lulling her to sleep. But it was the soft bed beneath her, the warm blankets acting as a cocoon, the wires crisscrossing her body that were confusing.

"Why…" She swallowed, but it felt like her throat was laced with the sand outside her summer home on the Cantabrian Sea. "Why am I here?" The dryness didn't dissipate, and her eyes were sensitive to the intensity of the lights above.

"Emilia?" The voice was as familiar but as disorienting as the rest of the scene. She rolled her head to the side, and her lips parted in surprise. Aiodhán sat in a chair looking unkempt. His hair stood on end, and the stubble on his chin said he hadn't used a razor in at least a full day. It…suited him. She swallowed again, but now it felt like trying to coax knives down her throat.

She winced.

"Can I get you something? Water?"

She nodded, bringing light to other injuries. There was a sharp pain pulsing in her head, a dull ache emanating from it. What was Aiodhán doing here? What was *she* doing here?

"Ow," she whispered.

"Do you remember anything from yesterday?" She shook her head more gingerly, but it still throbbed.

"My head hurts. Did I hit it?"

Despite the discomfort it caused, she sat up and focused her gaze on Aiodhán as he nodded. His smile was thin and barely masked the hurt etched in his eyes. Had she messed something up with a patient? The only time he'd appeared as concerned was when she'd set up an OR in a way that wasn't his "usual layout." It was the only reason that made sense for him to be in her room.

"You passed out in the ER. Your head hit the ground pretty damn hard. You have a concussion, but it could have been worse." Was that a shudder that rolled through him?

Heat rose up her neck, spread to her cheeks. "Is my patient okay?"

"He's fine. You finished closing what most other interns wouldn't have been able to do in better condition, and you did a great job, Emilia."

Aiodhán's palm cupped her head, which was good, because she felt dizzy all of a sudden. She'd done well? And he'd actually admitted as much?

Before she could think about her health or why she might have collapsed in the middle of a hospital ER, the doors opened and the privacy curtain parted. Chance appeared, and though the man likely thought of her as a thorn in his side, hot tears built behind her eyes at the sight of someone from home. Someone who truly knew her.

"*Princesa*, you're looking better."

Well, she probably was, until the color drained from her face at the mention of her title. "Chance!"

Aiodhán intervened. "It's fine. I know." And there went the blood, racing back to her cheeks and neck, painting her the color of mortification.

"I'm sorry I didn't say anything. The chief medical officer agreed it was best if the staff not be made aware—"

"It's okay. I don't care about any of that, Emilia."

What alternate universe had she awoken in? Aiodhán knew

who she was, that she'd been hiding that secret, and he didn't care? Something wasn't right...

"Now that you're aware of her status, sir, might I request that you refer to her as Your Royal Highness in private," Chance said.

"Absolutely not," Emilia said, sitting up straighter, mustering any semblance of courage and fortitude that might be hiding out in her body that ached everywhere. "You'll call me Emilia or de Reyes as you usually do, and Chance won't have anything to say about it."

"But—"

"I'm not *his* princess, Chance. Please, let me have my time here be as normal as it can be. That said, you probably have some questions about how we move forward with the staff. I'll be happy to give any insight I can."

The men looked at each other, and when Aiodhán dipped his chin to his chest, a chill tickled her skin.

"What? Have I been let go from the program because of my accident?"

"No, nothing like that. You're the top student, Emilia. I wouldn't kick you out unless..."

"Unless what?"

"I've contacted the king and queen, madam. They're concerned about your health here," Chance said.

"You shouldn't have done that, Chance. I'm fine, right, Aiodhán? Just tired."

The chills turned to icy tendrils of worry when Aiodhán began to pace the floor by her bedside.

"Can I have a moment alone with Emilia?" he asked.

"Need I remind you, Dr. Adler, that I have medical power of attorney—"

Emilia sighed. "If I'm unconscious or unresponsive. Neither of which I am. Please, Chance. Let me talk to him."

Chance bowed his head and left. The energy in the room was thick with tension.

"What is it, Aiodhán? You've always been straight with me, and I need that right now."

He slumped into the oversize chair she'd found him in when she awoke. Had she ever seen the man sit down? Once, when he laced up his shoes after their…night together. Beyond that, he was a workhorse, dragging the rest of them behind him. Anxiety jumped atop her nerve endings like they were springs.

When he didn't say anything, she spoke up. "Can you please tell me what the diagnosis is?"

"You're pregnant, Emilia."

"What? No," she whispered, her gaze somewhere beyond him. "No. I can't be. I'm—"

His lips opened as if he wanted to add something, but Chance poked his head in the room.

"They're here."

"Who is?"

"The king and queen," Chance said.

"My parents are where?" Emilia attempted to get out of bed, her head spinning with the sudden movement, the onslaught of information.

Her parents.

A baby.

Aiodhán's baby. She pressed the heels of her palms against her eyes. Aiodhán helped her lie back down.

"Please don't get up. You need your rest. And Chance, we need a minute."

"This is the king and queen. I don't plan on—"

"Chance. Please." He pointed to Emilia, whose lips trembled. She couldn't stop her teeth from chattering. "Trust me. We need a damned minute. Stall them," Aiodhán said.

She was grateful he spoke up for her. Somehow, she'd lost her voice. What could she possibly have to say in light of what she'd been told?

Aiodhán and Chance shared a look, but she couldn't comprehend it. Couldn't even try.

"I'll see what I can do." Chance left, and the room became silent again, save for the steady beep-beep of the machines in her room.

"Emilia, I am right that I am the father? You haven't been seeing anyone else?"

"Yes, of course," she whispered. "I'm not seeing anyone and haven't since you and I on that first night. Who has the time? I do my work, I come home and try for six hours of sleep, and go back to do it all again the next day. You know very well I don't have time for a social life. Not even those that happen in secret on-call rooms."

Aiodhán nodded, looking relieved and conflicted at the same time. Unease lingered around his eyes. "How are you? What can I do?"

She tried on a smile, her training superseding her biology.

"I don't know, honestly. I mean, I'm terrified, confused, and unsure how this even happened."

"Yeah, pretty much the same here. Especially that last part," he said, running a hand through his hair. "We used protection."

The corner of her lips quirked up.

"You're a brilliant doctor, Aiodhán. Go ahead and figure out the statistics on that while I wait."

He chuckled, lightening the mood enough she didn't feel as if she was suffocating. "What about your period? Didn't you realize something was off? It's been four months."

"It was light the first two months, and I didn't have one at all this month. To be honest, I thought I was overworked and severely stressed."

"I'm so sorry, Emilia." He held out a hand, and she took it. Only then did a rogue tear fall on her cheek. He wiped it away. "We'll be okay, though. I don't know how, but I know we will be."

Her smile dissolved.

"There is no *we*, Aiodhán. There can't be. I told you that when you tried to kiss me again."

Aiodhán shook his head. "No. You said it wasn't fair. I'm your boss, Emilia, and I get it. I messed up so badly." He squeezed her hand, and her heart cracked.

"You're right. I said it wasn't fair, but not for the reason you think. I said it because I can't have a normal relationship. I'm a *princess*, Aiodhán. Which means I'm going to be the queen of Zephyranthes one day, married to the prince consort."

The look on Aiodhán's face made her wish she'd never met him in that bar. Because she'd fallen for him, too, that day. Not in love, but she'd felt a deep connection that only intensified working alongside him. Sure, he was a tough boss, but he was fair, too. And brilliant beyond measure. But in letting him in, even a little, she'd opened them up to this heartache.

"But the baby—"

"The baby doesn't change anything," she said. Her voice cracked.

"The baby changes *everything*." He kneeled at her side. "Emilia, *please*. Please hear me out. There's got to be a way we can fix this so we have a chance."

She straightened her shoulders. Aiodhán was an amazing man, if not overly dedicated to work. But how could she fault that, when she saw the impact he made on his patients day after day? He was thoughtful with his patients, brilliant as a surgeon, and passionate as a teacher. She'd been lucky to learn from him.

It warmed her heart that no matter what happened, she'd also carry a part of him with her forever, even if she couldn't have Aiodhán as anything more than a colleague.

And she couldn't have him, that much she knew with absolute certainty.

"A chance at what? You weren't ever interested in a relationship. Do you really think this could work, even if we weren't up against my crown and country?"

"Then, what do we do?"

"I get a checkup. I must be nearly midway through my pregnancy, and I've not had any medical care. Then…we face the king and queen. They'll want to—" her voice broke "—they'll want me to come home with them."

He shot up. "You can't. Not yet. You've got a year and a half left of your residency. And what am I supposed to do without you both?"

It was terribly inconvenient that the way Aiodhán's lips, twisted in pain, looked so good on him. Especially since they did so every time he was around her. In a different world, they might have had a chance together, if she weren't a princess with another life that awaited her. She was always going to be an interloper in this world of medicine. In Aiodhán's world.

But now there was a tether between the two. An uncuttable tether.

He was right on one count. The baby changed everything.

"Can I see the test results?" He handed her the paper in his pocket, which she read over. "I don't see a way to avoid leaving. But I'll never keep you from her."

"It's a girl?" he asked. She nodded, tears flowing freely down her cheeks now as she pointed that out on her test results.

"I'm far enough along they must be able to tell from the blood test."

"I must have missed that."

Aiodhán paced again, worrying his bottom lip between his teeth. She wanted to know what he was thinking, but that wasn't as important as giving him time to process this.

She'd felt the pressing weight of her obligations since she'd arrived in America on borrowed time. No matter what her parents dictated, she wouldn't be staying long either way. Still, she'd just gotten started—on her dream, on putting the nightmare of her mother's betrayal behind her...on building a life and that was distinctively *hers*.

And Aiodhán was a pawn in a game so much bigger than himself. She felt horrible for involving him.

"What do you want to do, Emilia?"

She looked up at him, her eyes prickling with tears and her bottom lip quivering.

"I don't know. I... I want to be a doctor. I want to lead my country, however that looks. This wasn't in my plans."

"Mine, either."

"We should talk about how to address my parents, Aiodhán."

He blanched. "You mean like *Your Majesty* and all that?"

She smiled. "That would be a great start, and it reminds me we need to talk about royal protocol in general, but no, that wasn't what I meant. How will we address the pregnancy?"

"I get a say in this?"

"Of course. You're the father. I wouldn't dream of taking your choice in the matter from you."

"Well, I want to keep it, too, if that's what you're asking. As for what it means for you and me, I have an idea."

"I'm open to anything at this point," she said.

He opened his mouth to reply when the door opened again and Bridget peeked through the curtain.

"Hey, there."

"Bridget," Emilia whispered. There went the tears again. Good grief, she was emotional of late, wasn't she? She'd be leaving so much more than a job and the man she cared about when she went home. "It's so good to see you."

"Yeah. Ditto. Except you look like hell."

"*Bridget*," Aiodhán chided her.

"What? She does." Bridget sat on the edge of the bed, missing Aiodhán's withering look. "Anyway, I just wanted to check on you. There's some powerful-looking people right behind me. Are you involved with the feds?"

Emilia laughed. It felt good, after all the serious talk. That certainly wasn't over, but she needed joy while she could get it.

"You can let them in," she said.

The door opened, and sure enough, her father and stepmother strode through the door. Chance followed close behind.

They were tall, elegant, *polished*. They stuck out like lilies in a field of dandelions. One wasn't better, just…more regal.

What did that make her? Only one answer made sense in that moment, as she hugged her father tight.

"Bridget, Aiodhán, please let me introduce you to the king and queen of Zephyranthes, my parents."

CHAPTER NINE

"Emilia..." whispered her father, the king. He ignored the other two in the room, but Aiodhán knew he'd do the same if his daughter was in trouble. His daughter... He swallowed hard, risking a glance at Emilia's abdomen where his future grew. "Are you all right?"

The king wore a bespoke gray designer suit and was an inch shorter than Aiodhán, but sturdier. He looked like he might have lifted with Arnold Schwarzenegger back in the day. But it was his eyes that had Aiodhán staring. They were the same green as Emilia's, a jade-meets-the-Atlantic-after-a-storm color but with age lines fanning out from them. The woman was younger and didn't resemble Emilia at all. It was only then Aiodhán recalled that she was Emilia's stepmother.

A small gap opened in Aiodhán's chest. The concern her dad felt for her would most certainly evaporate the minute she let them in on why she was in a hospital bed instead of caring for a patient in one.

"I'm fine, Father. But we should talk."

Bridget slipped out the door without making a noise.

Aiodhán dipped his head low in greeting, as he'd seen Chance do. It might not be exactly right, but surely he couldn't be blamed for not knowing how to greet actual royalty. Royalty who would be his child's grandparents.

Wait...did that make the baby a princess?

Oh, God, he'd screwed this up royally. *Royally. Ha!*

"Your Majesty... Majesties. I'm Aiodhán Adler. Welcome to the United States, to Minneapolis. To our hospital."

Saying that out loud reminded him who he was. It'd been easy to forget his own power, worth, and choice in learning that Emilia was a member of the royal family. But he wasn't a slouch. And she was carrying his daughter. He stood up straighter.

"Aiodhán is in charge of the residents," she said, when her parents simply nodded at his introduction. Her voice was strong and regal. How hadn't he realized she was a princess before? Or at least a duchess or something similar. Her posture, the way she spoke and listened...

The man started rattling off concerns in Zephyr, the thick, syrupy language beautiful but incomprehensible to Aiodhán, even with his limited high school Spanish.

"*Papá*," Emilia said. She glanced around the room, jutting her chin out toward the others.

"Of course. Apologies," her father continued in English. "Let's get you home first, then our own doctors can find out what's going on with you." He looked back at Aiodhán. "No offense, Doctor, but we've got physicians on staff who can take better care of her."

For the second time that day, he was speechless. His mind and heart struggled to reconcile their conflicting feelings about Emilia's test results. But that was nothing compared to the other implications. He'd unknowingly created a new line of succession in a country he knew nothing about, except it was somewhere in the Mediterranean.

On one hand, this new information was life-ending, or life-altering at least, which for him might as well be the same thing. He didn't want to burden Emilia with his all-encompassing need to work away any residual longing for a family of his own that lived rent-free in his chest.

On the other hand, this was *Emilia* he was talking about.

And they'd made a *child*. It was kind of amazing, in a terrifying, stomach-dropping kind of way.

But it wasn't as if he'd knocked up a physician from Minneapolis. He'd gotten the princess of a European country pregnant out of wedlock. She'd said she wanted to know his ideas, his choice. That really was just an illusion though, wasn't it? A baby—a live, growing child was at stake here.

Yet…all of that wasn't as big a concern as what her father had said. He did, indeed, want to take Emilia home. Yeah, that wasn't happening. He might not be willing to love and care for someone in a traditional way—a lifetime of fighting against that had left his heart atrophied in that way. But he could help her stay, and maybe, just maybe, give him a way to see his daughter grow up.

Emilia couldn't have a real relationship, and he couldn't, either. They were, in that way, perfect for one another.

"I'm not so sure about that," Aiodhán said, his voice thick. A silence fell over the room, but Aiodhán didn't care if that was the first time anyone had dared disagree with the king. This was Aiodhán's hospital, and Emilia was carrying *his* baby. "Your Majesty, I'm the chief of general surgery and the trauma center director. We run a damn fine program here, and Emilia is an incredible asset. I'd like to talk to you both about the ways we can care for her so she can continue her career."

"Her career?" The king frowned. "Her career is serving her country and fulfilling her duty as the crown princess of Zephyranthes. This was a professional-growth opportunity. But seeing as how it's making her sick—"

"Father, that's not it," Emilia said. The king's face turned as red as the alarm bells outside the room. "Rebecca, it's good to see you," Emilia added.

The woman dipped her head in Emilia's direction but refrained from any other emotional reaction. Her father, on the other hand, issued a directive to Emilia, again in Zephyr.

"Doctor, I'll sign whatever forms you need, even if it's

against medical advice. We're taking our daughter home, and that's the end of it."

Aiodhán bristled. They hadn't asked her what she wanted, how her studies were going...*nothing*.

"Do you trust me?" he whispered to Emilia. She nodded up at him. He'd not had a chance to run this idea by her, but they didn't have time for that. It threw a wrench in his own plans, but that ship had sailed the day he met Emilia in the bar anyway. He took a deep breath and wrapped Emilia's hand back in his.

"I think we need to consider what Emilia wants in all of this," Aiodhán said. "This is her life, and I'll bet if you asked her, she'd call this life more than just a hobby. She wants to be a physician, and in my opinion we should get out of her way and let that happen. The world will be a better place with her caring hands available for patients."

The king's jaw clenched along with his fists. Aiodhán saw how he'd be a force to reckon with if someone came after what was his. But Emilia wasn't anyone's.

Chance stood back, a barely visible smile pulling at his lips. That meant Aiodhán was on the right track. He took her hand in his.

"Just who do you think you are?"

Aiodhán straightened his shoulders and glanced down at Emilia. She nodded and squeezed his hand, encouraging him. "I'm the father of the baby Emilia is carrying, and if she'll have me—" he said, kneeling on one knee. He wished it was more difficult to imagine he was doing this for real. "I'd like to marry her and be her proud husband."

CHAPTER TEN

THE ROOM ERUPTED into pandemonium. Her father's face just erupted, period. She schooled her features so the shock didn't register on her face. She'd expected Aiodhán to share the pregnancy, but what he'd actually done—*proposed?*

"Tell me he's kidding, *hija*," her father said. "After Luis—"

"He's *nothing* like Luis, Papa. Now, if you'll listen to us—"

"Why should I, Emi? You come here to pursue medicine, or so you say. But then I get a call that you're injured at work, only to arrive and find you're *embarazada*..."

"She doesn't have anything to be embarrassed about," Aiodhán said. Emilia bit back a grin because none of this was funny. But it was erring toward so tragic it became comedic.

"He means *pregnant*, Aiodhán," she said through gritted teeth.

"Oh." Her betrothed—or whatever she should call him since he hadn't really asked her anything, and she certainly hadn't said yes to his ridiculous proposal—said.

Start him on Zephyr lessons immediately.

Emilia adjusted in her bed. She was still on bed rest until more tests came back on the health of the baby she hadn't known she carried until moments earlier.

Her parents murmured to one another in clipped Zephyr she was too far away to hear. She had to admit she preferred their yelling to the hushed whispers.

"Fine," her father said. "Tell me your plan, then. Because it's obvious this wasn't a planned pregnancy."

Aiodhán stiffened beside her. "No," she said. Not to her father, who would believe her no matter what, but to Aiodhán. If he thought her capable of that kind of duplicity… "No, it wasn't planned."

Aiodhán squeezed her hand. His strength buoyed her.

"Your Majesties, I know it's quite a shock to be greeted with this kind of news the minute you've arrived, but we're committed to making it work and could use your support to do so."

"To making what work? A marriage? Do either of you have any idea what kind of commitment a good, strong marriage between *equals* takes? What raising a child in this world might require?"

Emilia cringed at the word *equals*. In so many ways Aiodhán was hers, if only her title and royal lineage could be taken out of the equation.

They both dreamt of a life of service to others in the medical field, they both were dedicated, hard workers, and as he'd mentioned, they were committed to making sure they gave their all to their unexpected gift.

A gift it was, too. Emilia was surer of that than anything else in her life.

"I do," Aiodhán said. She shot him a glance. What was he doing? She'd assumed the proposal was fake, a way to buy them time, but there went Aiodhán, telling her parents they had a plan in place. She hadn't even said yes. "To be honest, I never believed in love. To me, that word only equaled loss. But my friend convinced me to come to his wedding. If I hadn't, I wouldn't have met Emilia at the bar that night, and I wouldn't know the amazing passion your daughter holds for medicine, for life, and for her family. I know I have a lot to learn, but I'm willing to learn it. For her. For our daughter."

Emilia took in a sharp breath. She only released it when her father's frown softened ever so slightly along the edges. He sighed, and she, in turn, released the breath she'd been holding.

"You love her, then?"

"To be honest, sir, try as I did to avoid it, I care about her more than I've cared about anything in a long time. I want a life with Emilia and the child we've created, whatever that looks like." When he gazed over at her, she saw the truth in his statement and it simultaneously warmed her while sending shivers racing across her skin. What would happen if they went through with this—real or not—and she went back to Zephyranthes? Would he follow? What would he do there? The pressure was too much to put on him. But for now, it was nice to hear romantic words she never imagined she'd hear. "Like I said, we didn't plan on any of this, but I'll never let anything happen to either of them. I'll do what it takes."

Emilia's father and stepmother shared a glance, and Rebecca gave a dignified, subtle nod. It was hopeful.

"I see. I can see your dedication to my daughter, especially given the condition she's in because of you."

Emilia opened her mouth to object—like Aiodhán said, it took two of them to get here—but he'd already jumped in.

"And I'll make that right. Whatever it takes."

He squeezed her hand again, and heat built behind her eyes. If only this were real. She'd never wanted a family or love before, only because she'd assumed that wasn't in her cards: if she married, it would be for duty. But now...now she dared to wish for more than a life where she could love her duty to her country. She wanted love, period.

"Papa, can Aiodhán and I have a moment together? We've barely said hello to one another since my accident, and I need... I need to take a breath."

Rebecca and the king stood.

"We'll be right outside," her dad said.

Emilia nodded. "Thank you. I know you traveled a long way to see me and that you've been worried. So we'll be quick."

"Fine, fine."

When they were alone, Emilia glanced up at Aiodhán, who still held her hand.

"You can let go, you know. They're gone."

"What if I don't want to?"

She sighed and took her hand back. "Aiodhán, why would your idea include something as permanent as marriage? What the heck were you thinking?"

He leaned down, his breath hot on her neck. "To save you from going back there."

"*There* is my home, Aiodhán, and those are my parents—"

"Who want to sell you off to the highest bidder. While you're pregnant with my baby. They didn't even flinch when I asked if they'd still consider ripping you from this life you love."

He wasn't telling her anything that wasn't true. And maybe five months ago, fresh out of the media scrutiny around her mother and betrayal of Luis, she'd have agreed. But she loved her home. Looked forward to her duty. Sure, she had reservations about marrying someone she'd never met, but it's not like she could upend centuries of tradition just because she'd fallen for a commoner.

She gazed up at him, noticing the small tick in his jaw. She also took a minute to appreciate his strength and the gentle way he used his thumbs to rub circles on the heel of her palm. What she tried to ignore? The uniquely Aiodhán scent of soap and pine that worked its way past her defenses and made her woozy in a different way.

The kind of way that made her *want* to upend tradition.

"I'm sorry about that. I really am. But all I wanted was to guarantee you have time to make a decision you're comfortable with. You wanted something that would keep you here. Well, being my fiancée was all I could come up with in the thirty seconds we had to hatch a plan. It wasn't the perfect solution, but it's a start. You can still say no, you know. To being my fiancée."

Her pulse slowed enough she could catch her breath. She had asked for that, and to his credit he'd put himself in a terrible position just to help her. He just as easily could have run from this since it wasn't his concern, not really. But then, the idea of what would happen after his announcement made her shudder. "Perhaps you're right. But what is your plan, exactly? To marry me and make an honest woman out of me? I mean, you can barely stand to be around me most days."

He gazed down at her.

"That's not true, Emilia. Not even close. I just..." Nerves floated to the surface of her skin, making it itch. "I didn't know who you were when we spent that night together. When you showed up at the hospital that day, I didn't know if I could work alongside you and keep my feelings at bay. I think you saw how bad I was at it that day I..."

"The day you kissed me good and long enough I forgot my own name?"

He smiled, and her heart rate sped up. That was decidedly against doctor's orders, so she tried to get her mind off that searing kiss. What was her future without him?

Flying back home, a secret tucked away from her country.

Walking down the aisle toward a man she neither knew nor was capable of loving.

Saying goodbye to Aiodhán forever. Raising her baby alone. *Their baby*, she reminded herself again.

"Yep. That day. I tried to ignore the other feelings as they'd crop back up, but watching you work and laugh and be an amazing doctor isn't exactly a recipe for turning off how I feel for you."

"You feel things for me? Other than the obvious physical stuff?" She'd—wrongly?—assumed their fiery passion was a one-night thing, at least on his part. When he kissed her, she'd concluded he still wanted more of that. But to hear how he watched her work, appreciated more than her body, and without knowing her title...it was dizzying. Also against doctor's orders. "That's why you talked to me about moving past our night together that first day of work."

His smile warmed the parts of her that felt cold and exposed since the results of her tests had come back.

"Yeah. I sorta had to make that call. Survival, you know?" She did. It's why she'd offered to take extra shifts and longer hours: if she were wholly exhausted, she wouldn't have to let her mind wander to the handsome doctor in charge of her future as an OB resident. And what that doctor happened to look and feel and taste like bared for her greedy hands and lips. "But I guess it's for the best I did, now that I know who you are. Neither of us can have a traditional relationship, but maybe this is the best of both worlds."

She paused, giving herself a three count until she faked a laugh. Their love of medicine was the only thing they had in common.

"How is that? Because I don't see any way this actually works, Aiodhán. I mean, maybe we keep the pretense of an engagement up, but then when my parents leave we can—"

"No. I don't want to cut it off. I want to marry you, Emilia. Maybe we're not traditional, but I care for you—despite my best efforts not to," he said, winking. She laughed, but her chest rose and fell with nervousness. The beeping behind her picked up pace, likely from her pulse skyrocketing.

"Okay, so tell me what you mean."

"I mean we're perfect together because you can't have a so-called real relationship. You're sworn to your country and crown. And I can't give you traditional romance. I think I've worked too hard to surgically remove that part from my heart since I lost my parents. So if we go into this with realistic expectations, I think we can make it work."

Emilia couldn't believe it, but she was nodding. On paper, at least, that made perfect sense.

"We don't have to tell your parents all of that, just that we are committed to making this work for our daughter and our careers."

Emilia's cheeks flashed with heat. "What about—"

"Sex?" he asked. She nodded, biting her bottom lip. He surprised her with a kiss. "I don't know. Is that something you're interested in?"

"I'm not *not* interested," she said, smiling. The heat on her cheeks—and south—told a similar story.

"Fair enough." He laughed. "Any more questions in that beautiful brain of yours?" he asked. The heat intensified. She could get used to this attention, even as she knew she shouldn't.

"Just one." He kissed her again, almost making her forget. "Where will you live?"

"With you, if you'll have me. I'm guessing your apartment isn't a sparsely furnished studio like mine."

She shook her head. "Nope. One of the perks of being royalty. I have a rather nice apartment, actually, and would love to have you." Oh, my goodness. Reality set in as she realized she'd just said she wanted to move in with Dr. Aiodhán Adler. "But that's actually not what I meant. Will you follow us back to Zephyranthes?"

Aiodhán glanced at his lap. "I... I don't know, to be honest. I hadn't thought that far. I mean, I don't know anything about your country—"

"I'll teach you, of course. I'd never let you go if you weren't aware of our culture or language or customs."

"The language. I also hadn't thought about that. Man, I really jumped the gun, didn't I?"

Emilia felt his fear, could understand it on a cellular level. He'd thrown his whole future on the proverbial sword. For her. So she could stay and pursue her dream. He might not be royal by blood, but he was her white knight.

"You can still change your mind." But she didn't want him to. A small part of her—small enough she'd never admit it outside her own head—wanted to see where this went. Maybe there was a chance she would get the happily ever after she'd thought was forbidden.

Aiodhán leaned in. "I don't want to. It's just a lot to think about. If you don't mind helping talk me through some of the logistics, I'm in, Emilia. I mean that."

"Thank you, Aiodhán. For giving up so much to take care of me."

"I should have done it sooner. But I'm here now. Should we bring the king and queen back in?" She nodded. "I never thought I'd say those words out loud, by the way."

Emilia laughed again. She might be in a hospital bed, carrying a surprise pregnancy, but she was…happy. For the first time in a long time, maybe since she was seven, she had a sense of what life could offer her, and it was beautiful.

"Before they come in, you should know my parents will pull out all the stops. We won't be able to hide from the crown's influence or presence in our lives."

"I figured as much. It will be the same here. We'll have to start with HR here at Minnie Gen and let them know we're engaged. We might have been able to avoid that before, since we'd slept together before you were my intern, but it's protocol to disclose all consensual relationships between staff. You might get reassigned to another physician for your residency. That might take the trauma job off the table, but you'll still be able to practice."

"That's fine. That's all I need." *For now.* Aiodhán made her want things she'd never considered before… Her heart's desire took a different shape in a brief daydream in which Aiodhán wrapped his arms around her from behind, resting his palms on her swollen stomach. They were in their own home, flamenco music playing softly on speakers behind them, and he swayed his body against hers, kissing her neck while they danced barefoot.

"I'll make sure you get more than what you need. I want to take care of you and our child, Emilia."

Heat crept up her neck at being caught wishing for things that were wholly impossible.

Our child.

A wave of dizziness washed over Emilia. As much as it pained her to admit it, she needed him to get through whatever her life looked like next. So long as she could keep the pesky daydreams at bay, it wouldn't be too difficult to do that.

"Thank you," she whispered.

"Of course," he replied, helping her lie back in bed before finding a seat beside her. "How are you feeling?"

She tilted her head to each side. "All right, I guess. A little tired, and my head is sore, but otherwise normal."

"We need to get you seen by the team, Emilia. I know you'll want to keep this under wraps, but—"

"No. I agree. The baby's safety matters more than anything else. And this team, the Gold Fleece Foundation doctors—they're why I'm here."

"Okay, we'll set it up for tomorrow."

"Emilia, I'd like to talk now, if you two are done," her father said, poking his head in.

Emilia sighed but didn't take her hand off her belly. It offered her strength, reminded her why she was there and why standing their ground was important. It wasn't just her life at stake now; she owed freedom to her daughter.

"Yes, of course," she said, even if she wanted to close her eyes and sleep for a week.

When everyone was settled, her father dove in.

"We can't take him back to Zephyranthes," the king said. "Not like this. Not while the media is still hungry for information about your mother. They're looking for anything that would paint our family in a negative light. You know that, Emi."

She did. It was always that way: the monarchy wasn't a popular idea with some of the country. With poverty and homelessness on the rise due to global inflation, she understood. Even Aiodhán had his doubts about the necessity of royalty in the modern age. But she knew what others didn't: international relations relied on their political expertise, and their charity patronage donated to causes that kept citizens clothed and housed.

Even the top-tier education in Zephyranthes was funded by the monarchy, and each of the hospitals required no supplemental insurance thanks to her family's donations.

They did good work, but unless they took credit for all of that—something her father refused to do—they were bound to receive criticism.

"What do you suggest?" Rebecca asked. It was the first time she'd spoken. Emilia wanted to know what her stepmother must be thinking. She'd tried and tried in vain to get pregnant, only to be left without a child of her own, an heir for the throne.

And Emilia had had sex once—*once!*—in her life and gotten knocked up even with birth control. The unfairness of all of this knew no bounds.

"We create a story for the media they can't find fault in. A sympathetic story the country will believe. Princess studies in America, only to fall in love with a working-class man. It certainly isn't the first time such a thing has happened."

"And then what?" she asked. She *needed* to stay. Not just for herself anymore but to give Aiodhán time to figure out his place in her royal life.

"We give you two time here, working together, appearing for press engagements, items like that. Say a month. Prove this is more than a flash in the pan."

Okay. A month was something, at least.

"Then you two will marry in a public ceremony," he said. Emilia's blood ran cold. This was really happening. "She will continue her work here until the baby is born. We then bring you both back to begin your rule from there, the heir a part of its family." He waved his hand as if the rest of it was inconsequential. As if her and Aiodhán's futures were inconsequential.

Aiodhán's hand tightened on her shoulder and she couldn't contain her nerves. She'd wanted to go back, to live in Zephyranthes and raise a family there. But after her residency. When she'd had time to live.

"We'll offer our support in the name of love, of course, and tomorrow we'll announce the pregnancy and how pleased we are to welcome the next in line for the throne."

"The throne," Aiodhán whispered. Emilia wished she could see his face above hers. Wished she could cup his cheeks and tell him it would all be a lot, yes, but it would be okay in the end. She wouldn't let him go through this alone.

But how could she say this when her parents left her in the hospital room for the evening, chatting about details and governor's visits and so many other items that made Emilia feel as if this were snowballing out of her control?

How could she convince her husband-to-be that it would be okay if she didn't believe it herself?

CHAPTER ELEVEN

AIODHÁN GLANCED DOWN at his tie. It felt more like a noose.

"Isn't there a loophole in a royal decree that might get us off the hook for this?" he asked.

Emilia smiled up at him and a little of the panic that had raced through his veins slowed, dissolving into his bloodstream and allowing him a moment's peace.

"Unfortunately not. This is just part of the rigmarole. I wish I could say it's the hardest part of this transition, but that's not even remotely true."

"Um…thanks, Em. Love the vote of confidence." He faked a laugh, but it sounded as hollow as he felt. It wasn't like he hadn't known what he'd been getting himself into. He'd seen enough movies, read enough books to know that monarchies were a different breed. Meetings, classes, language lessons—all of it had been expected. But rubbing elbows with Emilia's family all week had made him into a phony—an unexplored side effect he hadn't considered when it came to caring about someone else.

Sure, it was impossible to constantly worry he could lose them—and he did. Every damned accident victim brought through the ER bay threw him into a spiral. Was it Emilia? He didn't know how he was supposed to let that go, even when he kept telling himself it was okay, she knew he had trouble with letting people in.

But worse than all of that was a new kind of fear as he slid into being Emilia's partner…

Being seen for who he really was.

He might be a stellar surgeon, physician, and scientist, but what else did he have to offer? Especially when he'd already witnessed his bride-to-be undergo a rapid transformation from overworked resident to a glowing, pregnant princess?

"Look this way," Paulo, part of the royal entourage, said, tugging at Aiodhán's sleeve. He did as he was told.

This was going to be a disaster, wasn't it?

When Emilia reached up on her toes and kissed him, though, he exhaled.

"It's you and me," she whispered, triggering their shared mantra.

"And our little bean." Okay, this was fine. Just another meeting, and he'd be doing it with her by his side. Regardless of how they'd arrived where they were—engaged and headed to the altar, then the throne, with an unplanned pregnancy—they were there together. And together was the only way to the other side of this, he was damned sure of that much. If his life looked different, that was fine as long as he could go to bed knowing he'd done the right thing.

Right now that meant cutting his hair, trimming his beard, and getting fitted for a suit. He didn't *do* suits, not when more than half his life was in scrubs. All for a single press conference and dinner with the governor of Minnesota.

He straightened his tie when Paulo's back was turned. Not one damned day in his life had he given his appearance any thought, aside from whether he looked professional or not. But now he had two stylists fussing over him, and he didn't like it.

"You look great," she said. "And I promise you will get used to this. It'll become part of the background to our lives."

He wasn't sure that made things any better.

"Okay, quiz me again," he said, ignoring the pervasive intrusion of the other stylist—what his name? George? Tomas?

"The royal values?"

"Family, country, loyalty."

"In Zephyr?" He glanced at her as Paulo put his tie back to where he wanted it. Aiodhán wished like hell he'd paid more attention to Spanish studies in school. Maybe then he could at least fake Zephyr enough not to be a total fraud. He could tell her each muscle in the human body, what they did, how they performed together, but he couldn't recall the first three words she'd taught him in her native tongue? He was failing her already. She waved him off. "Okay, we'll save that for later. But crest?"

"A crown on a field of blue, the green sea with fish and other sea creatures—"

"Symbolizing?"

He smiled. This he could answer, thanks to a very convincing study session where he got to kiss her wherever on her body she pointed if he got the question right. Maybe he'd draw her into another lesson that evening.

They were the only parts of his days that brought him any peace, curling up with Emilia. That had to count for something.

"The abundance Zephyranthes has to offer its citizens and its largest export, seafood." Truth be told, the more he learned about Emilia's country, the less he was worried about moving there. It seemed like an amazing place, and in the middle of a Midwest winter, time on the Mediterranean didn't seem like the worst idea.

As long as he forgot the other aspect of moving there: he'd be Emilia's husband. The prince consort of Zephyranthes.

"Hmmm. How about the line of succession?"

"Too easy. The king and queen, of course. You, next. Our daughter after that, and somewhere down the line, the dukes and duchesses on your father's side. I'll be a throw pillow on the throne—I'll look like one of the other pillows, but serve no actual use."

Sort of. The king and queen had been careful not to cross those lines, but he'd come pretty damned close the night before to being forced to choose between his job and his future family.

Emilia laughed. The sound was like soft rain on a warm afternoon. "Good job, future husband."

"Thanks, future wife." He leaned down to kiss her, and like always happened when they were close, he felt his pulse speed up and his body calm. She was like a lethal shot of adrenaline mixed with serotonin. He couldn't shake his new addiction to the drug that was Emilia de Reyes.

Aiodhán tucked a curl behind her ear. The scarlet waves were soft, but the color gave them an edge that made his breathing come a little faster. Kinda like the rest of the alluring woman—forgiving but with a determination that advertised her strength.

"I don't know how I didn't see right through those scrubs when I first met you." He paused and glanced around the palatial room with vaulted ceilings and crown molding that had to be turn-of-the-century. The lavish apartment was befitting a woman as dignified as Emilia. Funny how it took a woman from another country to show him places in his own city he hadn't known existed.

"I'm pretty sure you did." She winked.

"Not like that." He laughed, although there was a ring of truth to how he'd imagined her curves beneath those scrubs. "I mean, how didn't I recognize how regal you are? How you lead everyone with a simple smile. Your country is lucky. Hell, I'm lucky."

Another truth, one that dug into his self-imposed No Real Feelings wall and cracked it.

The way Emilia bit the corner of her lip made Aiodhán's heart beat hard against his ribs. It took all his restraint not to take her lip between his own teeth. Kissing Emilia with the hunger he felt wouldn't get them started on the right foot before the conference. He settled for a simple peck on the lips.

Paulo chastised them. "No kissing with her makeup finished. Save it for later." Aiodhán rolled his eyes. He might have to cut his hair and upgrade his wardrobe, but he'd damn well kiss his fiancée whenever he saw fit. It was the only perk in this whole arrangement.

"This is weird, huh? How quickly things changed between us?" he asked.

"It is. I'm glad to know you haven't hated me this whole time. I wouldn't be able to bear this, even temporarily, if I thought you despised me."

"Not even close, Emilia. I'll admit, you drive me to the edge of madness, but it isn't all bad."

"Ha ha, mister. You're funny when you're stressed, you know that?" She stepped off the pedestal and walked toward the exit. He considered that. He did rely on crappy, ill-timed humor when he was worried. She saw through him, just as he'd worried. He only prayed she liked what she saw. "And I love that about you. I love so many things about you."

The smile that spread over Aiodhán's face was the first genuine one he'd had in a while.

"And I think I have a plan for getting you to learn Zephyr. I'll give you an anatomy lesson later…" She winked at him. "With me as the mannequin since that seems to motivate you."

Heat flashed across his skin. What a whirlwind, to deeply desire this life with her one minute, then revolt against parts of it—namely the royalty portions—the next.

"You're onto something there."

"Like I mentioned earlier, I'm quite smart."

He squeezed her hand.

"You are. I wasn't ever in doubt there."

"So I've given you more information about my country and family over the past week than anyone should have to hear. Tell me about you. So far, all I know is that you're a tough boss, a brilliant surgeon, and—" she smiled "—that you've taken on a life of solitude so you can focus on medicine and not break any hearts in the process. Am I close?"

His laugh was stale. Again, he was struck by how deeply she saw through him. More like he didn't want his own heart to break any more than it already had. "More or less. But it's more—"

"Complicated?" He smiled and gave a curt nod. "I figured as much. What happened?"

The smile fell.

"My father died when I was eleven."

"Oh, my. I'm so sorry. How did he pass?"

"He got into a car wreck when he was too tired to drive one night. Ran off the road into a lake."

"Oh, Aiodhán, I'm so sorry."

"No, I mean thanks, but I'm not the only kid who had to go through that. Working at the ER every day, I'm reminded how normal my story actually is. Either way, it left a permanent scar that I never got over. I knew then and there I wanted to practice medicine so I could prevent other families from that kind of loss. Though, I think we both know it doesn't work like that."

"No, it doesn't. What about your mother?" Emilia had grown serious.

The stylists left them alone in the room, a gift, since Aiodhán's eyes burned with grief, even after all these years. That was the thing about loss. It stayed with you, tinted everything that followed a shade darker.

"She died, too. Years later, but also in a wreck. I'm not sure if you recall me talking about the I-35 bridge collapse?"

Emilia nodded and rubbed his hand affectionately. "The one you mentioned that day in the ER when the ten victims were brought in? That was my first day of residency."

"That's the one. My mother was one of the hundred-plus victims with severe injuries, and she died a few days later from them. It was my first month as a resident."

"That's awful."

He shrugged. "Now you know why I haven't let anyone in. Till you and the bean, anyway. The idea of losing you two is suffocating."

Emilia wrapped him in a bear hug and squeezed him tight.

"I understand that, you know."

He cleared his throat, which had gotten thick with decades of old emotions brought up from the depths. "Your family?"

Emilia chewed on her lip. "My mother."

"That's why you chose obstetrics?" A subtle nod had his chest constricting. Is this what it would feel like every time someone he cared about hurt? Like his chest was jolted by AED paddles? He didn't think he could take it.

"She died giving birth to my brother, and I never even got to meet him."

"God, I can't even imagine losing both in one day."

She waved him off. "It's okay. Well, actually it *was*." Emilia sat on the oversize love seat. "The man my father mentioned? Luis? He was my fiancé until he found out the child my mom was carrying wasn't the king's. He sold the information to the press, so I had to find out along with six million other Zephyranthians that my mother wasn't the woman—or queen—we all thought she was."

"Holy—" Aiodhán had to hand it to the monarchy. They took normal human problems and ratcheted them up a couple notches. "That's why your father is so worried about me and this, um, fast engagement."

"Yeah. More than what he said the other day about the media, he's worried about me. I can see it in his eyes, that he isn't sure I can take another heartache like that."

"I know you're strong enough to withstand any storm, Emilia, but I hope you know I'll block as many as I can for you. I may not have much to offer, but I can do that, at least."

"Thank you, Aiodhán. I believe you mean that. I just know the waves coming our way might make you rethink this whole arrangement. Being a part of this world, this life—I was *born* into it and have had time to fall in love with the opportunities it affords me. Choosing to be a part of it means giving up so much of what you used to be, and I don't want to ask that of you. I *can't* ask it."

Aiodhán gestured to his gelled, coiffed hair, his tailored suit, and his clean-shaven face.

"You didn't have to ask me, Emilia. I'm doing this because we made a child together, and she deserves parents who will do anything to keep her safe."

He couldn't read her smile but noted it didn't meet her eyes.

"We still really don't know much about each other, do we?" she asked.

He laughed, despite himself. "No, we don't. On one hand, you're surprising me around every turn, but on the other…" His gaze fell to her full lips, and he traced them with the pad of his thumb. She gave a barely audible gasp. "I know so much about you."

"Like what?" she whispered.

Aiodhán sat on the edge of the king-size bed then sank into the down-filled pillow beside her. The edge of his palm slid down her cheek in a caress that made him half-hard, a side effect that wasn't helped by the crimson glow on Emilia's cheeks, either. He'd done so well to keep this line drawn between them. But they'd agreed to take it as the moments arose and decide then. So he'd just let her decide what she wanted.

Please let it be me.

Like he'd said, he didn't have much to offer, but this—keeping the smile on Princess Emilia de Reyes's lips?—he'd do anything for.

"Like how your skin announces everything you feel with a different color red. This," he said, touching the nape of her neck that was a cherry color, "is when you're embarrassed."

"You're sure about that?" she asked.

"Mmm-hmm. I'd bet my salary I'm right. And the light pink from a minute ago? You were happy."

"I was." Her breath hitched when Aiodhán's fingertips traced the green lace of her nightgown. "What am I now?" she asked. Her gaze melted into his and anything halfway about his erection went out the two-story window with the pale flush of dark pink covering the top of her breasts, just visible above the lace.

"Aroused. You want me to keep going, I think."

"My body seems to agree."

"And your head?" he asked, cupping her breast through the thin satin. He teased the bud of her swollen nipple between his thumb and finger, and she moaned with pleasure.

"It's kind of quiet in there right now."

"How about your heart?" he asked, spreading his palm and fingers across her chest.

"It's racing. I think you might be right about what it wants."

Aiodhán leaned over Emilia, sliding her beneath him. He dipped his head so that his lips brushed hers softly.

"Are you sure about this? I don't want to confuse things, but goddamn do I want you, Emilia."

She nodded, the blush on her bared skin dappled with moisture. He kissed her again, this time tracing her lips with his tongue, tasting the vanilla from her coffee. Even since finding out she was pregnant, she wasn't ever without a cup of it, even if she had switched to decaf. She claimed it was her Zephyr heritage.

"I want you, too," she said, breathless. "There's no reason we can't enjoy one another while we figure out our new life. If it doesn't work out, we can do what all the other royals do."

He kissed her neck. "Trash one another publicly and have torrid affairs?"

She giggled and shook her head, even as his lips traced her earlobe. The gasp she released almost made him come right there.

"No, keep separate bedrooms and pretend everything is fine."

He laughed, his forehead touching hers, his hands wandering over her frame while she arched her back, pressing her chest against his. She pulled his bottom lip between her teeth and sucked on it.

"Tonight, Emilia, there's no way we're sleeping in separate beds."

He teased her lips open with his tongue and finally sated the desire that had been building for months, since the last time he'd tasted this delicious woman in the on-call room.

If only he could silence his own head and heart that were whining loudly that they still weren't ready to let anyone in. But it was too late; there was no going back to the man he'd been before Emilia. She'd dug her way through all of his walls and set up a home in his heart.

If he lost her, or the baby, there was no telling the husk of a man he'd become. All he could do was work like hell to make sure that never happened.

CHAPTER TWELVE

"Oh, Aiodhán!" Emilia let out a gasp of pleasure so divine, she wasn't sure it was legal, even in the United States. "Please. Please keep going."

His fingers slid along her lace undergarments, and one slipped beneath the fabric, flicking her sensitive center. She moaned and lifted her hips in response.

"You mean this?" he asked, dipping two fingers into her warm, wet folds.

"Mm.... Yes!"

"I aim to please, Your Highness." He traced the curve of her breast with his tongue, finally sucking the swollen tip into his mouth. Emilia hadn't ever known such exquisite pleasure was possible. Aiodhán's hands and tongue were medicinal, curing all that ailed her. Her worries, insecurities, and the predicament surrounding her pregnancy all dissolved with his expert touch and kisses.

"I want you," she said, pulling him up so she could kiss him, taste the peppermint she remembered from the night she'd met Aiodhán. It made her think of Christmas, of finally being given everything she'd ever wanted, but nothing money or a title could buy. "Please, Aiodhán. I want you inside me."

His eyes were stormy gray with shiny blue flecks, like the summer Mediterranean waters she'd played in as a child. Only this particular delight was for her and her alone, and she didn't have her meddlesome parents telling her to be careful since she was the sole heir to the throne. She'd gladly drown in Aiodhán's liquid depths.

Without moving from his perch atop her hips, he tore off his scrub bottoms and looked at the bedside table.

"We don't really need any more of those, do we?" she asked, her smile wide.

Aiodhán's matching smile was wicked. "I'm so happy that you're knocked up, Princess de Reyes."

She giggled and bit her bottom lip. This man sitting over her was so gloriously handsome, so divine a creature, both inside and out. Not to mention he was a superb lover, one like she'd only imagined on her loneliest nights in her palace bedroom. And he was to be her *husband.*

If only she could expect this kind of happiness for the rest of her life. A deep worry lived beneath the joy she felt around him; she'd seen what her lifestyle demanded of people. Her father might not recall, but Luis had been decent once. In her opinion, he'd succumbed to the pressure the monarchy put on anyone within its sphere. What would it turn Aiodhán into?

Right now she meant to enjoy every last second. She opened for Aiodhán, tangling her fingers in his hair as his tip nudged her core.

"You're sure?" he asked. She nodded and slid closer so his length was pressed firmly against her.

"So very sure."

With that assurance, he rocked into her, and she gasped.

"Are you okay? Are you hurt?"

She laughed. "No, darling. I'm fine. It just feels different now. Everything is sensitive." He tentatively shifted, and she released a small moan. "I'm very fine indeed."

"Well, then, let's make the most of this new sensation."

Dipping down to kiss her, teasing her mouth open with his tongue, Aiodhán didn't slow his gentle glide in and out of her. Each nerve ending, each cell in her body was on fire, brought on and quenched by Aiodhán, the father of the small life growing inside her. God, she was to be a mother, and this man, her equal partner in raising their child.

She wrapped her arms tight around Aiodhán's shoulders, drawing him closer to her in the hopes she could grant the gravity of her situation leave for an hour or two of pleasure and release. She laced her fingers together behind his head and deepened their kiss. His kisses ignited a part of her soul that worried she'd never know love or anything resembling passion, burning it to ashes.

His hands roved over her body like a surgeon searching for a cure. He filled and explored all of her, and yet the weighty knowledge her time with him was limited didn't dissipate. If anything, it made her hungrier, more desperate to see him satisfied.

Lifting her own hips, she moved against him until he growled into her mouth with a hunger that matched her own.

"Emilia." He groaned as she cupped beneath his erection. "Goddamn, woman. You feel...so...good."

"Igualmente, cariño."

His back tightened, and Emilia ran her fingertips down the strong length of him while he shuddered against her. Her own release came seconds later, and she couldn't help the cry of ecstasy that exploded from her.

Aiodhán stayed inside her but rolled them both on their sides. Her hands continued to trail up and down his muscular back. Appreciation for all he offered her, all he was sacrificing on her behalf, flooded from her fingertips and the soft kisses she peppered his chest with.

"That was..." he said, tipping her chin up so her gaze could fuse with his, "that was fantastic."

He kissed her before she could respond, forcing her to swallow the words on the tip of her tongue, forbidden words of love and promise and other things that should remain unsaid.

"It was," she said eventually.

His smile softened, and his eyes grew serious.

"I'm not the most emotionally available man," he said. Where she would have teased him earlier, his eyes—serious and gazing at her with intensity—said she should just listen. He paused, taking a deep breath. When he cupped her cheek, it simultaneously calmed and worried her. What was he having trouble articulating? "But I like this."

"Me, too. Very much." More words left unsaid. But this was enough. For now. In some ways it was more than she'd ever imagined. Yet somehow, the taste of Aiodhán left her greedy for all of it—all of him. He winked and squeezed her butt affectionately.

She kissed him then, for the confidence he exuded in their shared passion, for sharing child-rearing with her, for the nickname he'd coined for their unborn child. She only hoped who she was and had to become to rule a country didn't scare him away.

"We'll have the eyes of an entire nation on us, watching to see if we slip up. When you marry me, you're marrying into the crown and all that comes with that. Aiodhán, you'll be the prince consort of Zephyranthes after Friday. I don't say this to scare you, but we need to practice radical honesty if this is going to work. If things get to be too much, you need to talk to me so I can mitigate the effects on you and the country."

His thumb brushed her cheek, and she could feel the tension in his muscles beneath her hand. Neither of them would even be considering this if she weren't pregnant.

He'd said it himself moments before they'd just made love. He was only here because they had a daughter to raise together. Moments before they'd discovered her pregnancy, he'd been cool and indifferent to her. It was too much to hope the change in his heart would stick.

"Yeah, I've been ignoring that little addendum, actually. It's a lot."

She nodded. "At least we won't need those NDAs. The whole world will know about our marriage now, so what will a few extra nurses' eyes on us matter?" She'd tried for airy and playful but came up dreadfully short of trite.

His smile looked pained, especially the way his brows scrunched together in the center of his forehead.

"Will there be paparazzi at the hospital?"

"And outside our home. But that's where Chance comes in. He'll put a team together to ensure our lives remain as uninterrupted as possible. He's good at what he does, Aiodhán."

Aiodhán sighed and slid away from her, rolling on his back. She'd scared him. It hadn't been her intention, but it was better he knew what to expect now, before they made promises to one another they couldn't keep. All they really owed anyone was to put their child first; the rest was icing on a pretty top-heavy cake that might not be able to withstand the stress awaiting them.

"I wish I had known. You know, that night."

"Who I was?"

His hands were folded behind his head as he gazed at the ceiling. He'd gone from pulling her tight against his body to giving them all the space he could without rolling off the bed.

"Yeah." He glanced at her but didn't shift his body.

"Would it have changed anything?" Anxiety crept across her skin as she awaited his answer.

"No," he finally answered. "It wouldn't have. Nothing could have kept me from you, Emilia. But I would have liked to know more about you, where you came from, and what made you tick. Before so much was on the line."

"I agree. I'd only been in the country a few hours when we met, and to be honest, meeting you wasn't part of my plan, either. Not after Luis. I needed time to heal before I thought about anyone else. I did hope to try some American things like whiskey and hamburgers, maybe even put a song on a jukebox like they do in the movies."

"Sleeping with a stranger is about as ordinary and American as you could get."

They both laughed, and Aiodhán finally turned back toward her.

"Do you mind if I ask what happened with Luis? I mean, how did a sleazy guy like that get past your defenses? Hell, your dad's."

She sighed. The question was a fair one. And she'd agreed on radical honesty. "I think he was a good man trapped in an impossible situation, and though he was vetted and cleared, that wasn't enough to ensure he was supported in his role. He took the easy way out, but it cost him a lot. He'll never be allowed in Zephyranthes again, and we learned a lot about how to support newcomers to the family."

"Hence the lessons?"

"Hence the lessons."

Her smile didn't reach her eyes.

"Have I been vetted and cleared?" he teased.

She smiled. "If you hadn't, you'd be living in a prison somewhere south of Morocco," she teased back.

"Touché. But seriously, I'm sorry that happened to you. You deserve better, and as prince consortium—"

"Prince consort," she corrected, laughing.

"Yes, as that, I won't ever take the easy way out." The laughter faded, but her heart thumped against her chest.

She bit her bottom lip and nodded. "Okay, then. But you have to promise me something, Aiodhán."

"Anything."

"I don't want you to stay with me under some outdated sense of chivalry. I've had enough of that for a lifetime. If it's just about the baby, I can care for her alone."

Aiodhán laced his fingers around the base of her head and pulled her gently into him. His lips met hers, and where their earlier kisses had been passionate and fueled with something akin to desirous kerosene, this one was tender. Emotion passed from his lips to hers, carrying with them a depth that both frightened and calmed Emilia.

When he broke away, she was breathless and overwhelmed.

"It might have started that way, but it feels like there's more now."

"It does."

"I'll talk to you, Emilia, and I promise I always will, but you can be damn sure I won't let anyone in your royal entourage out chivalry me."

She giggled but grew serious when he kissed her again.

"I don't know what I'm doing, marrying a princess," he whispered against her skin. His breath was warm on her chilled skin, but his words still sent a shiver rolling through her. "But I can assure you, I'll rise to the challenge. Because I want to do right by *you*, Emilia the doctor and amazing woman."

He'd acknowledged the one thing that had been missing this whole time—that she was a woman affected by this decision, too, not just a womb for the infant princess.

"Oh, Aiodhán. I'm sorry for how this has all happened. But I'm grateful that it's you by my side."

"I'm not sorry. Even though it isn't what I thought my first go-around leading residents would look like, I'm glad that it happened."

Her giggle turned to a throaty laugh. "Give it time, Aiodhán. Give it time."

As he rolled on top of her, promising to make the most of the time they had before the crown pulled them for yet another press engagement by kissing her into submission, a small bead of hope rose to the surface of her thoughts.

If only she could ignore the world waiting just outside their door, ready to pounce on that hope and extinguish it in the name of curiosity.

CHAPTER THIRTEEN

Aiodhán had been out of the office for less than seventy-two hours, but it was still the longest stretch he'd gone without checking in or going through his emails at least. Stranger still was the fact that he didn't mind one damn bit. Instead of the steady thrum of noise in the back of his head urging him to work harder, to accomplish more, there was a peaceful silence.

The silence came with an almost magnetic pull toward Emilia, who quickly became his new obsession. If he wasn't making her comfortable after their press junkets, he was elevating her heartbeat with a passion-filled bout in her oversize bed. When he wasn't concerned about her food intake, he was licking chocolate sauce off her slightly swollen abdomen and trailing kisses south to an even sweeter spot. When he'd finished making sure the tiny life inside her was safe and healthy, he moved beside a sleeping Emilia and daydreamed about playing with a fake stethoscope with their little one, teaching them how to use the instrument.

Only once did he use his phone the whole weekend, and it was to work on something he figured they'd both need.

It was pretty easy to figure out—he was *happy*, and for maybe the first time in his life. If this was the payoff for the existential dread that plagued him each time he stepped away from her, he didn't mind.

When his alarm rang on the third morning away from the hospital, he almost hit Snooze to convince Emilia to wake him up in a far more sensual way than his coffee could. But she looked so peaceful, her eyes fluttering with dreams that must be good, given the sweet smile on her slightly parted lips.

Was he part of those dreams like she was in his? An ache to know the answer to that was as strong as his excitement to get back to the ER. He wasn't thrilled to go to work for the same reasons as before—to work away the loss that threatened to fill the cavernous spaces in his heart—but because he had a family to take care of now. A family that was filling those dark spaces with light.

He'd sworn to do what it took, and hell, if they could get off work and be together like they were the past few days, it would hardly be an imposition.

And in a few short hours, Emilia would be joining him at the hospital. He hopped out of bed, careful to shut the bathroom door quietly behind him.

It's going to be okay.

They'd already filled out all the HR forms and let the CMO know the plan, and he'd filled Mallory and Brian in. They were made aware of the minimum they needed to know, but it'd still been a surprise to hear Aiodhán had fallen for an intern, was marrying her in less than two weeks, and that she was a member of the royal Zephyr family. Oh, and he was gonna be a dad. Mallory had cried with happiness, and Brian had just sat there at the bar, his mouth agape, shaking his head.

"I can't believe it," his best friend repeated at least a dozen times in as many minutes. "You're actually gonna put a ring on her finger? Willingly?"

"I am."

He'd paid the tab and headed home, the smile remaining as he considered that word—*home*. Since the age of eleven he'd never really had one he looked forward to going to.

Brushing his teeth and heading out the door to the penthouse elevator, he contemplated his luck. It'd seemed like he'd stepped in some alternate universe when Emilia had strode through Minnie Gen's doors that first morning and he'd been forced to reckon with their one night of abandon every time he looked at her. But now he saw the fated second meeting for what it was: a portent of a future he was finally looking forward to. A future that would sustain him long after his career in medicine ended.

Emilia de Reyes was a gift he didn't plan on squandering.

When the doors opened in the lobby of the downtown apartment high-rise, though, he struggled to keep his focus. Flashing lights and a frenetic mob of people with cameras and microphones charged the doors. The noise was deafening, made worse by the way they charged him, bringing the chaos to his feet. Aiodhán glanced behind him as they approached, until it hit him.

They were there for *him*. The man about to marry Princess Emilia of Zephyranthes.

"Dr. Adler!" one reporter shouted from the back of the mob. "Is it true you're engaged to the princess?"

He ran through his talking points from the press secretary assigned to him and Emilia.

"Be brief. No details. Just good old-fashioned love that couldn't keep you two apart."

"I am. We're happy, and I'm sure she'll be willing to share more details soon, but if you'll excuse me, I'm late for work."

He pushed through the first membrane of reporters, surprised to find they were at least ten deep. Chance was shoving through on the other end, trying to make his way to Aiodhán, but the throng was relentless.

"How did you two meet?" another asked. He pretended he hadn't heard that one. Bar hopping and one-night stands were on the Do Not Mention list from the royal staff.

"Is it really love? How can you be sure when you've only known each other four months?"

"Were you aware she was one of the wealthiest people on the continent when you started dating? Do you think she'll ask you to sign a prenup after the fiasco with Luis Cartel?"

He used his shoulder to get through two more layers of the human shield blocking his way, refusing to answer the asinine questions from people who really didn't care about the answers.

Obviously there weren't prenuptial agreements in a royal marriage. He'd leave with nothing if he left, save a small stipend for his supposed troubles. He'd learned that much with an internet search. What happened to responsible journalism?

"Does this mean you'll be keeping up your medical practice? What about the proposed trauma center?"

Aiodhán frowned and turned to face the reporter who'd asked the last question. "Of course I'll keep practicing and building the center. Why wouldn't I?"

In the back of his head, he heard Florence, the press secretary's voice in his head.

"Don't get defensive. They'll try to rile you up, but don't let them."

"Will Princess Emilia stay on as an intern now that she's expecting?"

"You'll have to ask the princess." He tried for a smile, but damn if it didn't feel more like a grimace. A microphone was shoved in his face, actually slapping his chin when the reporter holding it was pushed from behind. Apologies were made, but the crowd didn't thin to make room for him to get to his car. How did Emilia do this every day of her life? No wonder she wanted a life of anonymity in America. One all her own without any prying eyes.

So much for that.

Chance finally broke through and snatched Aiodhán's hand.

"That's all the doctor has time for today. Please give him and the princess a wide berth so they can continue their lives without interruption," Chance said. It seemed to work, at least enough that Aiodhán could dive into the waiting car, Chance at his heels, before they sped off.

"Wow. That was intense." Aiodhán gazed out of the tinted window as the world he knew—usually by bike or on foot—

whizzed by. He got the distinct feeling he was a bystander in his own life, a nagging tic that had flicked him upside the head from time to time since he'd found out about the pregnancy.

"Was it? That was a smaller gathering than we anticipated, actually. This makes me concerned the real crowd is awaiting our arrival at the hospital."

The *real* crowd? Hell. All he wanted at that moment was Emilia's hand in his so he could make his way to work unscathed. She gave him strength, and without her, he was floundering. So much for *I'll act like the royal consort I'm supposed to be*.

Maybe closer to the truth was *Please be easy on me. I just want to work and then go home to the woman I've agreed to marry and care for*.

Only one thing held him up. The reporters mentioned love more than once.

How would I answer that?

It wasn't that he didn't feel strongly for Emilia. But love? That was a different animal altogether. On one hand, he couldn't imagine life without her at his side now. But on the other hand, he'd never let anyone in, beyond mild attraction. How did he know what love felt like? Or could withstand? He was giving up his dream of the trauma center and helping more people to follow Emilia to her country. Was that love?

It'd been easy to imagine it was when he was tangled in Emilia's arms. Outside, faced with the only world he'd ever known—one he'd built from scratch—the answer was more difficult.

Chance passed him a single sheet of paper with a list of times and places he was needed for appearances, distracting him from the give-and-take of emotions surrounding his new circumstances.

"You're kidding me." His skin went cold. "What if I've got surgeries scheduled during these times?"

Chance shrugged. "I'm only the messenger, Dr. Adler."

"How many times do I have to beg you to call me Aiodhán?"

"At least one more, sir." Chance smiled, his eyes twinkling with mischief. A small bit of the frustration dissolved. This wasn't Chance's fault any more than it was his. Hell, if anyone was scot-free in the whole mess, it was Emilia's guard.

"Is this what we can expect every day this week leading up to the wedding?" Aiodhán asked him. "I just mean with these events and stuff. I'd like to know how important it is so I can keep the surgeries and resident duties I need in order to keep the program running. Not to mention get the work done at the trauma wing that's overdue at this point."

Anxiety crept up his spine.

"I think that is something you should speak with the king about."

And just like that, the frustration reappeared.

"Sure. Easy for you to say, since you're carrying a weapon under that seersucker." Aiodhán rolled his eyes at the window, at the brisk walk he was missing because he wasn't allowed to, as Florence, doubling as his household manager, said, "take unnecessary risks." So he couldn't walk, couldn't ride his bike, couldn't know why he was being pulled off surgeries and other duties for his job, but he could shut his mouth and go along with the status quo.

Maybe he should have asked more questions when Emilia said there would be challenges to being the prince consort. The thing was, he had. And she'd been nothing but honest. He just hadn't wanted to believe his life would so irrevocably altered.

Or perhaps he'd just imagined it to be like in the movies: princess meets prince, they fall in love, and everything falls into place. Instead, it was like watching a bomb go off in his life, and he was surgically trying to piece together what he could.

"This gets easier, you know," Chance said, by way of an answer to Aiodhán's childish outburst.

Aiodhán sighed, his breath fogging the glass. He absently traced the outline of the stop sign they were parked by. The octagonal red warning was clear. He needed to knock it off. He'd made every choice that had led to that moment. And it wouldn't last forever.

"Sorry about my attitude. I knew what to expect, but I guess I wasn't prepared for what it would feel like."

"How is that, sir?"

"Like I'm not in control of anything happening to me. Between the reporters and the schedule changes for the wedding, I'm not sure I'm in charge of my life anymore. I want Emilia and the baby, but I wish the rest of it wasn't part of the deal."

"That will pass with time. You'll get used to it, and choices will be made available to you so it doesn't seem as if this life isn't yours. In fact, I have a few of them here."

Chance handed him another piece of paper. Aiodhán opened it, and sure enough, there were a list of possibilities laid out for him.

He could marry Emilia and move to Zephyranthes with her, where he could take on a role as adviser of medical policy, which sounded made up. It sounded like a lot of travel and not a lot of time with his wife and daughter.

The next option was worse. He could stay here "for a number of predecided years" to continue his practice and supporting his family. On one hand, that didn't sound half-bad. His life would largely stay uninterrupted, and he'd get to visit Emilia and his daughter whenever he could.

Nowhere did it say he could move, practice medicine in Zephyranthes, and come home to his family each night. Did Emilia know about this?

The choices they'd given him were only okay if he'd remained the same man he'd been the night he'd met her. Now, he was somewhere between the idiot who pushed everyone away and the prince he'd need to become.

Where did that leave him?

Somewhere in the middle of the Atlantic Ocean.

"You don't have to go with one of those options, you know.

You've usurped the royal lineage, so you hold more power than you think."

Aiodhán let that sink in. Chance was probably breaking three laws by mentioning that, but Aiodhán was only more confused than ever.

"I'm not going to blackmail them, Chance." He smiled. "But thanks for the talk. I'll work it out with Emilia."

He frowned at the crowd outside the hospital.

Aiodhán was a celebrity now, and everyone knew celebrities didn't get to keep the lives they left behind before they made the choice to step into the spotlight.

CHAPTER FOURTEEN

EMILIA GOT TO work without too much fuss. Of course, she'd been accosted by the gang of news folks outside the apartment and hospital, but that was to be expected. The questions were, too.

How long had she known the doctor?
Had they begun dating right after meeting?
What about Luis Cartel? Did he know?
Was it love at first sight?

That last one had given her pause, though she'd kept smiling, waving, and walking to the employee entrance of the ER as if nothing was amiss. On the surface, nothing was. She needn't think too hard on the attraction-at-first-sight aspect of her relationship with Aiodhán, but one word in that query had her heart aflutter.

Love. She'd never considered it possible, but here she was, living with a man she was to marry, a man whose baby she carried, and oh, it was everything she'd read about in the romance novels she'd stolen from her tutor's handbag when she was a young teen.

There was plenty of physical passion as she'd seen on the risqué pages of the romances she'd read, but there was also so much more. Aiodhán listened to her, and he took her ideas into consideration and built upon them. He laughed with her, and more than that, he invited her silliness.

It was just what she needed to face down the intense scrutiny awaiting her. Not from the cameras and writers attached to them; no, she could handle them as she had her whole life. But the peers she'd come to respect at the hospital were a different story. They wouldn't ever look at her the same way now that her true identity had been revealed. That, and the added judgment now that she was dating the boss. Would every good thing she'd done at the hospital be thrown into new light? Would they wonder if she received special treatment during her internship?

She knew how hard she'd worked, that they'd done everything above board, but still…worry tickled her skin.

"Are you sure you're ready for this, Emilia?" Rebecca asked her as the car came to a stop.

"I am. I've missed it here."

She felt stronger than she had since she'd arrived in Minnesota. Days of rest and good food and lovemaking could do that, she surmised.

"May I ask you a question?"

Emilia braced herself. She'd been waiting for Rebecca to come to her about the pregnancy instead of addressing the woman's own infertility trauma before she was ready.

"Of course."

"How did you muster the courage to chase this dream? Medicine, I mean."

Emilia was rarely surprised. Yet this question from Rebecca shocked her.

"Um… I'm not sure," she finally said. "I've wanted this life for as long as I could remember."

"Yes, I remember you trying to treat me for fatigue when I'd gone on a long ride through the Cyan fields."

Emilia laughed. "Didn't I prescribe you mints to take with every meal for a week after that?"

Rebecca offered a rare smile. "That you did. But what gave you the courage to pursue medicine as your passion project? Most nobles choose something like cooking in Italy or teaching in Africa."

"My mom." Rebecca's smile fell. "I'm sorry if that was blunt, but it's true. The woman may not have been who I thought she was, but her death affected me on a cellular level."

Rebecca gestured that Emilia continue.

"I didn't want anything to ever happen to anyone like what happened to my mother. When she asked for help, her doctors dismissed her as exhausted from labor—and she was a *queen*. By the time they realized she was bleeding internally, my brother had died in utero and my mother not long after. When I learned of the horrible conditions for women giving birth all over the world, my heart ached. I decided then and there I wouldn't let anything be more important than reaching that goal." Emilia got out and Rebecca sat in the car doorway. Reporters off in the distance hadn't noticed them yet, but their time was borrowed. "What did you want to do, Rebecca?"

Rebecca had been in Emilia's life since she was eleven. Only a year after Emilia's mother was buried, Rebecca walked down the aisle into the king's arms. Though it'd been almost two decades and Rebecca was legally Emilia's stepmother, she'd stayed just beyond Emilia's reach her whole life. Rebecca was only fifteen years older than Emilia, but that wasn't the only reason for the distance. Emilia had always sensed a jealousy emanating from the woman even though she was queen. She felt it even stronger now.

"To be honest, I'm sad we couldn't conceive, mostly because I know you and your father wanted it so badly—both for different reasons, I'm sure. But I never imagined being a mother. When your father met me, I was in graduate school to become an artist. I don't know if you knew that. He visited the school to see how the funds he'd donated were being put to use. Then…" she paused, a sad smile on her face.

"My father fell in love with you, and your life changed forever the moment you noticed him back."

Rebecca nodded. "And I fell in love back. I don't regret that, Emilia." For the first time since Emilia had watched Rebecca take her mother's crown, a peaceful understanding passed between the two women. It also helped her understand Aiodhán's struggles on a deeper level.

"Thank you for supporting me, Rebecca. And there's still time for you, too. Especially now."

Rebecca smiled as Emilia walked away. Their odd exchange weighed down Emilia's steps as she walked into the hospital with Chance. All it took was the familiar hiss of the doors opening for her to remember her purpose. A broad smile tugged at her lips, and her shoulders straightened with the importance of finding her life's work and performing her tasks with joy. That included becoming a queen worthy of the title.

She slipped past the main entrance without drawing the attention of the paparazzi outside. She could only hope Aiodhán had been able to do the same. This life was going to be a difficult enough adjustment for him; battling the unnecessary demons that plagued her position would only make it worse.

"Well, holy hell. I wasn't sure you'd come back," a welcome voice chimed in the moment she entered the lobby.

"Oh, Bridget, I've missed you."

The woman grinned and enveloped her in a hug. Emilia warmed at the affection. She'd never had a friend, but the gesture seemed to indicate she did now.

"Seriously, when you texted you were on your way in, I didn't believe you. Why the Sam hell would you come back here when you could, I dunno, run Zephyranthes and its wineries? I'd be back on the beaches of Cyana already, with a glass of Rioja and a plate of tapas on my lap."

Emilia let loose a laugh not becoming of a princess. "What? And give up our fourteen-hour-long days, the mystery meat in the cafeteria, and the nurse who I'm pretty sure tangles our picc lines on purpose? I wouldn't dream of it."

Bridget slapped her on the shoulder and led her to the locker room. Emilia inhaled the cool air of the hospital's lobby. The citrus-and-soap scent so endemic to the space slipped around her waist like the arm of a good friend, familiar and welcome.

"Don't forget about those flattering scrubs they gave us," Bridget added, cackling over her humor.

"Hey there. Don't disparage the pale blue wonders that are going to keep my belly hidden from all your prying eyes the next few months. Oh, and Rioja is off the menu for the time being."

Bridget grew serious. "I can't believe you're actually going through with the wedding," she whispered when the doors opened and the other interns strode in.

"Of course I am. I don't really have a choice, do I?"

Bridget shrugged, then her trademark smile kicked up in one corner of her mouth, matching the gleam in her eyes.

"I guess not, but you'd better promise me a dish session about you-know-who," she said in a hushed whisper meant only for Emilia. "I can forgive you for not telling me who you were in the beginning, but keeping the fact that you slept with the hottest doctor in the Midwest a secret? That's criminal."

Heat crept up Emilia's neck and cheeks. She could feel others' eyes on her as she changed into her scrubs. But the mention of Aiodhán calmed her. He was her partner in this. They could handle the pressure of the job, so long as they supported one another.

"If you can keep those interns off my back, I'll tell you everything."

"You're on. What about tonight? A wine and sparkling non-alcoholic cider date to celebrate your return?"

Emilia cringed. "I'm sorry, I can't. Aiodhán and I have dinner with my parents and the governor."

"No worries. How about tomorrow?"

"A press engagement at City Hall. We're pretty booked out, but I could probably sneak out for coffee one morning this weekend."

Although, as she mentioned it, she frowned. If she recalled, they had brunch Saturday with the mayor of Minneapolis and a champagne breakfast—sparkling cider for her—with the

Department of Health of Minnesota on Sunday to discuss maternal care foundations she'd like the crown to donate to, including the Gold Fleece program.

The door shoved open, and Aiodhán called in. "Interns, out here now. We've got a lot to catch up on, and you're slowing us down."

The heat on Emilia's cheeks turned to molten lava at the sound of his voice. Her stomach flipped, and the warmth fled south.

Bridget gave her a weak hug laced with disappointment. This wasn't how Emilia imagined her reunion with Bridget. But her duties had to come first.

"It's okay. We'll find time. Oh, hey. Did your man tell you he asked me to join him at the new trauma center in the peds wing?"

Emilia nodded, hoping the jealousy she felt rising up her throat with bile didn't show. She'd love to work with them both, but not at the expense of her reputation or Aiodhán's.

"It's exciting!"

"I'll keep you posted about how it's going. If you want to say screw those other interns and what they think, you could always join us, you know."

If only it was just the interns talking about her behind her back.

"Thanks." Emilia tried for a smile, but even forced it barely worked. She wasn't sure she'd wanted the trauma position with Aiodhán—until she found out she'd be able to work with the neonatal patients. Giving it up was another loss she'd mourned in the privacy of her own heart, another price levied for the life she was born into. She couldn't afford to have anyone question how she earned her experiences. Especially not when their opinions could derail Aiodhán's career. This was one thing she could control, and she would, for them both. "Good luck, Bridget, and thank you for being there even though this is hard."

"Of course. You're my girl, Em, no matter what you are to the rest of them."

Aiodhán nodded that Bridget leave the locker room with the other interns, and when they were alone, he took Emilia in his arms and embraced her tightly.

"God, I missed you."

"I was only an hour behind you."

"An hour too long," he teased. His phone chimed twice in quick succession.

"Do you need to get that?" she asked.

He shrugged her concern off and ignored his phone, a liability as a doctor.

"It's nothing. Just something I'm working on."

She regarded him through a sidelong glance. "Care to share?"

"Not yet. When the time is right." His smile took the edge off her worry, but not completely. When his phone made a different chime, his smile disappeared. "Maybe we should just run away and forget all this mess."

"What happened?" she asked, pulling back. His eyes were hard, his jaw set.

"Just what you warned me would happen. Did you see our schedule? All but one of my surgeries have been canceled. I'm barely able to squeeze in time across the street."

"Oh, no. I'm so sorry. I actually don't think we have the same schedule. You'll be needed for more fittings and instruction on protocol that I've been learning since I was a child. But I can talk to my parents if it's too much."

Aiodhán pulled back, and the cool air between them chilled where his heat had been.

"No. No, that's fine. I'll be okay." His lips brushed hers, but they were devoid of the affection they'd shared earlier. "Have a good day with Dr. Thomas. Are you sure you want to do this? You can stay on my service, hon."

"No, not if I want to make a name for myself. This is okay for now, if it means people will look at the medicine I practice and not think I'm good because I'm getting help from my fiancé."

"I could always tell them to shove off."

She smiled. "I don't need you to fight my battles for me, Aiodhán. This one I need to do on my own."

"I'll support what you choose. But let me know if Bob doesn't work out. There's other options, Emilia."

"It's fine. Good luck over there."

They'd each said they were fine in the span of a couple minutes, so why didn't Emilia believe it? Because she wasn't, not really. So much was changing. Though much of it was good, she used to find peace and stability in the routine of royal life. Now the uncertainty circling her future left her feeling untethered and tossed around a stormy sea.

Aiodhán walked out, leaving her very alone and very unsure of how to fix this. How could she keep her friendship with Bridget, her duty to her country, grow a tiny life inside her, work hard at her profession, *and* build a relationship with a man she truly cared about at the center of it all? A moment ago, she'd had everything she'd ever wanted, and yet it felt as if it were slipping from her grasp.

And no one was coming to save her. There was no other heir, no one else's shoulders on which to share the burden of her crown when it became too heavy.

As she grabbed her lab coat and found her way to her new boss, her heart hammered against her chest. *Something is going to have to give*, it whispered to her.

That she believed.

CHAPTER FIFTEEN

Aiodhán finished the final stitch of the biopsy and lifted his gloved hands.

"Bridget, you may close."

"Really?" Bridget asked. "Far out. I'll do you proud, boss."

Aiodhán simply nodded and headed out of the OR, stripping the gloves and face mask off when he was out of the sterile field. He sighed, watching on as Bridget—a fully competent, if overenthusiastic doctor—sutured the wound. It was their first patient together, and the procedure had gone as well as he could have hoped.

In an ideal world, Aiodhán would be able to keep Emilia on as an intern, but with the added scrutiny from their upcoming shotgun wedding, he understood why she'd opted to train under another physician. He respected her for the decision, even if he didn't care what anyone else thought of them.

Damn if he didn't miss her, though. Not just the warmth of her body he'd come to crave at the end of each long day, or the way her kisses could transform from soft and tentative to hungry and feverish within seconds. Yeah, he ached for those when he wasn't around her to claim them—especially now that the only hospital time he had was building up the trauma center across the street from him—but more than that, he missed *her*.

The wit he'd somehow overlooked, ebbing just below her intelligent responses at the hospital.

The way she knew just what he'd need moments before he asked for it.

Her ability to lead the interns without so much as a nudge. She commanded with her quiet strength and charm, and everyone just sort of fell in to learn from her. If he was honest, they'd all gotten more from Emilia than they had from him in the past five months.

But something nagged at him. She'd alluded to not knowing about his schedule, so did that mean she hadn't been aware of the king's ultimatum, either? Was it a boilerplate deal—marry the pregnant princess and pick one of two half-lives?

His pager went off and it startled him.

Surgery room 2, vehicle collision.

A second page went off.

Patient is 22 weeks pregnant.

Fear roared like a forest fire in heavy winds. Only repeating "She's here in the hospital" to himself took the edge off.

Still, the worry didn't dissipate. It never had, not since meeting Emilia. It'd only gotten worse after she'd collapsed in his ER.

He should give this case to someone else. But who? He pulled up the sheet of paper with his schedule from the king. If he took this on, he'd be late for the cocktail hour he and Emilia were scheduled for.

Well, that was too damned bad. Saving lives trumped drinks with strangers any day of the week. He pocketed the schedule and jogged down the hall to the surgery suites. Over the past few days, he'd grown used to being interrupted by Emilia's parents or their staff in the middle of his day, but this would make two surgeries in a row without being yanked out. He needed this. If for no other reason than to calm the part of him that relied on putting families back together for his own peace.

Aiodhán pushed open the doors and strode into the sterile corridor to wash his hands and stopped short.

"Hey there, gorgeous. What are you doing here?"

Emilia beamed at him as she turned off the water with her wrists and shook them off.

"Dr. Thomas was annoyed with me, I think. He got the page and sent me instead."

"What an idiot. You can still work with me, you know."

She shrugged, then gestured to the stainless steel washbasin that looked out over the sparkling new surgical suite. "This place is amazing, Aiodhán. I wish I could." Her voice was wistful and tugged at his heart. Was there a time when he hadn't known the lilt of her vowels, the way she placed her bottom teeth between her lips when she was reticent? Of course there was, but he couldn't remember, nor did he want to. As challenging as it all had been, with the schedule interruptions and worry about what would come next for them as a new couple, he appreciated every minute he got to spend with Emilia.

In fact, he kept looking for more, *craved* more. As a physician, he understood the feverish draw of an addict to a drug. Emilia was his, and he wouldn't mind being a lifetime user of the high she gave him.

"I do, too. Someday, hopefully, it'll matter a lot less to people how you got your start. They'll realize you're amazing, and that'll be all that counts."

"I hope so. The gossip in Middle America is certainly not for the faint of heart. I heard a man in front of me at the salad bar in the cafeteria, who I've never met mind you, comment on *the royal princess who was only hired to make the hospital look good*."

"Good grief. I'm sorry, Em." He was, too. He'd heard the rumors himself, but aside from telling the interns and other physicians to mind their own business, Emilia had asked him to stay out of it for fear of making things worse. He understood: the white-knighting wasn't going to help her show her own competence. Still, he wished there were more he could do besides stand by and support her decision. "You know the administration doesn't care. They know you're a good doctor and are fine with us sharing service. Just say the word, and I'll start pulling you over here until you're back to being mine."

"I'd like being yours." Her frown dissolved into a soft, lip-biting smile.

"Ditto." Aiodhán shook his head, the fear and worry fading like mist under a strong summer sun. "Well, I for one am glad Thomas is an insufferable tool who doesn't know greatness when he sees it. His loss is definitely my gain."

"You're sweet, but I'm not sure how I'm going to win his favor back."

"How so?"

Emilia bit the corner of her mouth in a way that made him half-hard and filled with the roaring desire that took over his good sense whenever he was with her. He threw on the cold water, hoping it would shock his system into remembering why he was there.

"He doesn't seem interested in instruction of, as he puts it, *a stuffed-shirt royal who won't be here long anyway.*"

"I know you want me to stay out of it, but when we're done here, I'm giving that jerk a piece of my mind. He has no right—"

"You'll do no such thing, Aiodhán Conor Adler. I can fight my own battles, thank you very much."

"And I love you for it." As soon as the words came out of his mouth, they both froze. Mortification spread from his toes to the tips of his ears as fast as a forest blaze in the middle of summer. Thankfully, she shook her head at his idiotic, purely unromantic way of telling her he loved her for the first time. "Sorry. That sure as hell isn't how I meant to tell you how I felt, but…"

He shrugged, his hands out in front of him, drying. When he bent in for a kiss, she met him halfway. The heat passing between them seared his feelings for her, capturing them in his heart.

"Well, I love you, too. But maybe we can talk about it after we're done saving lives and planning to overthrow the Zephyr monarchy with our unconventional marriage?"

Ask her about the letter from the king, his subconscious said.

No. Not right now. There was time.

"I'd like that."

"Dr. Adler, we could use you in here," the nurse came out to tell him. He nodded, pulled his mask over his face and hid his smile.

That is, until the phone buzzed in his pocket—the phone he'd been instructed to keep for de Reyes family communication. He let it buzz until curiosity finally got the best of him. Knowing he'd have to rewash his hands, he extracted the phone and read the stream of texts that followed.

There is a mandatory meeting at City Hall at three p.m. Please bring all documentation needed to procure a new passport, as well as your out-of-date items.

He frowned. They were making him renew his passport?

Of course, dummy. How else are you supposed to get to Zephyranthes to see your new wife?

It was two o'clock now. He wouldn't make it. Oh, well. Saving this woman—and her child's—life mattered more than some appointment that could be made up.

"What is it?" Emilia asked. "Is it my family?"

"Yeah, but it's not a big deal."

Wasn't it, though? Because this was the first step in his move to Zephyranthes someday so he could marry a woman who'd eventually rule a place he'd never even visited. His stomach hardened like it had been lined with lead.

"Talk to me, Aiodhán. Remember our radical honesty promise?"

He sighed. If he told her about every reservation he had, they'd never move past it. Some of the issues he had to work through on his own if he wanted to be the kind of partner Emilia deserved. The prince consort her country needed.

"I'm sorry, that's not what I was doing." He rewashed his

hands and slid gloves on them. "Your family's staff asked me to get to City Hall to renew my passport."

"I understand, and I'm sorry. To say they operate with royal efficiency wouldn't be hyperbole. But after Friday, we don't need to move on their timeline. We'll ask to take things slow, to figure out what we'd like to do as a couple."

A bit of the weight in his abdomen loosened.

"Okay. I like that. And I'm sorry I let it all get me wound up. It's just a lot to think about."

"I know." She nudged him with her shoulder. "But we're doing it together, and whatever choices we make will benefit our growing family."

She was right: they had a kid to think of now. He needed to stop getting so hung up on the small things when that was obviously the most important.

"All right. Let's do this, de Reyes."

She gloved up and put her surgical mask up as well, then followed him into the suite.

It was brightly lit, the instruments gleaming. This was Aiodhán's pulpit, his sanctuary, his Eden. Every patient he brought back helped smooth over the scar of a life interrupted. His life and childhood.

It might never be enough, but he had to try, right? At least this way, he put a little good in the world. Would he be able to say the same if he became the prince of another country, more or less a figurehead?

"Are you okay?" Emilia asked.

Aiodhán stood over the patient, the life in front of him heavy and difficult to imagine. Who was she, and more importantly, who was waiting on her to come home?

It hadn't occurred to Aiodhán to care much about those details. His job was to eviscerate unwanted illnesses and foreign objects, then suture together a new future for whomever ended up on his table. Who they were when they left wasn't ever his concern.

So why wouldn't his brain let that go just then?

It was Emilia.

If anything happened to her or their child she carried, he'd be the person in the hospital waiting room, desperate for her safety, for a second chance. She'd changed his motivations for working, living, and dreaming, and damn if that ripple effect didn't change the way he worked in his OR.

But was it enough to negate the after-effects of the texts still buzzing in his pocket since he'd ignored the first? To learn a new language, a new way of living, and all but give up medicine in the process?

He cleared his throat. He was working on at least one of those concerns, but it was slow going, reminding him of the noose tightening around his neck. *Time.* He was running out of time, and all the little unimportant engagements tugging at his schedule were removing the slack in the rope, cutting into his skin and plans.

"I'm fine. Let's get to work. Number five scalpel, please."

Emilia's gaze bore into Aiodhán, but he couldn't let it control the outcome in this room. She handed the instrument to him and grabbed the suction before he requested she do just that. His entire being was at war with itself. She made him better in so many ways, but she also made him vulnerable where he should be impermeable.

The patient had suffered injuries on the entire right side of her body, leading to a fractured rib, subdural hematoma, and a bleed he couldn't find.

An hour into cleaning the wound and searching for the cause of the destruction, Aiodhán shook his head in frustration.

"I can't find the bleeder," he said. His hands were deep in the patient's chest cavity, smeared with blood coming from a wound he couldn't see. The X-ray had shown the area, but it wasn't there. The infant's heart rate spiked. They were running out of time.

Emilia moved the suction, then followed the rib cage down

with her hands. She mumbled in Zephyr and for the umpteenth time, he wished he'd paid more attention in his high school Spanish class. But he understood more than last time: that was something.

"I've looked there." The patient's heart rate slowed, while the baby's continued to rise, triggering both alarms. "I need more suction, de Reyes."

She used the suction wand while her other hand investigated, before announcing, "I've got it. There's trauma to the right kidney where it separated from the blood vessels. I've got my finger on the separation point. Should we suture?"

Aiodhán exhaled a breath he hadn't realized he'd kept locked in his chest.

"Good job, de Reyes. How big is the tear?"

"Enough that the bleed is consistent."

"Let's cauterize what we can then suture the vessel once she's out of immediate danger."

"Can I take lead?" she asked.

Aiodhán shivered as if a chill had draped over the room. When she'd stepped back, he could see the swelling of her abdomen. The only thing preventing her from ending up on this table was sheer luck. Being a royal didn't protect her, or them. And he was willingly signing up to care for this woman and this child, knowing he'd never know a day's peace again.

Yeah, but you're together for other reasons now.

Were they, though? His thoughts spiraled out of control quicker than he could rein them in.

"Aiodhán?" she asked. "I'm taking the lead." He nodded and watched on as she asked the nurse for the cautery pen. In minutes, she was done and requested the sutures necessary to perform the vascular surgery. He assisted, but other than talking her through the closing, he hadn't done a damned thing.

The patient was wheeled to the recovery room, and Emilia wheeled on him.

"What was that, Aiodhán? You looked at me, at my stomach, and froze."

"I wasn't sure you could be objective." He nodded to her belly, housing the thing that brought them together in the first place.

"You have to trust that I'm going to be able to do this."

"I trust you, but this woman didn't end up in here of her own accord. The world's a scary place, and seeing her on the table made me think of you there. How do you separate it?"

She rested a hand on her abdomen. "If I let myself worry about our similarities, I wouldn't be able to do my job. And I'm training for neonatal surgery, Aiodhán."

"Should you be? I mean the stress of the baby with everything else going on—"

She froze, her bloodied hands held in front of her chest like a macabre offering.

"Is this about me or you right now?"

He ignored the sharp look from the anesthetist as she and the nurses left the room.

"Me. I get that, but this patient, Emilia... I can't protect you." There it was, his greatest fear laid on the table between them. "I mean, I can save all the lives in the world, but does it matter if I can't save you when it counts?"

She walked around the OR table to his side, dragging him out of the OR into the scrub room.

"You can't, you're right. Luckily, I can take care of myself. You're my partner, but it's not your job to save me. Nor is this a zero-sum game."

"How do you mean?"

"I mean, if you save a thousand people, it isn't bringing your parents back. And it won't protect anyone you love from harm."

She was right. He'd been racing the clock, trying to keep his heart safe while he protected other families. But that didn't change how he felt or why he'd avoided caring for anyone until now.

"It's just that... What about our child? When I'm a royal medical adviser, who's going to help keep her safe?"

Because even if Emilia could take care of herself, who would protect their daughter when he was working in some job he didn't understand on behalf of a country that wasn't his?

Shock registered in her wide eyes before her brows crashed together in a small act of fury.

"What the hell are you talking about? That's not even a real thing, Aiodhán. If you don't want to marry me and move, just—"

He'd stripped his gloves and tore out the letter that had been burning a hole in his shirt pocket.

"Then, what's this?"

She stripped her own gloves, and he watched her eyes widen with every line of the letter from her father.

"I—I don't know. But they must have a plan for you if that's what they came up with. Most likely it's a way to get you medical privileges without you having to be credentialed in Zephyranthes."

The naked truth of her statement fell on him like a thousand tiny paper cuts, stinging him but leaving him open and burning. Her parents had made up a position to pacify him, so not only was he losing his homeland, his friends, and freedom but he'd lose his practice as well. Unless he stayed here, which, he recalled, was their second option. Or was it their first? Were they hoping he'd take the easier route and they wouldn't have to come up with a job description for the royal medical something-or-other?

"Oh."

"Don't worry about it right now. We'll get it sorted."

Her dismissal was salt in his wounds.

"Sure. I'm sure it's going to work out."

"It has to," she whispered.

He pulled her into him and closed his eyes. This was his partner, the woman he'd just admitted loving and who carried his child inside her. She was struggling, too, despite being strong so much of the time—strong enough to carry him through his worry, too. He could do this. He had to, for her.

But would it be enough?

When he secured his arms around Emilia in a viselike grip, it was for himself. Maybe, if he held on tight enough, he could keep the outside world from taking what he loved this time around.

The door cracked open, and Bridget stuck her head in.

"Hey, you two. I've been waiting out here until you finish up, but since it looks like you're moving in here for the night, I figured I'd just interrupt."

"What's going on, Bridget?" Emilia asked.

"Your parents are in the lobby."

Aiodhán cringed. Shoot. He'd forgotten about his appointment with them.

"Why didn't they call me?"

"They're not here for you," she said. "I guess they had some sort of meeting with you, Dr. Adler. You're two hours late, they said."

"What's this about?" Emilia asked him. "And why didn't you say anything? I could have paged another doctor."

"Who? Who could have done what I did back there, Emi?" He raked his hands through his hair as Bridget slipped from the room.

"You can't play God like this, Aiodhán. You're a fabulous physician, but you're not the only one here."

"That's not the point."

Her hands rested on her hips. God, he both loved and despised when she did that. It was sexy as hell but usually meant she was pissed at him.

"Then what, pray tell, is?"

"Do you see what's happening? I love what I do, Emilia, and they're taking it from me."

"It'll only be—"

"For a few more days. I know." He shoved out of the doors, leaving Emilia behind in the scrub room. It wasn't right to take this out on her, he knew. But he was powerless to stop the royal wheel that was already in motion. Even though it was rolling right over his dreams and career.

"Aiodhán, look at me." He did and saw the hurt in her eyes. He wasn't the only one giving things up in this exchange.

He kissed the top of her head. "I'm sorry. I'm frustrated—"

"No. No apologies. But no wallowing, either."

"What's the alternative?" he said, only half-teasing.

"You find a way to get what you want out of this spin on your life, so you don't feel as steamrolled."

He considered that. What did he want? Besides the woman already in his arms, that is. And there was his answer. He'd been selfishly thinking about what he was losing if he married Emilia, but not how she must be feeling in all the upheaval. Hell, the woman had given up her position on his service to protect them both.

"Okay, hon. I can do that."

He changed out quickly, the sleek black suit and slicked back hair uncomfortable but necessary.

The pager buzzed again, and he wished he could chuck it at the door. The hospital would have to find someone else to perform the surgery: Aiodhán could no longer afford to ignore the king and queen. A whisper of an idea—an idea that had been nagging him—fluttered around in his head as he strode toward the lobby.

No, he didn't want to keep his future in-laws waiting, not when they had the power to help him out with a project he'd been thinking about. Maybe it was time to use this relationship to get something *he* wanted for a change.

CHAPTER SIXTEEN

EMILIA CHECKED HER TABLET. Only two more patients left on her rounds. Both were OB patients, which sent a thrill of excitement coursing through her veins. This was what she'd come to America for, what she'd pushed back her familial and royal obligations to do.

She stopped at the first room to find the patient sleeping. It always bothered her to rouse patients who clearly needed rest, but that was the job. As was working with men like Bob Thomas. Emilia shuddered, even though she hadn't laid eyes on the man in almost two hours.

"How is he?" Bridget had asked her at lunch on Emilia's third day back. "I've heard he's like the troll from the kids' story, guarding his patients like the troll guarded his bridge."

"Dr. Thomas is brilliant, and I'll learn a lot from him," Emilia replied, her practiced response.

Liar. You actually called him a jealous troll under your breath after he took credit for your last save.

Bridget had eyed her suspiciously, and for good reason. Emilia found it hard to complain when she'd put herself in this situation. But regaining her reputation as a top-notch intern had been more important at the time than working with him. Now, she wasn't sure that choice had been worth it.

"Ew... Like that's the point." Emilia had laughed at how different she and her friend were. "I'm just saying, you'd better learn enough to graduate early. Because Dr. Thomas isn't a quarter as good-looking as your last boss," Bridget had teased before snatching an olive from Emilia's salad. She didn't mind; she hadn't had much of an appetite the past few days. And of course her friend would bring up Aiodhán. As if Emilia could put him from her mind for more than a moment.

Between her pregnancy and the impending wedding, Emilia was a bundle of nerves. Her focus was pulled between the two, and she still strove to learn and take in as much as she could before this was all taken from her.

But the truth was, she'd never become the type of surgeon she wanted to be by watching.

It was frustrating to be sure, and it made her appreciate the intensity of Aiodhán's first weeks of instruction. At least he'd acknowledged when she'd done something well or allowed her to correct her own mistakes.

Speaking of Aiodhán, and of his grumpiness, he'd become distant at work again. Not emotionally—no, he was as supportive as ever. But she hardly ever saw him anymore. Their lives had changed, and it was time she accepted that. It would only be truer after their daughter was born.

She'd asked him where he went at lunch or after his shift, and Aiodhán had said, "You're just going to have to trust me." The soft smile she'd received consoled her, but barely. She trusted him, of course, but she also missed him.

She'd just have to dive into the kisses and tender caresses of their nights together, to cherish what they were able to share when they were able to share it.

She'd yet to ask her parents about the advisory position they'd created for him. It was clear it was a fake position, a way to make him feel a part of something he might never fully acclimate to.

That small worry nagged at her, but aside from talking to her father, what could she do? She was at the mercy of royal protocol as much as Aiodhán was.

And yet…a matter of days remained until Aiodhán became her husband. Then, her parents would return to Zephyranthes until the birth, and she and Aiodhán could go back to concentrating on their shared love of medicine. There was a world of time to plan the future beyond that.

"Good morning, Mrs. Reynolds. How did you sleep?" Emilia asked as she entered her last patient's room. She checked the chart at the end of the bed as well as the monitors, and her mouth twisted into a frown. She'd feel more confident if Mrs. Reynolds's numbers were a little better. She was only two centimeters dilated and thirty percent effaced, but her heart rate and that of her infant were a tad high for Emilia's liking.

"Okay, thanks. I'd have slept better if I could convince Sarah to come out a little early."

"Did you decide on Sarah, then?"

Mrs. Reynolds laughed, then winced, holding her belly. "I'm just trying it out. Mark likes it since it was his great-aunt's name, but I'm not sure."

"Okay. What are some of your other choices?"

While Mrs. Reynolds told her the other names topping their list for the baby, Emilia discreetly paged Aiodhán. The OB attending was with another patient, and Dr. Thomas was out for the afternoon at a seminar, which left all the interns under the purview of her future husband. Less than a minute later, he strode through the door as Mrs. Reynolds shared the final name on her list.

"If I had my way, I'd go with Eleanor. That was my mother's name and could be shortened to Ellie or Elle."

"My mother's name was Eleanor, too," Aiodhán said. Emilia's curiosity was piqued. She hadn't known that about Aiodhán's mother. The list was so long about what they didn't know, at times it overwhelmed her. "I'm Dr. Adler, the doc on call today, Mrs. Reynolds. It's nice to meet you."

"Where is my OB? She knows I'm here and said she'd come by."

"She'll come by after surgery to take a peek at the baby." Mrs. Reynolds nodded, pacing her own breathing. But her skin was warm and damp, not a good sign. Aiodhán sent Emilia a knowing glance. "Dr. de Reyes just wanted me to take a look at things to make sure you're doing okay. How do you feel?"

"Mmm. Okay. Hot, I guess? Maybe a little dizzy."

"Okay. I'll see what I can do to help."

Emilia pointed out the numbers on the machine next to the patient. He frowned as well.

"Wow. Are all doctors as handsome as him?" Mrs. Reynolds whispered to Emilia.

"Not a single one. He's quite the charmer, too." She winked and tracked Mrs. Reynolds' smile. It was sharp, forced. They'd be meeting her daughter sooner than expected.

"Mrs. Reynolds," Aiodhán said, "I'm afraid I don't like what I'm seeing. I'd like to wheel you into surgery so we can make sure your daughter is delivered safely. It would be a lot better for both your hearts, which are pumping a little fast for me to recommend a natural birth."

The blood drained from her face. Her bottom lip quivered.

"But my husband isn't here yet," she whispered. Just then, another contraction rocketed through her, and she let out an ear-splitting groan before losing consciousness.

"We've got to move, Emilia. Now."

Emilia nodded and tore open the door for Aiodhán to push the gurney through. She raced behind him until they got to the OR suite in the maternity ward.

"I've called ahead to the anesthetist," she said as they slammed through the doors of the OR. "He'll be here soon."

"Good. See if you can find her husband. Fill him in, and then get back here to assist."

Emilia nodded, her nerves frayed, though she hid it beneath the royal stoicism that had been bred into her and served her well. After turning the corner, sure she was out of sight of Aiodhán, she let her hands fall to her abdomen, the hint of the small human growing inside it swelling against her skin. Heat built behind her lids, but she would not let the tears fall. Mrs. Reynolds's story wasn't her mother's. It wasn't hers, either.

Though, the other day in the OR with the woman who'd been in the car accident, she'd felt the edge of fear sneaking up on her. It had been obvious Aiodhán was terrified, so she'd shoved the worry aside.

She didn't want to add more to his plate, though, so she'd hide it until the stress of the wedding was over. Besides, her pregnancy was normal so far, a miracle since she'd received no prenatal care before her sixteenth week.

That was the thing about pregnancy: it was such a seemingly similar, benign event that occurred to an impressive percentage of people who experience pregnancy at some point in their lives. Yet each one was like a fingerprint, unique and special.

She headed down the stairs to the lobby, keeping an eye out for the red-haired, tall man she'd seen in her patient's room before.

Worry plagued her as she scoured the bustle of faces milling about. Distinct births could mean unique complications. Her mother had died from internal bleeding no one caught, barely outliving a son. She'd collapsed much the same as Mrs. Reynolds and hadn't woken up again.

Emilia noticed she'd thought of her mother without going first to the betrayal of the woman. She was healing, largely due to Aiodhán's influence on her life.

A steady warmth flowed over and through her as she considered her husband-to-be. If she could have designed a more perfect match for herself, she didn't think she would be able to do better than the physician who'd stolen her heart. What would she change? Most certainly their circumstances. If left to their own devices, she had no doubt she and Aiodhán wouldn't have found their way to one another. Her pregnancy had brought them together, but it also brought the stress of the baby, the shotgun wedding, and the pressure to move to Zephyranthes…

It was a lot.

A flash of red dashed in front of Emilia, capturing her attention.

"Mr. Reynolds," she shouted across the lobby. The man stopped and turned in her direction. She sighed with relief as he walked toward her. "I'm a resident here at Minneapolis General, and your wife has been brought to surgery to have a C-section."

"Oh, my God. What—what happened?" he asked. "I just went to get her some thicker socks and figured I'd pick up this..." he choked on a sob "...this blanket for our little girl."

Emilia placed a hand on his arm. "Mr. Reynolds, we have the best team working to help your wife and daughter. I'll update you personally as we progress through the surgery, but you should know cesareans are common, even emergent ones such as your wife's. Hold onto that blanket—you'll be needing it soon."

"Thank you for coming to tell me. Should I wait here, or..."

Emilia shook her head, an idea forming. "No, come with me. You can sit in the gallery if you'd like to watch, or you can sit in the maternity lobby. She won't likely go back to her old room for a bit until we make sure she's stable enough."

"Okay. Yeah. I'll come watch."

Emilia led the way and showed Mr. Reynolds where he could watch the birth of his little girl before scrubbing in to join Aiodhán.

"Is he aware of his wife's condition?" Aiodhán asked as soon as she entered the sterile surgical field where Mrs. Reynolds lay, still unconscious but anesthetized as well.

"We've invited partners to watch the birth before," Emilia replied. "He's scared."

What she didn't say? *I'm scared. Please, let me control what I can.*

"I understand, and I'm not questioning your choice. I just want to be prepared. This is bad, Emilia." She'd thought of that, but she also imagined not being able to see Aiodhán in his last moments. Suddenly it was clear what had happened to her: like Aiodhán, she had something to lose, and that was unimaginable.

"What do you need me to do to support you here?" she asked. He glanced up, scalpel in hand. His gaze brushed over her, but she didn't miss the way it lingered ever so slightly on the swelling of her abdomen.

"Exactly what you're doing." Emotion overwhelmed her; the baby had changed so much between them. "Help me assess the damage from her placenta abruption. She's bleeding, and I need to get it under control."

"It's placenta?" she asked, a slight wave of fear hitting her like a Mediterranean winter storm. Mrs. Reynolds's case and her mother's were more similar than she'd initially suspected.

"Yes. And it's severe. I'm a little pissed Dr. Young missed it, to be honest. It's not a mild case, and Mrs. Reynolds must've been presenting with symptoms this whole time. She was lucky to have had you on her service tonight, Emilia."

Was there an element of luck to what they did?

Emilia steeled herself, pulling strength from within. She owed the mother on the other side of the fabric her full attention. She stretched her fingers until the tremble abated. There was a reason she'd chosen this focus.

"She will get to meet Eleanor, and her husband will give them the baby blanket he picked out for her."

"Damn straight. Now, let's get to work."

As soon as the words were out of his mouth, Mrs. Reynolds coded, the long slow beep announcing her loss of sinus rhythm deafening.

"No way," Aiodhán muttered. "Not today."

He started chest compressions while Emilia performed CPR.

"Bag her, Emi. It'll be easier on your body." She nodded and worked the oxygen bag until the steady *beep-pause*, *beep-pause* returned.

"Whew. That was close. We've got to get that baby out and see what's tearing her up."

They moved together as one, suturing and clamping and suctioning until the bleeding stopped. They delivered the baby, who offered the world a blood-curdling scream. It was the best sound Emilia had ever heard. Especially when it was paired with the steady hum of the heart rate monitor. Mrs. Reynolds would be okay.

Emilia was the furthest thing from happy in that moment, but an infinitesimal bloom of hope blossomed in her heart. Aiodhán was wonderful. Giving and intelligent, kind and dedicated, handsome and humble.

Emilia took the baby to the incubator to be measured and checked out, but not before holding her up so her father could see her sweet, cherub face from the gallery. Tears streamed down his face, and Emilia felt her own tears dampening the inside of her mask. He mouthed *thank you*, and a crack as wide as the Pyrenees opened in her chest.

"That was a good save, Emi. You made your mark today and should be proud."

She was.

"Thank you, Aiodhán. I appreciate you being there when Dr. Thomas leaves me behind. Especially when you're so exhausted."

"I'm always going to support your choices, Em." He bit his bottom lip and shook his head. "Even when I'm tired or frustrated. I love you. Already, despite your family or this job we've committed to... None of it matters. *I love you*. It just might come with some stuff I've got to work through."

Curiosity flirted with her.

"What stuff?"

He sighed and motioned to the scrub room where they'd be alone. She followed him out.

"I *am* exhausted, Emi. I'd rather work twenty-hour days saving lives than eight straight hours of the meetings and press releases and stuff they're pulling me for. I just..." He sighed as he ran the water over his hands while his gaze focused on something in the distance she couldn't see. "If I'm being honest, I don't know that I'm meant for this life, one split between medicine and...and politics. Have you had a chance to talk to your parents yet?"

"I haven't." She told herself it was because they had time, but the reality was deeper, darker. What if her family was complicit in taking Aiodhán's career from him? That made her complicit since she'd never do anything to get in the way of what was best for the crown. Was taking on a husband she loved part of that? Until her father had married Rebecca, no Zephyr monarch had married for love.

She knew then who she had to talk to, and hopefully it would solve two questions at the same time.

"I haven't, honestly. But I will today. I'll get our lives—and our careers—back."

His smile didn't meet his eyes.

"What else is bothering you?"

He paused before shaking his head.

"I'm just proud of you."

"What do you mean?" she asked.

He grasped her hand. "Those two women almost lost their lives, and their babies'. And their spouses? You can't imagine what it's like going from not caring about anyone to loving two people so completely your heart feels like it's walking around outside your body. I'm terrified all the time and you." He kissed her. "You're doing what you came here to do. It's amazing, Emilia. You make me a stronger doctor, even if I'm scared senseless every time I see a pregnant woman in the OR."

It was as if Emilia carried her own fear like a secret, even from Aiodhán. Aiodhán met her gaze, then looked up through the glass at their patient, who would be wheeled to the ICU until she recovered enough from the traumatic birth to be released.

"You're a brilliant doctor who makes the tough calls and seems unfazed."

She laughed, but it lacked any humor. It was time to tell him the truth. She was scared, too.

"I'm the furthest thing from unfazed, Aiodhán. My mother died from pregnancy complications. I was already hospitalized for my own, and I'm terrified that I'm dragging you into a world that might not hit you with a bus but kill you slowly over time."

He smiled. "Well, that's a relief. I'm glad we're together on that, but I meant what I said. In spite of it all, you're doing your job, and the hospital—and I—are better for it. Thank you."

She tucked herself into Aiodhán's arm. He squeezed her tight.

Aiodhán smiled and gazed down at her. "You can tell me, you know. When you're struggling. I won't rush to fix it, but I would like to know when I can be a shoulder to lean on. Radical honesty, Em."

"Radical honesty."

But before she could make good on that promise, there was a conversation she needed to have.

CHAPTER SEVENTEEN

EMILIA DIDN'T BELIEVE in regrets the same way she didn't believe in fate. Which was probably how she found herself in this position in the first place. She'd looked Lady Fate straight in her eyes and laughed at the bar the night she'd met Aiodhán thinking she was oh, so clever. Now, here she was, pregnant and alone since Aiodhán had taken on extra shifts the past two nights to make up for the cases he was pulled from during the day.

Try as she did to wait up for him both evenings, her will had succumbed to the needs of the tiny life growing inside her, and she never made it more than an episode into whatever police procedural she was watching.

She'd tried to talk to Rebecca about the letter they'd given Aiodhán, but her stepmother had been vague. It was boilerplate, just an outline to get them all thinking…blah, blah, blah.

Emilia didn't buy it, but she also had no brain cells left to figure out her parents' plan. On one hand, it seemed as if they were supportive of Emilia and Aiodhán, even going so far as to bring him into the security briefings they attended via remote server. On the other hand, Emilia felt as if she were being held behind a smoke screen.

She'd worry about it after work. Right now, she needed to keep her pregnancy brain—and energy—focused on her job.

She yawned and tied the scrub cap tight against her head, tucking any errant hairs under the soft fabric patterned after her home country's flag. Bridget had bought it for her as an early bridesmaid gift, though Emilia was still a little foggy on the point of such a thing. Not the scrub cap, but the idea of having a celebration to mark the end of being, as Bridget put it, *single AF*.

As if she'd ever been single a day in her life. She'd been married to the crown, betrothed to an idea of a man who'd bring her country stability, even engaged at one point to someone they'd thought would fill that role.

But Emilia had never been single.

Which is why her relationship with Aiodhán was so peculiar. He'd not only upended her so-called dating status but her *life*.

Even though she loved him, could clearly see the new life laid out for them, if pressed she'd admit it wasn't what she'd hoped for when she came to America. Not even close.

"You ready for tonight?" Bridget asked, slamming open the locker room door. She glanced at Emilia and frowned. "You okay?"

Emilia sighed. "Sorry, I'm just a bit grumpy because I haven't seen my fiancé in days, it seems."

"Aww, you two are too cute. Well, I'm happy to distract you tonight so you don't get too lonely."

"Lonely? No, I'll be asleep. You made the party after dinner, which is my new bedtime." They shared a laugh. "Can't we just call in a movie and wear comfy robes while someone rubs my feet?"

Emilia pasted on a cheesy grin, complete with pleading hands that looked close to begging or praying or something she wasn't above if it would get her out of this night.

Bridget laughed and hooked her arm in Emilia's. "Nice try. You're getting married Saturday, in America, so you're taking part in this ridiculous American tradition. You need this. You just don't know it yet."

"Oh, I need something," Emilia muttered under her breath as they left the room, tablets in hand.

"What was that?"

"Nothing. Let's get this set of rounds over with so I might sneak in a nap before you drag me across the city. You'd better let me wear my trainers, at least."

A couple hours and two tough cases that brought Emilia to her knees physically and emotionally, and the sight of Bridget strolling down the corridor toward her didn't bring with it the joy it normally did.

"So are you ready to par-tay?"

Emilia was decidedly *not*, but she put on her bravest face and nodded. This was important to her best friend, so she'd go along with it.

When they got in the car, Bridget had a soft smile on her face.

"What is that look you're wearing?" Emilia asked.

"What, my smile?"

"You're up to something…"

Bridget shrugged. "What if I am?"

If she was, and she wasn't mentioning it to Emilia, then it must be bad.

"If you make me so tired I look awful in my wedding photos Saturday, so help me…"

"You'll look fabulous. I promise."

Yeah, well, your promise couldn't hold up the weight of a feather, she wanted to tell her friend, who kept the mischievous grin on her face the duration of the ride to Emilia's apartment.

When they pulled up to the front, Emilia got out, and Bridget locked the car door behind her. She rolled down the window, though.

"Aren't you coming up with me to choose an outfit?" Emilia asked.

"Have fun tonight, and don't say I never gave you anything. Oh, and I'll be expecting the real thing when you have that kid, okay?"

With that, Bridget winked and zoomed out of the parking lot, leaving Emilia alone and terribly confused.

She parsed the last few minutes on her way up in the elevator, but when the doors opened to the penthouse, it all vanished in the breath she gasped out.

"What...what is this?" she asked Aiodhán. He held a bouquet of lilies—her favorites, and the national flower of her country—in his hands, but she hardly saw them when he took up all the space, all the air in the room. Bare chested, barefooted, and clad only in baggy gray sweats, he was the picture of comfort. If comfort was supposed to make one warm and tingly inside, that was.

"It's for you. All of it." He gestured to the sepulchral space that had been done up like the inside of a spa. "Well, for all three of us, actually." There were fresh lilies and hydrangeas on every surface, as well as Zephyr tapas beneath them. Emilia inhaled deeply; the floral aroma mixed with the spices of her country, a place she'd only recently come to miss. It undid a locked box in Emilia's chest, and the tears built quickly.

"It's beautiful," she said. "But what about Bridget? She has this whole evening planned for me."

"No," Aiodhán said, putting the flowers on the dining table and wrapping Emilia up in a hug that both calmed her and sent her heart racing at the same time. That was the power of the man she was to marry. "This is it. Her only job was to get you here so you could have a night of relaxation—so *we* could have a night to relax together. Do you like it?"

She nodded, and only then did Emilia notice there were three stations with people beside their setups.

Two masseurs were on hand with massage tables next to a woman with a pop-up nail salon, and another spot was tucked in the corner for hair. The strangers all dipped their eyes to the floor so as to give the couple some privacy. At least they would stop her from jumping her fiancé like she wanted to at that moment. Emilia wasn't sure if it was the pregnancy hormones or the man himself that made her crave him as she did. Probably a combination of them both.

"It's amazing, Aiodhán. How did you pull it off?"

"Very carefully and almost not at all when a few of our plans got waylaid by Zephyranthes and Minnie Gen."

"Zephyranthes?" Confusion swirled along with lust in her stomach, making it flip.

"Yeah. I had some help from your parents, but of course it had to happen between royal duties, which pulled them away a couple times. I've got to say, if the people there are as demanding as the king and queen, maybe it's better we're here."

He winked, drawing out a smile from her.

"My parents helped with this? I never imagined…"

"I didn't think so, either, but they just want you happy, Emi. They were so glad to take part in this night."

"I… I don't know what to say," she said. "Rebecca was so vague when I talked to her about your letter—"

"That's my fault. I addressed it with her when I asked about this, about the lilies and tapas."

"And?"

He shrugged. The light in his eyes dimmed ever so slightly, but his smile was fixed in place.

"It's a starting point. I can practice, but with the added security to the hospital over there, it might not be worth the hassle. We'll see."

"Oh, Aiodhán. I'm so sorry."

He waved her off. "It'll be okay. I promised to take care of you and the bean, and that's what's most important. But enough about that. Tonight is about pampering *you*."

Her gaze fell on the massage table, and her hand went to her stomach. "Oh, I can't get a massage because of the preg—"

"She's a neonatal specialist. It's safe, I promise."

"Thank you for thinking about that. But what about the hair—won't that be ruined by Saturday?"

He cupped a hand along her cheek, tangling his fingers in her curls. God, how she'd missed his touch, his scent, his body…

He softly kissed her lips before handing her a cerulean silk robe the same color as her wedding palette.

"The hair person is for Saturday morning so you don't have to go anywhere. She just wants to try a couple styles tonight so she knows what you want on the day." Tears sprung behind her eyes. Between her pregnancy, her internship, and Aiodhán's work, she'd barely had time to consider the smaller facets of her wedding day. And he'd done it all for her, even despite his hectic schedule.

"Is this where you've been in the evenings?"

"Sort of. I've actually been working since my days have been spent getting this together along with the growing to-do list from your parents. It's why I needed you to trust me when you asked about my late hours: I couldn't pull this off at home, with you lying on my chest. I wish I could have said something, but I wanted to give you something special and hoped it would be a surprise."

"It is, and it's lovely."

"I'm glad you like it. We took care of everything, Em. Change into this when you're ready, then just relax and enjoy." She smiled, biting her bottom lip. "Oh, but Bridget did say this gives her full access to you after you give birth. She's gonna want to do this night the good old-fashioned Southern way, she told me."

Emilia laughed, a heavy weight lifted from her shoulders. "That's fine. She told me as much, but I didn't understand why at the time. It makes sense now. But, Aiodhán?"

"Yeah?"

"Why... I mean, when? No, I guess I meant *why* as well."

Aiodhán chuckled.

"Because you deserve more from all of us. After my last meeting with your folks, I talked to them about my needs for the hospital and trauma center while we're here so I can leave it in good hands, but also for you. They can't keep pulling me from their daughter, or something was going to give. I told them I didn't want it to be you. You deserve everything, not scraps."

"I just can't believe how much you did. For me."

He pulled her into his chest. "For us. For our daughter. I know work has been running me ragged, but you have to know how much I care about our little bean. It's worth it to keep you both safe."

A small tinge of worry bubbled up amid the joy. He kept repeating his mantra—keeping her safe—no matter how many times they talked about what was within their control and what wasn't. And it all came back to their bean.

Another worry bubbled up, this one always at the edge of her thoughts. What if this was just another version of fixing what had happened with the loss of his parents, another tally in his attempt to right the scales?

"Aiodhán," she whispered, "are you happy?"

His eyes narrowed, but he tried on a smile for her. It was a shadow of the one he'd worn when they met.

"I will be. I've got so much to be happy for."

A tremble of worry rumbled in her chest. There was a breaking point for this man, and mercifully, they hadn't discovered it yet. But they were close, and when it came, she was certain it would take her under, too.

There was only one way to prevent all of this, to save the man she loved from a life that was running him ragged and might take his career away from him...

From being miserable and pretending he wasn't.

She wished there wasn't a room full of people, that she could sit him down and tell him how she felt. After they left, perhaps?

I have to set him free.

He could support her and the baby, visit even. But going forward the way they were was untenable.

There has to be another way, her heart screamed.

She ignored it. Try as she might, she couldn't see any other possibility, not one that would protect Aiodhán. Emilia was a princess; her life was never going to be her own. But the man she loved deeper than she'd ever dreamed possible?

She could—and would—save him from the same fate. Even if it cost her any chance at happiness.

Even if the heart she'd silenced broke into a thousand pieces.

CHAPTER EIGHTEEN

AIODHÁN SLEPT WELL for the first night in who knew how long. Actually, he knew exactly how long it'd been since he'd hit the pillow and crashed without spinning out: five months and eighteen nights. Coincidentally, the same amount of time since he'd met Emilia.

And now, stretching and feeling muscles that, with time to rest, decided to remind him how overworked they were, he actually felt…good. Not as tired. Maybe a little energetic.

Well, at least energetic enough to cuddle with his fiancée. He slid against her compact frame, her naked back pressed against his bare chest. The warmth emanating from her stoked a flame that was pretty much always lit around her. Blood and lust pooled south of his waist, and he rocked into her, eliciting a moan from Emilia.

God, how he wanted this woman. Every hour of every day, his need for her grew. It didn't hurt that she was carrying a life inside her made from their shared desire.

Wrapping a hand around her waist and clasping her hips, he drew her tight against him so his erection slipped between her legs. He traced the soft swell of her belly up to full, swollen breasts. He cupped them, gently massaging the firm, suppleness in the hopes it would wake his sleeping bride-to-be so they could start their day off with what he'd been dreaming about all night.

It was nice to see Emilia relaxed all evening, even if she'd seemed a little preoccupied. But when she'd sighed, slipping out of the new cerulean robe he'd given her at the end of the night... All he'd wanted was to kiss every inch of her gorgeous, curvy frame. But he'd promised her sleep, and hell, he'd needed to catch up on the elusive stuff, too. Now, though, the hunger for her roared in his chest, waking him up better than any espresso could.

Emilia didn't stir, and as his hand settled on her chest, it felt more than warm. It was hot. He placed the inside of his wrist along her forehead, and it burned. She had a fever.

Dammit. How had he missed that? He jumped out of bed and raced to find a thermometer, throwing on his sweats from the night before on the way to the bathroom. It didn't take him long to find the medical supplies under the bathroom sink. When he got back to her bedside, Emilia's skin was damp and clammy. He pulled back the sheet, and she shivered, but her eyes didn't open. She was burning up, though. As he tried to roll the thermometer across her forehead, she groaned and shifted.

And Aiodhán froze, fear seizing his chest and each cell in his limbs. Blood. Not a lot, but enough that it meant something was wrong. It had stained a small circle of the sheets and her skin on her thighs, but it might as well have been a bucket of the stuff the way it filled Aiodhán with dread.

"Chance!" Aiodhán shouted. The man stormed in like he'd been waiting just outside the door.

"What is it?" One glance at Emilia and his face lost its color. "What happened?"

"She's bleeding, and her pulse is erratic. I need you to call her parents. Have them meet us at Minnie Gen."

"Shouldn't I call for an ambulance?"

"No time." Aiodhán already had Emilia in his arms, a nightgown covering her slight frame. "I can get her there quicker."

Chance blanched when he saw the spot on the bed where Emilia was. Aiodhán swallowed hard and grabbed his keys.

"Is she—" Chance asked.

"I don't know. It's not enough yet, but if we don't figure out what's going on, it'll be bad."

What if...?

No. He couldn't think that way. His only focus was Emilia's health. And the baby's, hopefully.

"I'll drive. You make sure she lives," Chance said. Aiodhán nodded, tossing him the keys as they all but ran out of the apartment.

The drive to the hospital was short—made quicker by Chance's expert maneuvering of the city streets—but it still felt interminable. Emilia was in and out of awareness, and her skin was hot, pale, and damp. Not good signs.

As Chance tore into the ER entrance, Aiodhán was out of the car with Emilia in his arms before the car could fully stop.

"Meet me inside," he yelled to Chance. He didn't turn around to make sure the man heard him, just raced inside the doors as fast as they'd open for him.

"We need help," he yelled. "Now!"

Nurses, residents on call, and Mallory came rushing to the entrance when they heard Aiodhán's booming voice.

"What happened?" Mallory asked, already putting a stethoscope on Emilia's chest as Aiodhán gingerly placed Emilia on a gurney. Memories of doing something similar just weeks ago sent a storm of grief crashing against Aiodhán's fortitude.

This. This was his greatest fear realized. Had he made it happen by being too greedy, too happy?

"She was unresponsive this morning. Running a hundred-and-two fever, thready pulse."

"Okay. Anything else I need to know before I do a workup?"

"I'll come with you and assist."

"You're too close, Aiodhán. You're her fiancé." His chin hit his chest with blunt force. He nodded his agreement. "How far along?"

"Twenty-three weeks." Far enough that he'd felt safe. She'd been doing so well.

She offered him a gentle pat on the shoulder, a paltry consolation to the fear mounting in his mind.

"How bad is the bleeding?"

"Light, but enough to bleed through her undergarments." Aiodhán's voice cracked, along with his composure.

"I need to take her now, but I'll take good care of your family."

Emilia just looked so...small. The woman herself was a beacon of strength in every way—taking care of patients, of him—all with a smile on her face despite her own exhaustion. Yet, as the shell of her human form lay there, lifelessly being rolled toward a trauma room, she appeared fragile for the first time.

"Please. She's...she's everything to me."

Mallory nodded and jogged after the gurney carrying the only things Aiodhán cared about. He looked around the waiting room, and his chest ached. What he should do is get to work so he could distract himself from the crippling dread. But how the actual hell was he supposed to give a patient his best self when the best of him was in a trauma ward being poked and prodded while she tried to live and keep their child alive at the same time?

No, work was off the table, but just as terrifying was waiting. Because it allowed the doubt to creep in and take root in his chest, making it hard to breathe. Faced with losing Emilia, their baby or, God forbid, both, he couldn't believe he ever cared about work or anything as menial. Because he'd give it all up if doing so would ensure her safety and health.

But that's not how it worked, so all he could do now was wait. Wait and hope that everything he loved wasn't ripped from him again. Because no amount of surgeries or saves would make up for what losing Emilia would cost him.

Aiodhán tapped his feet on the tile floor with impatience. He'd paced the entire lobby and every place the staff allowed him to be. He'd checked in with Mallory who told him Emilia was taken into surgery—all she was able to tell him because, injustice of all injustices, she still wasn't his wife.

It wasn't for a lack of trying. But now, twelve hours before their wedding, he was in a standstill hoping she *lived*, let alone could become his wife.

So he waited for news, or her parents to arrive, or the chance to see her. Chance had some issues contacting the king and queen since they were at the governor's mansion and all phones had been relinquished.

"This is asinine," he muttered.

"There are so many ways your language fails you, Dr. Adler, but in this case, I'm inclined to agree. Might there be a way we can find what we're looking for without the traditional means?"

"You mean sneak up to her room?"

"I wouldn't dream of suggesting such a thing. However, you should do what you think best, and I would happily support the future prince consort's efforts from here."

Aiodhán chuckled, the levity a welcome respite. The man had bugged him at first, but now it was nice having a sidekick in his efforts to keep the princess safe.

Fat lot of good it'd done any of them. Emilia was right, per usual. There wasn't much anyone could control when it came to keeping loved ones safe in a fast-paced world like they lived in.

But where he'd really been wrong? Believing that keeping himself separated from anything resembling love would prevent him from being hurt. Sure, he'd been unattached and content, but he hadn't been *happy* before Emilia. And he wouldn't trade knowing her, no matter the outcome.

"Okay. I'm gonna…go check on a surgical patient upstairs. If her parents get here, you'll call me?"

"Of course," Chance replied. He looked as stoic as ever, but Aiodhán knew the man by now and caught the glint of mischief in his eyes.

Aiodhán didn't waste a minute. He took the back stairs by the employee entrance to the fourth floor, the OB surgical suites. Ducking his head, he circumvented the staff until he found the surgery board behind the nurses' station.

His pulse raced as he found what he was looking for.

E. de Reyes. Premature labor. Room three.

Oh, God. Premature labor. A miscarriage most likely. He inhaled deeply, the cool air doing not a damn thing to keep the tears—hot and heavy—from burning the backs of his eyes. A few fell, but he couldn't let the pain itching beneath his skin out. His job was to be there for Emilia.

Closing his hands into tight fists, Aiodhán made his way to Emilia's recovery room. Mallory's voice drifted into the hallway, calm but hushed.

Aiodhán ducked behind the wall. She wouldn't appreciate his subterfuge to come up against her advice. But she didn't get it. Emilia was his world. Supporting her through this was too damn important to bring nuance into it. He might not be her husband—yet—but that didn't mean she wasn't his world.

"You're still on bed rest. Premature labor puts the mother through hell, Emilia. You need to heal."

Aiodhán clamped his eyes shut. Nothing about the baby.

"What about…what about having children later?"

"Let's not worry about that right now. Our focus is on your health and getting you through this. Okay? I'm going to get a couple labs ordered, but I'll be back soon."

"Thank you, Mallory. Um, can I ask you something?"

"Sure." Aiodhán leaned in to hear what Emilia asked.

"Can you not tell my parents or Aiodhán what's going on? I'd like to talk to them myself."

"Of course."

Aiodhán turned his head as Mallory passed by, issuing orders to one of her interns. She didn't see him as he slipped around the corner and into the room where Emilia lay, facing the window. Her face was turned from him, but he could see the shine of tears on her cheeks. All he wanted to do was run to her, to take her home and hold her while she healed on his watch.

That feeling was amplified when she turned to look at him.

"Aiodhán," she whispered. He moved to the edge of the bed, which was topped with at least a dozen blankets and pillows. It only served to make Emilia look smaller, more tender and breakable. But she was still there, and he sent up a silent prayer to whomever was in charge of such things in the universe that she was safe.

He couldn't process the potential loss of their child, wouldn't go there yet, not if he needed to be there for Emilia. They could cross that bridge later, when they'd both grieved and settled back into their jobs and new marriage.

"What are you doing here?" she asked him. He wiped a tear with the pad of his thumb.

"I couldn't wait to see you. No one was telling me anything, and I was so scared."

"I'm fine, Aiodhán."

"I'm so damn glad you're okay. I was so scared." He kissed her. "And the baby—"

Her hand fluttered to her abdomen.

"It's okay. We don't need to talk about the baby now. Or the wedding, or the move. We can just let you heal." He didn't care how hurt he was: he'd be strong for her if it was the last thing he did. "I'll make sure you get to stay here and practice medicine, and you don't have to go back if you don't want to. Hell, you don't have to get married if it'll keep you here. Just tell me what you want."

Tell me what will take the pain of losing our daughter and smooth it into something we can live with.

The look on her face—vacant with a faraway stare—combined with the sweet, simple gesture of reaching for the swell in her stomach cracked his chest open for her. She'd lost so much.

"Aiodhán," she said, looking at him again.

"Yeah, Em?"

"The baby is okay. For now. I got a cervical cerclage that should help."

He felt the relief as it spread to his limbs. A sob escaped his chest. He squeezed her hand, but she pulled back.

"Oh, thank God. I was so petrified—"

"You weren't ever going to get married, were you?"

Shock twisted his lips in confusion. "What do you mean?"

"Before you met me. You were happy at work, with your career and not dating or getting involved with anyone."

"That's true, sort of, but—"

"And the baby shifted everything. It shifted things that shouldn't be moved. You are who you are, and this baby didn't change that." That wasn't true. He *had* changed. And it wasn't the baby, it was Emilia. Sure, the baby had woken him up to just how much Emilia meant to him, but he loved her for who she was to him.

"Maybe at first, but..." He drew a breath he hoped would fortify him. "I love you. It showed me that."

"Enough to move to Zephyranthes and lead a life tied to the monarchy? Because that's still the plan, you know. For me to go back. I *want* to go back. It's my duty, but it's a part of who I am. I'm raising our daughter in Zephyranthes."

"Okay, then we'll talk about it sooner. I'll take the advisory position until we can work out the challenges with my medical practice. Whatever it takes."

Emilia shut her eyes, and the overpowering desire to kiss her pressed against her heart. But it wasn't the right time. Not when she was struggling with almost losing a pregnancy and what it all would mean.

"Aiodhán, you say you love me, but the woman you see here isn't the same woman who is duty bound to Zephyranthes. Here, I can laugh and be free and eat takeout with you. But there? I'm a princess, Aiodhán, and if you don't like the king and queen, you won't much like your wife."

"You don't know that." His hands shook now.

"I do. It's why Luis sold my secrets. It was easier to betray the crown than marry into it. So I'm letting you off the hook. I don't need you to go through with this wedding for me or the baby. I'll take care of my parents and the press. You go back to being the man I fell in love with, the man who is going to save so many people's lives."

Aiodhán stood up, his mouth open in protest.

Mallory came into the room, stopping the words that sat thick on his tongue, waiting for a way out.

"Okay, Emilia—" She took one look at Aiodhán and frowned. "What are you doing here?"

"Mallory, you know damn well that rule isn't for people like us. I need to talk to my fiancée." They needed a few more minutes, a respite where he could gain his bearings and they could talk this out. There had to be some middle ground he was missing.

"Fine. You can stay if the patient agrees."

"Are my parents here?" Emilia asked, ignoring Aiodhán's desperate, wordless plea. Mallory nodded. "Can you send them up? I'd like to tell them what's happening."

"You bet. I'll ring downstairs and have them sent up."

Emilia turned to Aiodhán, the tears falling freely on her cheeks now.

"That's it, Aiodhán. We tried, and you were wonderful. But I don't need you to cover for me anymore. The rest I have to do on my own."

Breathing was all of a sudden difficult. Letting go of her hand impossible.

"You can't think that just because we lived different lives before we met—"

"That's exactly what I think. And it doesn't mean I don't love you. Because I do and probably always will, Aiodhán." Her voice broke, spilling emotion into the sterile room.

"Just not enough to do this with me."

"So much I'd never drag you through this with me if there was a way to let you live the life you'd planned for yourself. This is it. You're free."

"And if I don't want to be free? If I want you?"

She settled her gaze on the window again. "You don't want to be the prince consort of Zephyranthes, and in marrying me, that would be your fate. Do you want that?"

He squeezed her hand. "There has to be another way. When we found out we were pregnant—"

"The baby was a delay. This was always going to be the outcome. I go home and rule my country with my parents by my side. Our baby is royalty, whether we like it or not. She can come stay with you from time to time, but her place is in Zephyranthes, too. You stay here and save lives."

"You can't say goodbye just because we've had a hard time—"

"Please don't make this harder than it already is for me, Aiodhán," she said. "We don't work outside of the one thing that flung us together in the first place. Even then, we were struggling to blend our lives so much that it was killing both of us. It almost killed our child."

"So, what do you want from me?"

She glanced back at him, her tear-stained cheeks an ache that wouldn't abate.

"I want you to go, to make yourself happy and fulfilled again, and to let me do the same from home."

"Home? You mean Zephyranthes? You won't even stay so I can meet our child?"

"I can't stay in this place and be reminded of everything I want that keeps being pulled just out of reach. The universe is telling me to let you go, and everything that comes with that. Besides, I can't practice surgery like this. I'm on partial bed rest. What use would I be?"

Aiodhán opened his mouth to argue, when Emilia's parents ran in. Rebecca looked scared, and Emilia's father as if he might cry. Aiodhán understood.

"Good-bye, Aiodhán," she said, turning her focus to her parents.

He walked out of the room, but there wasn't a cell in his body that could tell Emilia goodbye. Not if he expected to walk out of this place in one piece. She'd said she was giving him back the life he'd planned, but he didn't want it. Maybe he never had: it'd been a coward's way out, and Emilia had showed him how to be brave and long for more.

It was then he realized the hardest part of loving someone. It was hard to cope with the loss of them unexpectedly, and she'd been right that he couldn't control that, nor should he try.

But harder still—impossible, even—was the idea that he could lose the two things he loved most, and both of them would still be out in the world, living without him.

She might have to let him go, but he'd never be able to release Emilia de Reyes from the hold she had on his heart.

Never.

CHAPTER NINETEEN

EMILIA DE REYES might be gone, but damn if Aiodhán didn't see her ghost everywhere. The alluring combination of vanilla and coffee seemed ingrained in his clothes, even though her side of the closet comprised just a few empty hangers.

Call him crazy, but he swore he heard her laughter ringing down the halls when he was in the main campus of the hospital. And then there was the way everyone looked at him like *he* was the ghost. Like he was fragile and might disappear at any moment. That was, when they didn't actively avoid him.

The only people in his corner were Mallory and Brian.

"Have you heard from her?" Brian asked over a beer the second week after Emilia had packed up and went back to Zephyranthes.

Aiodhán took a long pull from the bottle of amber. It tasted sour, but then, so did everything these days.

"Not a thing. And I won't. She said goodbye, man, and for the life of me, I'm not sure what I should do with that."

Brian gave him a sideways glance. "What's there to do but the usual? Throw yourself into the clinic, into your patients, and wait for the sting to wear off. I'm happy to tell dad jokes if you're up to hearing them."

Aiodhán chuckled, shaking his head. "Nah, but thanks. And don't think I haven't tried the usual. But can I tell you something? Something you have to keep to yourself?"

"Of course. But in the spirit of full disclosure, I can't keep anything from Mal. Believe me, I've tried, but it's like the minute we got married, I couldn't wait to tell her everything and anything."

A small twinge of jealousy tweaked Aiodhán's heart, leaving behind a dull ache. He understood completely. Because he felt the same way about Emilia. She'd been his person, the one he wanted to share every mundane case from work or silly idea for decorating the trauma waiting room with, and everything in between.

"I figured. That's fine."

"So...spill."

Aiodhán glanced across the spacious living room of Emilia's penthouse. She'd left with almost ten months remaining on the lease and invited Aiodhán to stay and use the space since his closet-sized apartment in the lower downtown wasn't exactly comfortable. He hadn't planned on taking her up on it, but how could he leave? Especially when an overwhelming part of him hoped he'd come home from work one day and find her there in the living room, her growing belly propping up a book while she sipped the decaf coffee she was never without.

"I don't want to work."

Brian's mouth dropped open. Aiodhán didn't blame the guy for his surprise. The realization had hit *him* like a ton of bricks falling from a ten-story building.

"I'm sorry, who are you, and what have you done with my best friend? You don't want to work? The one thing that's driven you since we met in med school?"

"I know. It's not like I don't love medicine and helping patients anymore. But the clinic and the extra hours and the chasing down some magical elixir that'll erase decades of guilt... None of it worked. The only thing that's actually made me happy was Emilia."

"Even knowing you'd be marrying into some crazy royal drama?"

"Even then. Especially then. Watching her navigate that

and still pursue her dreams was inspiring as hell. It made me think…"

He shook his head, drank down a third of his beer.

"What?"

"It made me think I've been prioritizing all the wrong things my whole life. And I want a do-over."

Mallory sipped her drink, a pink cocktail in a rocks glass, a half smile tugging at the corner of her mouth.

"I know. I'm just glad you finally figured it out."

"What?" Brian asked. His eyes were as wide as his open mouth. "Am I the only one here surprised by this turn of events?"

"Yes," Mallory and Aiodhán replied in unison.

"You love her, and love changes your mind and heart when it comes to deciding what's important."

"Yeah, but what good does all that do?" Aiodhán asked. He got up and went to the window overlooking his city. It didn't feel like home anymore, not since the best part about it skipped town and crossed the Atlantic. "She's gone and told me to shove off. The thing is, I get it now. How hard I tried to keep it all together when all I really wanted was to be with her. How it looked when I only let her know how much she meant to me when I found out about the pregnancy. The medicine would always come back around when I needed it, but her? I lost that chance."

He couldn't talk about their daughter: it was too damned hard to think about. Being a father was never on the table until it was dropped there in front of him, and now he couldn't imagine his child growing up without getting to be a part of every single moment. But losing the love of his life to his own stupidity took that chance with it as well.

"Would you give it up to be with her?"

Aiodhán barked out a humorless laugh. "I already have, even if it doesn't do any good."

"What do you mean?" Mallory asked.

"I handed over the clinic to Bob Thomas. He's been vying to be involved since it's been up and running, and to be honest he's a better fit over there where he won't have any interns to pretend to teach. I just want a life of helping people for the sake of helping people, and to hell with the tally. Emilia was right—that was never within my control. My parents lost their lives, but I'm not giving mine up out of guilt or some misplaced sense of playing God."

The silence behind him wasn't as disconcerting as the whispers that followed. He spun around, and the couple broke apart like they'd been caught at something nefarious. All Aiodhán caught was a hissed "No. It's patient confidentiality" from Brian.

"What's supposed to be kept confidential?" Aiodhán asked. Brian stared at Mallory, whose gaze was pinned to Aiodhán's. Brian shook his head, finally relenting and falling back against the couch. "If you two know something and you aren't telling me…so help me I'll never forgive either of you."

"You want this to work, right?" Mallory asked.

"I do. More than anything else. I mean, I gave up the one thing I've been working on my whole career, if that's any indication."

"Okay, then you need to call her parents. Talk to them and see how you can make it work. Because I know you, Aiodhán, and you can love Emilia all day long, but if you don't have something that's yours, you'll go crazy. They can help with that."

"How are you so sure they'll want to help me with anything? I mean, I let their pregnant daughter leave here without a fight."

She shrugged, sipping her pink drink like she was the royal. "I got to know them pretty well while they were here taking care of Emilia. They only want her to be happy, Ad. And you made her happy."

"Would…" He struggled to find a way to articulate the swirl of thoughts buzzing in his head. "Would Emilia hate me for that?"

"My guess is no," Mallory said, her smile as wide as it had been on her wedding day. It was a flotation device while he was drowning. "She misses you."

"Mallory," Brian exhaled at the same time Aiodhán said, "*What?*"

"It's not patient confidentiality when this had nothing to do with her surgery," Mallory said, kissing her husband until the shock made way for a contented smile.

"How the hell do you know how she feels? Are you still talking to her?"

"Okay, since my lovely better half can't keep anything to herself, she's right. Emilia's been checking in on you, wants to know how you're doing and all that."

Aiodhán got up and paced in front of the couch.

"But she left me."

"No. She thought you were only marrying her because of the baby, and she gave you an out. You're the one who took it."

"Dammit. Well, I'm untaking it."

"I mean what I said, Ad. You need to make sure you have a plan before you jet across the ocean with nothing but love in your suitcase. Upending both your lives will take more than that."

"Oh, I know. And for the first time in my life, I'm more than a little sure what *I* want and that the work will be worth it."

Mallory's smile turned soft like it did when she looked at Brian.

"Then, go get her," she said. Brian's arm wrapped around his wife's waist, and he pulled her into a deep kiss as Aiodhán strode to the closet, whipped out a suitcase, and started throwing stuff in it. For the first time, he didn't resent the extra minutes in the elevator or waiting on labs that he had spent practicing his Zephyr. He'd need it, now.

"If you two lovebirds are done making out, I could use your help getting a ride to the airport so I can make a call that's long overdue."

CHAPTER TWENTY

EMILIA PACED THE marble floor of her suite, unable to concentrate on the beauty of the cerulean sea beneath her. It met the pale yellow sand of the shoreline with gentle caresses, the sound of the water's crashing and receding dance usually calming. But not today.

No, today, her focus was pulled to the meeting her parents had set up for her. She'd been expecting it since she'd arrived back in Zephyranthes, the thick, salty sea air greeting her like an old friend. Part of her was delighted to be back in her home country—especially since she'd be keeping up with her medical studies in the Hospitál Real de Cyana—the Royal Cyana Hospital.

She'd been surprised when her stepmother suggested it and even more shocked when Rebecca made the king see how necessary it was for Emilia to continue her studies—both for her country and her well-being.

It'd brought her a measure of pride to know her father was still growing as a leader and a man she could look up to.

But she'd left behind her heart in Aiodhán, which she wouldn't need here, anyway, it seemed. It was time to take a suitor and fill the role she'd been born into. At least that's why she assumed she was being called to the Great Hall by her parents. Why else would they ask her to dress befitting her role and, Rebecca had added, wear those earrings she'd received from her stepmother as an engagement present in Minneapolis?

Her stomach rolled with disgust as she got ready. It didn't

matter who they'd picked because it wasn't Aiodhán Adler, the love of her life and father of the precious child she carried. But if she made waves about this, would they strip her of her internship?

Did it matter? Yes. To the people—the women and children—she'd save, yes, it mattered.

Even if...

The throbbing ache in her chest hadn't abated since her plane had landed in Zephyranthes. If anything, it grew each day, each moment she went without Aiodhán's crooked smile shining down on her, without his arms pulling her close, without his lips grazing hers and making her feel like it would all be okay.

She'd marry, she'd practice medicine and rule her country when it was time for her to take over, but there wouldn't be a breath she took that wasn't laced with regret and grief at what that life would cost her and her daughter.

A knock on the heavy oak door of her suite roused her from her bout of self-pity.

"Come in," she commanded. The door opened to her father and stepmother, her father dressed in military blues and Rebecca a cream gown that showed off her grace, elegance, and beauty. Would Emilia, clad in a jade gown Rebecca chose for her, ever feel that natural in this space?

Maybe she would have with Aiodhán by her side, but alone she felt adrift and every bit a royal impostor. Being a doctor and Aiodhán's fiancée were the only times she'd truly felt at home in her own skin. She could have ruled the world with him by her side.

"Are you ready?" they asked. She nodded, even though it took every ounce of her strength to perform that simple gesture. Her footsteps grew heavier with each one she took.

They led the way out of the living chambers and to the Great Hall. She'd always loved the regal space as a child, with its grand painted ceilings and the molding from centuries before her time. But now it felt like a well-adorned prison cell, a frozen space where her life would cease to carry meaning.

Throwing her shoulders back and her chin up, she strode into the room as if this wasn't the last day of the rest of her life she'd be free to love another man, even from afar.

She could see the tuft of brown hair in the chair reserved for guests at the formal table in the center of the hall, and her chest cracked open, spilling out thoughts of the man she loved, a man a million miles from where she was. The espresso-colored waves only reminded her of Aiodhán.

"Your Royal Highness, Princess Emilia de Reyes of Zephyranthes, may we present to you your betrothed."

So it was true. She was to marry. Even suspecting it didn't cushion the blow. She would never love him like she loved Aiodhán...

The man stood up and turned to face her.

The eyes gazing back at her were the same eyes that had captured her interest seven months ago and her heart not long after that. They broke through whatever fears she'd built into a fortifying wall, and they came crashing down around her.

"Aiodhán," she whispered, "you're here."

"There weren't many paparazzi to greet me, either," he said jokingly. "I could get used to that."

His gaze fell to her abdomen, which had grown considerably now that she was in her third trimester. He took a tentative step toward her, and her hands trembled with anticipation.

"I could get used to this, too. She's grown."

She nodded her head, which was still fuzzy with disbelief. Aiodhán was in her home, sitting at her dining table, looking every bit like he belonged there. Her heart almost couldn't handle the stress of her dreams coming true. She could show him her birthplace, her birthright... She could kiss him in plain daylight for the world to see. He could hold their daughter when she was born and every day after.

She hoped.

Wait—her parents had said *betrothed*, hadn't they?

Tears pricked the back of her eyes that she wouldn't dare blame on the mess of hormones coursing through her veins. They were tears of happiness, nothing more.

"Well, my dear, we'll leave you two to discuss your future and how you'd like to proceed. But Emilia?"

"Yes, Father?" Her voice sounded far away, muffled under a million questions.

"We've given Dr. Adler our blessing and want you to have the same."

She nodded, her gaze still on Aiodhán—*there! In her home!*—until Rebecca's hand fell on her shoulder.

"You should know I'll be opening an art gallery as well. It will have a space dedicated to teach art classes to children whose circumstances wouldn't allow it before. I wanted you to know you're the reason I'll finally chase my own dreams. Thank you, Emilia."

Emilia could only smile and hug her stepmother before her parents left, leaving her alone with Aiodhán. So much information was shared with her in the past few moments she wasn't sure where to start.

"Aiodhán," she said, walking toward him. He'd crossed the Atlantic for her; it was the least she could do to meet him where he stood. "You're here."

"You said that already."

They shared a laugh before he grew serious.

"I am. And as long as you'll have me, I'm here to stay."

Her smile twisted with concern.

"But your job—"

"I talked the board into giving control of the clinic to Dr. Thomas before I talked to Mal and Brian." He took her hands in his and brought them to his lips. Her heart fluttered like a thousand butterflies were trapped inside it. "I gave over my service to Mal, and she'll take on the role of chief now that I'm gone." He kissed her knuckles, sending a flash of heat straight to Emilia's stomach.

"Oh," was all Emilia was capable of saying. She swallowed. "Why did you do that? Your life and practice are in Minneapolis. I know meeting me steered you off course."

The subtle shake of his head made Emilia's mouth go dry.

"Meeting you didn't steer me off course, Emilia. It changed my course. *You're* my life—everything that matters in it, anyway. And my practice is now as a general surgeon in the... Real Hospital in Cyana?"

She laughed. "Hospitál Real de Cyana?" she asked.

"Yeah. That."

"But...why?"

Aiodhán released her hands only to draw her into an embrace that gave her strength. *Dío*, how she'd missed that. Missed this man who, she had to admit, pulled off his gray seersucker suit very nicely.

"Because no number of people I save will matter if I don't save myself. When I took a look—a real, honest, hard look—at myself, I realized only one thing mattered. Well, two actually."

"What were they?" she asked. Aiodhán dipped down, his lips brushing hers.

"You. And this little bean." He laid his hand on her belly, and as if on cue, the baby kicked. "Was that her?"

"It was. It seems she likes hearing such sweet words from her father."

"I like hearing you call me that. But she's not the reason I proposed to you. When you woke up on the table after hitting your head that day in the hospital, I knew I wanted to be with you and keep you safe—" She opened her mouth to protest, but he kissed her silent. "Just a sec. I have to get this out. I know now I can't control that, so I want to make you a new proposal."

"First, how did you get the job at *el hospital*? Not the adviser?"

He laughed. "My headstrong princess. Your parents offered

it to me. Apparently, when your girlfriend is the princess, the king pulls special favors. They were looking for a trauma surgeon, and he said he knew a guy. They rushed the reciprocity of my medical license."

Emilia was mildly annoyed they hadn't done that earlier but understood their reticence. Her parents had stuck their necks out to support Emilia and Aiodhán and had wanted to know they were committed to one another.

"So you're really here? And you're okay with…" she spread her arms to indicate the castle they stood at the center of "…all this?"

"If it comes with you at the end of the day, I'm excited to take it on. Plus, it seems like the trauma center idea sounded good to the hospital board, so I'll be building one up here. Would you do me the honor of creating it with me?"

"I would love that, Aiodhán."

He released her, though, and the inches separating them brought a layer of cold that hadn't been in the room before. Until he dipped to one knee, and her skin flushed again.

"Now for the proposal. I want to grow old as long as we have together. I want to love you every day like I'll lose you tomorrow and celebrate every day we're given. The pregnancy might have brought you to me, but we're choosing this life together from here forward. Or at least, I am."

She'd thought the same thing when she'd been on her way to her bachelorette party with Bridget. That seemed like a thousand years ago. She nodded, unable to speak.

"Okay, then, now on to the important question." Aiodhán drew a small oak box from his pocket, and when he opened it to reveal a princess-cut diamond the size of her knuckle, she gasped. Not at the ring, which was stunning, yes, but at the love pooling along the edges of the eyes of the man offering it to her.

"Yes!" she said.

"Well, that's the answer I was hoping for. But I haven't even asked the question yet."

They both laughed, and she wiped a stray tear from her cheek.

"Emilia de Reyes, Dr. de Reyes... Will you do me the honor of being my partner in medicine and in life? I want to raise kids and travel and practice medicine and even drink that stuff you call coffee every day with you, for the rest of our lives. So, what do you say? You in?"

She smiled, and the kick from their daughter giving her own version of an answer filled Emilia's heart more than it was already.

"Yes, I am. Every day for the rest of time."

Aiodhán swooped her up in an embrace and kissed her thoroughly, the taste of vanilla and promise on his lips. Her parents strode in, shouting congratulations as Emilia let the truth of it all settle on her heart.

She wasn't going to get everything she'd ever wanted—she already had it all.

EPILOGUE

A year later

EMILIA ROCKED NORA, named after her mother, humming a Zephyr lullaby.

"There's the two most beautiful women on earth. I've been looking all over the castle for you."

Emilia smiled and leaned in for a kiss. The passion that blazed when her lips met Aiodhán's still surprised her. She didn't see a day that she'd ever tire of wanting the man.

"I wanted to show her the sunset over her country now that she's finally old enough to be awake for it."

"You mean you walked her all over the castle and she still didn't fall asleep?"

Emilia laughed. Aiodhán held out his arms to take their daughter, and she begrudgingly handed sweet Nora over.

"It took four hours of walking and singing. I've run out of melodies to hum. I daresay I'm excited to take my exams tomorrow, so I'll give my voice a break." Emilia was getting certified as a neonatal surgeon tomorrow, if everything went well. Then, she'd be a colleague to the hottest doctor she'd ever met.

"I think our little princess must be as lively as her mother."

"*Sí*," Emilia agreed, starting the long walk back from the grotto overlooking the Mediterranean. "I do love this view, though," she said, gazing out over her country. Aiodhán smiled.

His gaze was fixed on her. "So do I."

The fire in her stomach rolled and burned, flooding her with need.

"Let's drop her off with Sofie," Emilia told him. "I'd like some time alone with you."

His brow raised, letting her know he appreciated the thought.

"I promise I won't fall asleep, no matter how many melodies you hum me, my love. As long as you keep those lips on mine."

She winked at him, marveling at how in love with her life she was. She'd enjoy all of it as it came to her. Right now, that meant giving her attention to her husband, the love of her life and chief of surgery at their hospital.

She had plans for him that didn't involve sleep.

Tomorrow she'd delight in making the rest of her dreams come true. As fairy tales went, hers really was the sweetest.

* * * * *

*If you enjoyed this story,
check out these other great reads
from Kristine Lynn*

A Kiss with the Irish Surgeon
Their Six-Month Marriage Ruse
Accidentally Dating His Boss
Brought Together by His Baby

All available now!

CITY DOC FOR THE SINGLE MUM

KATE MacGUIRE

MILLS & BOON

For Nate and Megan:
every day you inspire me to tell—and live—
the stories that matter.

CHAPTER ONE

"Winter Storm Isabella's cross-country trek is underway, but the worst of its impacts are still to come as it spreads heavy snow and blizzard conditions through the Rockies, Plains and upper Midwest. Folks, the National Weather Service is calling this storm historic *for our area, so please avoid all unnecessary travel and be prepared to hunker down for a few days."*

Lily switched off the radio as she glided to a stop alongside the Shop-n-Go, the small, locally owned grocery store on Twin Creeks's Main Street. Stocked with everything from milk and butter to deer corn and cast-iron cookware, the Shop-n-Go was pretty much the hub of activity in the final hours before any big storm. So it was no surprise to Lily that all the parking spots in front of the store were taken.

But luckily for her, a brown sedan was backing out of its space. She flicked her turn signal on to let the cars behind her know she was waiting for that spot. The sedan driver gave her a little wave before motoring off, the car's exhaust pipe emitting white smoke on this bitterly cold day.

Lily smiled and waved back, not sure if she knew the driver. She had met her fair share of neighbors and friends since she had moved to the former mining community of Twin Creeks five years earlier with her newborn daughter, Alexa. But it didn't matter. Even if they were strangers, the driver would have waved. That was just how it was in Twin Creeks, especially during the off-season when the tourists were gone and the town returned to a slower, more civilized, pace.

Lily eased her foot off the brake. Her truck made a creaky, wheezy sound as it slowly coasted forward. She loved this old truck, as much as she had loved the cherry-red convertible sportster that had been her ride when she lived in Chicago. But that little cutie was no match for the unpaved road riddled with divots that wound through thick forests to her tiny cabin. The old, sturdy flatbed truck that once hauled produce for a hydroponic farm had no trouble grinding its way up the hills to the cabin Lily rented from Jennifer Wilkins, a widow who lived in the main house. One of these days she'd get around to removing The Lettuce Lab's company decals from the truck's doors.

Lily was about to pull in to her spot when a streak of black whipped past her and claimed her parking space. Music—loud and thumping—pulsed from the car's interior. The streak turned out to be a midnight-black expensive luxury car, its sleek, aerodynamic lines and shiny, rust-free paint hinting at faraway places. Her hunch was confirmed by the car's blue-and-white license plate that said the car was registered in the coastal state of California.

The music stopped. The car door opened, and a man unfolded himself from the driver's seat. He was tall and

CHAPTER ONE

"WINTER STORM ISABELLA'S cross-country trek is underway, but the worst of its impacts are still to come as it spreads heavy snow and blizzard conditions through the Rockies, Plains and upper Midwest. Folks, the National Weather Service is calling this storm historic *for our area, so please avoid all unnecessary travel and be prepared to hunker down for a few days."*

Lily switched off the radio as she glided to a stop alongside the Shop-n-Go, the small, locally owned grocery store on Twin Creeks's Main Street. Stocked with everything from milk and butter to deer corn and cast-iron cookware, the Shop-n-Go was pretty much the hub of activity in the final hours before any big storm. So it was no surprise to Lily that all the parking spots in front of the store were taken.

But luckily for her, a brown sedan was backing out of its space. She flicked her turn signal on to let the cars behind her know she was waiting for that spot. The sedan driver gave her a little wave before motoring off, the car's exhaust pipe emitting white smoke on this bitterly cold day.

Lily smiled and waved back, not sure if she knew the driver. She had met her fair share of neighbors and friends since she had moved to the former mining community of Twin Creeks five years earlier with her newborn daughter, Alexa. But it didn't matter. Even if they were strangers, the driver would have waved. That was just how it was in Twin Creeks, especially during the off-season when the tourists were gone and the town returned to a slower, more civilized, pace.

Lily eased her foot off the brake. Her truck made a creaky, wheezy sound as it slowly coasted forward. She loved this old truck, as much as she had loved the cherry-red convertible sportster that had been her ride when she lived in Chicago. But that little cutie was no match for the unpaved road riddled with divots that wound through thick forests to her tiny cabin. The old, sturdy flatbed truck that once hauled produce for a hydroponic farm had no trouble grinding its way up the hills to the cabin Lily rented from Jennifer Wilkins, a widow who lived in the main house. One of these days she'd get around to removing The Lettuce Lab's company decals from the truck's doors.

Lily was about to pull in to her spot when a streak of black whipped past her and claimed her parking space. Music—loud and thumping—pulsed from the car's interior. The streak turned out to be a midnight-black expensive luxury car, its sleek, aerodynamic lines and shiny, rust-free paint hinting at faraway places. Her hunch was confirmed by the car's blue-and-white license plate that said the car was registered in the coastal state of California.

The music stopped. The car door opened, and a man unfolded himself from the driver's seat. He was tall and dressed in khakis, a light blue dress shirt and a rust-toned hooded sheepskin jacket, which was paired with a casually tousled haircut that would have cost two hundred dollars or more in Chicago. Lily couldn't help but stare at a man who looked like he had just stepped out of the catalog for a high-end outdoor retailer. Even without the California license plate, his whole vibe screamed *I'm not from around here!*

There was no apologetic wave to acknowledge he had just stolen her parking spot. Instead, the man opened his back door. A lean black-and-white dog jumped out, then sat attentively at his side. The man turned on his heel, pointing his key fob over his shoulder to activate the car's alarm system with a sharp *beep-beep*. He strode into the Shop-n-Go on long legs, his hands tucked deep into his jacket with the dog trotting obediently at his side.

"What the...?" Lily began, then forced her slack jaw to shut. She, like most locals, was used to summer visitors traipsing all over their town with little regard for basic manners as they explored the endless miles of hiking trails and top-notch breweries. But the winter months were for the locals, along with a few *respectful* tourists who craved Twin Creeks's quieter winter ski season.

Her gaze fell to the car's bumper where a decal declared the car's owner liked to *Work Hard. Play Harder!* So there it was. Just another winter visitor who was more focused on making the most of his ski weekend than practicing a little common decency.

But boy, had he picked the wrong weekend for a ski trip. Lily was no stranger to the mountains of snow that Montana winters could deliver. But even she was a little nervous about this *epic storm*. In a state accustomed to measuring snow in feet rather than inches, calling a winter storm *historic* was not a good omen.

Lily found a parking spot behind the Shop-n-Go. She slammed the truck's heavy door shut and headed inside, a cloth bag slung over her shoulder. Glass jars clinked against each other with every step. By the time she arrived, she had forgotten all about the rude tourist and was back to humming along with a tune that had been playing in her head all morning. She couldn't remember the lyrics, but it didn't matter. The tune itself was upbeat and positive, like something good was about to happen.

Before entering the store, Lily looked to the sky, where gray clouds were clumping into thicker, darker ones by the hour. Oh, yes, good things were definitely about to happen.

Because Winter Storm Isabella meant at least two days alone with her little girl. With any luck, the power would go out sooner rather than later, giving Lily a legitimate excuse to ignore her work for a few days. Being the clinical editor for a nursing journal sure lacked the thrill of her former job as a trauma flight nurse practitioner, but it paid the bills and kept her and Alexa safe, so she couldn't complain too much.

But first, a little unofficial business. Edith was running the cash register as always. Lily paused her whistling long enough to call out a greeting. As soon as she saw Lily's cloth bag, Edith rolled her eyes.

"Sweet Mary, not more pickles," she groaned. "I still haven't sold the last dozen you gave me!"

"This is the last batch!" Lily said with a laugh. Which

wasn't entirely true. All the energy she used to funnel into her work as a flight nurse was now directed to her new hobby farm. The result had been quite the bumper crop of cucumbers over the summer. There were at least a dozen more jars lined up in Lily's pantry that needed a home. But Edith didn't need to know that just yet.

Edith shoved the bag under the counter and gave Lily a look that let her know that she better not see any more pickles for a good long while. Lily scooted to the back of the store before Edith could scold her again.

The refrigerated cases were predictably empty. Lily didn't have much time to shop. She didn't want Alexa to be the last one to be picked up from her home-based preschool. That would do nothing to get their little winter retreat off to a good start.

Lily quickly scanned the shelves, looking for games or crafts that Alexa might like. A picture frame tucked behind the painting kits and modeling clay caught her eye. She grabbed the frame and studied its photo of a fake family. A dad, a mom and a little girl eating ice cream at some kind of carnival. Geez, they looked stupid happy. Did Alexa ever feel as happy as that little girl looked? Lily wasn't sure.

Alexa wasn't a tiny toddler anymore, content with playground adventures and library story times. She was becoming more adventurous and bold—the same traits that had once motivated Lily to become a trauma nurse in the army and then a flight nurse practitioner for an air ambulance company in Chicago.

But Alexa had never known that version of Lily. Because those traits died the same day her husband did.

Now all she cared about was keeping Alexa safe, no matter what. That meant saying no to Alexa's growing wish list of Grand Life Adventures.

Could I please ski something harder than the bunny slope?

Too much risk of head trauma, even with a helmet.

When can I go to a sleepover party?

The thought of Alexa being away overnight made Lily hyperventilate.

And Alexa's final, brazen request: *I want to go to kindergarten next year.*

Kindergarten. Whoever thought Lily would fear kindergarten? But Connor's death had changed everything. That was the day she'd learned gunmen could show up anywhere—even a hospital's emergency room—and steal the person you loved most for absolutely no good reason.

And if that utterly random act of violence left her a widow, what could happen to Alexa?

I don't know, Alexa. We'll see.

That was the best she could manage when Alexa would bring the topic up again and again. But the unresolved conflict had left its mark on their relationship.

So Lily couldn't wait for Isabella to arrive. It meant two days alone with her precocious daughter, surrounded by books and games and hot chocolate and cozy quilts. With any luck, she and Alexa would be able to regain the closeness they'd once shared.

Lily sighed and put the happy family back on the store shelf. She knew nothing in that photo was real, but she couldn't deny how much she wanted her and Alexa to feel *that* happy, just for one single day.

That was when she felt something cold and wet tickle the back of her neck.

Lily shrieked in shock and surprise and instinctively jumped away from the unfamiliar sensation. She landed awkwardly on her butt in a most undignified fashion.

Her abuser gave her a slow, thoughtful blink, then sat on its haunches and considered her with a cocked head and liquid brown eyes.

"What," Lily sputtered, "the hell?"

The dog stretched forward to press its muzzle into her hand. Its touch was gentle and seemed intentional. Not dangerous, at least not so far.

She reached down to stroke its silky head, finding a blue collar with black stripes and sparkly rhinestone diamonds.

"Daisy," she read. "Is that you?" The dog, some kind of mix of Border collie and who knew what else, wagged her tail slowly, enjoying Lily's gentle ear rub.

A man's voice rang out. "Daisy! You little minx. Where are you?"

Daisy cocked her head in the direction of the man's voice. Then she turned back to Lily with an open-mouthed pant. If Lily didn't know better, she'd swear the dog was laughing.

"We better get you reunited with your owner," Lily said. Then she added, under her breath, "And hey, do me a favor, would you? Tell him not to steal parking spots. It's rude."

"Who stole your parking spot?"

Lily winced at realizing she had been overheard. She stood and turned to find Mr. Work Hard Play Harder appraising her with captivating blue eyes.

By all appearances, the traveler was living up to his vehicular motto. His clothes were high-end but seemed casually tousled in a way that was probably anything but casual. He wore his dark brown wavy hair swept away from his face, revealing smooth skin, piercing blue eyes and a light stubble beard that had been precisely trimmed to perfection.

Lily's first thought was that he must be a tech bro. One of those guys who had created a social media app for teenagers and made a fortune larger than the GDP of most third-world countries. But he wasn't sporting the requisite tech bro hoodie or backpack, so maybe not. Stockbroker? Could be. He lacked that California-sunshine-and-avocado-toast vibe, so it was possible he spent his day in front of multiple monitors, tracking stocks and commodities. Lawyer or accounting executive worked, too.

Whatever he did for a living, he must be doing it well enough to afford the good life. But that didn't give him the right to be rude.

"Well, to be honest, you did."

His eyebrows, thick and precisely trimmed, arched as he quickly scanned her from head to toe. Her mouth went dry as she remembered the heavy-duty, super-functional overalls she was wearing. And the even more functional—and ugly—rubber boots she had donned before dawn to deal with the snow-and-mud slushy mix that was the current state of her farm.

She just hoped she didn't have any chicken feathers stuck to her hair. Or her butt.

He didn't seem particularly offended at her accusation. If anything, he appeared amused. He tucked his shopping basket over one arm and leaned against the shelving where jars of pickles and olives were lined up in neat rows.

His smile was disarming, as was his husky voice. "Sure it was me?" Mischief sparkled in his eyes like they were at a bar— instead of a small-town grocery store—and he wanted to buy her a drink.

She mentally replayed her first sighting of him. The sharp angles of his jaw and his confident stride as he walked into the Shop-n-Go. She swallowed hard, now aware that she had unabashedly checked him out in the parking lot. So yes, she was sure it was him.

"I remember your dog," was the best explanation she could conjure.

His brow furrowed as he seemed to search his memory bank. "Oh, wait! Were you in that old, beat-up pickup truck?" The words must have popped out before he could consider his tone. He grimaced. "Sorry. That came out wrong."

She waved off his apology. "Yeah, that was me."

"I had no idea you were waiting. I thought you were there to deliver produce or something."

So he thought she was a lettuce farmer, for which, considering her overalls and her ride, she could hardly blame him. It shouldn't matter what he thought—he was just a tourist. Still, his attention made her feel overly self-conscious.

"I don't know how things work where you come from Mr....?"

"Chambers." He stepped forward with an utterly disarming smile and offered his hand. "Joe Chambers."

His hand, warm and strong, clasped hers for just a moment, the simple touch igniting a spark that lingered long after his fingers slipped away. She looked up to find his gaze studying her, which only intensified the warmth that seemed to diffuse from his hand into her body.

She cleared her throat and massaged her tingling hand. She would have liked a moment to catch her breath, but Mr. California was waiting for a response while she was finding words hard to come by.

She cleared her throat. "Mr. Chambers, here in Twin Creeks, we use turn signals to show we're waiting for a parking spot. Perhaps you missed mine on account of how fast you were going?"

Good grief, she sounded just like her fourth-grade teacher. Formal to the point of brittle.

Joe chortled. "I doubt it. How fast could I go in Nowhere, Montana, with a giant produce truck blocking my lane?"

Nowhere, Montana? What the...?

He held up his hand in a defensive gesture. "I'm sorry. That was rude." His gaze drifted downward to his lace-up leather boots. His smile slipped and she saw fatigue in the crinkles around his eyes, a slight slump to his shoulders. He looked up to meet her gaze, his blue eyes intense and sincere. "It's just...been a day."

His comment *was* rude. But her irritation refused to stick. Those prominent cheekbones and deep blue eyes were making it hard to stay focused on a stupid parking spot.

"Well, okay then," Lily replied, her words having decided to take an impromptu vacation. "Just, you know, look where you're going next time." She mentally face-palmed herself for her schoolmarmish scolding. Why didn't she just waggle her finger at him for good measure?

Joe smiled as his gaze lingered on her lips. She saw some kind of shift in his expression that she couldn't quite read. Less fight, more…*what*? Interest? That didn't make sense. She had literally come straight from farm chores to the Shop-n-Go without a smidge of lipstick or a decent outfit.

"Thank you, ma'am. I will be sure to do that." He gifted her one last wistful smile before he turned on his heel and whistled. Daisy whimpered softly, then fell in step with her person, her hips swaying in rhythm with her foot strikes.

Lily watched them leave, her hands still fisted on her hips. She felt disoriented and faintly flustered. What had just happened? Did she win? She wasn't sure. If so, winning had left her with a hollow, unsettled feeling.

Just then, her cell phone alarm beeped, warning her of Alexa's impending school dismissal. She chose the rock-painting kit, tossed it into her basket and headed for the checkout.

Lily took her spot behind Grace Brown, the town's sole art gallery owner, in the checkout line. Lily checked the weather radar on her phone. Blizzard conditions would start after nightfall. She had plenty of time to get Alexa from preschool, then spend the afternoon baking and watching movies.

Lily had just started scrolling through cookie recipes when Grace suddenly dropped to her knees. Her shopping basket slipped from her hands, sending batteries skittering across the floor.

Then she fell forward, unconscious.

Edith screamed and pressed her hands to her mouth. "Oh, my God, she's having a heart attack!"

Maybe. But it could be a stroke. Or low blood sugar? Lily knelt down and gently rolled Grace to her back. She hadn't used her nursing training for over five years, but she remembered everything she'd been taught.

Lily placed a hand on Grace's forehead and gently tilted her head back, making sure her airway was open. Then she placed her ear over Grace's mouth, hoping to feel Grace's warm breath on her cheek or hear sounds of her breathing.

Nothing.

Lily reflexively reached for the stethoscope she used to drape around her neck. But of course, it wasn't there. So she placed two fingers on the side of Grace's neck, desperately hoping she'd find a steady pulse. But there was no flutter beneath her fingers. Not in her neck nor in her wrists.

Grace was in cardiac arrest. For reasons Lily couldn't know without testing, her heart had stopped beating. There was a small chance she would survive, but only if she received intensive medical care very soon.

Lily knew exactly what she needed to do—tear Grace's coat aside and yank up her shirt, then brace the palms of her hands against Grace's sternum and deliver a staccato of hard chest compressions.

But Lily's hands remained fisted at her sides.

Oh, no, not now. Not with Grace.

Her body was a stubborn, useless statue. She desperately wanted to leap into action to save Grace's life. Her brain even screamed *Move!* so loud, Lily flinched.

But she remained frozen in place, her tight chest sucking in tiny gulps of air.

She's going to die, Lily, right in front of you, if you don't do something.

Just like Connor had died. His body sprawled on the floor of the emergency room where he saved patients every day, but where his trauma team could not save him. Not even with Lily crouched at his side, futilely trying to contain the red flower that bloomed across his chest.

We're losing him! Get the crash cart now!

Frantic voices crossed five years of memories to slam her right back into the worst day of her life. She wiped her sweaty palms on her overalls. She didn't want to be here. Didn't want to experience these muscle memories that made it feel like that night was happening all over again.

The door was so close. All she had to do was drop her basket and run. Maybe if she could get outside, this fog would lift and she would be able to think again. To breathe.

But no, she couldn't do that. Not with Grace in her

arms, slipping away. She squeezed her eyes shut against the horror unfolding before her.

Because she knew she couldn't save Grace. Her body wouldn't let her.

She never knew when these panic attacks would flare. They had started a few months after Connor died, when she'd tried to return to work. She'd thought it was a fluke at first—just a bad day, fatigue, whatever, but she was wrong. The more urgent or traumatic the call-out was, the more likely she was to stand frozen on the sidelines, hands fisted at her sides, watching helplessly as her trauma team did all the hard work without her.

Her coworkers had been kind, and her boss was understanding. There was talk of more time off, support groups, counseling. But Lily knew the rules. There was no room on a medevac helicopter for someone who couldn't pull her weight.

That was why she had left everything she loved in Chicago. Her job, the fast pace of city life, her friends and neighborhood.

All so she could keep Alexa safe from the unpredictable side of city life. And make sure that her flaws never, ever hurt a sick or injured patient.

But her past had caught up to her here in Twin Creeks. She bowed her head in despair, barely aware of Edith's frantic cries for someone to please, for Pete's sake, help Grace!

But then a streak of rust-toned coat and dark hair appeared in her peripheral vision. Before she could register what was happening, the dark-haired stranger who stole her parking spot slid to Grace's side on his knees.

"What happened?"

"She's having a heart attack!" Edith screamed. "We need a doctor!"

"I *am* a doctor," Joe replied. He lifted Grace's eyelids, using his cell phone's flashlight to check her reflexes. He seemed utterly calm and focused, as if he had come to the Shop-n-Go for the sole purpose of saving Grace's life.

After checking Grace's pulse, Joe whipped off his jacket, rolled up his sleeves, and pressed the palms of his hands against her chest.

His quick action and laser focus was enough to shock Lily out of her panic attack. Daisy had followed Joe and seemed to know this was serious. She dropped to the floor and appraised Lily with her serious brown eyes.

Lily's vise grip around her chest loosened just a bit. It felt good not to be alone anymore. Joe's steady pace and single-minded focus on Grace gave her something to concentrate on. She started silently counting each of Joe's compressions, then pinched Grace's nose shut and delivered a full breath while Joe waited. Soon, they were working in harmony, his chest compressions to her breaths. Her anxiety slowly receded, allowing her mind to clear so she remembered something important.

"Edith! Call the high school! Ask them to bring the defibrillator over—stat!"

Joe's gaze caught hers. "Shouldn't emergency services be here by now?"

"We share emergency services with six other rural towns in western Montana. They could be here in five minutes…or an hour."

Joe was utterly focused on his work. His arms were straight and rigid, his entire body working to deliver the deep, hard chest compressions that Grace needed to keep her heart and brain oxygenated. Sweat beaded on his forehead and upper lip. Maybe he was a jerk when it came to parking spaces, but Lily felt profoundly grateful their paths had crossed that day.

"I can take over. You've been working for two minutes," she said. "You run lead on the defibrillation when the AED gets here."

Joe glanced up, his eyes searching hers, filled with unspoken questions.

"I used to be a flight nurse," she explained. Lily waited until his twenty-count was done before lacing her hands together and taking Joe's place. "But that was a long time ago," she added, her tone somber as she began her count to twenty.

CHAPTER TWO

THE SOUND WAS very far away—muffled and indistinct, like it was coming from a deep tunnel. And so annoying, like a persistent bee.

It was a bell, ringing over and over and over.

Joe groaned and reached for his phone. His thick *Practical Medical Oncology* textbook slipped from his lap and landed on the floor with a thud, startling Daisy from her nap.

A booming male voice started talking before Joe could even say hello. "Bill needs his insulin."

"I'm sorry...what?"

"Bill Parker."

Joe recognized the caller as George Benson, the mayor of Twin Creeks. George had led Joe's video interview with the town council to be Twin Creeks's interim doctor until they found a permanent replacement. The previous doctor had run the town's sole medical clinic for four decades before succumbing to heart disease. Despite months of running job postings around the country, the council had not found anyone willing to relocate to the former mining community nestled at the foot of a mountain.

"Lives over in Blue Sky Valley. He's out of insulin and he's going to need it before he gets shut in by the blizzard."

Joe unfolded his bone-weary body from the recliner where he had fallen asleep watching a hockey game. He tossed his blanket back on the chair and rolled his shoulders and neck, feeling a deep ache from the grueling marathon session of saving Grace's life at the Shop-and-Go.

It had taken the EMT team forty-five minutes to arrive. By then, he and Lily had performed CPR nonstop, pausing only to deliver shocks with the portable AED machine. He'd never been so happy to hear the sound of sirens in his life. Even happier to learn that the EMT could detect Grace's persistent, if tachy, pulse.

Joe opened his front door to look at the storm. Snow fell sideways, driven by a steady, brisk wind. The cold air sliced through his T-shirt and stung his eyes.

"You want me to drive to Bill Parker's house in this weather?" Tiny shards of ice pelted his face, driving him back into his warm, dry house.

"Well, he's out of insulin, isn't he?" The mayor's tone was matter-of-fact, as if driving through blizzards was a normal occurrence around here.

"Couldn't the pharmacy courier the insulin to him?"

"Courier? What?"

Of course not. Joe was acting like he was still a resident doctor back in Los Angeles, working in a top-tier hospital with armies of medical specialists at his beck and call. Back there, he could have phoned in a script from the comfort of his recliner. The pharmacy would have filled the prescription and delivered it by private courier, charging it all to the patient's insurance.

But those days were long behind him now. His residency was over and his plans to train for a career in oncology had ended in a spectacular plot twist he had never seen coming. Instead of being halfway through the first year of a top oncology fellowship, he had been exiled to Nowhere, Montana, and now had to figure out what on earth the mayor wanted from him.

"Never mind. Could this wait until the storm passes?"

"No can do, Doc. Bill's caretaker saw my wife at the feed-and-tack store this morning. She said that Bill dropped his last vial of insulin when he did his injection this morning. So now he's out and needs more."

"And I'm just hearing about this now?" Joe ran a hand through his hair. Good grief, what if the council member's wife hadn't gone to the feed-and-tack store? Would Bill just muddle through without his insulin, risking his body going into diabetic ketoacidosis?

Joe could practically hear the man shrug. "First I thought of it, I guess."

Joe opened the front door again, squinting his eyes against the wind and ice. He could barely see a foot beyond his front door. "I'm sorry, but these roads simply aren't drivable."

Not in his luxury sedan anyway. He had only been in Twin Creeks for a few days, and he already knew his prized possession would be a liability here. Maybe he should trade it in for something sturdier, like the lettuce-hauling flatbed that had blocked his path that morning. But no, Joe could never give up that convertible. The sleek luxury sedan wasn't just a car—it was a symbol of everything he had worked so hard for, a reward for the long hours and endless sacrifices. As was the luxury townhome he had rented near the hospital in LA, and the trendy clubs where he easily attracted the attention of beautiful women for a night or two.

Most days his work and play kept him busy and satisfied. But sometimes he felt a strange emptiness tugging at him. A sense that there was something more he was still searching for.

Whatever it was, he sure as hell wasn't going to find it here in Twin Creeks, Montana.

It was impossible to think of the truck without remembering the nurse who drove it. If he were still in LA and he had spotted her in one of the city's trendy clubs, he would have gladly crossed the room to buy her a drink, chat her up and see if he could get something started. He would have shown her the night of her life, then driven her home along the Pacific Coast Highway, feeling the salt and wind against his face as he drove with the top down, racing the waves and the seagulls in sync with whatever music he had blaring on the radio.

Most women he met were looking for what he had to offer. A few nights of glamour and passion, nothing more. And if any woman did get the wrong idea about him, he took her to brunch at his favorite resort where he would gently explain, over quiche and mimosas, that he just wasn't a mortgage-and-minivan kind of guy. Being honest and up-front had allowed him to enjoy the occasional connection he craved without leaving a string of angry, bitter ex-lovers behind.

His casual dating life would probably be one more casualty of this forced exile to Twin Creeks. It was just another handful of salt in the fresh wound of losing his fellowship. But a setback was not destiny, and Twin Creeks was not his forever. So that sweet, midnight-black convertible wasn't going anywhere.

Joe's thoughts drifted back to the ex-nurse he had met that morning. She was a pretty woman with her jet-black hair cut in a short bob. What was her story anyway? She was obviously skilled in trauma care, but she said she wasn't a nurse anymore. What happened? Was she injured? In some kind of professional trouble? That was hard to imagine. She didn't seem the type.

He had looked for her after handing Grace over to the EMTs. But by the time Edith had finished hugging and kissing him and declaring him a *hero* to anyone who would listen, the nurse in the bright pink wool hat with the white tassel was long gone. He hadn't even gotten her name.

"Take the snowmobile, then," the mayor bellowed.

"The what?"

"The snowmobile. It's in the barn. Just fire her up and zip over to your medical clinic in town for the insulin. You can jet over to Bill's place and be back home in no time."

A shock of electricity rippled down Joe's spine as he realized he had two new things to tackle today. Learning to operate a snowmobile and surviving a blizzard.

Joe pressed his thumb between his eyes where a throbbing headache was ramping up. What the hell was he doing here? He should be in Florida where he belonged, on the fellowship he had sacrificed so much for. Instead, he was here in this crazy place with crazy people who expected crazy things in the middle of a crazy snowstorm.

Hey, now, Chambers. It's not the mayor's fault or Bill Parker's fault that you're here.

Whose fault had it been? That was hard to say. All he knew was that his department chair, whose recommendation he'd needed to get that fellowship, had politely declined to support his application.

Not this time, Joe.

He had been completely stunned by her refusal. And confused. His grades were stellar. He had taken every overtime and on-call shift during his residency. While his peers were living it up over drinks at the off-campus bar, he had been at the medical library, researching the latest treatments and pharmaceuticals for cancer. No medical student had sacrificed more to accomplish their goals than he had. So why on earth did his top mentor lack faith in him?

His mentor had tucked a pencil behind her ear, crossed her arms over her chest.

Tell me your most difficult case this week.

That was easy. He rattled off the health metrics of his thirty-four-year-old patient with a history of Type One diabetes. He went into great detail describing the extent of her rapidly worsening renal function, severe hypertension and episodes of hypoglycemia despite careful insulin management. He listed the medication adjustments he had made and the extensive testing he had ordered.

And what is her name, Dr. Chambers?

He was utterly stumped.

Who does she love? And what is she willing to fight for?

He couldn't believe that after eight years of hard work and sacrifice, these were the questions that were tripping him up.

His mentor had scooted her chair closer so she could meet Joe's gaze. *Do you know the difference between a good doctor and a great doctor, Joe?*

Normally, he would say being committed, knowing your stuff and working harder than everyone else. But he didn't think those were the answers she was seeking.

Curiosity, Joe. Because when we are curious, we ask questions. When we ask questions, we learn things. We're in the business of treating people, Joe, not diseases. Know your patient, and you'll know their cure.

At that point, she had pushed away from him, scooted her chair back to her desk, then handed him a sheet of paper. She had a twinkle in her eye he had never seen before. "I'd like you to spend some time in Twin Creeks, Joe. It's a small town in western Montana where I grew up. Their long-time doctor has passed away and they need an interim doctor for a few months. It's your choice, of course, but I think you'll find it a special place where you can expand some of your people skills. Go there and come spring, I'll recommend you for the oncology fellowship in Florida."

Joe had questions—so many questions—and lots more fight in him. But she had already turned back to her computer—her way of saying the meeting was over.

Joe thought this was the most idiotic thing his medical

training had asked of him. But there wasn't a damn thing he could do about it. Without her blessing, he had zero chance of landing an oncology fellowship anywhere. So after packing all of his worldly possessions into a moving truck, he and Daisy had set off for the west coast drive to Twin Creeks, Montana. Just in time for Winter Storm Isabella.

Joe shook off his frustration and rooted through the kitchen drawer for paper and a pen. "And where will I find Bill Parker?"

"I told you. Blue Sky Valley, just past the widow's place."

Joe's pencil hovered over the paper, waiting for something useful. "I have no idea what that means."

The mayor sighed. "Blue Sky Valley is on the north side of the county, butted up against the mountains. Set your GPS to 46.1263 degrees north and 112.9478 degrees west and you'll be in the general area. Use forest roads when you get out of town. You'll pass a small homestead—that's the widow's place. Keep heading north and stick to the tree line. You'll find Bill's cabin soon enough. If you leave now, you should get back before the storm gets going real good."

Joe glanced out the window at the mess of snow and ice. This was going to get worse?

Joe ignored the feeling of dread coiling in his chest and wrote the directions on his pad. The staffing recruiter had warned him that rural medicine was different from what he was used to. But he thought that meant less access to specialists and hospitals, fewer resources.

He hadn't counted on doing house calls on a snowmobile in blizzard conditions.

Joe hung up, shrugged on his jacket and went out to the small barn that flanked his rented home. Daisy followed close at his heels.

He pulled off the snowmobile cover. It was black and sleek with a few dents and scratches from its previous adventures.

"Snowmobiling," Joe said to Daisy. "How hard could it be?"

Daisy yowled and flopped to the floor, dropping her chin to her paws and looking up at him with her soulful brown eyes.

"Oh, who asked you?" Joe muttered. He ran his fingers over the various gauges. The key dangled from the ignition. The left grip was the throttle; right was the brakes.

"See, this isn't so hard," Joe said, as much to himself as to Daisy.

There was also an open box-shaped sled that looked like it could haul a good number of supplies. Maybe even a person. If house calls were going to be part of his job description, a utility sled like this would be pretty handy.

Joe returned to the house to dress in his warmest winter gear and enter the GPS coordinates in his phone. He made a mental note to purchase a rugged, heavy-duty GPS unit as soon as possible. For now, his cell phone would have to do.

Daisy positioned herself between him and the door, her tail wagging wildly like a metronome.

"Not this time, girl. You're safer here."

Daisy threw back her head and yowled in protest. Joe's heart sank. He didn't know how she did it, but Daisy was some kind of expert at reading human emotions. And right now his heart didn't want to leave her behind. Unlike his father, who had found his solace at the bar after his mother died, Daisy had never abandoned him.

Joe crouched to stroke her ear the way she liked. "Aw, Daisy. You don't want to be alone, do you?"

Daisy tilted her head to rest it in his hand, just as she had with the pretty nurse back at the Shop-and-Go. Cripes, there he went again, thinking about the mysterious nurse. This had to stop. The fellowship application cycle would open again in a few months. If he wanted to get his shot at that fellowship, he needed to trust his head, not his heart. There was something his mentor wanted him to learn here in Twin Creeks, and the mysterious woman at the Shop-and-Go had nothing to do with it.

He could hardly blame Daisy. Everything here was strange for both of them.

"All right, girl, let's go."

Daisy sprang to her feet and glued herself to his hip as he locked the house. Then he hitched the box-freight sled to the snowmobile, layered it with blankets and gave Daisy the command to go. She jumped into the boxy space, spun once and settled into the soft bed he had made for her.

"Stay put," he warned her in his *I mean business* voice. "Even if you see a squirrel!"

So long as he took things nice and slow, they should be fine. But he had to be careful. Sometimes he revved the throttle when he meant to use the brake, resulting in a frightening surge forward.

Joe found the supply of insulin in the refrigerator at the clinic where he would start seeing patients in a few days. He was settling Daisy back in the sled when his cell phone rang. Joe checked the screen, desperately hoping it might be the mayor telling him to never mind, Bill had found extra insulin at home so Joe could go back to bed. But he had no such luck. It was his father's photo on the screen.

Joe studied his father's image. Recovery looked good on him. He was no longer the man Joe remembered from his youth, overwhelmed by grief and parenthood. Back then, he had found his solace in working far too much, then stopping at the bar for a "bite to eat" on the way home. Which turned into a pint...or four. As a father, he did most of what he was supposed to do. He made sure the house was stocked with food and that Joe's homework was done. *High-functioning alcoholism* they called it. But emotionally, he was long gone, drowning in grief after losing his wife just two months after she was diagnosed with ovarian cancer.

Joe sent the call to voice mail. He knew what his father was calling about and he didn't want to talk about it again. He had no intention of taking the newly developed test that would determine if he carried the same gene that had caused his mother and four other relatives to develop cancer before their fiftieth birthday. He knew his father loved him and was worried for him, but what was the point? Knowing he carried the gene only meant he would be screened more often and aggressively. It didn't mean he could beat his genetic fate.

So he'd decided long ago that he would rather not know. It was better to throw himself into a career of fighting cancer. It was too late to help his family, but maybe he could help others. Maybe he could be the doctor his family had needed in their darkest hour.

And it was why he wasn't a mortgage-and-minivan kind of guy. He had no intention of ever having a serious relationship. Losing his mother had almost destroyed his father and left him with memories of a dark and lonely childhood. It wasn't fair to let someone fall in love with him, knowing that one day they would have to watch him prematurely grow sick and die. And he sure as hell wasn't going to knowingly pass these genes on to an innocent child.

So there would be no love, no wedding bells, no tiny feet pitter-pattering through his home. He loved his work, and he loved Daisy...period. Most days, he was happy enough. And if he felt a little lonely from time to time, well, that was just the cost of doing the right thing.

Joe tucked his phone into his pocket, then settled Daisy back in the sled. He kept the pace nice and slow all the way to Bill's cabin, making sure to check his bearings often on the GPS app to ensure he was still on course. It was impossible to tell with the low visibility.

By the time they were ready to head back home, both he and Daisy were wet and miserable from the snow and wind. They were on a well-marked forest trail now, which made him feel a little more confident of his bearings. Thoughts of getting back to his warm house and starting a crackling fire spurred him on, making him a little more reckless.

He revved the throttle, taking the snowmobile up to thirty mph, then forty. At this speed, they would be home in no time.

Up ahead there was a curve in the trail, marked by a thicket of trees and some huge boulders. Joe reduced the throttle to slow the snowmobile for the curve.

But a rough patch in the ice-covered trail startled him. Instead of braking, he hit the throttle…hard.

CHAPTER THREE

"I'm ready, Mommy!"

Alexa emerged from her room wearing adorable snowman winter pajamas with a matching robe cinched tight against her little round belly. She had her favorite teddy bear stuffed under her arm.

Lily looked up from the kitchen where she was putting the final touches on their winter snack. "Okay, I've just decided. Five is my favorite age for little girls like you."

"I'm five!" Alexa said, her tone full of wonder.

"Yes, you are." Lily filled a ceramic teapot with homemade hot chocolate, then set it on a serving tray alongside small bowls of marshmallows, peppermint sticks, whipped cream and little snowman cocktail napkins.

The oven timer dinged, signaling that their chunky monkey brownies were ready. Ooey-gooey brownies packed with caramel and white chocolate chips.

This was probably the unhealthiest "dinner" Lily had ever served her daughter, but she wanted to start their snowy retreat off right. There would be plenty of time to make Alexa eat her veggies later.

For now, they still had power, so they planned to watch their first holiday movie of the season with this carb-centric snack. Later, when the power was out, they would rely on the fireplace for heat and the generator to keep the refrigerator and lights on. That was when they would switch to the healthy granola bars Lily had baked, along with strawberry smoothies that had a secret handful of spinach blended in.

Alexa plopped herself on the couch and patted the spot next to her. "Come sit by me, Mommy!"

"Just where I want to be!" One of the many nonsense rhymes they had created over the five years of being a family of two.

Oh, it was so nice to have this time with her. For the first few years in Copper Ridge, Lily had been able to survive on Connor's small life insurance policy. Getting a part-time, work-from-home job with a nursing journal was the perfect way to help the insurance money last longer while still filling Alexa's days with nature hikes and library trips. Lily knew she probably tried too hard to make up for Alexa's not having a father.

Lily had let Alexa pick out any movies she wanted from the library's holiday collection. Just a few minutes into the film, she realized that might have been a mistake.

Because this movie featured a class of first graders who did a silly science experiment with a snowman in their playground, then discovered that they accidentally brought him to life. Mayhem and misadventure ensued.

It was a cute and charming story that had Alexa mesmerized. But Lily gritted her teeth and sipped her hot chocolate, desperately hoping that Alexa would just enjoy the story and not focus too much on…

"I want to go to school," Alexa said suddenly and with great determination. "Like those kids."

"Well, you will go to school. Even if we decide to homeschool, there's lots of classes we can take at the library."

"Not like that!" Alexa was adamant. "I want to go to a school like them." She pointed to the television. "With a teacher, and a classroom, and recess and everything!"

This was Alexa's last winter attending a home-based preschool in their neighborhood. The following fall, she would be old enough to board the yellow bus that drove by their house every morning and afternoon.

Oh, gosh, she didn't want to argue with Alexa. Not now, when everything was starting so well. Maybe a little distraction was in order.

"You know what we forgot? The popcorn!"

Lily headed to the kitchen and filled the popcorn machine with kernels. She slid a bowl under the chute, then snuck a peek into the living room. Alexa was busy examining the rock-painting kit that Lily had brought home from the Shop-n-Go. If Lily waited just a little bit longer, Alexa might focus on rock painting instead of kindergarten, giving them a much-needed peaceful evening.

Lily glanced out the window. It was snowing quite hard now. Not quite whiteout conditions, but close. She grabbed her sweater from a hook near the back door and went outside to the screened-in porch, then flipped on her porch light so she could watch the beauty of a powerful winter storm.

The storm was picking up momentum now. Snow fell steady and hard, covering her house and driveway in a thick white blanket. She shivered as wind whistled through the screened-in porch, chilling her to the bone.

Her thoughts turned to Grace. She had called the hospital twice since she got back from the Shop-n-Go and was heartened to hear that Grace was in critical but stable condition. She involuntarily shuddered as she remembered how close Grace had come to dying. If it hadn't been for Joe Chambers, who knows what might have happened?

"Joe Chambers..." She whispered his name out loud and it tasted like candy.

Lily wasn't prone to infatuations, but she couldn't quite put memories of her encounter with the sexy stranger to rest. Jennifer, her good friend and landlord, would be thrilled. She had started working on Lily a year or two after she moved to Twin Creeks.

You're a young, beautiful woman, sweetie, she had said. *You deserve to be looked after, you know?*

People kept telling her that she needed to find closure, move on, that sort of thing. Lily didn't know—maybe Jennifer was right. So she'd tried. She hired a sitter to go out with the men Jennifer had thought would be just perfect for her. Her dates had been nice enough, and she couldn't deny it felt good to enjoy some attention and laughs over dinner and wine.

But she'd known soon enough that she could never go beyond dinner. Her heart had barely survived the loss of Connor. How could she ever let herself fall in love again, knowing that at any moment, some random act of fate could snatch it all away? Even if she wanted to fall in love again, she couldn't risk breaking Alexa's heart, too, if love wasn't going to stay.

Jennifer had been disappointed when Lily told her there would be no more dates.

I understand, she told Lily, giving her arm an affectionate squeeze. *But honey, sometimes love finds us, whether we're ready or not.*

That had been the end of her dating life. That is, until today. Ugh, there it was again. The image of Joe braced against the grocery store shelf, flashing her that brilliant smile as they pointlessly bantered about a parking space. He'd been flirting with her and damn if she hadn't liked it...a lot.

Who was he anyway? His out-of-state plates made winter tourist seem likely, but he didn't have a ski rack mounted to his car roof and he didn't look like a hunter. He was probably just passing through Twin Creeks on his way to the bigger city of Billings. Which was for the best, really. She might be lonely from time to time, but being lonely was better than being heartbroken.

She'd feel a lot less lonely if she could stop thinking about Joe Chambers and his perfect jawline. She left the shelter of her porch and stepped out into the storm. She wanted to feel the wind and ice battering her body instead of the loneliness making her heart ache.

She was instantly pelted by snow and tiny ice shards. The wind howled through the courtyard between her little cottage and the main house. Snow and ice chafed her cheeks and made her eyes sting.

She closed her eyes against the storm and realized that if she tilted her head just right, the wind howling through the ponderosa pines sounded a little like the blades of an emergency rescue helicopter. It was enough to conjure memories of rescue calls from long ago.

Loma Linda base, this is Medevac 2646...
Medevac 2646, on call out to Apple Valley...
Medevac 2646, requesting space in your emergency room...
Patient with positive LOC...
Patient with a fractured left ankle...

Even though it was five years ago, she could still remember so many patients. Their names and faces. The accidents and injuries. Their fear and pain.

She missed that job *so* much. She missed being there for people at their darkest hour. Holding their hand as they crossed the city skies, far above the bustling city that had its own problems and worries. In every call, she strived to be the beacon of hope someone needed when their entire world had crashed around them.

The wind was whipping into a frenzy now. Soon, they would be in whiteout conditions. She was chilled to the bone but didn't want to leave. It felt too good to imagine herself back in the action and thrill of her former work as a flight nurse.

Medevac 2646, we have a patient with partial facial paralysis...

"Help...we need help!"

This is Medevac 2646...recommend that the orthopedic team be on standby...

"Help me! Please! Can you please help me?"

At first, she thought the cries for help were part of

her memories. But when she opened her eyes, she could still hear the cries.

The cries were very faint, just barely audible in between the howling wind gusts.

She waited; her head cocked…yes! There it was. Someone was crying out for help.

She ran inside and turned on the switches for her exterior lighting around the barn.

There, off in the distance, she could see something moving toward the farm. The barest impression of a dark shape headed her way.

"What is it, Mommy?" Alexa joined her at the back door, her brow furrowed with worry.

"I don't know, baby. I think someone might need our help."

She didn't even know that for sure. But her trauma rescue skills were kicking in, and she felt a familiar surge of adrenaline for the second time that day.

She dashed to the hallway closet, donning her heavy winter coat and boots, then slammed on her gloves and winter hat before heading for the door.

"I'll come, too, Mommy!" Alexa trailed after her mother, her teddy bear dragging behind her.

"No, baby—you're not dressed warm enough. Stay here in the kitchen. I'm just going to take a look."

Lily grabbed her most powerful flashlight, kissed Alexa's cheek and went outdoors.

At first, she couldn't see a damn thing. Nothing but snow flurries and pitch-black night. She strained to hear the voice calling for help again, but the howling winds were no match for a human voice. After several long and cold minutes, she was starting to think she had imagined everything. But somehow it felt wrong to give up and go back indoors, even though the wind was practically pushing her that way.

Then she saw the figure moving between the barn and house. She couldn't tell what it was exactly, but it was definitely not her imagination.

She ran off the porch to the figure. It was a man, stumbling through the thick snow, cradling one arm with the other.

If he was yelling before, he wasn't yelling anymore. Maybe he was too tired or weak, or maybe it was because he got a mouthful of snow every time he tried.

She caught up to him and gripped his arm. "It's okay!" she shouted. "You made it!"

He looked up at her, startled, as if he didn't expect his cries to actually rally help. His eyebrows and lashes were frosted with snow. He had a flannel scarf wrapped tight around his face, so all she could see was his eyes. Eyes that were very familiar.

Lily tugged at his arm. "Let's get you inside!" she shouted.

But he resisted her pull, shouting something that was hard to understand between his scarf and the wind. Something about a snowmobile…an accident…

"I don't understand!" she yelled.

He pulled down his scarf and shouted as hard as he could. "Daisy…! Injured…" He gestured wildly at the direction that he'd come from.

Under the lamplight, with his scarf removed, she could see why his eyes seemed familiar.

It was Joe Chambers. From the Shop-n-Go!

Her heart fluttered for a moment, stunned to see him here in her courtyard. Had she somehow managed to conjure him into her life with her incessant thoughts of him all afternoon?

"Daisy?" she screamed back, remembering the sweet dog who had befriended her in the store.

"Yes! Have to...help her!" He pointed to his arm and then she understood. He was too injured to help Daisy on his own.

He gestured for her to follow him, but there was no way they could just jet off into the night in the middle of a blizzard. They would end up lost or injured for sure.

And she couldn't leave little Alexa here all by herself.

Joe had already turned back in the direction he came from. She grabbed his arm and hauled him back.

"We need supplies!" she shouted, hoping he could hear at least half of what she said. "Come with me!"

He looked behind him, where he had left Daisy, and then to her cabin with its brightly illuminated windows and warm, crackling fire.

The look on his face was pure anguish.

He was stuck; she could see that. Stuck between doing *something* to help Daisy, even if it got him killed, and following her.

She needed him to trust her if they were going to help Daisy. The same way she had needed her trauma patients to trust her before she strapped them into a helicopter and whisked them off to unknown places.

So she told him what she had told her patients. "Everything's going to be okay, Joe. I will make sure of that."

* * *

Lily swung the cabin door open with a crash and waved Joe inside. "Come in, come in!" she gushed.

Joe was nearly frozen numb from all the time he'd spent in the fierce winter storm. First, on the snowmobile trip to Bill, then spending who knows how long stumbling through the snow, hoping against all odds that he might catch a glimpse of lights from the tiny cabin he had passed earlier.

He stood just inside the doorway, still mystified that he had managed to make it here safely. The woman pulled off her pink winter hat with the white tassel. The same hat she had worn that morning when he first saw her at the Shop-n-Go. Then she slipped out of her boots covered in slush and put on a pair of slippers shaped like soft white bunnies.

She disappeared for a moment, then returned with a mug of hot coffee and a few rolls of bandage wraps. "What happened?"

Joe didn't know if she meant the throbbing arm he had pressed protectively against his side or what brought him to her doorstep. "Snowmobile accident," he managed to get out, because that would answer both questions.

It was warm in the foyer. Warm enough that his teeth had stopped chattering though he still felt frozen to the core. The unmistakable aroma of something hot and delicious wafted from the kitchen, making his mouth water against his will.

"And you had Daisy with you?"

Hearing it from her lips made it sound completely

ridiculous. Reckless even. But he lacked the energy to explain the whole story, so he just nodded.

"Where is she now?"

"Pinned under the snowmobile. It flipped when I took the corner too fast. She was in an attached trailer, but somehow she ended up pinned under the snow machine. I tried, but I couldn't lift it." He indicated his injured arm with a frustrated shrug.

Then she was right in front of him, the mysterious woman from the Shop-n-Go. For a moment, he thought she might hug him. But no, she was looping something over his head. It was a makeshift sling she had created with the bandage wrap. She held it open wide so he could wriggle his arm inside. That small motion was enough to launch another explosion of fireworks deep in his shoulder and neck, but then she wrapped his arm snug against his body. The combination of support and stabilization provided a small measure of comfort.

"Here, take these." She offered him two orange pills from her pocket. "We'll check you out later, after we've found Daisy. Until then, hopefully these will help your pain a bit."

He swallowed the pills dry. They were just garden-variety anti-inflammatories sold at any drugstore. He doubted they would do much to combat the ripping, searing sensation in his shoulder, but he appreciated her effort all the same.

She patted his good arm gently. "I've got to gather a few things before we leave. Why don't you come into the kitchen and have some soup. It'll do you some good to warm up before we go find Daisy."

Joe shook his head in confusion. The warm house, hot coffee, homemade soup, soft bunny slippers—these were the trappings that came with a normal day. But today wasn't normal. It was a disaster, and it was all his fault.

He started to protest but it was as if she could read his mind. "Everything will be okay. But it could be a long night. Leave your jacket and boots here—we'll get you fixed up with something to eat."

He followed her to the kitchen and went on autopilot, sitting on the chair she pulled out for him and accepting the bowl of soup. Until that moment, he'd been functioning from a comfortably numb place. Just doing what he had to do, moment by moment, to survive his ordeal. But the heat of the ceramic bowl, the fragrant steam of the soup, the tantalizing aroma of basil and tomato broth with hunks of hearty stew meat—its simple pleasure was almost overwhelming.

She smiled at his expression. "Like it? It's a family recipe." She dropped into the chair next to him. "I'm Lily, by the way."

"I remember you from the Shop-n-Go this morning."

"I recognized you, too." He wondered how, with his face all bundled up against the snow and cold.

That was all he could manage. The heat and aroma of the soup was getting to him. She had served it in a blue ceramic bowl with a slab of what appeared to be homemade bread. And a glass of cold milk.

Just a few bites, he told himself. *Then I'll insist we get going.*

But the first bite completely felled him. Stew beef, root vegetables and a thick, satisfying broth utterly did him in. Once he took that first bite, he could not stop. He devoured bite after delicious bite while Lily quizzed him on his journey, trying to get a bearing on where he had crashed. He knew he had been on a forest service road, following the route based on his GPS directions. He described the landmarks he had passed, including her cabin, before the accident.

"I think I know where Daisy is," she said, her brow furrowed in thought. Then she jumped to her feet. "I'll be right back. I need to ask my landlord to stay with Alexa."

She disappeared, leaving him to wonder who Alexa was. He was more concerned with scraping the last drops of broth from the bowl. He was so engrossed that he didn't notice a little scrap of a girl standing by his elbow, her expression quite solemn.

"Hello," he said. "You must be Alexa."

She neither confirmed nor denied his assumption. Instead, she blinked twice. "Mommy says your doggie is hurt."

"That's true. She's trapped in the snow, but your mom and dad are going to help me rescue her."

The girl gave him a funny little frown. "Daddy can't help."

"No?"

She shook her head hard, making her auburn curls shimmy and shake. "He's with the angels now."

"Oh." Joe's heart squeezed with sympathy. He had been older than Alexa when his mother had died of cancer. Old enough to understand, but not old enough to accept the feckless, random hand of fate. He didn't know if he would ever be old enough to accept the *c'est la vie* canned advice that some people doled out in the face of incomprehensible loss.

He put his hand over his heart. "Ouch," he told the little girl with the big brown eyes. Because what else could he say that would let her know he understood? She nodded in return, as if she understood him perfectly.

Lily returned, her arms full of supplies, and dumped them on the table. A topo map and GPS unit. Water bottles, ski goggles, flashlights, medical supplies, headlamps and a handful of granola bars.

"Jennifer's on her way," Lily told Alexa.

Alexa groaned and dropped into the chair next to Joe. "Aww, I want to come, too!"

"'Fraid not, kitten. The weather's too rough. You'll be safe here with Jennifer—I'll be back in a jiffy!"

Joe stood so he could return to the foyer and put his boots and jacket back on. He'd lost track of time since he'd come to Lily's cabin, but it felt like too long. Every minute in her safe, warm home was one more minute that Daisy was alone, cold and afraid.

Lily bit her lip. "I just need one more thing from the shed."

Joe's heart sank. He could understand Lily's need to find someone to stay with her daughter, but with that taken care of, he wanted—no, he *needed* to get back in the storm and find Daisy.

She must have read his expression because she paused, her hand on the doorknob. "I'll be quick, Joe. I promise."

And then she was gone. He watched helplessly through the paned window as her dark figure crossed the open courtyard between her little cabin and the barn that was illuminated by the exterior floodlights. She was so small and the storm so ferocious that he momentarily feared she would get lost, too; swallowed up by a storm that seemed intent on obliterating everything in its path.

He wanted to scream with frustration, but Alexa had joined him in the foyer, and he didn't want to scare her, too.

"What's your doggie's name?"

He dropped to the bench, then winced at the bolt of red-hot pain that zipped from his shoulder down his arm at the sudden movement. "Daisy," he said through gritted teeth.

Alexa spied his wool cap on the bench next to Lily's pink one. She picked it up, then carefully climbed on top of the bench so she could reach his head and tug his hat down over his ears, though it felt wildly askew. It was cute how she bit her bottom lip when she concentrated. Just like her mother, he realized, when she had been counting his chest compressions on Grace before she gave a deep, hard breath.

He waited until Alexa wasn't looking to straighten his cap. Just then, Lily burst back through the door, a shovel in one hand.

A shovel? Why the hell did she need a shovel? All they needed to do was find Daisy and lift the snowmobile away from her.

Unless Lily thought that Daisy might be beyond rescue?

The lump that formed in his throat was enormous. He forced the terrible image far from his mind. Daisy was going to be fine. She had to be.

She slipped her winter gear back on, leaving those

memorable white bunny slippers in the foyer, then helped him back into his winter gear, too. This time she left his injured arm close to his body and just zipped up his jacket, leaving the empty sleeve dangling at his side. After loading their gear onto a sled, she gave Jennifer a hug to thank her for staying with her daughter. Alexa got a quick kiss on the cheek and off they went, abandoning the safety and warmth of Lily's little cabin to head back into the raging storm.

CHAPTER FOUR

As soon as they left Lily's screened-in porch, the icy wind snatched away all the warmth and coziness of Lily's warm cabin. But that was okay. All Joe wanted was to get back to his best friend.

Lily led the way, creating deep depressions in the snow that he could follow to conserve his energy. The stress of his injury plus exposure from being outdoors made him the weaker partner.

At first, it felt like Lily was leading them farther away from where he felt the crash site was. But then he saw her logic. By sticking to the tree line, they had some perspective of the landscape despite the poor visibility from the blizzard. And when the path suddenly became an open corridor in the forest with yellow blazes tacked into the trees, he knew she had led them back to the forest road he had traveled before the accident.

Joe felt a sudden surge of energy when he recognized his bearings. So much so that he stopped following her tracks so he could walk alongside her. He couldn't see much of her profile with her yellow goggles and her face wrapped tight with a thick winter scarf. But she gave him a single curt nod to acknowledge him, and he felt like there was intention in that gesture. That whatever happened next, he wouldn't face it alone.

Despite the poor visibility, Joe could just make out the clump of trees that he had passed seconds before the snowmobile crash. He tugged on Lily's arm and pointed toward the field. The wind was too strong to even attempt to speak. She nodded and gave him a thumbs-up. Their pace quickened as they passed the trees. It was then that he could just barely discern lumps in the snow—the boulders! His heart soared with hope. This *was* the crash site. He was sure of it!

All his exhaustion disappeared as he broke into a run, searching for the snowmobile. There! Off in the distance he saw twin beams of light—the lights of his snowmobile were still glowing, thank goodness.

He ran awkwardly through the snow, every jostle making his arm howl with pain. The thick, fresh-fallen snow seemed intent on grabbing him with every step. Still, there wasn't anything that was going to stop him from getting to Daisy.

He cleared the snow machine and dropped to his knees. Daisy was right where he left her, but now she was almost entirely covered with snow. Her head and muzzle remained visible, probably because she kept shaking it off for as long as she could.

But she wasn't moving. And her eyes were closed.

No. No, she couldn't be.

Before he could register that terrible thought, Lily's pink-gloved hands began sweeping snow away from Daisy's muzzle and body. She whipped her goggles off and threw them aside, laser-focused on clearing the pup's airway. Then she cupped her hands around Daisy's muzzle and blew hard, until Joe could see Daisy's chest rise in response.

No, no, no! We're too late!

But Lily didn't seem to think so. She kept repeating the breaths over and over.

"We need to get this damn snowmobile off of her!" Joe screamed, having no idea if Lily could even hear him with the wind howling through the ponderosa pines.

She nodded. Joe struggled to his feet, hoping to rock the snow machine away from Daisy with his one good arm. But before he could try, Lily grabbed him. She pointed to where the machine had landed—on a small outcrop of tree roots that were preventing the full weight of the snow machine from landing on Daisy's body. She was pinned but not crushed.

"Too! Much! Ice!" she screamed, pointing at the ground. He saw her point. Messing with the snowmobile could send it skittering off in the wrong direction.

She grabbed the shovel from her backpack and returned to Daisy, then began digging. He immediately understood her plan. If they dug out enough space from under her body, they could slide her out instead of trying to lift the machine off her. It would be safer and faster.

And it would never have been an option if Lily hadn't insisted on bringing the shovel.

Joe dropped to his knees and began digging at the snow with his one exposed hand. Soon, they had cleared a deep depression under her body.

Lily looked at him, her brown eyes calm and focused. "Ready?"

He read her lips more than heard her words, and he nodded. He held Daisy's head steady with his good arm while Lily braced Daisy's body with her hands.

"One! Two! Three!" she screamed.

Together they guided Daisy's body away from the snow machine. The sudden motion made the machine lose its precarious balance and crash-land into the space where Daisy's body had just been.

Joe felt a sudden, sickening wave of nausea roil his gut at the thought of how close Daisy had been to disaster.

But there was no time to think about that.

Joe grabbed the sled with his good arm and arranged the blankets into a makeshift bed. As Lily lifted Daisy's body, she gave a soft little whimper that made Joe's heart soar. She was alive! Not in great shape, but alive! They worked together to cover Daisy with more blankets, then improvised a safety strap system using the extra bandage wraps Lily had packed.

His fingers were numb to the bone, but he just had to rub Daisy's ear the way she liked. Lily slipped her goggles and gloves back on, then pointed at the trail. He got the message loud and clear.

Let's get the hell out of here.

She grabbed the sled pull and he followed behind, his heart in his throat. Lily had thought of everything they might need out here, while he had just wanted to bolt out the door. If they had followed his instincts instead of hers, they might still be searching for the crash site.

He felt greatly humbled by this terrible day. All he had wanted when he accepted the temporary job as town doctor was to escape the humiliation and shame of losing his fellowship after years of hard work. He thought Montana would be a refuge and a reprieve. A place he could hide away until his mentor deemed him ready for the Florida fellowship program.

But Montana was nothing like California. And if he didn't figure things out here pretty quick, he could get himself or someone else killed.

He kept his eyes on the determined woman leading the way back to safety. She didn't even know him, yet she had jumped in with both feet when he needed help. Unlike him, she knew what she was doing.

I used to be a flight nurse...a long time ago...

There had been sadness in her face when she said that. He had no doubt that she must have been a spectacular flight nurse. She was calm under pressure, had quick planning skills and was determined and focused.

All qualities that a medical professional working in this rural, wild place needed to be successful.

His mentor had told him that the state wanted to recruit more doctors and nurses to their rural communities. He even had a budget to add a nurse and a medical technician to his downtown medical clinic. But no one seemed to want to relocate to a rural area like Twin Creeks, so the towns had to rely on traveling doctors and nurses to rotate through on a monthly basis.

That lack of medical care was dangerous for the farmers and ranchers who worked the land. People put off seeing a doctor because the closest city was a hundred miles away. Small problems became life-threatening ones, and emergency care was sketchy at best.

Yet, Lily lived right here and clearly had top-notch

skills and could work under challenging conditions. So why wasn't she working at the clinic?

It was flat-out none of his business. Maybe she'd had a workplace injury. Or some kind of professional trouble.

Whatever the reason, it was none…of…his…damn…business.

I used to be a flight nurse… Those sad brown eyes. *But that was a long time ago.*

It wasn't just a matter of curiosity anymore. This town needed her.

And maybe he needed her, too.

Lily quietly closed the door to her daughter's bedroom. Alexa was totally exhausted after spending the evening tending to Daisy like a little mother.

Somehow, despite the accident and her exposure to the cold, Daisy seemed to have survived her accident unscathed. Lily had called the town's sole veterinarian who guided her through the basics of a veterinary exam. Daisy was resting now, curled in front of the fire on a pile of blankets that Alexa had fluffed into a little bed. Though her eyes were shut tight, she had kept one ear cocked in Joe's direction all evening, opening her eyes only if Joe moved or coughed. All things considered, Daisy was a very lucky dog.

Lily paused before descending the stairs. Joe sat where she'd left him, on the couch with amber light from the fire casting dancing shadows across his face. Her coffee table was strewn with plates, mugs and playing cards from where they had played games with Alexa after dinner.

Joe was engrossed in his phone, so it took a moment for him to notice her return, affording her a long look at his profile. He had an excellent nose, she thought, narrow and straight, and a broad, smooth forehead. His flannel shirt was unbuttoned at the neck, revealing a strong throat and a glimpse of his smooth, athletic chest.

Her body thrilled at the sight of this man in her living room. It had been just her and Alexa for so long. Not that their tiny family wasn't enough. She had everything she needed for a lifetime of happiness—a safe, dry home, a few good friends and a bright, healthy daughter. She had never felt any lack in her new life in Twin Creeks.

And yet... Joe's masculine energy was stirring something in her that she thought had died long ago. It was like realizing that cake was pretty good, but cake with icing... Well, that was a tempting, decadent treat. She wasn't sure if this was good or not. On the one hand, it meant she was still alive. A healthy, vibrant woman with robust sexual appetites. But it felt dangerous, too. Like opening a Pandora's Box of forbidden desires that could trample her fragile life if she surrendered. She swallowed hard, straightened her sweater and joined him in the living room.

He looked up from his phone with a furrowed brow. "I think you have to restart your router. I can't get internet access."

Lily cast her gaze to the window where the blizzard continued to rage. "Yeah, I don't think it's the router."

Joe's eyes widened. "So, no internet until tomorrow?"

She nibbled the edge of her nail, a nervous habit she couldn't quite give up. "Or the next day."

"You've got to be kidding. How the heck do you function without internet service for two days?"

She laughed at his incredulous expression. "The same way people functioned before the internet existed. Chores, books, baking...we even take a hike once in a while."

Joe held up a weary hand. "Stop. You're making me tired just thinking about all that."

"Speaking of tired," she said, noticing how the tiny muscles around his eyes were tensed, the hitch of his shoulders. Joe was in more pain than he was letting on. "Looks like you could use a rest yourself. And another dose of pain meds?"

"That would be great." He lifted his mug. "And maybe something a little stronger than hot chocolate?"

Lily swiftly cleared the coffee table of plates and cups, then returned with two crystal tumblers filled with ice and a bottle of single-malt whiskey. It was a farewell gift from her trauma team when she'd left Chicago.

Save it for a special occasion, her boss had told her. A historic blizzard and her surprise visitor certainly qualified.

Joe had gathered the cards and was shuffling them one-handed as he gazed into the fire. There was an awkward moment as she considered where to sit. There was a chair opposite the couch, but it was far enough that it felt distant and rude. She opted to join him on the couch, putting him within arm's length. Which felt a lot different than when it had been the three of them playing cards and board games all evening.

He smiled as she sat down and waggled the cards in his hand. "Up for another round of Go Fish?"

She wrinkled her nose. "Nah, let's play something more grown-up. How 'bout poker?"

She plucked the card deck from his hand. The fire was going, making the room quite warm and cozy. The candles and camping lanterns she had set out when the power went out added a hazy warm glow to the room.

She counted out five cards for both of them. "So, Dr. Joe Chambers. You just passing through our little town or will you be staying a while?"

"Both, I suppose. I just completed my residency training in Los Angeles and I had hoped to start an oncology fellowship this winter. But my mentor—" Joe took a sip of his whiskey "—strongly encouraged me to spend some time in Twin Creeks, serving as the interim doctor until a permanent replacement is hired."

"Oh," she said. "I wonder how she knew we needed an interim doctor? I thought the town was planning to rely on traveling doctors for now."

"She said she grew up here. She called Twin Creeks a *special place*."

Lily smiled at the description of her quirky new hometown. "That it is. But I wonder why she thought Twin Creeks would be good preparation for an oncology career? We don't have any cancer treatment centers here."

"I think she wanted me to have the opportunity to… get a little more life experience." He shifted in his seat, his jaw tight and his words clipped, clearly uncomfortable and frustrated with the details he was sharing.

Lily had no idea why his mentor would send him to

their tiny town for more life experience. But clearly, Joe wasn't happy about it. "I'd say you're off to a good start," Lily said, hoping to turn the conversation back to easier topics.

"How's that?"

"You have life experience with a blizzard now."

He chuckled wearily. "I guess that's true."

Lily tried to keep her focus on the cards in her hand and not on the gorgeous man next to her. But the firelight played against his angular features, and it was hard to ignore the soapy fresh scent of his aftershave. She took a deep, bracing breath to steady herself.

"We don't have any poker chips," she said apologetically. "Hold on." She stretched to reach the baskets where she stored Alexa's small toys below her TV cabinet. She found a handful of plastic safari animals and dropped them on the coffee table.

Joe laughed. "A bit unconventional, but okay. I propose an opening bet of two tigers."

"I'll see your two tigers and raise you one camel and one hippo."

"Am I being hustled here?" he fake groused.

She laughed but felt the heat in her cheeks rise as she caught his gaze lingering on her features. Electric tingles of anticipation zipped up and down her spine. She was so out of practice with socializing with someone new. Especially someone who looked like him.

Joe checked the cards in his hand, then threw two bears into the pile. "So how long have you been in Twin Creeks?"

She matched his bears with two of her own, then

tucked a wayward strand of hair behind her ears. "I moved here five years ago from Chicago. Alexa was just an infant."

"So, you left Chicago for—" he gestured to the window where Isabella raged on "—this paradise?"

She made a face at him. "Twin Creeks isn't that bad. You've just got to give it a chance."

"I *am* giving Twin Creeks a chance. Just long enough for a new doc to be hired."

She liked his mischievous smile. After considering her hand, she took another card from the pile. "I don't know, Doc. Twin Creeks just might grow on you."

"Like a fungus? There's medication for that, you know."

Joe leaned back into the couch and stretched his arms across its length. Lily was suddenly very aware of how close he was. If she leaned back, too, his arm would brush her shoulders.

"Seriously, how did you get here? Did you lose a bet? Owe someone money in Chicago?"

She smiled and tucked a strand of hair behind her ear. "My husband and I used to ski here every winter. He died shortly after I found out I was pregnant with Alexa. When Jennifer heard, she insisted I stay in her vacation rental for as long as I liked. But once I got here," she said, shrugging, "I didn't want to leave."

Joe sat in quiet contemplation, his brow slightly furrowed as he listened.

She looked around her cabin. The mantel over the fireplace was filled with framed pictures of her, Connor and Alexa—but none of them together as a family. One corner of her tiny living room was filled with a miniature-size kitchen where Alexa spent hours preparing snacks and meals for her stuffed animals. The bookshelves were stuffed with books and puzzles, and a basket near the fireplace overflowed with soft blankets for her and Alexa's nightly snuggle sessions.

"I think everything worked out okay. As okay as they can be considering our circumstances."

Joe regarded her for a long minute before setting his whiskey on the coffee table. "At the Shop-n-Go, you said you used to be a flight trauma nurse. What do you do now?"

"I was a nurse practitioner, actually. Now I'm a writer and editor for a medical journal about emergency nursing."

"Big change from jumping out of helicopters and keeping critically injured patients alive."

True, but there were no abusive husbands here, armed and angry. The only threat she had to worry about was whether her internet access would last long enough to get her articles uploaded by their deadline. "Yeah, that's true. But I'm able to work from home. It's great."

"*Great* like this is your dream job or *great* like it keeps the bills paid?"

He was looking at her in a way that made her feel a little too seen. She bit her lip and looked away. "Bill paying is important."

"No doubt about that. But would you ever…" He trailed off, then snapped his mouth shut and gazed down at his drink.

"What?" she prompted, now curious.

He shook his head and shifted his weight away from her. "Nothing, sorry. I'm just glad you found a good place to land when you needed it." He reached to set his glass on the table, the sudden motion making him wince with pain.

Lily noticed. "All right, Joe. Let me check out that shoulder."

CHAPTER FIVE

It was reflexive, really, his urge to wave her off and swear he felt fine. After years of his father being emotionally absent, he had learned not to draw attention to himself. What was the point? There wasn't anyone around to care.

But his shoulder was starting to ache like crazy despite the painkillers she'd given him. He didn't know what she could do for him out in the middle of nowhere, but she was right. Getting some sense of what might be wrong was a good start.

She leaned into his space until she was close enough that he could smell the soap from her recent shower mixed with nutmeg and cloves from the kitchen. Her hands were gentle as she helped extricate his arm from the sling.

"Extend your arm. Thumb down, please."

He tried to follow her directions, but the pressure of her soft, cool hand against his arm was incredibly distracting. Maybe she was better medicine than those little orange pills. He forced himself to concentrate on her words.

"Does this hurt, Joe?"

Heavens, it hurt a lot, but he didn't want her to stop touching him.

"Sorry about that. Can you raise your arm straight up and then lower it slowly?"

He gave it a try, his gaze lingering on her lovely mouth as she spoke. The upward motion wasn't too bad, but when he tried to lower the arm slowly, his shoulder just completely gave out and he felt a sudden shredding sensation with a lightning bolt of intense pain. He cried out before he could stop himself, pulling his arm into his body for protection.

"Oh, no, I'm so sorry!"

The waves of pain rocked him to the core but even that couldn't distract him from how she curved her hand over his knee. "I didn't mean to hurt you. Here, may I?"

She leaned into his space with outstretched hands, and he wasn't sure what she wanted. But she was so beautiful and earnest as her smoky brown eyes studied his face. She had the cutest pointy nose and a sharp little chin that jutted just so. It was impossible to imagine any request she could make that he wouldn't move heaven and earth to grant her. But at that moment, with the deep ache in his shoulder, all he could manage was a nod.

She reached for him, her hands hesitating at his collar. He watched, mesmerized, as her tongue darted to lick her lips before she unbuttoned the top button of his shirt, then the next and the next. She glanced up to catch his gaze, then gave him a tentative smile. Using his knee for leverage, she pushed herself off the floor, then sat on the couch behind him.

He felt the light brush of her hip against his shoulder,

her hands slipping under his shirt. Light as a feather, she carefully slipped his shirt off his shoulder. The cool air of the cabin wafted over his skin, chilling him, but he knew the goose bumps that prickled his flesh weren't from that. It was from her—the thrill of her leg against his shoulder, the softness of her hands sliding across his skin. Her fingers were gentle but probing and he knew she was searching for signs of dislocation or a fracture. But all he could think about was how good her touch felt as her fingers swooped and glided over his skin. The intoxicating blend of her touch and fragrance, the warmth of the fire and the delicious aroma of soup on the stove all threaded together into a blissful feeling that was familiar and yet foreign.

Home. This was what a home felt like. These feelings stirring deep in his psyche were memories of a time long ago, before cancer stole his mother and, by extension, his father, launching his crusade to become an oncologist. For the first time in a long time, he didn't feel a pang of guilt because he wasn't studying or caring for patients. Instead, he felt completely content to just be here with her. *She* made it okay in ways he didn't understand.

But then her hands were gone and the absence of her touch shocked Joe back to reality. The spell was broken—that was if it was ever there in the first place. Lily had hardly asked for some stranger to show up at her front door, let alone hit on her. And he didn't need to get himself mixed up in a relationship when he still had no idea what his future held.

She cast a glance upstairs where he guessed the rest of the bedrooms must be, then back at him. She chewed her lip for a moment, an utterly devastating gesture that tested his resolve to keep his distance.

"Here, let me fix that," she finally said, reaching for his shirt again. Her deft fingers rebuttoned his shirt, affording him one last long gaze at the beauty of her features.

She paused when done, giving him a wan smile that made him want to ask if everything was okay. But that wasn't his business. She had friends and a daughter. A life of her own in a town that cared about her.

"I'm not finding any breaks, Joe," she said, and he could hear the strain in her voice. "Which is good news. But I think you have a torn rotator cuff. You need an MRI to know for sure, but I do know this. There's no way you'll be able to open the clinic this week."

Joe's chest tightened with resistance. "That's impossible. The clinic hasn't had a doctor for months!"

"The town council will just have to keep relying on temporary health-care workers until you're healed."

Joe broke his gaze with her to frown into the fire. Playing country doc in Twin Creeks had never been part of his life plan. But taking care of people had always been. Maybe his original plan to be an oncologist hadn't worked out like he hoped…yet. But there was no way he could hang out on his couch for weeks while people like Bill ran out of insulin because no one checked on them.

But the deep burning fire in his shoulder told him Lily was right. Whatever that accident had done to him, he was as helpless as a baby. There was no way he could run the clinic like this. At least, not alone.

He looked away from the fire, his gaze finding Lily.

"You're a nurse," he challenged.

"What?" Her brow knitted in confusion. Then realization bloomed as she read his expression. "Oh, no, Joe. There's no way."

"Why not? You used to be a trauma nurse in Chicago. And you know this town, and the people who live here. Besides, you looked a heck of a lot happier fighting your way through a blizzard to save Daisy than you did when you talked about your journal work."

"That's different."

"Why?" he pressed again.

"Because I'm not a nurse anymore."

"But why not?" He knew he was being intrusive, but it made no sense to close the clinic for another month or two when they both had the skills to keep it open. "What's the deal? Were you injured? In some kind of trouble?"

"Because I can't do that work! Okay?" she shouted, then leaned back against the couch, defeated. Joe tried to make sense of the moment. Clearly, he had touched a nerve in her, but he didn't know why.

"My husband didn't just die, Joe. He was killed. Connor was a doctor in the emergency department at the hospital where my team and I delivered many of our trauma patients." She fidgeted with a loose thread on her shirt. "He wasn't scheduled to work that night. But we had just found out that I was pregnant with Alexa, and he wanted to start saving to buy our own house as soon as possible."

She folded her arms across her chest, drawing her sweater tighter around her body. "My team was completing a patient handoff when we heard shouting. Someone was approaching the emergency room. A man, very angry, screaming for his wife. We learned later that his wife was a domestic violence victim. He was yelling, demanding to see his wife. Connor wasn't going to allow that. He intercepted the man and tried to get him to calm down. But that only made the man more angry."

She closed her eyes against the memory. "I never saw the gun, but Connor did. All I remember is him yelling *Lily, run!* and then he lunged in front of me."

Joe listened, a heavy knot forming in his chest. Guilt washed over him, realizing how blind he'd been—so consumed with his own need for help at the clinic that he hadn't once stopped to consider why Lily had walked away from nursing. Now, hearing the depth of her pain, her unspoken wounds too raw for him to fully grasp, he felt ashamed, knowing her trauma was far beyond anything he could have imagined or understood.

"I tried to go back to work after Connor died. But something in me broke that night. I thought it would get better with time, but it didn't. I started having anxiety attacks when my team got the call to respond to an emergency. I froze up when I needed to help. I never knew what would trigger me. But I knew there was no room on a medical helicopter for someone who couldn't pull her weight."

Her eyes welled with tears, and she dropped her head to her hands. Instinct more than thought impelled Joe to reach for her hands, pull them away, so he could look into her eyes. "But you *can* do this work. I saw you do it today...for me and Daisy."

"That was different."

"How?"

She shrugged in frustration. "I have no idea, Joe."

"Maybe if we take it slow, like just part-time at first. You take whatever cases you want and leave the rest to me. If I can't help them, we'll arrange medical transport to a facility that can. I think if we give it enough time, you'll get your sea legs back under you. I think you need this, Lily. And I *know* I need you."

He held his breath, hoping she wouldn't say no. Suddenly, his mission wasn't just to make sure Twin Creeks had a functional medical clinic. It was also to break through the fog of guilt and despair that had convinced this woman she was too broken to ever heal and reclaim the life she wanted.

"I don't know, Joe. I don't want anyone to get hurt."

"Fine. Then let fate decide." He indicated the cards in his hand. "Finish the game. If I win, you work at the clinic. If you win…well, it's up to you what happens next."

"We're going to decide my future based on a round of poker?"

"Why not? Who knows how much of human history has been shaped by wagers, chance and sheer dumb luck. What about the circumstances that led to us even being here right now? What if my mentor had supported my fellowship application in the first place? I never would have come to Twin Creeks and never would have stumbled my way through a blizzard to find you."

"Sometimes fate is awful," Lily whispered.

Sometimes it was. Why did his mom have to inherit

the cluster of genes that caused her ovarian cancer? Why did his father lack the strength to go on when she died? And what had fate tucked into his own genetic code?

But the events of the day—saving Grace, then being saved by Lily—were so random and fortuitous, it was hard to ignore the gifts that fate could bring, too.

Lily bit her lip and stared into the fire. "Okay," she finally whispered.

"Okay?"

"Yeah, okay. Let's finish the game. See what happens."

She laid her cards down first, one by one. A two, three, four, five and six...all hearts.

Joe's eyebrow arched as she laid out her cards. He looked down at his hand, his smile melting into a frown. Then he laid his cards out one by one. A five of hearts, followed by a five of spades, diamonds and clubs.

Her straight flush beat his four of a kind. She had won. Her fate was in her hands now.

The fire burned low in the fireplace. A chill crept into the room. The weak afternoon light had surrendered to the dark, so that the light from her lanterns made shadows dance on the wall. Joe braced himself for her answer.

When she spoke, her voice was so soft, he had to strain to hear. "Part of me wants to keep things just as they are. I've worked hard to create a little bubble for me and Alexa, and it's kept us safe for five years now."

He held his breath and willed himself to be still. He wanted to smash the hell out of that little bubble, set her and Alexa free of a life that seemed too small for this vivacious woman. But it wasn't up to him.

"I'm grateful to the bubble. But I hate it, too. Because every day that I try to find my happiness in growing cucumbers and fact-checking articles is one more day that my soul seems to die just a little bit more." She looked away from the fire and to him. Her gaze was different. Something had shifted. He saw it in her clenched jaw, her pointed gaze.

"Okay," she said.

Joe's breath caught. "Okay?"

She stiffened her spine and steeled her gaze. "Part-time, mornings only, while Alexa is in school. And only four days a week. I'll need a day to catch up on journal work."

Was he hearing this right? Was this a yes? "So, you'll do it? Work at the clinic?"

She repeated her terms, slowly and deliberately. "Just until your shoulder is better. Or the town council hires a permanent doctor. No promises, Joe. Okay?"

He nodded slowly, deliberately. "Okay, Lily," he repeated in a soft voice, as if speaking too loudly might make her change her mind. "No promises. For either of us."

Joe used his teeth to tug his glove off, then fished the clinic keys from his jacket pocket with his good arm. It was cold and dark outside, making his breath crystallize into tiny, misty clouds. Starting early on his first day of working at the clinic would give him some time to get his thoughts and the space organized. It also meant he was the only soul in sight on Main Street, where the Twin Creeks Community Clinic sat in an old-fashioned shopping center, tucked between a hardware store and a vacuum repair shop.

His cold, numb fingers nearly fumbled the key. His injured shoulder was still stabilized in a sling, making everyday tasks difficult. But this was a temporary hassle. As soon as the roads were clear after Winter Storm Isabella, he had visited an orthopedic clinic in Billings and gotten good news. The snowmobile accident had badly wrenched his shoulder, but he didn't need surgery. With a few weeks' rest, he should be fully healed and ready to work at full capacity.

He jiggled the key into the door lock and was surprised when the knob turned freely in his hand. The door swung open to reveal a waiting room already full of people. Joe froze and scanned the room. Two elderly women in floral dresses and matching ballerina buns sat shoulder to shoulder on the couch. A lean, pale man in green rubber wading boots sat in the chair beside them, fidgeting with his winter wool hat. A young mother had properly commandeered the only rocking chair in the room and was rocking a small dozing infant. A middle-aged woman who wore her blend of black-and-gray hair in a long braid was the only person not inspecting him from head to toe. She was too busy working furiously at a knitting project that sprawled across her lap.

As surprised as Joe was to find his predawn waiting room already packed with patients, they seemed only curious at his appearance. Time stood still for a moment as everyone except the knitting lady stopped what they were doing to study him.

One of the elderly ladies squinted at him, then leaned close to the other, shouting in her ear. "Look at that, Ruth. He looks just like one of them TV doctors."

The other woman startled, perhaps from a nap. "What?" she shouted.

"Oh, never mind," the first woman groused.

"Um...hello," Joe said, trying to recover. "How did y'all get in the office?"

The knitting woman didn't look up. "With the key, of course."

"And what key would that be?" So far as Joe knew, only he and the mayor had keys to the clinic.

"The key that Dr. Smith kept under the front doormat, of course." *Click-click, click-click*. "Sometimes Dr. Smith went out on house calls, or needed to help if one of his mares was delivering breech. He left a key so folks could let themselves in and be comfortable till he made it back to the clinic."

Joe nodded, trying to take in so much foreign information all at once. "I see. But um, the clinic doesn't usually open until nine, right?"

"That's right." *Click-click, click-click*. "We'll wait."

"All right, then," Joe said. "See you soon, I guess."

There went any plans he had for getting organized before work. It was impossible to focus on anything besides the steady drone of chatter coming from the waiting room.

He might as well get his workday started. Maybe if he started early, he could close a little early, too. This was his first time leaving Daisy alone at home since they had moved to Twin Creeks. He already missed her steady presence by his side.

Joe returned to the waiting room and introduced himself as the new doctor for the community. "At least for a short while as your town council continues to search for a permanent replacement." The knitting woman snorted to herself but didn't look up from her work. He wasn't really sure what that meant, so he refocused on the expectant faces looking his way. "So then, who's first?"

Everyone in the waiting room cast glances at each other with a puzzled expression, as though he had just spoken in a foreign language.

He tried again. "I mean, does anyone have an appointment?"

No one raised their hand or spoke up.

"Okay, who was here first?"

The elderly ladies who looked a lot like sisters just kept beaming big smiles his way. He doubted they heard much of what he said. The young man in the green waders thought that the knitting lady got there before him, but the mother was sure that he had been there first because he'd held her diaper bag while she got the baby out of her car. Soon, they were all talking at once, the din becoming a cacophony of voices until someone shouted, "This isn't how it's done!"

It was the knitting lady again, of course. "Dr. Smith always saw the sickest person first." Her tone held an edge of exasperation, as if this should be perfectly obvious to Joe.

And it did make sense. If you were going to operate a medical clinic without appointments, triaging the walk-ins based on the severity of their illness or injury made sense.

"That's a good idea." *But an appointment system would be better.* "Does anyone have a fever?"

The young mother raised her hand. "My baby woke up feverish this morning and won't nurse."

The knitting woman clucked in sympathy. "He's probably teething, poor thing."

"All right. One fever. Does anyone have a serious injury, shortness of breath, chest pain?"

No one ventured a hand or spoke up. Joe did not like this makeshift system. He was basically asking his patients to triage themselves. That was dangerous because heart attacks could feel like indigestion. A stroke could be confused with a headache. There was too much risk of making a mistake.

He checked his watch. Another hour until the clinic officially opened and Lily would show up for her first shift. He desperately hoped she hadn't changed her mind. He needed someone with her expertise to decide who needed urgent care before the others.

Joe took one last look around the room. Other than the tall man who was a little pale, everyone seemed to be in decent shape.

Joe led the young mother and her baby to the larger of his two exam rooms. Once the blizzard had cleared and the streets of Twin Creeks were drivable again, Joe had spent some time at the clinic getting to know his new workspace. The community clinic was poised at an interesting crossroads between modern conveniences and old-world sentimentality. There were old, faded posters showing various aspects of human anatomy, and glass jars filled with cotton balls and tongue depressors. Peeling linoleum tiles that should have been replaced a decade ago were topped by a surprisingly modern surgical table that could be risen or lowered to Joe's perfect height. It concerned him that Dr. Smith had felt the need to order a surgical table—what kind of cases had the old doctor seen that made that seem like a necessary purchase?

There were also cameras positioned at various points in the room, along with a smattering of microphones built into the walls and added to the surgical table. Joe knew these were a recent investment in the clinic, thanks to the town council. They had signed a contract with a telehealth company that specialized in connecting rural medical clinics with medical specialists all over North America using state-of-the-art, on-demand telehealth equipment. All Joe had to do was press a button on the wall and he was instantly connected with a trained dispatcher who would arrange a virtual consultation with the right specialist for his case.

The baby's ears were clear, but she had plenty of chest and nasal congestion to confirm his suspicions.

"Looks like a run-of-the-mill winter cold," he assured the young mother. "Just give her plenty of fluids and run a humidifier in her room. Maybe some antihistamines for the drainage so she can sleep. She'll be right as rain in a day or two."

He handed baby Mabel back to her mother, who settled

the baby on her hip. "So do you have her medication in stock or will you send her prescription to the pharmacy?"

"She doesn't need medication," Joe assured her. "It's just a little virus that will run its course."

"But Dr. Smith always...."

"Mrs. Hawthorne, the protocol for viral rhinitis that is characterized by copious amounts of clear drainage is best treated initially with an antihistamine that has anticholinergic side effects. Now, if it turns out that Mabel has viral-induced rhinitis that is refractory to an antihistamine, I might consider an intranasal ipratropium bromide zero point zero six percent. But at this point, I do not believe Mabel needs that intervention."

The mother's brow furrowed in confusion. "What?"

"It's just a cold, ma'am."

"But she has a fever!"

"Completely normal for viral rhin..." The expression on the mother's face stopped him. "It's normal for a virus. I promise you that Mabel will be just fine."

But instead of looking reassured, Mabel's mom looked angry. "So, you're not going to help my baby?"

"I *am* helping your baby."

"By denying her medicine? When she has a fever?" Mabel began fussing on her hip. "Ugh, you've been no help at all..." She flicked his chest with her finger, right where his name was embroidered in navy blue thread above the breast pocket. *Dr. Chambers.*

As she stomped out of the office, she passed Lily, who was heading in.

"Hey there, Sophia!" Lily said with a big smile. "How's that sweet baby Mabel today?"

"Practically dead, thanks to him!" Sophia indicated Joe with an indignant chin thrust. She headed down the hallway, then paused to turn back and shout, "And I thought a California doctor would have a better tan!"

Lily's mouth gaped as she watched Sophia leave. She turned back to Joe, her eyebrows arched impossibly high. "What did you do?"

"Nothing!"

"Well, I suggest you do *something* next time," she said, her tone full of mirth. She stepped aside to reveal the elderly sisters behind her. "Joe, meet Betty and Ruth, twin sisters who are here for their annual physical. Which exam room would you like to use?"

"I can see them here," Joe said. It was the larger of the two rooms and included the adjustable surgical table along with the telehealth equipment. Not that he expected to need all of that, but the room was much better equipped and comfortable.

Joe was able to tease out their health history in bits and pieces. Betty was the elder sister by two whole minutes. She was talkative and funny but blind as a bat. Ruth, the younger sister, was hearing impaired to the point of deafness, but still able to see well enough to drive their ancient sedan to church and back.

"Between the two of us, we make a whole person!" Betty cackled, and he couldn't help but laugh along.

"So, what brought you in today?" Joe poised his pen over a legal pad. It seemed a terribly unprofessional way to record his patients' visit, but the clinic lacked the tablet computers he was used to using in LA.

They were there for their annual physical. Betty

leaned in and asked, in a conspiratorial whisper, if she might get an eye exam done so she could get her driver's license. She cast a sly glance at her sister, who seemed blissfully unaware of the conversation.

"Of course," Joe said, eager to recover from the bad start he had had with Mabel's mother. Betty read the chart perfectly, which was surprising considering her thick eyeglasses, but she didn't hesitate once.

"Practically twenty/twenty," he told her as he signed off on her DMV form.

Just then, he heard Lily shout for help.

"Ladies, could you give me a moment?" He passed the vision form to Betty, who looked like she had just been handed a fabulous prize.

Joe dashed to the waiting room, an uncomfortable surge of adrenaline making his heart rate soar. There had been an unmistakable edge of panic in Lily's voice.

Joe found Lily in the waiting room, crouched in front of the tall, pale man and taking his pulse.

"Joe, why is Luke just sitting here? He's white as a sheet!"

Joe was at a loss for words. "He was fine just a few minutes ago." But was that true? The man had been pale ever since he arrived. But since the man hadn't spoken up when Joe was doing triage, Joe thought that was just the way he looked.

"Sir, what brought you in today?" It was a question he should have asked a long time ago.

The man turned his leg out, revealing a knife handle protruding from the back of his boot. He looked up with an embarrassed grin. "I borrowed my wife's utility knife to scrape some tar off my boot." He shook his head with despair. "She's gonna kill me."

Lily plucked Joe's penlight from his lab coat pocket, then peered into the man's boot. "Would you look at that? You've been quietly bleeding to death in your boot."

Joe rubbed his brow. "You've been stabbed? And you didn't say anything?"

"You asked if anyone had an emergency." He glanced down at his boot. "And this knife wasn't going nowhere."

Joe groaned with frustration. He and Lily helped Luke to the back room for an X-ray.

"Oh, thank God," Lily whispered as she scanned the films.

Joe didn't have to ask what she meant. The knife was short and stubby and had managed to miss Luke's bone. And with the injury in his lower leg, they didn't have to worry about damage to a major artery.

"I'll numb him," Lily said. She went off to prepare a dose of lidocaine while Joe prepared the supplies they would need to remove the utility knife and clean and repair Luke's injury.

Luke watched the entire operation with keen interest. When Joe was done, he turned his leg this way and that, appreciating the vertical line of sutures that ran from midcalf to his ankle.

"That's so cool, Doc. Hope it leaves a Franko scar!" He chuckled and hopped off the table, his gait awkward from walking with one foot in a wading boot and the other barefoot.

Joe watched him leave, shaking his head. "He didn't think it was an emergency..."

Lily was eyeing him from head to toe.

"What?" he said. It was clear she didn't like what she saw. He couldn't imagine why. He was wearing his usual doctor attire. Italian leather loafers, pressed wool pants, a navy blue dress shirt and a gray-and-blue tie to match.

"Nice threads," she said. "Are you the keynote speaker for the—what did you call us?—the Middle-of-Nowhere Medical Conference?"

"Hey," he said. "I already said I was… Wait, what's that sound?"

Lily stopped and listened, her head cocked. "I don't know. But it's coming from your other exam room."

Joe headed that way with Lily close on his heels. He paused to knock before entering but then they both heard an angry whining sound, like someone was standing on a cat's tail. All pleasantries aside, Joe flung the door open and discovered things were not the way he had left them.

The surgical table was the source of the angry whine. The head of the table was tilted as high as it would go, nearly five feet in the air, and the foot side was down almost to the floor. Ruth, the petite half-deaf sister, had slid down the table and landed in a little ball of Queen Anne's lace and sensible shoes. Betty was frantically trying to keep Ruth from falling onto the floor, but Ruth seemed rather oblivious. She just smiled serenely as Betty tugged on her arms.

Joe tried to make sense of the crazy scene. Why was this happening? The table was perfectly fine when he left. Then he looked down and noticed that Betty was standing on the floor pedal that raised and lowered the head of the table. She clearly didn't realize what she was doing, too focused on trying to keep her sister in a semi upright position.

Lily rushed past him. She helped to get Ruth back on her feet, but by now she was so dizzy, she could hardly stand by herself. But the table's motor continued to grind on.

"Your foot," Joe yelled to Betty. She beamed back at him. "You have to move your foot off the pedal!" Joe hollered.

"My foot?" she repeated, confused.

Exasperated, Joe hooked an arm around her waist and lifted her tiny frame off the foot pedal. The grinding, screeching sound came to a merciful end.

"Oh, my," Betty said, smoothing her skirt. "I believe your table may be broken, Doctor."

"Thank you," Joe said through gritted teeth. "I will be sure to look into that."

Lily's mouth was a tight, thin line, but she was having a difficult time suppressing her smile. Somehow, they managed to get through the health concerns of the sisters. Joe wrote a round of prescriptions for both and then they walked them out to the waiting room.

Lily took one last look through their paperwork before they left. "Wait a second—what's this?"

Betty cast her eyes downward.

"Joe, did you sign this form?"

Joe peeked over her shoulder. "Sure. She passed her vision exam with flying colors."

Lily frowned at Betty. "Nice try, Betty." Then she ripped the form in half.

"Damn it," Betty swore under her breath. For some

reason, she took it out on Joe. "Dr. Smith left some pretty big shoes to fill, young man! I'm not sure you're up to the task."

He stood there helplessly. "What happened?"

"Betty's legally blind, Joe. She memorized the vision test years ago."

The sisters left and Joe felt like he could finally exhale. He dropped into a chair opposite Lily's desk as Lily flipped the closed sign for their lunch break.

"Well, let's see," Joe said, using his fingers to tick off his list. "That's two patients who hate me and one I almost killed. Not the most auspicious start."

Lily settled into her chair. "Aw, don't take it too personally. Twin Creeks is a special place, Joe. Folks are going to need a little time to get used to the change."

Special place. Where had he heard that before? Oh, yes, his mentor had told him that when she had exiled him to the American northwest.

Lily zipped open her insulated lunch bag and laid out her lunch. "Trust me, Joe. Folks around here just need a little time to get used to your face. Before you know it, the waiting room will be standing room only."

CHAPTER SIX

Joe reclined on the couch in the clinic's waiting room, bouncing a rubber ball against the wall.

Bounce-bang-bounce. Bounce-bang-bounce.

"How does our morning look, Lily?"

Lily didn't need to open their appointment scheduler to know the answer. "The schedule is wide-open, Joe."

"So, no appointments at all? Not a single patient on the books?"

"Nope."

"And how many people are in the waiting room?"

"Including us? Two."

Bounce-bang-bounce.

"So, just to recap, we have no patients today. Just like yesterday. And the day before. And last week."

Lily rolled her eyes and closed the filing cabinet. It had been like this for over a week, ever since Joe's disastrous first day. Even though Winter Storm Isabella was long gone and the roads were clear and dry, the clinic remained stubbornly empty. Except for one teenage boy who had brought his goat in for an X-ray because the veterinarian's machine was down.

Joe was flummoxed but she had a pretty good idea why the lobby was empty. Joe's first day had been…

less than spectacular. There was no doubt in her mind that word had spread all over town at warp speed. So now everyone was avoiding the big-city doc and his big-city ways.

"Look on the bright side," she chided Joe. "With all the downtime, your shoulder should be healed in no time!"

Lily had been thrilled to hear that Joe didn't need surgery. But now she wondered how long she should stick around the clinic. Being alone with Joe had been terrible for her peace of mind. Without a steady stream of patients and problems, she had way too much time on her hands to wonder where he had come from and what his story was. He was friendly enough when it came to clinic business, but otherwise, he kept his nose buried in a book, endlessly preparing for that oncology fellowship he wanted so much. She knew all about that fellowship—it was all he ever wanted to talk about—but he was frustratingly vague about his personal life. Was he being obtuse? Or had he really built his entire life around medicine and oncology?

Eventually, she did what any modern woman would—she checked his social media. Joe didn't post often, but when he did, it was clear he lived by his "work hard, play harder" mantra. His social media was filled with photos of medical school achievements, but just as many showed him enjoying his downtime—ski trips, boating adventures and bonfires on the beach. In every picture, there was a pretty girl on his arm or in his lap, but never the same girl twice.

Honestly, it was a relief to know that he wasn't the

committed type. Somehow, over the past few weeks of working together, she had managed to develop the teeniest little...what? *Crush* seemed too strong of a word. *Infatuation* was more like it. And who could blame her? He was handsome and charming and just a little mysterious. It gave her understimulated mind plenty to think about on her long drives back and forth to the clinic. A just-right blend of angst and excitement that added an edge of surprise to a life that was otherwise pretty dull.

But she needed to stop playing these mind games with herself. Nothing would ever become of her little infatuation. Even if Joe didn't spend every minute of his day plotting his escape from Twin Creeks, there was no way she could let herself fall for him. Losing Connor had broken her into a million tiny pieces, and it had taken her most of the past five years to put herself back together again. There was just no way she could let herself fall for Joe—or anyone, really—and risk having her heart broken like that again.

But it was also a good reason not to spend too long working at the clinic. She wasn't worried about falling head over heels for Joe, but she didn't need to indulge in romantic fantasies that would just leave her feeling lonelier when he left. Still, she'd rather be lonely than head over heels in love with Joe and terrified that any day, he could be snatched away without warning.

Lily checked her watch—an hour till they closed for lunch. She had time to run an errand or two before she needed to pick Alexa up from her morning preschool program.

She closed the file on her desk and pushed away from

the counter. "Well, if you don't need anything, I think I'll head out a little early."

Bounce-bang-bounce.

"That's fine."

Lily busied herself finding her purse and winter coat. It was cloudy and cold, and the dim light was making the waiting room look sad and dingy.

She paused at the door, her gloves in hand. "You want the lights on?"

"No need."

Bounce-bang-bounce.

"Okay, then. See you tomorrow."

Maybe it was the low light that made her pause a moment. This wasn't the Joe she had seen on social media, full of confidence and a passion for adventure. This version of Joe looked a little…lost. Maybe he had a revolving door of girlfriends in California, but here in Twin Creeks, he was all alone. And the entire town snubbing him wasn't helping matters at all.

The doorknob felt solid in her hand. Joe's reputation in Twin Creeks wasn't her problem. At least, it didn't have to be. All she had promised was to help at the clinic until his shoulder was healed. In just a few weeks, he would be fine and she could return to her simple, sane life.

Bounce-bang-bounce.

She let out a soft sigh, her gaze drifting downward. It wasn't that simple, and she knew it. After Connor died, she had been all alone in the world. And then Jennifer had offered her a home and friendship in Twin Creeks. Who would do that for Joe?

Joe's head snapped up when she groaned out loud. "You okay?"

Dammit! I hope I don't regret this.

"You like pie, Joe?"

"What?"

"Pie. It's a dessert item with crust and some kind of filling. Sometimes fruit…sometimes custard…"

He rolled to a sitting position. "I know what pie is. And yes, I like it."

Lily silently kissed her uncomplicated life goodbye. "Well, come on, then."

"Where?" But he was already grabbing his coat.

"The Snowy Owl Café. Best pie in town 'cuz it's the *only* pie in town."

Joe closed the door behind them. He started to slip the key into his pocket, but then stopped to look at Lily.

"Don't bother."

"Right," he said before returning the key under the mat.

Lily parked her truck in front of a quaint log cabin-style building with a snow-dusted roof and twinkling fairy lights strung along the eaves. Joe followed Lily up the wooden steps to the front porch of the café, pausing to check out the intricately carved Snowy Owl that hung over the café's wood door.

"I guess Twin Creeks can be kind of charming," Joe said. "Even if that charm is covered in snow and ice."

Lily laughed and led him into the foyer where they hung up their jackets and hats. A lean woman with silver threaded through her hair recognized Lily and crossed the café to give her a huge hug. "Lily! It's so good to see you."

Lily returned the hug, then introduced the woman as Denise, owner of The Snowy Owl Café.

Denise shook Joe's hand politely. "Pleased to meet you, Dr. Chambers. I've, um—" she suppressed a smile "—heard a lot about you."

Lily smiled, too, in a way that made Joe doubt this was a ringing endorsement of his reputation.

After they ordered, Lily's gaze shifted to something happening behind him. She chuckled at what she saw.

"What?"

"The Twin Creeks gossip line has been officially activated."

Joe glanced over his shoulder and caught sight of the barista, her gestures lively and animated as she pointed in his direction, her eyes lighting up with whatever story she was telling.

"Don't look now!" Lily hissed.

"Why not?"

"Because they're talking about you!"

"Why would they be talking about me?"

"Because that's what Twin Creeks does, Joe. We eat pie and talk about people."

He studied her face like a detective. "And this is good?"

"It could be. Or it could make things a lot worse. All depends on what they're saying."

"I don't get it."

"Listen, Joe." She leaned in, her eyes locking on to his with an intense gaze. "The only way we're going to start filling the clinic with patients is if Twin Creeks accepts you—both as a resident and as their doctor."

"I don't see how that's going to happen if no one comes to the clinic."

"Exactly. That's why everyone needs to know who you are," she said. "More importantly, they need to *like* who you are. You could make a difference by fitting in a bit better—maybe ditch the tie and lab coat. Dr. Smith always looked like he came straight from his barn to the clinic. People felt like they were visiting their neighbor, not a scary doctor."

Joe frowned, mulling over her advice. His lab coat was more than just a uniform; it was also a badge of honor, marking his place in the medical hierarchy and reflecting the sacrifices he'd made to earn it. Of course, there was no way she could know that these symbols of status were also his consolation prizes. His early-onset cancer risk meant he would never have a wedding or hear a chubby toddler call him "Daddy." So he clung to trophies like his lab coat, his convertible and off-duty adventures as a source of solace and validation in a world where he would always be alone.

"So that's it? I dress more like a rancher and suddenly I'm the greatest thing since sliced bread?"

She sipped her coffee. "Probably not."

"What else, then?"

Lily set her fork at the edge of her plate and steepled her fingers.

"Folks around here are hardy, prideful people who try not to burden others with their problems. So, if you're going to help them, you have to…you know, show you care about them."

"Well, of course I care about them. Isn't that what doctors do? Take care of people when they're sick or injured?"

"I'm not talking about taking care of their bodies, Joe. I'm talking about caring for *them*."

Joe felt his brow furrow. "I don't get it."

"Take Mabel's mom. She came in with her sick baby, right?"

"Right. But Mabel just had a cold. Once I ruled out allergies and bacterial infection, I correctly recommended plenty of rest and a humidifier to keep her comfortable."

"But her mother wanted medication, right?"

"Right. And I didn't prescribe any antibiotics because Mabel didn't need them."

"What made you think she wanted antibiotics?"

"Because she…" Joe was about to say *asked for antibiotics* but then he realized that wasn't true. She had just asked for medicine.

"Joe, Mabel gets frequent ear infections because she has acid reflux. She's been on an H2 blocker for a few months, which has helped. But sometimes her reflux flares and causes her to develop symptoms of a cold. Dr. Smith prescribed extra acid blockers when she's symptomatic, to try to prevent an ear infection."

Joe frowned. "I took Mabel's medical history before the exam. Her mother didn't mention any of this." Joe felt his patience fraying at this misunderstanding with Mabel's mother. "She should have told me. It's important to consider familial input when choosing a course of action for your patients."

"Mabel's mom didn't want to give you *familial input*. She wanted to tell you how Mabel started crawling last week and how her fine blond hair is finally growing in. Then she wanted to tell you she spent all day making homemade baby food and, oh, by the way, I think her acid reflux might be flaring." Lily cocked her head. "See how that works?"

Joe groaned and leaned back in the booth. "Good grief, Lily. If I have to play this cat-and-mouse game with every patient, appointments will take forever!"

"They'll take exactly as long as they need to take."

Joe considered Lily's suggestions. Sure, he could be a little more social—that wouldn't hurt. Ditching the lab coat and tailored suit? He didn't really want to do that but whatever. He could make it work.

But trying to forge an emotional connection with every patient? That was way outside his comfort zone. It was why he had chosen medicine as his career. Decisions were made on data and studies, not hunches or feelings.

"Listen, Lily. I *do* care about my patients, but at the end of the day, they are still my *patients*. I have to maintain emotional distance so I can be an effective doctor. After all, when we care *too* much, it can make us want to do the easy thing, instead of the right thing."

Lily opened her mouth to protest, but then Denise reappeared at their table to take their order. She was about to leave when she turned back. "Hey, I guess you two will be taking over the blood drive this year?"

Joe noticed how Lily's shoulders tensed and her gaze faltered. "Oh," Lily said, her voice wavering. "I hadn't thought about that when I agreed to work at the clinic."

Joe's gaze pinged back and forth between Lily and Denise. "Blood drive?"

Denise set down her coffeepot, happy to explain. "Well, Twin Creeks organizes a blood drive twice a year—winter and summer—to make sure that our blood bank is stocked for the year. Dr. Smith was a genius at getting all the tourists to donate. Now that he's gone—" she cast her gaze upward "—I guess it'll be up to you and Lily to run the show."

Lily fiddled nervously with the hem of her sleeve, avoiding Joe's gaze. This was the first time Joe had seen her look so vulnerable, and his concern deepened as he wondered what could be troubling her.

As soon as Denise left, Joe leaned toward Lily. "What's wrong?"

Lily glanced out the window. "Nothing. It's fine. I just hadn't expected that the blood drive might be part of my job."

"You scared of blood or something?"

She rewarded his lame joke with a half smile. "No, I'm fine." But clearly, that wasn't true.

All his resolve to maintain emotional distance vanished in an instant. Lily's distress about this blood drive stirred a deep concern within him, and he needed to understand what was wrong.

He ducked his head so she couldn't avoid his gaze. "Lily, what's up?"

She grabbed a napkin and began twisting it in her

hands. "Connor and I planned a winter wedding so we could take our honeymoon in Twin Creeks. We both loved skiing, and Twin Creeks has some of the best skiing in the northwestern US. We were here for the first blood drive and we were two of those tourists Dr. Smith roped into donating blood. We didn't count on it being such a huge community event. The town council provides a huge pancake breakfast and there's all kinds of activities for the kids. What should be a mundane donation event turned out to be so much fun. We just fell in love with Twin Creeks and from then on, we spent every anniversary here."

There was so much emotion in her voice and the story was so sad. Joe almost felt like he was intruding as she shared her story.

"There's a dance, too," she confided, her voice just barely above a whisper. "About a week after the blood drive, the town hosts The Healthy Heart Gala, which is a fancy—or at least fancy for Twin Creeks—charity dance where we raise money for heart disease research."

Sweet mercy, were those tears trembling on her eyelashes? *No, no, Lily, please don't cry.* He wouldn't be able to take that. People cried when they were upset—he had seen plenty of that when he had to deliver difficult news to patients and their families. But that was his cue to escape those hospital rooms, leaving the emotional fallout to those who knew what to do. Like social workers and chaplains.

But sitting here in this little café, with the scent of freshly ground coffee and sweet pie hanging in the air, he was surprised as hell to realize he didn't want to escape Lily and her tears. He wanted to be the reason she didn't cry anymore.

Get a grip, he silently scolded himself.

Lily was a vulnerable widow with a young daughter. The last thing she needed was him complicating her life with signals he had no right to send. He had nothing to offer her—nothing lasting, nothing real. Just the brief time he'd spend in Twin Creeks. And if the universe had any mercy at all, that time would be over soon.

But there had to be *something* he could do to help Lily through this emotional event. Some small action that could make life a little better for her.

"Let me handle the blood drive, Lily. I'm sure I can do that on my own."

Her eyes flickered with hope, and he felt certain she would take him up on his offer. But then her brow furrowed, and she gazed back down at the table. "I can't do that, Joe."

"Why not?"

"Because next to our high school football season, the Healthy Heart blood drive and gala is *the* town event of the year. *Everyone* will be there. Which makes it the perfect time for Twin Creeks to meet their new doctor. And I should be there to help."

He couldn't believe she was willing to put herself into such an emotionally loaded event just for him. There was no reason for it—she barely knew him.

"Okay," he agreed, reaching across the table to clasp her hand. Wanting to give her strength and let her know that she wouldn't be alone.

But what about the gala? The blood drive he could

handle. It was predictable and medical and completely in his wheelhouse. But the gala was something else entirely. That was dancing and dresses and elegant flutes of champagne.

Unbidden, an image of Lily in a sexy dress, her body pressed against his as they danced, came to mind. He could practically feel the warmth of her hand in his, see the flecks of gold in her eyes as she gazed up at him. Suddenly, he was flooded with an aching desire that left no doubt in his mind—he had no business taking his colleague to the gala.

He swallowed hard. "But if it's all the same to you, I'd like to skip the dance. That is, if you agree."

Lily's expression remained pleasant and neutral, but for just a split second, Joe thought he saw a shadow cloud her eyes. It was there and gone so quickly, he wasn't sure if he had imagined it.

She picked up her fork and gave him a brilliant smile. "Oh, no, we don't need to do the dance. Absolutely not!" Then she shifted her attention to her pie, and Joe wondered if he had said something wrong.

"Well, good," he said, clearing his throat and picking his fork back up. "I'm glad we're on the same page!"

What a relief. He had found a way to help Lily through a difficult situation without risking any sticky, confusing emotional stuff. He should feel triumphant, really, at managing all this without losing control of the situation.

Yet, he didn't feel in control at all.

CHAPTER SEVEN

"Forty-eight...forty-nine...fifty!"

Joe rounded the corner just in time to see a young woman in yoga pants and a ponytail finish her last jumping jack before bending over to lean her hands on her thighs to rest. She was panting hard, but she looked pleased. Joe paused, his hands full of supplies, trying to make sense of the scene.

They were in one of the many classrooms at the community center, where he and Lily had arrived before dawn to set up for the blood drive. With assistance from The Healthy Heart Association, they'd transformed a craft room into a passable temporary donation site. Four recliners were set up for donors to relax in during their donation, but only three were occupied—because the fourth donor was busy doing jumping jacks.

Lily was perched on a rolling stool next to the empty recliner. "Awesome!" she told the young woman. "You ready to get started?"

The young woman had bright blue eyes that seemed to sparkle. She seemed incredibly energetic.

"Almost! Just twenty push-ups to go."

She got right to it, dropping down and bracing her

hands on the floor. Joe grabbed a rolling stool and joined Lily.

"What's going on?" he asked under his breath.

"Joe, meet Maggie O'Hara. She owns the fitness studio on Main Street."

"Pleased to meet...oh, you don't have to do that," Joe said.

But somehow Maggie managed to balance herself on one hand so she could shake his hand with the other.

"Maggie's getting ready for her donation," Lily said. As if that explained anything.

Joe's eyebrow arched. "With push-ups?"

"Helps with blood flow!" Maggie panted.

"That's very conscientious, Maggie, but you don't really need to do that. The Healthy Heart Association just recommends that you have a light meal and hydrate well before..."

Joe trailed off as he caught the look that Lily gave him. He was doing it again—focusing on rules and protocols instead of what his patient might need. He gave Lily a baleful smile.

"But you know, I'm sure a few push-ups won't hurt."

"Twenty!" Maggie huffed. Somehow she bounced catlike from a prone position on the floor back to her feet, brushing her hands off when she landed. "So, you're the new fancy doc I've been hearing about."

It was more of a statement than a question.

"Fancy? No. But yeah, I'm Dr. Joe Chambers."

Maggie gave him the once-over. "You work out much, Dr. Chambers?"

"Sure, when I have time."

"You should stop by the studio. I think you'd love my six-week Build-a-Booty Boot Camp series. Good for flat butts."

Joe fought off the urge to look at his backside. "Thanks for the tip, Maggie. I just might do that. So, you think you're ready to donate?"

Maggie paused and put two fingers on her wrist, checking her pulse. "I think so."

Lily started snapping on a pair of latex gloves while Maggie settled in the chair. Joe picked up his box of supplies, preparing to restock before he helped the next donor.

"Thanks for being patient, you guys. I just wanted to make sure I didn't get any heart flutters during the donation."

Joe froze and turned back, his gaze immediately meeting Lily's. She looked concerned but kept her gaze steady and calm.

"Flutters?" Lily asked. Her tone was light, but Joe could hear the undercurrent of worry.

Maggie waved her off casually. "It's nothing, really. Only happens when I go for a run."

Joe felt a surge of alarm. He couldn't let this slide. He began firing off a series of medical questions about the flutters, but the more he pressed, the more anxious Maggie became, her earlier ease disappearing.

Lily shot Joe a warning look—a reminder of what she'd tried to tell him back at The Snowy Owl. Patients weren't just their symptoms; they were people, with lives and fears that couldn't be reduced to medical charts.

Realizing he needed a softer approach, Joe shifted

tactics. Maggie was passionate about fitness—maybe he could use that to get her to the clinic. "You know," he began, his tone more casual, "we could use some help designing fitness programs for patients recovering from surgery or illness. Do you think you could come by the clinic and talk about the classes you teach?"

Maggie lit up, thrilled at the idea of helping Twin Creeks stay fit. "I'd love that!"

After she left, Lily turned to him with a playful grin. "Not bad, Doc. But you know she's never going to agree to testing unless you take that booty class, right?"

Joe groaned, realizing she was probably right.

Lily shrugged. "Think of it as your Twin Creeks souvenir."

"Does it come with a T-shirt that says *I went to Twin Creeks and all I got was this lousy booty*?"

"More like *Welcome to Twin Creeks. You Must Be Lost*."

"Now that's a T-shirt I would buy!"

Lily shook her head with an amused smile. "I don't know, Doc. I still think Twin Creeks is gonna grow on you."

The rest of the afternoon passed with few complications, as a steady stream of donors came and went, many of them curious about the new doctor they'd heard so much about. Joe and Lily crossed paths repeatedly, her quiet encouragement keeping him grounded as the endless small talk frayed his nerves. Lily seemed to know nearly everyone in Twin Creeks, and the townspeople were thrilled to see her at an event she had avoided for so long. Though she remained poised and gracious all day, Joe noticed the shadows behind her smiles—the way her lips would fall into a soft frown when she thought no one was watching.

Joe tried to stay focused on his tasks, but Lily's quiet struggles gnawed at him. She barely knew him, yet he couldn't shake the urge to ease the sadness that seemed to cling to her all day.

When a lull came in the donor line, he saw his chance.

"Hey, I'm gonna step out for a minute, if that's okay."

"Sure." She looked up from the computer where she was updating their records, giving him a soft smile that made him forget, just for a moment, the exhaustion of the day.

Joe headed to the recreation room, guided by the rich aroma of coffee, bacon and sweet treats. He filled a large mug with strong coffee and doctored it just the way she did at the clinic—two creams and one sugar. When he returned, Lily was alone at the sign-in desk, her attention on the paperwork. Quietly, he placed the coffee next to her elbow.

"What's this for?" she asked, glancing up.

"Just something to make your day a little better."

Her wry smile faded into a slight frown. "It's that obvious, huh?"

"Not really. You're doing great."

"I thought I was holding it together pretty well. But I can't deny that being here stirs up a lot of memories for me."

Joe paused, then spoke softly. "I once overheard a hospital social worker tell a patient that grief is just all the love we didn't get to give. So maybe feeling sad is just...another way of loving."

She looked at him, her eyes softening. "I like that, Joe." Her smile grew warmer. "I'm so glad you're here."

Before he knew what was happening, she stepped into his arms, surprising him. Instinctively, he wrapped her in his embrace, felt her head rest against his chest. A rush of emotion flooded through him—feelings he'd long since buried now unleashed by the simple, undeniable comfort of having her tucked against his body. The way she smelled, the way she fit so perfectly in his arms, was undoing him piece by piece.

Then she stepped away and it took every ounce of control he had to stuff those emotions back into their box. She gave him a look that was just a beat longer than it needed to be. Nothing dramatic or obvious. But enough to make him wonder if she was catching feelings, too.

Don't look at me like that, Lily. I'm not the guy. Trust me.

Joe took a step back, needing to put some distance between them, forcing himself to get his head on straight. He quickly rearranged his features into the neutral expression he'd perfected over the years. He wasn't always as in control of his emotions as he wanted to be, but he had mastered the art of making it look like he was.

But Lily was different. Her face was an open book, her heart's truths playing out for the world to see. She was honest and vulnerable in a way he couldn't afford to be. She didn't live her life with an invisible clock ticking down her fate. And if she knew he did, she wouldn't be looking at him like that.

"Well, we'd better get back to work, right?" he said, his voice thick with words unsaid.

Lily held his gaze for a few more seconds, searching for something he knew he could never give. Her expression faltered slightly, but she quickly recovered and turned back to the task at hand.

Joe threw himself into the work, grateful for the distraction. The final wave of donors kept them both busy, and the familiar routine of boxing up supplies to return to the Healthy Heart Association helped him push his emotions aside.

But just when he thought he had regained control, he turned from stacking the totes to find Lily bent over the last one, snapping it shut. The brief, unintentional brush of her body against his—her backside grazing his thigh—sent a jolt through him. The suppressed desire he'd been holding back all day surged like a storm inside him, a force powerful enough to wreck both of their lives.

Lily spun around, and in an instant he knew his mask had fallen. She could see everything he was trying so hard to hide.

Their eyes met, and the air between them seemed to thicken as he felt a magnetic pull drawing them closer despite the unspoken barriers. Lily's soft gaze lingered, her lips parting slightly as if she was about to say something but couldn't find the words. Joe felt a dangerous awareness settling in his chest. He could see it in her, too—the way her breath hitched, her cheeks flushing with the same tension that gripped him. But her vulnerability shimmered just beneath the surface, forcing Joe to step back. He couldn't—wouldn't—cross that line. Not with her, not when she deserved so much more than the heartbreak he knew he'd bring.

"Mommy!"

Alexa's sudden cry startled Lily, making her jump as she spun to face her daughter. Alexa raced across the room, her hands overflowing with the artwork she had created during the children's activities. Joe watched as Lily showered her with delighted praise, admiring each piece like a treasure.

The tension in Joe's chest slowly eased, his emotions settling. He was grateful for Alexa's interruption—it was a much-needed reminder of the boundaries he needed to maintain. The day's events had made that crystal clear. He had only wanted to support Lily through a tough event, but the depth of his attraction had blindsided him. From now on, things had to stay strictly professional.

"Mommy, what are you going to wear to the dance?" Alexa asked, her eyes wide with curiosity.

Lily smiled, gently smoothing her daughter's hair. "My pajamas, sweetheart. Because I'm staying home with you."

Alexa frowned. "But you have Dr. Joe now! You could go to the dance with him!"

Joe's pulse spiked as alarm bells rattled his core. Taking Lily to the gala was the *last* thing he needed. More space from Lily was what he needed to keep his head straight. But Alexa was looking up at him with those big, hopeful eyes. What could he possibly say to this adorable little girl? *No, I won't take your mom to the dance?* What would his next trick be—kicking puppies?

Of course, he could take Lily to the gala. He'd spent a lifetime giving beautiful women the night of their lives. He knew how to plan the perfect evening, full of romance and glamour, because that was *all* he had to give. A few dates, a little charm, nothing deeper.

He could do this for Lily, too. It felt right, in a way—giving her a night to remember at an event clouded by painful memories. He just had to keep his heart out of it. And make sure she did, too.

Lily gripped the steering wheel of her truck tightly as she navigated the familiar streets of Twin Creeks. Her heart was already pounding in anticipation of what lay ahead. She glanced over at Joe in the passenger seat. He was still talking to Denise on his cell phone, getting as many details as he could before they arrived on the scene of the accident.

It had been years since she had responded to a trauma call. Her old lettuce-hauler of a truck was a far cry from the state-of-the-art medical helicopter that used to whisk her between accidents and emergency rooms. She tried to stay focused on the road ahead of her, but she still felt haunted by memories of how her skills had failed her after Connor's death. Her hands felt clammy, and her breath came in short, shallow gasps as she tried to focus on the road.

The call for help had come in while she and Joe were working at the clinic. It was a week after the blood drive event and Joe and Lily had settled back into their clinic routine. Lily had recognized Denise's voice, the owner of the Snowy Owl Café, but she could barely understand what Denise was saying.

He won't open his eyes, Lily. I can't get him to open his damn eyes!

Denise had called emergency services, but there was no way of telling how long it would take for them to respond. So Joe and Lily had closed the clinic and were now speeding through Twin Creeks on their way to the quiet neighborhood where Denise and her husband, Matt, lived.

"We're almost there," Joe said, his voice calm and steady. He reached over and gave Lily a reassuring squeeze on the shoulder with his good arm. "Whatever happens next, Lily, remember that we're a team, okay? We'll handle this together."

Lily gave him a wan smile and tried to draw strength from his words. But they both knew the truth. Joe's shoulder injury meant that if there was any intensive hands-on work to do, it would fall to her. She wouldn't be able to sit on the sidelines this time and let her crew take over. Matt's life was literally in her hands.

Oh, please, let emergency services get there before we do.

They pulled up to a modest suburban home where Denise was waiting. She led them quickly to the backyard where Matt lay motionless. Denise frantically ran to his side to kneel beside him.

"Please, you have to help him!" Denise cried as they approached. Her eyes were wide with fear, and her hands shook as she reached for Matt's limp hand.

Joe knelt down, tunneling his focus on Matt. "Denise, I need you to step aside. We have to assess Matt's injuries."

Matt lay flat on his back, blood pooling around his head. A tall ladder was tipped over the border hedges to land in the snow. A rectangular chunk of ice in the snow told the story. Matt had been trying to clear an ice dam from his roof gutter when he fell.

Denise whimpered with fear and reluctantly let go of Matt's hand. Joe tugged his stethoscope from around his neck. "Lily, we need to assess his airway. Can you take a look?"

Lily's heart started hammering in her chest at the sight of all that blood around Matt's head. She felt that familiar cold dread creep up her legs to her torso and chest, as if her fear lived in the ground, just waiting to invade her in times of stress.

Move, Lily. Just get to Matt's side. You'll know what to do when you get there.

But her legs were like twin blocks of stone, refusing to move again. Her throat tightened with fear. This wasn't like the Shop-n-Go. Joe was injured now, and emergency services were nowhere to be found. If she wasn't able to help Matt, he might die. Her vision blurred for a moment, images of Connor's violent death flashing before her eyes.

"Lily!" Joe's voice was firm, commanding her attention. "You are the best person to help Matt right now. Just trust yourself. Like I do."

Lily gasped. *Trust.* Was that the missing piece of her life? Trust that the world was a safe place to raise her child. And trust that she still had the skills and mental toughness needed to work under crisis.

It was true. She hadn't believed in herself for a very long time. But Joe did. He *trusted* her. More importantly, he needed her.

"Okay." Lily swallowed hard and she walked stiff-legged to Matt's side. She dropped to her knees so hard, she knew she'd have angry purple bruises on her kneecaps the next morning. Her hands were unsteady as she checked Matt's airway.

She looked up to find Joe's steady gaze. "He's not breathing," she told him.

Joe swore under his breath. "And his pulse is weak and erratic." He reached up to cup his injured shoulder with his hand. "Lily, I don't trust my shoulder for something this important. You're gonna have to intubate him."

Joe had stopped wearing his sling to work, but he was not yet fully healed. Lily knew he was right—his weak shoulder was a huge risk right now.

A wave of nausea washed over Lily. Intubations were tricky and complex even for experienced medical professionals. Other than ongoing training to keep her nurse practitioner license current, she had barely touched a real patient for the past five years. Intubating a real patient with head trauma was nothing like working on a mannequin. She knew what she needed to do, but her panic was rising again, threatening to overwhelm her.

Joe's calm voice cut through the haze. "Lily, listen. I'm right here with you. You won't be alone. Just remember your training."

Lily's hands trembled as she took the intubation kit

from Joe. Her chest felt so tight, she feared Joe might have to resuscitate her when this was over. Joe moved closer, leaning his hip against hers so that his body became her steady anchor.

"Lily, look at me," Joe said, his voice like a lighthouse beacon through the storm of her panic and fear. "Take a deep breath. In and out."

She did as he asked, even though her breaths were shallow and ragged.

"Now focus on Matt. You know what to do."

Lily forced one more choppy breath, keeping her gaze focused on Joe's deep blue eyes. She found no panic or doubt there. Just his unwavering confidence and calm demeanor. Slowly, her breath steadied, and she felt a small measure of control return.

"That's it," Joe soothed. "Now, let's do this. Together."

Lily nodded, feeling something inside her sharpen and focus. She smeared a thin layer of lubricant on the endotracheal tube, then guided it into Matt's airway. She held her breath as she connected the ambu bag, then began to ventilate him, her hands steadying as she fell into the familiar rhythm of the procedure.

Joe pressed his stethoscope to Matt's chest. "We've got breath sounds. You did it, Lily."

A tsunami of relief washed over Lily's entire body. Denise watched from a distance, her hands pressed to her mouth. "Is he going to be okay?"

Joe looked up at her, his expression just as calm and reassuring as he had been with Lily. "We're doing everything we can, Denise. Emergency transport should be here soon. But until then, he's in good hands with us."

With us.

His words lodged in Lily's heart, knowing that it was their teamwork that had made the difference. Joe had not only found a way to snatch Matt from death's cold, sharp claws, he had also managed to break through the brick wall of fear and doubt that had paralyzed her for so long.

Minutes felt like hours as they kept Matt stable and waited for help. Finally, she heard the distinctive *whomp-whomp-whomp* of an approaching helicopter. A few minutes later, a nurse and EMT in flight suits rushed into Denise's backyard.

"What have we got?" the nurse asked Joe.

Joe didn't answer, instead indicating they should get the patient handoff from Lily.

She cleared her throat. "We have a male patient, age forty-five, found unconscious after falling off a ladder. Patient was not breathing and had a weak, erratic pulse. Intubation was performed on scene using a seven point five millimeter endotracheal tube to secure the airway. No medications given. Recommend continued mechanical ventilation and immediate transport to a level three trauma center."

The trauma nurse nodded. "Good work getting him stabilized. We'll take it from here." She and the EMT prepared Matt for transport, then ran with his stretcher back to the helicopter. Lily followed, with Joe and Denise close behind.

"Where are they taking him? Can I go with him?" Denise couldn't contain her tears anymore. They spilled down her cheeks. Lily instinctively wrapped her arms around her friend as tight as she could, wanting to shield her from everything bad that could happen. She and Joe had managed to stabilize Matt, but he had a long way to go.

The pilot started the helicopter, and Lily's pulse thrilled at the distinctive whirring of the helicopter's rotor blades as it prepared for takeoff. There was a rush of wind as the downwash from the rotor blades intensified. Ice and snow swirled about, adding to the dynamic atmosphere.

Lily caught a brief glimpse of the flight nurse's profile as she worked on Matt. For the next twenty minutes, it would be her sole responsibility to keep Matt stable until he reached the emergency room. Lily bit her lip as she watched the nurse work. That was her once, not that long ago. For the first time in five years, she wondered if one day, that might be her again.

The sounds of the engine and rotor blades grew more distant, gradually fading away as the helicopter disappeared from view.

Joe and Lily helped Denise arrange a ride to the hospital with a neighbor. When Denise was on her way, Joe walked Lily back to her truck where Daisy was waiting patiently. The sun dipped low in the sky, making the cold day even more bleak.

Lily was happy to hand her truck keys over after the emotional afternoon. Joe fired up the truck and looked her way. "I don't know about you, but I'm famished. Wanna grab something to eat?"

"I would love to," Lily said, settling her weary body against the truck seat. "But I've got to get back to Alexa. I don't want to abuse Jennifer's free babysitting offer."

She also just wanted to see Alexa and smell that sweet-little-girl scent that pooled in the hollow of her throat. Days like these were terrible reminders to keep her loved ones close, because every day brought its own surprises.

"Why don't we bring dinner back to your place?" Joe suggested, casting a sideways glance at her.

Lily hesitated, her mind swirling with uncertainty. For days, she had wanted to talk to Joe about the upcoming gala. It was clear he didn't really want to go—he'd made that obvious back at The Snowy Owl. He had only agreed because Alexa had put him on the spot.

But the clinic had been bustling ever since the blood drive. Joe's charm and warmth with the donors had endeared him to the town, and now their waiting room really was standing room only.

Joe waited for her response, looking effortlessly handsome. Exhaustion from the stress of saving Matt after his fall weighed heavily on her, and she was ravenous. It just didn't seem like the right time to tell him she was canceling their plans.

So yes, she would invite him back to her house. They could have dinner with Alexa, and once she was in bed, Lily would let him off the hook for the dance. It was only right.

Still, when Joe gave her that smile that made her toes curl in her boots, she couldn't help but wonder why doing the right thing sometimes felt so lousy.

CHAPTER EIGHT

Lily watched with a smile as Joe and Alexa huddled over the board game spread out on the living room floor. Joe was dramatically pretending to cheat, slipping extra cards into his hand with exaggerated stealth, just so Alexa could catch him and scold him indignantly. Daisy sat between them, her gaze ping-ponging back and forth as the drama played out. She seemed just as amused by the game as they were. Lily cupped her coffee mug with both hands and felt her heart swell with joy as she watched her daughter have the time of her life.

Joe, with his easy charm, had embraced the role of playful accomplice effortlessly. Lily had to give him credit—he hadn't even flinched when Alexa roped him into taking her mom to the gala. It was sweet of him to play along, but Lily planned to let him off the hook as soon as they were alone.

"Come on, Alexa—time for bed, sweetie," Lily said gently.

Alexa groaned and protested, dragging her feet, but Lily managed to get her settled into her room. After reading her favorite story twice, Lily closed the door softly and headed downstairs.

When Lily walked into the living room, she was taken

aback. Joe had transformed the space into a cozy retreat. He'd cleared her coffee table and draped one of her gauzy scarves over it, setting out two glasses of wine that glowed a rich ruby in the firelight. Soft instrumental folk music played from the Bluetooth speaker—a tune that wasn't on her playlist, suggesting Joe had connected his phone to her speaker.

She settled onto the couch, taking a glass of wine, her nerves barely contained.

"Any more news on Matt?" she asked.

"He has a skull fracture with some bleeding in the brain. He's in the ICU while the neuro team figures things out."

"That's terrible. Poor Denise," Lily said, her heart aching for her friend.

Joe sat down beside her, his warmth making her shift closer. "I went to med school with one of the neurologists treating Matt. He's a good guy. He says the neuro team is top-notch."

That was reassuring, though Lily couldn't shake her nervousness. Joe's smile was warm and genuine, but it set a flutter of butterflies loose in her stomach. She looked away, trying to steady herself.

Could she ever have a cozy domestic scene like this? It was the first time she'd thought about it since her disastrous attempts at dating. Yet, she realized she didn't want to open her heart to just any man—only Joe. What was it about him that made her want to push past her boundaries and hope for more?

"You don't have to take me to the gala this weekend,"

she said, trying to keep her voice steady. "It was very kind of you to offer, but you really don't have to."

"But what if I want to?" His response was quick and firm, leaving her momentarily speechless.

What was his story? Why was he spending time with her and Alexa? Joe was a drop-dead gorgeous doctor, and Lily had noticed the parade of young singles dropping by the clinic with vague complaints. In a small town like Twin Creeks, a handsome single doctor was bound to attract attention. So why was he here, in her living room, spending the night playing little kid games and hanging out with her?

"Well, I'd say that would be…weird," she said.

He laughed. "Why would that be weird?"

"I don't know…" She didn't want to tell him the truth. That she spent most Saturday nights on the couch with a good book and an oversize bowl of popcorn. "I didn't think you'd be into small-town traditions like the gala."

Joe shrugged, his arm casually draped over the back of the couch. "Who knows? Maybe this middle-of-nowhere town is growing on me." He smiled as he threw her words back at her, his fingers grazing her shoulder.

Lily laughed, feeling the warmth of his touch and the sincerity in his eyes. For the first time in a long while, she let herself entertain the possibility of more.

"How did you end up here, Joe? I know you mentioned your mentor sent you, but I don't really know why. Did you lose a bet? Owe someone money back in LA?" She laughed at how she had recycled Joe's joke, then tilted her head, admiring his handsome profile.

Joe rolled his head to face her as they lounged on the

couch, his smile tinged with something more somber. "Not quite that sordid. My mentor has known me for a long time. For the past eight years, I've been focused on a career in oncology. But I guess she thought I'd become too fixated on my goals."

He paused, his gaze distant. "My mom died of cancer in her forties. My dad was devastated and turned to drinking. I was just a kid when my mom passed—helpless to support her or my family. I chose oncology as a way to fight back against a disease that caused so much suffering for my family and so many others."

Lily's heart softened. His intense focus on his oncology fellowship suddenly made sense. It wasn't about status or prestige, as she'd first thought. He was driven by a desire to create something positive out of his own profound loss.

She considered his words, reflecting on the power of his commitment. "What a powerful way to show the world all the love you didn't get to give, Joe."

He returned her smile, and as his warm hand rested on hers, a shiver of electricity ran through her. It brought her back to their moment at the blood drive, when she had brushed against him while packing up supplies. In that fleeting instant, she had seen a spark of passion in his eyes that mirrored her own feelings. But as quickly as it had appeared, it vanished, leaving Joe's expression once again as unreadable as ever.

"Oh, crap. Tell me my watch is broken," Joe groaned, tapping his watch face.

Lily glanced at the clock on the mantel. "That can't be right."

"It is, I'm afraid. I'd better head out," Joe said, getting up from the couch. Lily felt a pang of loss as his warmth left her side.

She followed him to the hallway, where he shrugged into his coat and scarf. The tension in her body was palpable as their flirtation was coming to an abrupt end. It left her feeling restless and unsatisfied.

As he opened the back door, the cold air rushed in. Lily followed him out, wanting to make sure the exterior lights were on so he could see his way back to his car.

"Thanks for dinner," he said, leaning in to kiss her cheek.

But she turned back from the light switch just then, and his kiss landed on her lips.

She registered the warm, light pressure of his mouth. Could feel his breath drift across her skin and scent hints of plum from the wine they had shared.

Both shocked, they broke off the stolen kiss to stare at each other. Neither moved and the space between them seemed to crackle with energy. She scanned every inch of his face, lingering on the fullness of his lips and the tiny endearing mole that sat just above the curve of his smile. Her eyes traced the line of his jaw, the slope of his cheek, until she found him staring down at her with those hypnotic blue eyes.

Dammit. I hope I don't regret this.

A sense of certainty she had not felt in years warmed her body and strengthened her resolve. She laced one hand around the nape of his neck to draw him in, but he was already moving toward her, his eyes hazy with lust.

She stood on tiptoe, her lips brushing against his

with a tantalizingly soft touch. The heat from his mouth surged through her, igniting a fire deep within her core. As his hands curved around her waist, pulling her closer, their kiss grew more intense. Their tongues met in a dance of longing, and she felt as if an invisible weight had been lifted, setting her heart free.

She clung to his jacket, her grip tight with a desperate need she hadn't felt in years. The kiss was all-consuming, a hungry reunion after a five-year hibernation of solitude and unfulfilled desire. She never wanted it to end, but as time passed, their lips finally parted. She glanced at her hands still clutching his coat and wondered with breathless anticipation—if this kiss was so electrifying, what would it be like to make love to him?

With the greatest of willpower, she pushed herself away from Joe's embrace. She kept her eyes averted, hoping he couldn't read her stormy emotions. There was nowhere to go with this attraction. Twin Creeks was not where Joe wanted to be. And she had no idea if her heart could handle what promised to be a short, incredibly passionate fling.

"I've got to get back to Alexa," she said. She had to do the right thing for her daughter. If Alexa woke in the morning to find Joe and Daisy there, her happiness would shoot her to the moon and back. She would never want to let that feeling go. And she wouldn't understand when it was time for Joe to leave in a few months.

The night was getting too cold and her toes were going numb, so they parted for the last time. He waved as he rounded her driveway. She stood in the doorway, hugging herself hard, and watched until his taillights disappeared into the cold, dark night.

But the struggle within her wasn't over. Something fierce in her wanted to call him back, to seize the fleeting chance they had. Joe wouldn't stay in Twin Creeks forever—she knew that well enough. Yet, he was here now, and she couldn't help yearning for something just for herself. A primal and restless need that would awaken her soul from its long slumber and make her feel alive again. The thought of calling him back was almost intoxicating. But she hesitated, knowing that saying yes now would only lead to a heart-wrenching goodbye later. A goodbye she wasn't sure her heart could bear.

CHAPTER NINE

Joe set the parking brake and turned off his car's ignition. Lily's small cabin sat nestled in a blanket of pristine snow with a tidy stack of firewood neatly arranged by the door. Even though it was winter, Lily's love for gardening was evident in the carefully pruned bushes and the dormant flower beds lining the path to her front door. Something about her cabin always beckoned to him, inviting him to please come in, have some coffee, stay awhile. Or maybe it was just Lily who made him feel like that.

Joe glanced at the passenger seat, where a stunning bouquet of roses and an expensive bottle of champagne awaited. These luxuries were rare in Twin Creeks, so he had made the long drive to Billings on a Saturday afternoon while Lily was occupied with Alexa. He'd also treated himself to a fresh haircut and picked out a new shirt and tie. To top it off, he'd had his car meticulously detailed, ensuring the midnight-black exterior gleamed and the rich, buttery leather seats smelled fresh and a little soapy.

Joe checked his reflection in the rearview mirror and made a few last-minute adjustments. He didn't understand the undercurrent of nervousness that had been dogging him all day. He had crafted the evening with fastidious care, determined to give Lily the night of her life. Usually, he looked forward to dates with eager anticipation, knowing he could pour himself into the role of charming bachelor date for the night because there would be no second date.

But tonight felt different. Probably because of that passionate kiss. Ever since he had tasted Lily's lips, she had haunted his thoughts with an intensity he hadn't anticipated. Memories of how she had pulled him closer and the fierce passion in her kiss had left him feeling completely disoriented. Something about that kiss had shaken him in a way that said Lily was different. It had left him feeling vulnerable and, for once, unsure of his own usually unshakeable demeanor.

So he had done his best to keep his distance at the clinic, trying to get his emotions back under control. It was pure agony to hear her voice in the hallway or catch sight of her between patients and know that he needed to stay away. But Lily seemed to avoid him, too, so he had to conclude that she also felt uneasy with that unexpected kiss. Maybe she even regretted it. He did not, but he was wise enough to know that allowing this attraction to grow would only end badly for both of them.

Despite the nervous flutter beneath the polished image he had cultivated for the evening, he was determined not to let it show. He could manage this—he had spent a lifetime perfecting the art of compartmentalizing his desires from his duties. Tonight Lily deserved an attentive and supportive companion, someone who could help her navigate an event that might stir up painful memories. He was ready to be that person for her.

That realization shook him to the core. Somehow Lily had slipped past the wall he had erected between himself and the world. He was no longer satisfied playing the role of perfect romantic suitor for the night. He wanted more—not for himself but for Lily. He needed her to feel safe and protected, so her heart could finally heal and she could reclaim her life. Letting his guard down—letting these hopes see the light of day—left him feeling bewildered and confused. But he had never felt so acutely alive in his entire life.

Jennifer answered the door, her eyebrows lifting in approval at the sight of Joe's bouquet and champagne. She was watching Alexa while Lily finished getting ready for their date. While he waited, Joe entertained Alexa with amusing tales of what Daisy had been like when she was a mischievous puppy. The more time he spent in Lily's home, the more confident he felt about handling the evening. He just needed to channel the old Joe—charming, self-assured and perfectly in control.

"Hey."

He had been so absorbed in deciphering Alexa's still babyish dialect that he hadn't noticed Lily coming downstairs. But the look on Jennifer's face made him suspect that tonight might not be the surefire success he had anticipated.

He turned to find her on the stairs and in that moment, he knew he was in deep trouble. Because Lily was nothing short of sheer perfection.

She was gorgeous in a strapless black dress that

showed off the curve of her shoulder and the delicate skin of her collarbone. A deep slit on the side of the dress revealed her long, shapely legs. She must have gone shopping, too, because the warm, airy blend of spices and fresh florals in her perfume was not familiar and it set his head swimming. It made him think of warm, faraway places he would like to take her to where they could finally be alone.

Joe's heart beat harder as his mouth went dry. All of his senses went on full alert. She was a beautiful woman on any day of the week, but tonight she left him speechless.

"Hey, yourself," he managed to say. "You look beautiful." Which sounded so stupid. Because saying Lily was beautiful was like saying the sun was warm—obvious, undeniable and utterly inadequate to capture the way she lit up everything around her.

She flashed him a dazzling smile that sent Joe's emotions into a dizzying spin. So much for being the epitome of stoicism and control. All he could hope for now was to keep these tumultuous feelings well hidden.

Lily kissed Alexa for the night and thanked Jennifer for babysitting again.

"It's my pleasure, sweetie," Jennifer said, giving Lily a warm smile. "In fact, if it's okay with you, I'd like to keep Alexa at my place. She can stay up a teensy bit past her bedtime and camp out on the couch if she likes."

"Sure," Lily said with a shrug. "If you're sure you don't mind."

Joe carefully navigated the dark forest roads that led back to the highway that would take them to Twin

Creeks's downtown. He kept both hands curved around the steering wheel and his eyes on the road, trying hard to keep his thoughts where they belonged. But he couldn't stop stealing glances at her profile. Her black hair was soft and glossy, and her lips were full and red. He wasn't used to this version of Lily, and it was scrambling his thoughts.

Lily glanced at him with a teasing smile. "I can't believe you're wearing a tux, Joe. You clean up pretty well."

Joe grinned but kept his tone light. "Me? What about you? Not bad for a lettuce farmer—not bad at all."

Lily covered her mouth with her hand, embarrassed and amused at the same time. "Oh, my gosh, I remember that morning. I was so worried I had chicken feathers stuck in my hair!" She shyly glanced his way. "You look really nice, Joe."

Joe kept his eyes on the road, not wanting her to see how her compliment affected him. "Nice? That's it? I was going for devastatingly handsome."

Lily rolled her eyes but her smile lingered. "Well, I didn't want to inflate your ego *too* much before we even got there."

Joe couldn't stop himself. "You look stunning, by the way."

She looked down at herself and smoothed her dress with her hands. "Thanks," she said shyly. "Jennifer made me go shopping."

They fell into a brief silence, the air crackling with unspoken tension. Lily's gaze wandered out the window as she nervously toyed with the pendant on her necklace, and Joe couldn't help but wonder if she, too, felt the simmering attraction beneath their playful banter. The anticipation of this night had been a constant thrill for him all week. She crossed her legs, making the fabric of her dress slip to reveal the soft, inviting skin of her thigh. He felt an irresistible urge to reach across the car's cabin so his pinky finger could graze the delicate skin of her knee and feel the warmth of her touch.

By the time they reached the community center, Joe's head was spinning with desire. He was happy to get out of the car and deeply inhale Montana's cold, brisk winter air. It revived him a bit and brought him back to his senses. Even though Lily was a gorgeous, desirable woman, he was not going to make a move on her. She deserved better than the one-and-done dates he had to offer, and there was no way he could step into the unknown and risk sharing his uncertain future with her.

Thankfully, the evening started as a whirlwind of meeting and greeting Twin Creeks's many residents and friends. Lily had been right. Working the blood drive together had been the perfect icebreaker to introduce Joe to the community. Now his night was filled with hearty handshakes and polite inquiries as to where he came from and how he found his way to Twin Creeks.

People were thrilled to see Lily attending the gala for the first time in years. She accepted all of their hugs and well wishes with grace. Joe watched closely for any signs of the sadness that he had seen at the blood drive. But she seemed relaxed and happy to be there.

"I can't believe how much people have changed," she commented thoughtfully. "Rebecca Morales just asked me to write a recommendation letter for her application to medical school. When I first moved here, she had just gotten her first job at The Snowy Owl!" She took a sip of her drink. "I guess life just keeps moving on, whether we like it or not."

Joe understood perfectly. Not so long ago, his social media feed was a parade of adventures with friends, snapshots of their carefree moments between hospital shifts. Now his notifications were filled with wedding invitations and photos of his friends' new babies. He knew why he couldn't have those comforts in his own life, but the reality still left him feeling isolated and abandoned. He had once buried these feelings in relentless work and fellowship preparation, but here, standing in the community center beside Lily, he couldn't outrun the ache of loneliness that struck him with a piercing clarity.

Joe left Lily for a moment to fetch drinks for both of them, feeling parched from all the mingling. As he made his way back, the DJ transitioned from lively music to a slow, romantic song, dimming the lights to create a softer, more intimate, atmosphere.

He caught a glimpse of Lily's profile as he approached. She watched the dancing couples with a wistful sadness that tugged at his heart. But as soon as she noticed his return, her face brightened with her usual warm smile, masking the fleeting melancholy he had seen moments before.

So Lily was just like him. Presenting one image to the world—the version of her the world wanted to see—so that no one would see the turmoil in her heart. He wished she didn't feel she had to do that for him. He wished she felt safe enough to show him all of her, even the parts the world didn't understand.

She accepted the drink with a smile, then leaned into his space to speak close to his ear. "I'm glad we came here, Joe. Thank you for bringing me. You didn't have to do that."

Joe's fingers brushed the warm, soft skin of her inner arm, tracing a gentle path from her elbow to her wrist. He watched as a range of emotions flickered across her face. She looked down, surprised by the tender touch, and then met his gaze as he took her hand in his.

"Care to dance?"

"Oh, Joe. You don't..."

"I know, I know. I don't have to be here." He slipped her hand into his and gently tugged her to the dance floor. "But have you ever considered that maybe I *want* to be here?"

Lily hesitated, her steps slowing as Joe gently pulled her toward the dance floor. "Here?" she asked, glancing at the gala's homemade decorations and the array of potluck dishes. "What would your friends in LA say if they saw you now?"

Joe looked down at the stunning woman beside him, feeling a surprising surge of emotion that only intensified at the thought of having her pressed close to him on the dance floor. But his feelings didn't matter right now. Tonight was about giving Lily a chance to create new memories in Twin Creeks, memories that would help her move forward when he was gone.

He gave her a playful grin. "I think they'd say Twin Creeks has grown on me."

She smiled at their shared joke and squeezed his hand. "All right, Joe," she said with a flirtatious shrug. "Let's dance."

Joe's shoulder had healed enough that he no longer needed to wear his sling, a freedom he now treasured for the way it allowed him to hold Lily close. He gently guided her hand to rest against his chest and let his free hand travel the length of her back until it found her enticing curves. As Lily melted into him, tucking her head under his chin, the scent of her shampoo filled his senses. He closed his eyes against the rush of emotions he felt. The sounds around them magnified. He could hear every note of the romantic song they were swaying to, and the low murmur of couples as they chatted, laughed, gossiped. Joe felt the warm and gentle press of Lily's body against his. He gazed at the delicate skin of her shoulder, longing to press his lips there and trace a tender path along the curve of her neck to her mouth. But that could never happen. Lily wasn't one of his casual just-for-fun flings that used to fill his days. And he could never promise her any sort of future that wouldn't break her heart if his family's cancer gene one day caught up to him. All he could have with Lily was this—the sweet torture of holding her in his arms, knowing she would never be his.

Lily pulled her head away from Joe's chest. "Joe?"

Joe opened his eyes, adjusting to the disorienting return to reality after being lost in Lily. "What?"

Lily stopped dancing and pulled away. "Something's wrong with Beth."

* * *

Joe and Lily hurried to Beth's side. She was bent over, her hands pressed to her swollen abdomen. Beth had visited the clinic for her prenatal checkup just before the dance. She was still a month away from her delivery date, but she hadn't been sure she should attend the event because she was feeling so many practice contractions. Lily had given her a thorough exam and encouraged her to attend.

But now, with Beth leaning against her husband for support, her eyes squeezed tight against the pain, Lily wasn't sure she had made the right call.

"Come on, let's get you some privacy," Lily said. She and Joe supported Beth as they walked her out of the gala event and to the classroom where they had held the blood drive. The Healthy Heart Association had not yet come to collect their borrowed equipment, so Beth was able to get comfortable in one of the recliners still there.

"It's okay," Beth said through gritted teeth. "This should pass in just a minute."

Lily thought back to Beth's last exam. Her readings on the fetal monitor had been low—much too low to indicate true labor. And her cervix was barely dilated. It was all consistent with a mother who was weeks from delivery.

Still, she opened her phone and noted the time. Just then, Beth gasped with pain.

Joe and Lily made eye contact. She could see unease in his eyes, too. This seemed too intense for practice contractions.

Lily gave Joe a little nod. A silent acknowledgment to keep things nice and calm until they knew what they were dealing with.

"Hey, Beth," Lily said. "Why don't we head over to the clinic? Let's get you back on the fetal monitor, see what's going on."

Beth held her husband's hand tightly. "But I'm not due for another month."

Lily tried to keep her laugh natural and light. "Well, you know. Sometimes babies have their own ideas."

Joe helped Beth get to her feet, then looped her arm around his neck. "Here we go, mom. Nice and easy."

But just when they got her back to her feet, Beth cried out and dropped to her knees.

"It's okay," Joe assured Beth, moving to support her weight.

"No, it's not!" Beth yelled, then started to cry. She wrapped her arms around her swollen midsection. "It hurts so much."

Lily knelt so she could look in Beth's eyes. "I think you're in labor, Beth."

That only made Beth cry harder. "But the hospital's two hours away."

Lily took charge. "Listen, Beth. I don't know if you're going to be having this baby in the hospital tonight. Joe has called emergency services, but I need to check you so we know what to expect. If there's time, we'll get an air ambulance to take you to Billings."

"What if there's not?" her husband asked, his voice tight with tension.

If they were lucky, Beth would make it to the clinic

where they had the equipment to monitor mom and baby. Along with the labor and delivery kit, medications and support for the new baby.

"And if we're unlucky?"

Lily had to push the thought away. It was time to think like a trauma nurse now. "We're just going to take this one minute at a time, okay?"

Joe sent a volunteer to the clinic with instructions on where to find their labor and delivery kit. Then he shouted orders for supplies like soft blankets and a large lamp.

The sudden shift in energy made Beth even more nervous. Lily took her hand and stroked it gently. "Hey, Beth? You have just one job here, okay? Keep your eyes on me. Everything's going to be okay. Let's keep taking nice deep breaths now, all right? Let's give that baby plenty of oxygen."

Lily snapped on a pair of latex gloves, then checked Beth's cervix. She couldn't believe it. Beth was fully dilated. Something round and hard pressed against her fingers.

Lily looked at Joe and tried to keep her voice calm. "She's ready."

Beth suddenly moaned. Lily felt Beth's abdominal muscles contract hard under her hand.

"This…baby's…coming!" Beth moaned through gritted teeth.

"Yep, she sure is," Lily said, using her nurse-in-charge voice. But inside she was feeling waves of panic start to swirl. Even in a hospital with all of its fancy technology, there was so much that could go wrong. It was terrifying to think of what could happen right here.

Part of her wanted to run. To escape this stuffy dance hall and Beth's pain and the fear of all that could go wrong.

Her gaze frantically swept the room, finally settling on Joe. He watched her with calm eyes. "We've got this," he said, and she wasn't sure if he was talking to Beth or to her.

But it calmed her. Because he was right. *They* had this. She would be okay because Joe was there.

In nurse mode, she gave Joe the update. "She's fully dilated, baby is crowning. Mom appears ready to push. Let's have a baby!"

Joe doused his hands and arms in sanitizer, then pulled on the sterile gloves from the dance hall's kitchen. "All right, let's get this show on the road."

Lily timed the contractions while Joe guided Beth through pushing. He must have done a good job, because after just three contractions, a full head of dark, curly hair crowned.

"Almost there," Lily assured Beth.

With the next push, the newest resident of Twin Creeks made her debut.

Joe guided the baby into the world, cradling her tiny body in his hands. Lily watched his face as he worked to clear the baby's airway. But instead of relief or joy, she saw concern etch deep lines in his forehead.

Oh, no... she thought. There was no wail. The tiny newborn lay limp in his arms.

Beth looked up, her eyes full of questions and fear.

Lily's heart sank. This was her worst fear. Some babies had trouble making the change from getting their oxygen from the placenta to breathing on their own. As a trauma nurse, she had resuscitated a few babies, using an ambu bag to force air into the baby's new lungs and get breathing started.

But they didn't have anything like that here. There was only one thing she could do for Beth's tiny baby.

"Hand me that dish towel," she demanded.

She took the baby in one arm and rubbed her body vigorously with the towel. Warming and stimulating the baby's body could trigger her to breathe on her own.

Chest and body, turn baby over, now the back.

"And the bulb syringe!"

She used it to clear the baby's airway again and again, then returned to rubbing the baby's body as hard as she dared.

Beth's eyes welled with tears. "Is my baby..."

"She's going to be fine," Lily said with fierce determination. There wasn't a bone in her body that didn't believe this baby would make it. She just needed a little more time.

Rub the chest and body...now the back. Clear the nose and mouth.

Joe said, his voice soft, "Lily..."

Lily shook her head hard. "No, Joe," she said, her tone fierce. Nothing bad was going to happen to this baby. Not tonight. Not on her watch.

She was just about to repeat the process when suddenly, a beautiful, perfectly pitched, tiny cry pierced the air.

* * *

Lily gently turned the baby over, watching in awe as her purple color transformed into a radiant pink. A wave of relief washed over her, leaving her feeling weak and unsteady as she realized Beth's baby was going to be okay. With a tender touch, Joe took the baby from her arms, quickly assessing her breathing and heart rate before handing her back to her elated parents.

Lily sank back onto her heels, her heart full as she observed the powerful scene before her. Though she hadn't delivered many babies in her career, the sight of Beth and her husband's astonished faces meeting their daughter was breathtaking. It stirred a flood of memories for Lily—her first meeting with Alexa, a poignant mix of joy and heartache. Joy for Alexa's safe arrival and the painful realization that she would never know her father.

Swiping at her eyes with her fingers, Lily forced herself to focus on the moment at hand. This was a time for celebration, not self-reflection. With a determined smile, she turned to the proud new parents. "Congratulations, Mom and Dad. What's your daughter's name?"

CHAPTER TEN

Lily stayed with Beth and her family while Joe ensured Beth was stable and healthy. When the EMT crew finally arrived, she felt the tight grip of tension release. Joe took care of the patient handoff, giving her the chance to slip away to the quiet solitude of the deck overlooking the rose garden.

The cold air hit her immediately, and she wished she had grabbed her jacket. But the chill was also a welcome relief, bracing her emotions and offering a reset after the long, emotional day. Alone now, the adrenaline from delivering Beth's baby faded, leaving her feeling weak, drained and exposed. The emotions she had been holding back began to rise, impossible to ignore.

She heard the sliding glass door open behind her. "Lily?"

Her heart lifted slightly at the sound of Joe's voice. "Over here."

His footsteps echoed across the wooden deck, a faint creaking accompanying each step. She stood still, trying to steady herself, but then she felt the warmth of fabric as Joe draped his coat over her shoulders. His gesture, so tender and kind, was too much. She lowered her head, unable to stop the tears that overtook her.

"Lily! What on earth is wrong?"

Joe's voice was full of concern as he spun her gently to face him, trying to read her expression. But all she wanted was to disappear, to melt into the shadows. Instead, she moved closer, feeling his strong arms wrap around her, pulling her into a protective embrace.

"Lily, talk to me. What's wrong?"

For several minutes, she couldn't speak. All she could do was let the tears flow, and for once, it felt good not to be the strong one. To let someone else take care of her, just like Jennifer had told her all those years ago.

When the sobs finally subsided, she pulled away slightly, wiping her face and wishing for a tissue. Like magic, Joe produced a handkerchief from the pocket of the coat draped over her shoulders.

"What's wrong?" he asked again, his voice soft.

"Beth's baby came early!" she choked out.

"But she's okay," Joe reassured her.

"I know," Lily whispered.

"So why are you crying?"

"Joe…" She pulled away, dabbing her eyes with his hankie. She hoped she didn't have mascara streaked down her cheeks. "That baby wasn't supposed to be here for another month."

Joe laughed. "I know, Lily, but you're a nurse. You know life doesn't always go precisely as planned."

"Exactly."

His brow furrowed, searching for an answer to her inexplicable response. "I am so confused."

Lily led him by the hand to two deck chairs overlooking the garden. "Beth did everything right. She kept all of her prenatal appointments and took care of herself during her pregnancy, yet her baby still arrived early for no medical reason that would explain it. It just… happened."

"Right…"

"And Connor left for work like he always did. He made a thermos of coffee, kissed me goodbye and then he left like he had a thousand times before. But he never came home."

Joe's eyes were full of concern and protectiveness. He knew she was upset, but he didn't know why.

"For the past five years, I've tried to create a perfectly safe world for me and Alexa. A world where I can protect both of us from heartbreak and loss…because we don't *do* anything that might break our hearts.

"I call it our *bubble world*, and to be honest, I find it stifling as hell. But I have truly believed that I was doing the right thing for Alexa and me. I didn't want her to hurt like I had when I lost Connor, and I sure as hell didn't want to ever grieve the loss of my daughter.

"But tonight I'm just not sure I believe in that bubble anymore. Because there was nothing Beth or you or me could have done to stop her daughter from coming early. It was just…"

"Fate?" Joe offered.

"I guess you could call it that. It's just the way things were going to be."

Lily trailed off, exhausted by the long night and her emotional outburst. Joe seemed to understand that she needed some quiet. He just held her hand as she sat and thought about the past five years of her life. She had never questioned her desire to protect herself and Alexa from danger and pain. But she had also never questioned the toll that this battle had taken on her. The signs were everywhere. Her anxiety to let her daughter grow up and experience life. Giving up the work she loved because it was too painful to talk through her memories in therapy.

How much more was she willing to sacrifice for the illusion of peace and safety? She looked down at the hand that was holding hers. Joe was out here in the freezing cold without his coat because he didn't want her to be alone. He wasn't even supposed to be here. Had his life gone the way he planned, he'd be in Florida right now, and she might never have attended the gala again.

Joe's life plan never included Twin Creeks, yet here he was.

She'd never planned to love again. But she could if she wanted. Because he was here.

"Joe?"

"Yeah?"

"Take me home."

Half an hour later, Lily flung the front door of her cabin open so hard, it crashed against the wall.

She backed her way into the cabin, clutching fistfuls of Joe's shirt as she met the passion and intensity of Joe's kisses with her own desire.

She slapped her hand along the wall, searching for the light switch, but knocked a stack of library books off the hallway table. "Crap," she mumbled against Joe's lips.

"Don't worry about it," he answered, breathless against her mouth. "We don't need any light."

She kicked off her shoes and threw her purse on the floor, then led Joe up the stairs the same way she led him into the house. Joe steadied her backward ascent with his hands on her hips.

Eventually, they dead-ended at her closed bedroom door. She fumbled behind her, trying to wrench it open, but the handle wasn't budging and she was so distracted.

"Wait," Joe said against her mouth.

"Oh, my God, for what?"

Joe pulled away, obviously reluctant to break off the passion that had consumed them as soon as they got in his car. Driving home had been a spectacular form of sweet torture as she could only allow her hands to roam his body, nothing more.

Joe pulled away so he could meet her gaze directly.

"What are we doing here, Lily?"

Lily looked at the chest she had managed to bare as she led him up the stairs. Her fingers traced the contours of his taut belly as she cocked her head and arched an eyebrow.

"No, I know what *this* is," he said, indicating their shared space with an impatient hand gesture. "I mean, what are *we* doing here?"

"Oh. Right."

She let her hands drop from his body and leaned her full weight against the door. Her breath was coming in ragged pants, and she could feel her heart thumping in her chest.

She pushed hair away from her forehead. "I don't see that there is a *we*, Joe. You're leaving in a few weeks."

"So this is it—just a casual fling between friends, then?"

Her heart squeezed with something that didn't feel good. Neither *friends* nor *fling* really described how she felt about Joe. But she wasn't going to dwell on that. Theirs was passion with an expiration date.

"Exactly. A friends-with-benefits setup."

Joe leaned into her so he could nuzzle her neck. Her hands automatically searched for and found his thick, wavy hair. "And when it's time for me to go to Florida?"

She closed her eyes against the image. She would be lying to him and herself if she said it wouldn't hurt when he left. But she would know it was coming. She could prepare.

"We'll celebrate with pie at the Snowy Owl."

"Seems fitting." He leaned in, ready to resume their passionate kiss, when she remembered something that was important to her. She pressed her hands to his chest, stopping his approach.

"One more thing... Alexa can never know."

"That might be tricky seeing as she lives here, too."

She shook her head to show she meant it. "We meet at your place. Or the clinic. Never here, unless Alexa is gone. Agreed?"

Joe nodded solemnly. "Agreed." He studied her face for a moment, as if he wanted to memorize the planes and curves of her. Then he traced her jawline with the back of his finger before bending to kiss her so tenderly, so slowly, that she thought surely she'd fall to pieces right there.

The frantic sexual energy that had propelled them to this moment was maturing into something tender and sweet. His mouth hovered inches from hers. Her chest rose and fell in tempo with his shallow breaths.

He leaned closer, until his breath stirred her hair, tickling her cheek. "Are you going to open the door, Lily?"

"Oh. Right." She found the door handle, gripped it hard and felt the stability of the door fall away, leaving her weightless for a moment. She might have fallen if Joe hadn't stepped forward, his good arm finding her waist so he could pull her to him.

Her bed was unmade, and her pajamas were thrown over the overstuffed armchair, but she could not give a damn. All she wanted was to feel his skin against hers. Her hands helplessly tugged at his pants as he kicked the door shut behind them.

They stumbled across the floor toward her bed in a flurry of kisses and hungry hands. She strained to meet his kisses, her weight balanced on her tiptoes. She felt his fingers, light and teasing, as they followed the contours of her neck. Every nerve she possessed went on full alert.

"You are so damn beautiful," Joe said, his tone reverent.

She didn't know about that, but she knew his hands were making her skin sing as they trailed from her neck to her waist. His hands found the curves of her breasts, then wandered to her back, found her zipper, and slowly, inch by inch, tugged the zipper from her back to her bottom without ever breaking their kiss. The strapless dress slipped from her body to pool at her feet, leaving her standing naked save for her black lace panties and high heels.

Joe's gaze traveled the length of her body. "You are

the hottest lettuce farmer I've ever seen," he said, and that made her chuckle. Until he palmed her bare breast with one hand, flicking his thumb over her nipple until both were tight and beaded. The flock of butterflies Joe had set loose with his flirting was becoming a manic swarm of bees, their incessant humming felt behind her navel and at the apex of her thighs.

"My turn," she whispered. She found the buttons of his shirt in the dark. She slipped each one through its buttonhole, then slipped his shirt from his shoulders. She smoothed her hands over his chest, followed the hard muscles of his forearms and biceps. The curves of his shoulder reminded her that he was injured, which meant she would have to take the lead.

She took him by the hand and guided him to the soft, overstuffed chair in front of the window where she liked to drink coffee and read. She pushed him into the chair, and he laughed at her bossiness. She laughed, too, but it was a husky, knowing laugh. Her power was coming back to her. For the first time in a long time, she knew what she wanted.

She followed him into the chair, tucking her knees against his hips. That made Joe's eyes go all smoky, and his hands found her hips, bringing her down so that the hot, damp vee between her legs pressed against his stiffness.

Her hands found his hair and burrowed into its wild waves. Joe arched forward to meet her mouth, his hands still bracing her hips. His mouth and tongue were demanding more now. She felt it, too. The need, so long denied, was building in her. She ground against his manhood, feeling fireworks of sensation in her core. *Damn, this was good*, but not nearly enough.

Her fingers trailed the skin above his belt buckle, making his muscles tense and shiver. His fingers were stroking her back, neck to bottom. It felt delicious and shivery. She unbuckled the belt and pulled it loose, then unsnapped his pants.

"We need a condom," she whispered. But then she remembered that she had some in her bathroom. A dusty memory tickled the edges of her mind as she rummaged under the sink, past boxes of tampons and bottles of hairspray and gel. Something that felt like a warning.

But she was tired of her mind always warning her to *be careful...be careful...be careful.* Beyond using protection, she wasn't going to be careful. She was choosing to be alive and accept all the risks that came with living the life she had been given.

Tucking the foil package between her teeth, she slipped off her panties, making Joe's gaze go hazy again. His obvious desire for her made her feel powerful and wanted.

"Get over here," he murmured. He lunged forward to pull her to him. She straddled his lap, then his mouth was on her breast and his fingers stroked her sex, stirring passions in her she thought she had put to rest long ago.

What a fool she had been. She hadn't put anything to rest. She had only buried this part of herself deep inside her soul where it had lain dormant. Joe was like a mage, finding all of her missing pieces and putting her back together.

She tore the foil packet open and rolled the condom

on. Joe palmed her breast with one hand, her curves filling the palm of his other one. She watched Joe's lids go heavy and his eyes dreamy as she sank down on him. She gasped at the sublime sensation of their joining, letting her head fall back with pleasure.

Joe thumbed her nipple as she rolled her hips over him. Liquid heat rippled from his thumb throughout her body, making her shiver with pleasure.

"God, Lily, you feel so good."

Lily wanted to agree, to tell him how every roll of her hips was making him hit that magic spot that made her moan. Joe's breaths were coming shallow and fast, his fingers digging into her hips. She doubted he would hear a word she said, if she even had the strength to speak.

She could smell his clean sweat and hints of his aftershave—woodsy and warm—and it made her squeeze around him, loving him deeper.

"Damn it, Lily. I...don't...please..." The edge of lust in his tone was all it took to send her orgasm rolling over her like a tsunami. From deep in her core, pleasure rippled outward, making her melt into Joe. He grabbed her shoulders and yelped as his bliss peaked into a series of shuddering rolls.

For many long minutes, they clung to each other like survivors of something death defying. Lily curled into Joe's chest, inhaling his scent. He was like a raft, ferrying her back to the safety of the shoreline with every gentle rise of his chest.

The buzzing bees that moved from her core to her brain, pestered her with demands to know *What does this mean?*

It didn't mean anything; that was what they had agreed. But she couldn't deny that all she wanted to do was bury under the covers with Joe and feel safe and loved for the first time in forever.

But that was not what Joe was offering, and she had to accept that.

CHAPTER ELEVEN

Joe woke in the early-morning light, the soft glow streaming through lacy curtains. An unfamiliar clock ticked steadily beside him, and the faint sound of a crow—or maybe a woodpecker—filtered in from outside.

Slowly, he became aware of the warm body nestled against his. Eyes still closed, he traced the arm draped across his torso, then lightly stroked the leg that was wrapped over his hips. Her head rested on his shoulder, her breath deep and steady, almost to the point of snoring. Without thinking, he let his fingertips begin to glide along her arm, savoring the smoothness of her skin, still in disbelief that this moment was real.

Memories bubbled to the surface of Joe's sleepy mind. He recalled the way they danced, how stunning Lily had looked, the torturous drive home and finally, the moment they were alone. He remembered her passionate body beneath him as they lost themselves to each other in the quiet of the night. They'd agreed—this was casual, no strings attached, no expectations. The only rule: Alexa could never know.

Lily had understood and agreed without hesitation, and Joe was relieved they were on the same page.

Though he knew he'd already fallen for her, he was determined to keep that to himself. As long as Lily wanted nothing more than a fling while he was in Twin Creeks, this could work. He'd deal with his tangled emotions later, when he was alone in Florida.

Joe let his hand wander along Lily's leg until it found the round curve of her backside. An incessant buzzing was ramping up behind his navel. He rolled over so he could curve around her, then let his hands explore the soft feminine curves of her body.

Lily softly mumbled. "Whatever you do, do not wake me up. Because this is the best dream I've ever had."

Joe smiled as he began nibbling the back of her neck. That made her shiver and laugh, then she turned toward him, loping her arm around his neck. He was just about to devour her mouth when they both heard a door slam downstairs.

Lily's body went stiff, then she sat straight up in bed. "Oh, no."

"Mommy! I'm home!"

Lily suddenly swore, then threw off the bedsheets. He watched in a sort of fascinated confusion as she began flying around the room, first in one direction, then the other. She snatched her robe from its hook in the bathroom and lashed the knot tight and fast.

"Joe. You've got to get out of here!"

"What?"

But she wasn't paying any attention to him. She dashed around the room grabbing his pants, belt and shoes. "Get out of bed!"

She was obviously upset and he didn't want to make

things worse. They could both hear Alexa calling for Lily. "Where are you, Mommy?"

"Lily, it's going to be okay. We'll just tell her..."

"No, Joe! Don't you understand? We're not even one day into our deal and we're about to get busted by my daughter! I do *not* want Alexa to know about this. You've got to go!"

"But how?"

Lily stopped and thought, her expression frantic. "You parked out back by the garage, so hopefully Alexa and Jennifer haven't seen your car yet. Get your stuff and hide in my closet. I'll go distract her and when the coast is clear, I'll come for you."

"Mommy?"

Alexa's voice was impossibly close.

Joe jumped out of bed naked, his arms full of his clothing, and made it into Lily's closet one split second before he heard Alexa say, "There you are, Mommy! I was calling for you. Did you hear me?"

Joe felt a rush of relief that he had managed to get out of sight before Alexa saw him. He stood frozen, afraid to even breathe, as he listened to the sounds of them descending the staircase. When he was sure they were downstairs, he began getting dressed in the dark. It wasn't easy and he hoped he hadn't put his shirt on inside out.

Long minutes passed as Joe waited for Lily's signal that it was safe for him to leave. He could hear them downstairs, but he couldn't make out their words. He heard the sounds of breakfast being prepared—the refrigerator door opening and closing, the rattle of silverware being laid out for breakfast, and Alexa's giggles. Then the grind of the blender and then the smell of bacon.

As Joe stood there in the dark, holding his shoes so he could silently escape the house, the strangest feeling came over him. It was something he had never felt before—the desire to go downstairs and join them for breakfast. And the fact that Lily wanted him up here in her closet and not downstairs with her and Alexa left him grumpy and out of sorts.

But he deserved this—he knew that much was true. How many women had gotten the same lecture from him? Boundaries around his time, his attention and most certainly his affection. He had never really thought about what it felt like to have someone tell you that they can only love you "this much." That you aren't important enough to be their everything. He'd always thought that as long as he was honest and up-front about his limits, everyone was happy. But Lily had been honest with him, yet being left behind in her closet was not making him happy at all.

Why couldn't he just open this door and join them for breakfast? Because of that damn cancer gene. He knew his odds—they weren't good. If he had inherited the gene, there was a 60 percent chance he'd develop cancer before midlife.

But that meant he might have a 40 percent chance of being fine. And what if he hadn't inherited the gene at all? It was only on his mother's side of the family, so there was a not small chance that he didn't have any risk at all.

What if he took that test and discovered he was fine?

Joe heard the oven timer ding, then the smell of sweet hot rolls made his mouth water. If he didn't have that cancer gene, then things could be different. He could be downstairs with Lily and Alexa right now. Maybe he could be a mortgage-and-minivan kind of guy after all.

The closet door swung open violently, startling him out of his reverie.

"Joe, get out."

He blinked against the sudden light after being in Lily's dark closet for so long. He felt disoriented and confused and now Lily was hissing at him. "I've sent Alexa over to Jennifer's to borrow some eggs. You've got to get out of here now!"

She pushed his car keys into his hand, then grabbed his wrist and pulled him from the closet. Everything was happening so fast. All he could do was surrender to her urgent requests and follow her downstairs. Before he knew what was happening, she had shut the back door behind him and was headed back down the hallway. She turned back one last time and mouthed the word *go!* before she disappeared into the kitchen.

After a few seconds of getting his bearings, Joe turned to leave. It was a long trip back to town from her cabin in the woods and he had plenty of time to think.

Apparently, Lily hadn't exaggerated when she said she was up for a fling. A fling and nothing more because she had made it quite clear that she didn't want to risk any part of her "real life" being affected by their fling.

It was wrong for him to feel rejected—they had both agreed to the terms. Casual, fun, passionate and short-lived. He sighed and decided there was no need to get that cancer test done. Cancer or no cancer, his life worked better when he put work first.

It was the end of the day, and Lily had just finished with her last patient. She sat at her desk, reviewing patient files, stifling a yawn—exhaustion weighing heavy on her.

No surprise, really. For the past month, she and Joe had been meeting at his place almost every morning before work. Their clandestine affair continued, and she couldn't help but smile at the thought of the creative—and undeniably sexy—ways they made use of that hour. Occasionally, she'd manage to arrange for Alexa to spend the night at a friend's house, allowing her to slip over to Joe's, parking in the back to keep their rendezvous under wraps. Still, she wasn't entirely sure they'd gone unnoticed.

Joe exited his exam room with Maggie following close behind, assuring her that he'd send her test results to a cardiologist in Billings.

"You can call me tomorrow morning," Lily said, offering a reassuring smile. "I should have some news for you by then."

Maggie's eyes sparkled with mischief. "Should I call here? Or at Dr. Chambers's place?"

Lily kept her smile in place, playing dumb, but inside, her heart sank. There were signs all over town that people knew what she and Joe were up to. Just the other day, the mailman handed her Joe's mail to deliver, and Edna at the Shop-n-Go had been suspiciously inquiring about Lily's health every time Joe bought flowers. She should've known better than to think they could keep their affair a secret. After all, no one keeps secrets in a small town—that was what she always said.

But as long as Alexa didn't know, that was all that truly mattered.

After Maggie left, Lily and Joe settled in to review their cases for the day, including Maggie's. They talked over the results as Joe went through the list of tests he'd performed on Maggie: blood pressure, cholesterol, EKG and a few others.

"Anything conclusive?" Lily asked, hopeful.

"Not really," Joe replied, leaning back in his chair. "Her blood pressure, cholesterol and EKG all look like those of a very healthy young woman. The only thing she reports is feeling these heart flutters during her daily run."

"Any suggestions?" Lily inquired, her curiosity piqued.

"Maybe," Joe said thoughtfully. "We'll need to see what the cardiologist in Billings has to say. She might need to go there for a more comprehensive test."

Lily yawned, standing up to stretch. "It's getting late," she said, her voice trailing off. "I better get…"

Suddenly, her head started to spin, and the room grew dim. She wanted to call out that something was wrong, but the words wouldn't form. From a distance, she heard Joe shout her name before everything went black.

"Lily… Lily… *Lily!*"

Someone was shouting her name from the end of a long, dark tunnel. Lily struggled to open her eyes, her vision blurry. There was Joe, crouched over her, his penlight darting back and forth as he called her name with a firm, commanding tone. The edge of panic in his voice made her want to reassure him that everything was okay, but her mind felt too foggy to form the words.

"What happened?" she managed to croak, her throat parched. She tried to sit up with his help.

"You fainted," Joe explained, his concern evident.

"That's weird," Lily murmured, trying to piece together what had happened.

"But you seem to be okay. Your heart rate and blood pressure are normal, so I don't think it's anything serious. Have you eaten today?"

"Yeah, eggs and pancakes at your house. Remember?" Lily said, struggling to get her footing. Joe assisted her, staying close.

"Right," he said, hovering nearby as she steadied herself. "I think it was just a fainting spell, Lily. Has that ever happened to you before?"

"No, I'm not really the fainting type," Lily said, attempting to brush off Joe's concern. His intense focus made her feel a bit self-conscious. Once she felt steady on her feet, she made her way to the restroom, needing a few moments to freshen her makeup and regain her composure.

As she walked, a nagging memory surfaced. She turned back to Joe, hesitating before speaking. "Actually, there was one other time…when I was pregnant with Alexa."

The color drained from Joe's face, leaving him looking as if he might faint himself.

"Come on," Lily said, taking his hand and guiding him to the waiting room couch. He sank heavily into the cushions.

"Maybe it's not related," Lily reassured him. "Just because I fainted during my pregnancy with Alexa doesn't mean it's the same this time."

"Right," Joe replied, his voice sounding distant, his expression one of sheer, stunned horror.

"Besides, we used protection every time, so there's very little chance that—" Lily began, but then she remembered their first night together after the Healthy Heart Gala. As she rummaged through her bathroom cupboard, she had felt uneasy. At the time, she had brushed it off as her overcautious nature trying to shield her from getting hurt by Joe. But now she realized it wasn't just that. The condoms had been under her sink for years, never replaced because she had never needed them. That night with Joe, she hadn't been thinking about the expiration date or their integrity; she had simply been grateful they were there.

Joe stared out the window, his hands pressed together in a tense steeple. "You can't be pregnant, Lily. You just can't."

Her concern for Joe's reaction was giving way to a deeper, more painful, emotion.

"Would it really be so terrible if I was?"

She knew Joe had been eagerly counting the days until he could leave Twin Creeks and start his career as an oncologist. She understood his reasons were noble and good, but she had given up pretending that she didn't care. The truth was she had fallen for Joe in a way that left her disoriented and vulnerable. She had tried to savor every moment with him while maintaining the facade that their relationship was just a fling. But she had never imagined that he might see her as an obstacle to his plans.

Joe opened his mouth to respond, but Lily cut him off. "You know what? Let's just find out."

In a haze of shock and frustration, Lily stood up and headed to the clinic's medical supply cupboard. Joe's reaction had stung deeply, making her feel like a problem in his life rather than someone he cared about. Grabbing a pregnancy test, she made her way to the bathroom, hoping Joe wouldn't follow. Her emotions were on a knife's edge, and all it would take was a single word from him to send her spiraling into tears.

She peed on the stick and set it aside, waiting for the three minutes to pass. As she waited, she couldn't make sense of Joe's intense reaction. She hadn't planned on getting pregnant, and it was just as difficult for her as it was for him, but his horror seemed more profound than just shock. She knew how important his career was and that he was eager to return to his oncology training.

Despite her best efforts to keep their fling casual and free of commitment, she had fallen for him. She wasn't expecting him to change his plans because of a pregnancy, but it hurt to see that his shock seemed to go beyond the immediate news. He appeared truly horrified at the thought of her carrying his baby.

She glanced at her watch—three minutes had passed. Closing her eyes, she inhaled deeply, silently praying for the best. When she opened them again, she checked the results.

Joe was exactly where she had left him, slumped on the waiting room couch, his head buried in his hands. As she walked back in, he lifted his gaze to meet hers, his once-bright eyes now dull, filled with a hollow emptiness.

Without a word, she handed him the test. She watched as his breath caught in his throat, the color draining from his face.

Her heart broke. She sank onto the couch beside him, the weight of the moment pressing down on her chest. "Joe, I don't know what you think I expect, but... I don't have any illusions. I know you're not going to stay in Twin Creeks or...get married, or—"

Joe's hand gently curved over her knee, the warmth of his touch making her hate how her body instinctively responded to him.

"Lily, stop. This isn't about you."

"Then what is it?"

He sighed, hesitating, before finally speaking. "I should've told you a long time ago...but I didn't think it mattered."

Her heart thudded painfully in her chest. "What didn't matter?"

He took one of her hands, folding it gently between both of his. His voice was soft but heavy with grief. "My mom wasn't the only one in my family to die young from cancer. Her brother, father and my aunt—they all did, too."

"Oh, Joe...that's terrible."

"We didn't know it back then, but there's a gene. It runs in families. Different types of cancer, but the common thread—they all developed it before turning fifty."

Lily sat in silence, her mind racing as she pieced it all together. She couldn't even begin to imagine what it must feel like—so much loss in one family.

"We can test for that gene now," he whispered.

Shock rippled through her. "Joe, do you have the gene?"

"I don't know," he admitted, his voice low. "I've never been tested."

Her eyes widened in disbelief. "Why on earth not?"

"Because it didn't matter," he said, his frustration raw. "I had no plans to get married, no plans to have kids. I didn't want to risk passing it on."

Lily's mind flashed with memories of social media images—Joe at parties, on yachts, at the beach. Always with a beautiful woman, but never the same one twice. He hadn't been tested because he never planned to stay long enough for it to matter.

Not even with her.

A wave of emotions hit her—sympathy for Joe, who wasn't the player she'd thought, but a man hiding behind a mask of detachment. And fear—gut-wrenching fear. What if Joe did have that gene? He could have fewer than twenty years before facing the devastating diagnosis that haunted his family.

No wonder his oncology fellowship meant so much. It wasn't about ambition; it was his way of fighting the disease that had destroyed his family—and could one day destroy him, too.

But the fear didn't stop there. What if their child carried the gene? What if their baby had to watch Joe die young and face the same terrifying future?

"Joe, you have to..." Her voice broke, her chest tightening.

He raised a weary hand. "I've already called a doctor friend of mine in Billings. As soon as I can get there, the test will be ready."

"I'm going with you."

"You don't have to—"

She grabbed his hand, gripping it tightly, her heart pounding with determination. She loved this man—desperately—and there was no way she was letting him face his worst fear alone. "This affects me, too."

Joe's gaze dropped to her belly, then back to her eyes, softening with understanding.

"Okay."

Lily fumbled through her purse, her hands shaking as she finally found her phone. She quickly arranged for Alexa to stay overnight with Jennifer, giving herself enough time for the two-hour drive to Billings. Everything felt surreal, like she was watching her life unravel from a distance.

At the hospital, the staff was expecting them. Joe was whisked away to the back, leaving Lily alone in the waiting room. The silence was unbearable, thick with dread.

Her mind raced, thoughts spiraling in every direction. What if Joe did have the gene? What would that mean for him? For their baby? The fear clawed at her insides, cold and unrelenting. She couldn't shake the thought of their child growing up without a father, just like Alexa had. But unlike Alexa, this baby would grow up knowing their father, only to suffer the pain of Joe being taken from them far too soon, just like the others in his family. The grief felt suffocating—grief for something that hadn't even happened yet but lingered like a dark cloud, casting shadows over every hopeful thought.

And what if the test came back positive? Could she handle watching Joe, this man she had fallen for so deeply, battle the same disease that had taken so many from him? Could she really survive the heartache of losing Joe like she had lost Connor? It was her very worst fear coming to life before her horrified eyes.

Maybe it would be easier to let him go to Florida. Let him run from Twin Creeks and from her. Let him slip back into his life, away from the constant reminder of what could be lost. She could return to her safe little bubble, where she controlled her world, and her heart wasn't at risk of being shattered.

When Joe finally returned, the nurse followed closely behind, telling them that his doctor friend had put a rush on the results. "We'll call you as soon as we have them."

The drive back to her house was painfully quiet, both lost in their own thoughts. The tension between them was heavy, unsaid words hanging in the air like storm clouds. Once home, Lily numbly put on the kettle for tea, going through the motions while her mind felt paralyzed by all that had transpired.

Suddenly, Joe's phone rang, its shrill tone piercing the dark quiet of her house. They both froze, eyes locking, the weight of a thousand emotions passing between them. Fear. Hope. Love.

He answered the call, his hand trembling slightly. Lily reached for him, her fingers entwining with his. She wouldn't let him face this moment alone.

Joe listened in silence, nodding slowly as the voice on the other end of the line spoke. When he finally hung up, his eyes were wide, disbelief washing over him. "It's good news," he said, his voice thick with emotion. "The results are negative. I don't have the gene."

Lily's breath left her in a rush, her knees nearly giving out as the overwhelming relief washed over her. She felt like she could collapse, the weight she'd been carrying for hours suddenly lifted. Their baby was safe. Joe was safe.

For now, everything would be okay.

But the relief was short-lived. Lily knew they couldn't go back to what they were before the pregnancy test turned positive. This was supposed to be a fun fling—a few passionate weeks until Joe left. But now everything had changed. They both understood too much, had seen the risks they were taking, and there was no pretending otherwise.

A wave of exhaustion crashed over Lily, making her body feel heavy. All of a sudden, all she wanted was sleep. Joe looked at her, and for a moment, they were frozen—trapped in a mess of emotions and unspoken feelings, neither of them knowing what to say.

"Maybe I should go," Joe finally said, his voice quiet, almost hesitant.

It felt like a test. Should she ask him to stay? Would it make any difference?

"A lot's happened tonight," she said softly, her heart aching. "We probably need some time to process everything."

His eyes searched her face, trying to find something—anything—that would help him make sense of her emotions. But Lily didn't know what she was feeling herself, and she had no idea what he'd see.

"You're probably right," he murmured, the sadness in his voice unmistakable. It felt like defeat.

"I'll see you at the clinic tomorrow," she replied, the words feeling hollow. When they kissed goodbye, it was a chaste, closed-mouth affair, the passion that had once burned between them now overshadowed by the uncertainty of their future.

Lily stood on her front porch, watching as Joe's taillights grew smaller, fading into the distance as he disappeared into the forest. A soft, distant sound—a rustle in the trees—pulled her from her thoughts, making her wonder what, indeed, the future would hold for them now.

CHAPTER TWELVE

Lily smiled as she checked Beth and her newborn, marveling at how the baby was thriving. Beth's husband beamed with pride, unable to contain his excitement. He was the picture of a proud father, doting on his wife and baby, bragging about their little one's first month of life.

Lily, exhausted from her long, emotional night with Joe, could barely keep her eyes open. But there was no way she'd miss this checkup. Being part of moments like these, caring for families and watching them grow—it was what she loved most about her job.

After walking Beth and her family to the waiting room, she noticed Joe emerging from his exam room at the same time. It was clear he hadn't slept much, either. They exchanged a brief glance as he wished his patient well.

"Lily, do you have a moment?" Joe asked, his tone serious.

She nodded, said goodbye to the family and followed him into his office, her stomach twisting with anticipation. She'd been thinking about him all night, wondering what the test results meant for their future. But now, seeing the look on his face, she wasn't sure she wanted to know.

Joe closed the door behind them and turned to her. "I have some news."

Her heart raced. What could possibly top the bombshell of last night?

"The oncology program in Florida had a candidate drop out. They've offered me the spot—if I can start a month early."

Lily quickly did the math. A month early meant...now.

"I have to leave immediately."

Her mind scrambled to process the words, and she sank into the chair opposite his desk. Just hours ago, she had been trying to figure out what Joe's test results meant for their future. Now it seemed like there was no future at all.

"Well, that's great news," she forced herself to say, her voice hollow. "I'm really happy for you."

"Thanks." But there was no joy in his eyes, just exhaustion and something else—something that looked like guilt.

"I was thinking...maybe you and Alexa could come with me," Joe said, his voice tentative.

"Oh?" Her head spun as she tried to reconcile his offer with the defeated look in his eyes. She cared for him deeply. Maybe more than she had realized until now. But this—this didn't feel right. Some secret part of her had hoped their fling might become something real, something lasting.

But his eyes told a different story. He looked strained, burdened. "I don't want to leave you here all alone," he added, the weight of his words heavy in the air.

That was when it hit her. Joe didn't want to leave Twin

Creeks. But he wanted Florida more. And now, she and Alexa—and their baby—were complications.

"Take the fellowship, Joe. You deserve it."

"What about the baby?" His words struck her like a dagger. No mention of love. No confession of feelings. Just the obligation of a child.

Lily thought of Beth's husband, how he doted on his wife and their baby. That was what it looked like when a man chose you—when he wanted to be a father and partner above all else.

Her heart clenched, but she held steady. *You knew what this was* she reminded herself. They had never promised each other anything beyond a few weeks of good sex and fun. She had been the fool to fall for him, especially when his carefree social media feed had shown her exactly what would happen: good times, good sex then goodbye.

And that was okay. She didn't need Joe. She loved him—God, she loved him—but she didn't need him. And she wasn't about to love someone who didn't truly love her back. Beth's husband had shown her what real commitment looked like, and that was what she and Alexa—and her baby—deserved. Nothing less.

"You can see the baby anytime you want, Joe. Just let me know when."

Joe blinked, clearly shocked. He hadn't expected this. It felt like a breakup, but with so much more at stake.

He opened his mouth, as if to protest, but then stopped, thinking better of it. "And the clinic?"

"I think I can manage until the new doctor is hired."

He gave her a long, appraising look, as if waiting for her to change her mind. But Lily didn't waver.

"I have no doubt," he finally said, though his voice was soft, defeated. His shoulders slumped as he let out a breath. "Okay, then. I guess I'll go pack."

Lily merely nodded, her heart breaking as she watched him gather his briefcase and personal belongings, shutting down his computer with an eerie finality.

"I'm sorry, Lily," Joe said quietly, his voice full of regret.

For what? For getting her pregnant? For leaving early? She couldn't be sure. Other than the pregnancy, everything seemed to be perfectly on schedule for him.

"I know," she replied softly.

He gave her one last searching look, but she held firm, refusing to let her emotions betray her. Moments later, the clinic door closed quietly behind him, and he was gone.

Joe leaned back in his chair, rubbing his eyes as he glanced at the clock on the wall. It was nearing the end of his shift, but his mind was still racing with thoughts of his patients. The oncology ward was always busy, filled with the quiet hum of machines and the soft murmur of conversations. He took a deep breath, refocusing on his computer screen to update his notes before his next patient.

His cell phone alerted, signaling another hospital task at hand. Joe stood up, smoothing down his white coat, and made his way to Room 214. He stopped by the nurses' station first for an update on his new patient.

"Hey, I just got a page regarding…" He checked his phone. "Mr. Roger Allen in Room 214. What's the story?"

The nurse paused her typing on the computer to roll her eyes. "Mr. Allen's here for evaluation and treatment of advanced colon cancer. The attending put orders in for a full battery of tests, which the patient has completed. But he's refusing a colonoscopy because—and this is a quote—*I know my wife says I have my head up my butt, but I don't think she meant that literally.*"

Joe chuckled. "Well, at least he has a sense of humor, right?"

"Yes, but Dr. Atkinson is losing his cool. Mr. Allen's treatment plan can't be finalized until he's completed all the testing."

Joe rapped his knuckles against the counter. "Right. Let me see what I can do."

Joe knocked on the door, then entered Mr. Allen's room. He found a middle-aged man staring out the window, his shoulders slumped and eyes distant. The man's pallor and gaunt frame were stark reminders of the battle he was facing. Joe approached with a warm smile, hoping to ease the tension in the room.

"Good afternoon, Mr. Allen. I'm Dr. Joe Chambers. How are you feeling today?"

Mr. Allen turned slowly, his expression wary. "Not too great, Doc."

"I can imagine," Joe said. "I think we can get you feeling better soon, Mr. Allen. But we need to complete all your testing first."

The man groaned and turned away from Joe. "This will be my fourth colonoscopy, you know."

Joe winced. Not a fun procedure for sure. "I'm sorry about that, Mr. Allen. Can I answer any questions to make this easier for you?"

"Yeah," he said softly. "When can I go home?"

Joe's phone went off again, alerting him that his department meeting would start in five minutes. The next ninety minutes of his life would be about budgets, protocols and research updates.

It was tempting to give Mr. Allen a quick pep talk, then rush off for his meeting and hope for the best. No one would blame him. His entire team spent their time bouncing around patient care, administrative meetings and endless hours spent documenting every single thing they did. He had learned a lot about bureaucracy since joining the oncology team here, but patient care seemed to get lost in the shuffle.

Joe checked his watch. He really didn't want to spend the next two hours in a stuffy meeting listening to administrators tussle over budgets.

"May I?" Joe asked, indicating the chair next to the bed. Mr. Allen nodded. Joe slipped his lab coat off and folded it over the back of the chair. He removed his tie and unbuttoned his shirt a bit. Not the same casual attire he wore in Twin Creeks, but maybe it would help. "Where is home, Mr. Allen?"

"A little town called Pine Hill. Not much there, but it's home."

Joe's heart ached at the familiarity of the story. "I know a little about small towns, too. I spent six months in Twin Creeks, Montana. It's tough being away from the people and places you know, especially during times like these."

His mind's eye formed a perfect image of Lily as she lay sleeping serenely in bed with him. Her jet-black hair fanning across her pillow, her lush full lips slightly parted in sleep.

He couldn't believe how just the thought of her was enough to make his throat go tight and his vision get misty. It had been six weeks since he had left Twin Creeks. He thought that his busy schedule would ease his pain, but it was as fresh as if it had happened yesterday. Daisy seemed to feel the loss, too. He had found a five-star doggie daycare for her to attend while he was working, but she never seemed happy when he dropped her off. The director said she would adjust in time, but every day he found her by the gate, ignoring the other dogs and looking up at him with big, soulful eyes that seemed to say *take me home*.

He had heard hardly anything from Lily since he left Twin Creeks. She did send him some of Alexa's artwork, though, which he clung to like a lifeline, each colorful drawing a reminder of the family he'd left behind. He knew she was running the clinic alone and he had a million questions about how everyone was doing, but she never sent any messages—just Alexa's drawings. And he didn't know what to say.

He got the message loud and clear. *Stay away.*

Joe and Mr. Allen talked for a while longer. Joe enjoyed Mr. Allen's stories about his family and life back in Pine Hill. It reminded Joe of the people in Twin Creeks, and all they had taught him about caring for patients. He couldn't shake the feeling of guilt for leaving them behind.

Just as he was about to leave the room, Joe heard a sharp voice behind him. "Dr. Chambers, a word please."

Joe turned to see Dr. Martin, his program director, glaring at him from the doorway. He nodded to Mr. Allen and stepped out into the hallway.

"Yes?"

"You're spending too much time with patients," Dr. Martin snapped. "We have protocols to follow, and we need you to be efficient. You can't afford to be so…sentimental."

Joe felt a flash of frustration. He was sorely tempted to ask his program director if he knew this patient's name and what he was willing to fight for. But he doubted that would improve their relationship.

At the end of his shift, Joe sifted through his mail. There were the usual conference announcements and advertisements from pharmaceutical companies. He was about to dump the pile in his waste bin, when a thin, creamy envelope caught his attention.

He immediately recognized Lily's handwriting. He held the envelope for a moment before he lunged for his silver letter opener and made a clean slit across the top of the envelope. He expected this might be another of Alexa's drawings but no, it was something else. Black-and-white glossy photographs.

He slid them from the envelope, laid them out one by one on his desk. He turned on his lamp so he could see them better.

His eyes welled up as he realized what he was seeing. Ultrasound images of his unborn child, taken at Lily's twelve-week checkup. A small, quiet smile spread across his face as he traced the grainy pictures with his finger. Never had he felt such an overwhelming mix of wonder and love.

He checked the envelope again, hoping there might be a note from Lily. Something to let him know how she was doing, if she was okay...if she missed him. But there was nothing to relieve the aching loneliness that had haunted him every single day since he had left her behind in Twin Creeks.

And why should she relieve his misery? He had foolishly convinced himself that he would be happier here in Florida, buried in a fellowship consumed by data and statistics, instead of being with the woman who had taught him what it truly meant to love. He deserved every minute of loneliness here.

Joe stared at the images for a long time, his heart aching with longing. He missed Alexa's bright smile, her infectious laughter. And he missed Lily's warm body, her sensuous kisses. Six weeks had passed since he left. He should feel more like himself by now. But he couldn't shake the feeling that he had made the wrong decision.

He was surrounded by a tropical paradise, but he never went anywhere but work and his apartment. He could say it was because he was too busy, but the truth was, there was no beauty in the world without Lily by his side. The ocean without Lily was just a shark-infested salty pool. A sunset dinner without Lily was like eating cardboard. Who cared about tropical breezes and sun-soaked days when you woke up alone every morning?

How many more signs did fate have to send him before he got the message? It was time for him to care for *people*. His people! His beautiful, quirky, delightful people.

He opened his computer again and composed a new email.

I regret to inform you that I will be leaving the Oncology Fellowship Program at Florida State University, effective immediately…

A huge weight lifted from his shoulders, and he felt joy coursing through his body for the first time in six long weeks.

Then he opened a new window so he could search for the first flight back to western Montana.

CHAPTER THIRTEEN

THE TWIN CREEKS COMMUNITY CLINIC was eerily quiet, a stark contrast to the daytime bustle of patients and activity. The hum of the fluorescent lights seemed louder in the absence of voices and footsteps. Stacks of patient files cluttered Lily's desk, each one a testament to the endless stream of ailments and worries she'd managed throughout the day. She leaned back, feeling the weight of exhaustion press heavily on her shoulders.

Her eyes drifted to the chair across from her desk—Joe's chair. It had been six weeks since he left, but the memory of him sitting there, laughing and joking, was still vivid. She could almost hear his voice.

"And then he says…" Joe had barely been able to get the words out between chuckles. "That's not a lab sample. That's my lunch!"

Lily had lost count of how many times Joe had teased her into fits of laughter, her tears smudging her mascara as she begged him to stop. The clinic had felt so alive back then. She could still see his broad smile, lighting up the room as they shared yet another one of his medical school stories. Those moments had made the world seem brighter, more enchanting.

She shook off the memory, her smile fading into a

deep, aching melancholy. Sighing, she stood to stretch her back and headed to the kitchenette, needing a distraction from the weight of the past.

Filling the kettle with water, she reached for a travel mug but paused. It was a memento from the Healthy Heart blood drive and gala. With a sigh, she pushed the mug aside and chose a plain one instead. *It's just a mug, Lily. Just a mug.* But that small act of denial tugged at her heart.

The tea brewed slowly, the steam curling upward, mirroring her tangled thoughts. She returned to her desk, opening the next patient file, but her gaze kept flicking to the empty chair across from her. Why was it even there? Other than the occasional visiting doctor or nurse, she worked alone.

"Stupid," she muttered. Frustrated, she pushed away from her desk, grabbed the chair and dragged it across the room, the legs screeching against the hardwood floor. She shoved it up against the wall. "There!" she said to the empty room.

But it wasn't enough. Joe wasn't coming back to sit in that chair with his mischievous grin and that perfectly tousled hair. No more end-of-the-day jokes or intense discussions about difficult cases. It was just her now, and the ever-growing pile of patient files.

The front doorbell tinkled.

Good grief, what now?

"We're closed," she called out, her voice tired and resigned. She waited, listening. After-hours drop-ins weren't common, and usually, they were quick questions or requests for medication refills. If it was urgent, they'd stay. If not, she'd hear the doorbell again as they left.

Please, just go away.

Her body ached, and all she wanted was to crawl into bed with a cup of tea, a good book and maybe a sleeve of chocolate cookies. But then she heard a soft jangle—metal on metal—and a rustling sound.

"What the—?"

Before she could finish, Daisy appeared around the corner. Her ears flopped, eyes bright, her tail wagging with each step. But what really caught Lily's attention was the pink gift bag clutched in Daisy's mouth, a silver heart embossed on the front, the white tissue paper rustling softly.

Lily stared, her mind struggling to make sense of what she was seeing. Daisy padded around the desk and sat in front of her, tail wagging, waiting patiently. There was a small tag attached to the gift bag.

Open me

Lily's heart skipped a beat as she reached out, her voice soft. "Daisy, give."

The dog released the bag, and Lily retrieved it, her emotions swirling. If Daisy was here, Joe couldn't be far behind. She had spent weeks wondering if he'd miraculously appear like he had that dark, snowy night. She hadn't just waited—she had *yearned* for him.

She opened the bag, finding a small white box wrapped in tissue paper. Her fingers trembled as she removed it. Inside was a titanium cuff bracelet, delicate snowflakes etched across its surface. She flipped it over, noticing an inscription on the inside.

Fate 46.1263° North and 112.9478° West

"It's beautiful," she whispered, sensing Joe standing in the doorway. "But what does it mean?"

"Those are the GPS coordinates the mayor gave me the night I got lost in the blizzard."

Lily rolled the bracelet between her fingers, its weight solid and grounding. "You really hurt me, Joe."

She heard his sharp intake of breath. "I know. I was a bona fide idiot."

When she finally looked at him, he was as beautiful as ever—those magnetic blue eyes and tousled auburn waves—but he also looked thinner, tired. He glanced at the chair she had just pushed against the wall, his expression questioning. She nodded, and he dragged it back to its usual spot in front of her desk, sitting with his arms folded.

Joe took a deep breath. "I didn't choose you or the baby when I left, and I regret it every day. My whole life I've been preparing to fight the disease that destroyed my family. I never thought I'd have love in my life because of that risk. But then I met you, and it changed everything."

Lily held the bracelet tightly, her heart beating faster.

"My mentor sent me to Twin Creeks to teach me to care about people, not just the diseases they carry. I didn't understand what she meant at first. But now I know—she wanted me to learn who *I* was willing to fight for. And that's you, Lily. You, Alexa and our baby."

Joe's voice cracked as he continued. "I don't deserve anything from you after leaving, but I want you to know that I'm staying right here in Twin Creeks. I want to be part of my child's life—and yours—if you'll have me."

Lily rolled the bracelet between her thumb and forefinger. "Fate can be awful sometimes. That's what I told you that night."

Joe smiled. "I remember."

Lily held up the bracelet so that the light from her desk lamp glinted off the snowflakes. "But now I know that it can be pretty wonderful, too." Unconsciously, her free hand found its way to the beginning of her soft round baby bump.

She set the bracelet on her desk. Joe visibly stiffened. "I can't go back to the bubble, Joe. I've tried. But nothing works…because I'm in love with you."

He seemed too restless to stay seated. Joe crossed the distance between them, kneeling in front of her, his hands resting on her knees. A rush of electricity surged through her, making her certain their baby felt it, too.

"Oh, Lily," he murmured, his voice filled with regret. "I'm such an idiot."

She smiled softly and reached out to run her fingers through his thick tousled hair. "Go on…"

Joe took her hand, intertwining their fingers. The warmth of his touch felt like being wrapped in her coziest blanket. "You once told me that people aren't just problems to be solved. I learned that here in Twin Creeks. And again in Florida. People are more than their diseases. They're families, friends…and with you, I realized, they're the people you're willing to fight for."

His gaze dropped to her baby bump, then back to her.

With a nod, she gave him permission. He placed his hands gently on her belly, his touch reverent.

"And I want to be here with you and Alexa and our baby, if you'll let me."

Lily's heart clenched as she fought off the voice that told her she was safer alone. Safety was an illusion anyway. Every day was an unknown, and maybe Joe or she would someday become a cancer patient themselves. But love was worth the risk.

"It's good to have you home, Joe."

Relief washed over his face. He slipped the bracelet onto her wrist, his fingers lingering as they both took each other in.

"Is this real?" she whispered, her voice trembling. "Or am I dreaming?"

"You tell me," Joe replied, his voice thick with emotion. He cupped her face in his hands, and when his lips met hers, the world faded away. She opened herself to him, mind, body and soul, ready to fight for their love for the rest of her life.

EPILOGUE

The whir of the helicopter blades was deafening, but Lily was used to it. The confined space of the medical chopper was her domain, and here, every second counted.

The call had come in just twenty minutes ago—a severe car accident on a remote highway. Now she was midair, speeding toward the crash site, her mind already racing through protocols and procedures.

"Let's move, people!" Lily shouted when they landed. She grabbed her flight bag and rushed to the patient, her heart pounding with adrenaline.

"Vitals?" she asked, kneeling beside the young man.

"Blood pressure's dropping, pulse weak," a paramedic responded. Sweat beaded on his forehead.

"All right, we need to get him stabilized before we can transport." She turned to her partner, Jake, who was already setting up the IV. "Two liters of saline, wide-open."

Lily assessed the injuries with a practiced eye. The man had a deep laceration on his thigh, likely from a piece of metal, and his chest was rising unevenly—a sign of potential internal injuries. She noted the pallor of his skin and the rapid, shallow breaths.

"He's in hypovolemic shock," she muttered. "We need to stop this bleeding now. Hand me the tourniquet."

With no hesitation, she applied the tourniquet above the wound, tightening it just enough to slow the blood loss without causing further damage. The man's eyes fluttered, and he let out a weak groan.

"Stay with me," Lily said through gritted teeth. "What's your name?"

"P-Paul," he managed to whisper.

"Hey, Paul, listen up, all right? Everything's going to be okay, Paul. I will make sure of that."

Lily and Jake worked together without saying a word. They had partnered on many rescue calls, and Lily had come to trust that he knew the right thing to do at the right time.

Lily secured an oxygen mask over Paul's face and checked the monitors attached to him. "Good job, team. Let's get him on the stretcher and into the chopper."

The transfer was smooth, Lily's team moving like a well-oiled machine. Once inside the helicopter, she secured Paul and rechecked his vitals. He was still critical, but stable enough for transport.

As they lifted off, Lily monitored him closely, her mind already running through the next steps. She mentally prepared the detailed report she would deliver to the trauma team waiting at the hospital.

"Hang in there, Paul. We're almost there."

The city's skyline appeared in the distance, then the hospital's helipad came into view. Lily's grip on Paul's hand tightened for a moment, a silent promise that she would see this through.

They touched down, and the trauma team swarmed in, taking over with practiced efficiency. Lily briefed them quickly, then stepped back, her job done for now. She watched as they wheeled Paul away, a mixture of exhaustion and satisfaction settling over her.

That was the last call of her shift with Jake. All that was left to do was let the medical helicopter take them back to the air ambulance headquarters where her gear was stored. She said goodbye to the pilot and to Jake, grabbed her gear and headed for the parking lot.

Joe's forest green SUV waited in the parking lot, as she knew it would be. Even though it meant traveling an hour each way from Twin Creeks, Joe insisted on picking her up at the end of her twenty-four-hour shifts. It was a good call. Sometimes she was so bone-weary from back-to-back trauma calls, she could barely keep her eyes open.

But this pickup was a little more special.

Joe stood outside his SUV for her, and her heart almost skipped a beat. He was wearing the same jacket that he had worn the first time they had met at the Shop-n-Go and had his beard trimmed to that same precise short length. There was such a strong sense of déjà-vu, it made her knees a little wobbly.

He looked the same, but everything was so different now.

Jacob, their son, was eight months old now—a cheerful babbling baby. Alexa was halfway through first grade and delighted in her new role as Jacob's big sister. Both were waiting in the back of Joe's new SUV for their next grand adventure.

Lily walked into Joe's waiting arms and buried her cold nose against his warm neck. He wrapped his arms around her and rested his chin on her head.

"How did Jacob sleep last night?" she asked, breathing in the mix of his aftershave and baby powder and that unique scent that was just Joe.

"Well, let's put it this way," he said, his voice gritty with fatigue. "Whoever coined the term *slept like a baby* has a pretty warped sense of humor."

She laughed and looked up at him. He kissed the tip of her very cold nose.

"You ready for this adventure?"

Lily's heart fluttered a little as she contemplated their family's first ever ski trip. It had been a long time since she had donned a pair of skis and hurled herself down a mountain, though she doubted that was how this adventure would go. With two kids under six, this trip would be less black diamond, more bunny hill for sure.

"I've been counting the hours," she told Joe, then handed him her flight bag. He headed to the back of the SUV to store her gear along with their suitcases and skis while she opened the back passenger door to find her two rug rats waiting.

"Mommy! Joe said we're going skiing!"

"That's right, baby. We're leaving right now."

Alexa's face furrowed into a small frown. "Will I get to go skiing, too?"

Lily's heart fluttered at the thought of Alexa on skis, but she pushed the fear aside. "Of course you can. But you have to wear your helmet and stick to the bunny slope…"

"Aww, Mom!" Alexa, her beautiful, stubborn, ambitious, adrenaline-junkie daughter protested.

"Until," Lily continued with a smile, "the ski instructor says you are ready for the intermediate ski runs."

Alexa's eyes widened at the prospect of more thrills ahead. "Okay!" she said with a beaming smile. She had something to look forward to now, and really, wasn't that what everyone wanted?

Lily leaned forward to give her dozing baby a kiss on his forehead. He still smelled like a baby, which was a source of endless delight. "No skiing for you, baby Jacob," Lily whispered. "You'll be having fun at the lodge's childcare center."

Alexa looked at Jacob like she was a little mother, too. "Don't worry, Jake. When you get bigger, I'll teach you how to ski."

Joe appeared behind her and wrapped his arms around her waist, tugging her into his chest. She took a moment to lean back into him, loving the solid feel of his body against hers.

"You ready for this?" he asked, his breath warm on her ear.

Lily paused for a moment to reflect on the adventure her life had become. After becoming a mother for the second time, she and Joe had worked together to design a new home for themselves, located a little closer to town so they were better able to respond to urgent calls at the clinic. Jennifer was sad to see them move away, but it also meant she could rent out her cabin to the many tourists who passed through Twin Creeks.

Joe and Lily ran the Twin Creeks Community Clinic

together now. They had developed a business plan focused on adding new services and technology to better serve Twin Creeks and its surrounding communities. Joe volunteered one week each month with Trailblazers in Cancer Care, delivering cancer treatments and doing preventative screening in towns in the wider area.

Lily had started taking a few shifts each month as a flight nurse with an air ambulance company based in a small town about an hour outside Twin Creeks. Working in trauma care again, even on a limited basis, thrilled her and sharpened her skills for emergency work that came up at the clinic.

It also made her feel connected to Connor in a mystical way. Of course she saw Connor in Alexa, too, especially in her beautiful hazel eyes. But it was in the skies where she most felt Connor's presence. They had bonded over the high stakes trauma cases she had delivered to his emergency room, and every patient she stabilized and saved made her feel close to Connor, even if it was just for a moment.

She glanced up at the skies now, and then to Joe, who had helped her weave her past into her future.

"I sure am," she breathed. Then she turned and took Joe's coat lapels in her hands, so she could pull his mouth down to hers. His kisses were like oxygen to her, and she inhaled him deeply, feeling his love permeate her body so that every doubt was subdued, every lonely corner filled with warmth and hope.

* * * * *

*If you enjoyed this story,
check out this other great read
from Kate MacGuire*

Resisting the Off-Limits Pediatrician

Available now!

MILLS & BOON®

Coming next month

A DADDY FOR HER BABIES
Becky Wicks

'Twins,' Theo announces, before Dr Priya can.

She nods and lets him wheel the monitor closer so I can see better.

Twins.

The word echoes through the room, doubling itself in my mind. Twins? I turn to Theo, who's still grinning in a way that makes him look ten years younger and twenty times more handsome. Here they are, right here. Two little beings, my babies, dancing in their own private universe.

'Twins are a huge part of my family. They have been for generations, but somehow I never really thought...' My voice trails off. I'm lost in a swell of emotions now, just looking at the screen. I am completely mesmerized by what I'm seeing and soon I'm hearing it, too—two tiny hearts beating in sync.

'They're cooking along nicely, Carter,' Theo says proudly.

'Would you like to know the genders?' Dr Sharma asks. My palm is warm and clammy now from my nerves, glued to Theo's. He's still mouthing the word *twins* to himself, and there's a look of disbelief and wonderment on his face that I've never actually seen before. Am I ready? I think I am. I tell her yes. I think I'm feeding off Theo's excitement.

Dr Sharma begins with another swirl of the cool wand over my abdomen. 'You're having a boy and a girl.'

'One of each, no...' Theo lets out a laugh, just as I do.

A boy and a girl. This is crazy. More tears gather in the corners of my eyes. 'Just like Rose dreamed,' I remember suddenly. Weirdly, Rose said she had a dream the other night, in which I announced this exact thing. I wish she were here now. She'd be wrapped around their little fingers already, too.

'Congratulations, Carter,' Theo whispers. I know I'm emotional, but his words tingle my ear and send a flush of adrenaline to my nerves. I can't help missing my sister, but I'm so relieved that someone's here to witness this. That *Theo* is here to witness this.

'Congratulations, *both* of you,' Dr Priya says, making me a printout so I can show Rose. She's going to be so thrilled. Just wait till she... Wait... *What did she say?*

'Oh, no,' I insert as it hits me what this lady just alluded to. 'Theo's not... I mean, we're not...'

'They're going to be so loved, right, wifey?' Theo finishes for me. He's still marveling at the screen. He really does look fiercely determined now and I let the comment go.

They will definitely be loved. But my friend and colleague has just been mistaken for the father of these babies, and more concerning, for a hot fleeting second there I caught myself wishing he really *were*.

Continue reading

A DADDY FOR HER BABIES
Becky Wicks

Available next month
millsandboon.co.uk

Copyright © 2025 Becky Wicks

COMING SOON!

We really hope you enjoyed reading this book. If you're looking for more romance be sure to head to the shops when new books are available on

Thursday 22nd May

To see which titles are coming soon, please visit
millsandboon.co.uk/nextmonth

MILLS & BOON

LET'S TALK
Romance

For exclusive extracts, competitions and special offers, find us online:

- **f** MillsandBoon
- **X** @MillsandBoon
- **◉** @MillsandBoonUK
- **♪** @MillsandBoonUK

Get in touch on 01413 063 232

For all the latest titles coming soon, visit
millsandboon.co.uk/nextmonth

FOUR BRAND NEW BOOKS FROM
MILLS & BOON MODERN

The same great stories you love, a stylish new look!

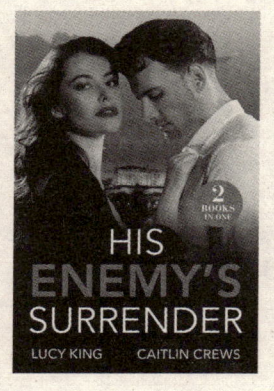

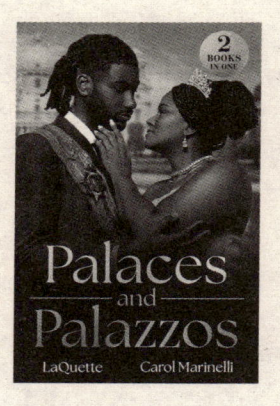

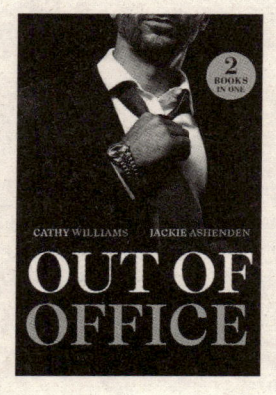

A Consequence Claimed — Louise Fuller, Clare Connelly (2 Books in One)

Palaces and Palazzos — LaQuette, Carol Marinelli (2 Books in One)

His Enemy's Surrender — Lucy King, Caitlin Crews (2 Books in One)

Out of Office — Cathy Williams, Jackie Ashenden (2 Books in One)

OUT NOW

Eight Modern stories published every month, find them all at:

millsandboon.co.uk

afterglow BOOKS

Afterglow Books is a trend-led, trope-filled list of books with diverse, authentic and relatable characters, a wide array of voices and representations, plus real world trials and tribulations. Featuring all the tropes you could possibly want (think small-town settings, fake relationships, grumpy vs sunshine, enemies to lovers) and all with a generous dose of spice in every story.

♪ @millsandboonuk
◉ @millsandboonuk
afterglowbooks.co.uk

#AfterglowBooks

For all the latest book news, exclusive content and giveaways scan the QR code below to sign up to the Afterglow newsletter:

afterglow BOOKS

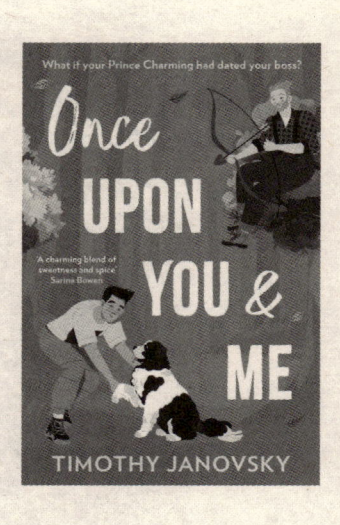

Ms. V's Hot Girl Summer
A.H. Cunningham
THE TEMPERATURE'S RISING...

Once Upon You & Me
Timothy Janovsky
What if your Prince Charming had dated your boss?
'A charming blend of sweetness and spice' Sarina Bowen

- ✈ International
- ☯ Opposites attract
- 🌶 Spicy

- 💻 Workplace romance
- 🚫 Forbidden love
- 🌶 Spicy

OUT NOW

Two stories published every month. Discover more at:
Afterglowbooks.co.uk

OUT NOW!

Opposites ATTRACT
MEDICS IN LOVE

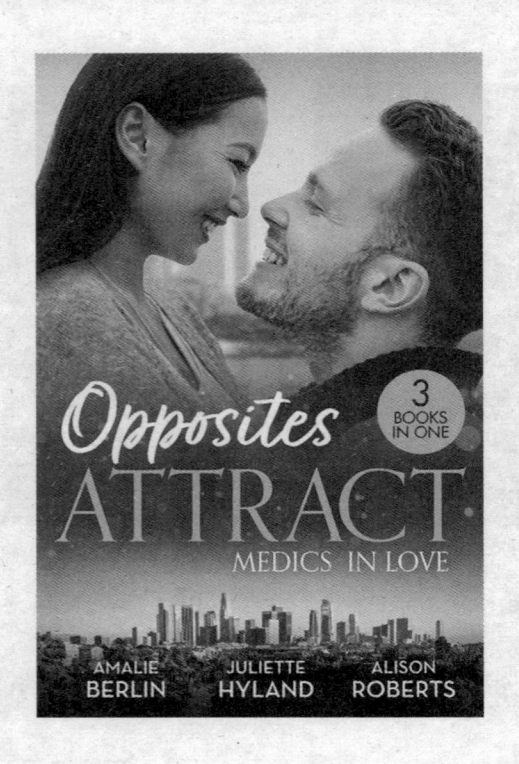

3 BOOKS IN ONE

AMALIE BERLIN JULIETTE HYLAND ALISON ROBERTS

Available at
millsandboon.co.uk

MILLS & BOON

OUT NOW!

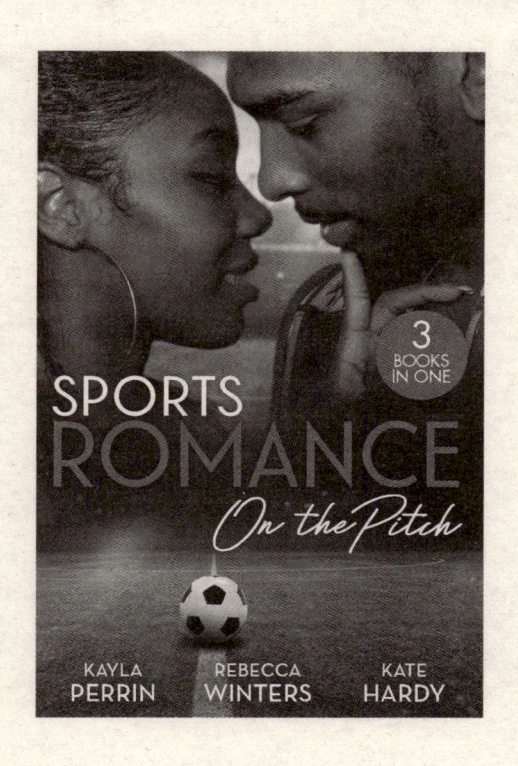

SPORTS ROMANCE
On the Pitch

3 BOOKS IN ONE

KAYLA PERRIN · REBECCA WINTERS · KATE HARDY

Available at
millsandboon.co.uk

MILLS & BOON

OUT NOW!

3 BOOKS IN ONE

― ROMANCE ON DUTY ―

LOVE IN *Action*

BRENDA JACKSON NICHOLE SEVERN CHARLOTTE HAWKES

Available at
millsandboon.co.uk

MILLS & BOON

OUT NOW!

Princess BRIDES
A CINDERELLA STORY

3 BOOKS IN ONE

MAISEY YATES
LOUISA HEATON
AMALIE BERLIN

Available at
millsandboon.co.uk

MILLS & BOON

MILLS & BOON
A ROMANCE FOR EVERY READER

- **FREE** delivery direct to your door
- **EXCLUSIVE** offers every month
- **SAVE** up to 30% on pre-paid subscriptions

SUBSCRIBE AND SAVE

millsandboon.co.uk/Subscribe